D0370343

HOWARD FAST

MOSES

Howard Fast is well known for a literary career that spans more than sixty years. He is the author of over seventy novels, including *Spartacus, April Morning, Citizen Tom Paine, The Immigrants,* and *Freedom Road,* which has been published in eighty-two languages. Among his most recent projects are the novels *Redemption* and *An Independent Woman,* and the screenplay for *The Crossing,* a television movie for the A & E Television Network.

After the loss of his wife Bette—to whom this book is dedicated—he is now living happily in Connecticut with his new wife, Mercedes O'Connor.

MOSES

HOWARD FAST

ibooks
new york
www.ibooksinc.com

DISTRIBUTED BY SIMON & SCHUSTER, INC.

For

Bette, Rachel & Jonathan

Introduction

To think of either Judaism or Christianity without Moses is impossible; and even Islam rests on this mighty, towering, half-mythical figure. I am a Bible student, and have been one since my teens, reading it for its beauty and literature, for its magnificent cadences, and for its wonderful, ruthless history. Of all people, only the Jews wrote their history without apology, putting down their worst moments, their best moments, and every violation of the law and code that had been given to them by Moses. They worshipped a God that rewarded the good and punished the evil.

What follows is the biblical introduction to Moses, taken from the beginning of the Book of Exodus:

"And there went a man from the house of Levi, and took to wife a daughter of Levi. And the woman conceived, and bore him a son; and when she saw him that he was a goodly child, she hid him three months."

(Pharaoh had ordered that male children of the Jews be put to death.)

"And when she could no longer hide him, she took for him an ark of bulrushes, and daubed it with slime and with pitch, and put the child therein; and she laid it in the flags by the river's brink. And his sister stood afar off, to wit what would be done to him.

"And the daughter of Pharaoh came down to wash herself at the river; and her maidens walked along by the river's

side; and when she saw the ark among the flags, she
sent her maid to fetch it. And when she had opened
it, she saw the child; and, behold, the babe wept. And
she had compassion on him, and said, 'This is one of the
Hebrews' children.'

"Then said his sister to Pharaoh's daughter, 'Shall I go and
call to thee a nurse of the Hebrew women, that she may
nurse the child for thee?'
And Pharaoh's daughter said to her, 'Go!'
And the maid went and called the child's mother,
And Pharaoh's daughter said unto her, 'Take this child
away, and nurse it for me, and I will give thee thy wages.'
And the woman took the child, and nursed it. And the
child grew, and she brought him unto Pharaoh's daughter,
and he became her son. And she called him Moses; and
she said, 'Because I drew him out of the water.'

The next thing we hear about Moses, in Exodus, is this:

"And it came to pass in those days, when Moses was
grown, that he went out unto his brethren, and looked
on their burdens. . . ."

Thus, from his birth to that moment when he strikes
down an Egyptian overseer and is forced to flee Egypt, we
know absolutely nothing of Moses, of his childhood, his
youth, and his young manhood.

Forty years ago, when I wrote this book, I steeped myself
in Egyptian history and ancient Egyptology; but that was
forty years ago. Much of the incident was suggested by the
large mythology created for Moses by those Rabbis who

wrote of him in the Talmud, but I have no notion of what this is worth as history.

I am far from sure that the Rabbis of a thousand years later knew much about the life of an Egyptian prince, but their tales are enchanting and I made full use of them, particularly those related to Southern Egypt, the Nile, and the mysterious land of Kush. Other parts of the book are fictional inventions, but I tried to stay as close to what was reasonable as I could.

Of all my historical fiction, this book, I feel, is the richest and most colorful. When I wrote it, I envisioned a second narrative to cover the years of Moses, the liberator, but I never got to it, and now, at the age of eighty-five, it is not likely that I ever will.

So here it is at the millennium. Read it slowly and savor it, and be with me in ancient Egypt—a fabulous, colorful civilization where monotheism began and where a man called Moses searched for God.

Howard Fast
December 1999

MOSES

Note

Ancient Egyptian writing was *hieroglyphic*, that is, picture writing developed to a point where it could record the spoken language completely and exactly. In order to accomplish this, the pictures or signs had to be employed in three different ways: first, as direct pictures of an object, an idea or word; second, syllabically, representing part of a word as direct picture or parallel sound; and third, as a limitation of a word already pictured.

While this method of writing was later modified to what is known as the *hieratic*, and still later the *demotic*, for most of the ancient era and for the time of which I write, the *hieroglyphic* was dominant. While these pictures defied translation for many centuries, the key to them was finally discovered, as most people know, through the Rosetta Stone; and today scholars in this field read Egyptian as well and completely as Latin scholars read Latin.

Nevertheless, there is a difference; for many questions of pronunciation are still unresolved, and the transliteration from pictures to our alphabet is chaotic, many scholars developing their own system of transliteration independently. For example, Amen-Hotep, the king who introduced Aton worship and changed his name to Akh-en-Aton, is so rendered by the eminent authority, John A. Wilson; another scholar of equal importance renders the names thus: Amenophis and Ikhnaton. Being unable to read heiroglyphics, I have taken the liberty of choosing those forms which appear to be most pronounceable and therefore most readable. I have tried to be both exact and consistent in rendering texts that exist in translation, but since I feel that modern usage best expresses the feeling of a time, I have eliminated *thee* and *thou* in speech.

I have not used the word *Pharaoh* as it is commonly used, since at the time of Ramses II, *Pharaoh* quite literally was the name of the enormous palace he built. Ramses was usually called the *God Ramses*, of the *God-King*. The literal meaning of *Pharaoh* is *Great House,* and it is only after the time of Ramses that it came into common usage as the king's title.

Most scholars in the field seem to agree that Moses is an Egyptian word, meaning *a child is given*. Connected with a prefix, it would mean *has given a child*. It should be remembered that Moses is an Anglicization; in Hebrew the name is pronounced *Mosheh*; in ancient Egyptian the pronunciation of *Mose* was probably identical. Just as *Mosheh* is Anglicized to Moses, so is the Egyptian "has given a child" most often rendered *Mose,* as in *Ka-Mose* and *Thut-Mose*. In order to avoid confusion and to strike a specific chord in my readers, I have spelled the word *Moses* in all cases.

The "Hymn to Aton" has been slightly changed for purposes of style. *Kosen* is rendered *Goshen,* both to avoid confusion and because the latter rendition is common to our literature; both are, of course, references to the same place. The substitution of modern measurements for the *royal cubit* and modern time measurements, as well, for the Egyptian terms has been done for the convenience of the reader. Because the word is still current, and because it has so much color of the time, I use as a measure of weight the *shekel*—then common to all the countries of the ancient Near East.

A List of the Main Characters in the Book

MOSES

ENEKHAS-AMON: The sister of Ramses II

RAMSES II: God-King of Egypt

AMON-TEPH: A priest in the Great House

SETI: Enehas-Amon's physician

SETI-HOP: Chief arms instructor in the Great House

RAMSES-EM-SETI: One of the sons of Ramses

NEPH: An engineer in the service of Ramses

RE-KOPHAR: Priest in charge of surgery in the Great House

SETI-MOSES: Chief steward of the Great House

SETI-KEPH: Captain of Hosts under Ramses

HETEP-RE: A Captain of Chariots

NUN: Servant of Moses, a Levite

SOKAR-MOSES: Second in command of the expedition to Kush

ATON-MOSES: A physician of Karnak

MERIT-ATON: The daughter of Aton-Moses

IRGEBAYN: King of Kush

IRGA: One of the daughters of the King of Kush

MIRIAM: The sister of Moses

DOOGANA: A witch doctor

PART ONE

The Prince of Egypt

[1]

WITH HIS TENTH year, on the day of his birth, his royal uncle agreed to receive him, look at him, lay a hand upon his head, and perhaps even say a word or two to him.

He was afraid. When his mother told him what was in store for him, he stared at her fixedly, his dark eyes wide and open, and she realized that he was very much afraid; but she was in no mood to offer sympathy. She was too much concerned for herself, and for months now this concern had deepened. The truth of it was that she had difficulty in remembering the old days when her health was good. If it wasn't a headache, it was a pain in the stomach; if it was neither, it was a general feeling of fatigue, an ache in her joints, a drawing sensation in her groin. "You're getting no younger," her physician had remarked, and she replied peevishly that thirty-nine was not old, not in a man and not in a woman, and that she paid him not for philosophical observation but for the practice of medicine. But her petty lie, born out of annoyance and anxiety—she was forty-two, a year younger than her royal brother—brought just a shade of a smile to the doctor's lips.

Afterward, she had looked in the mirror and wept for herself. Others had specified this or that tragedy in her life; but the truth of it was that she was a vain and selfish woman, and the only tragedy she had ever felt truly was the loss of her beauty; not even her illness, not even the pain and fatigue, but the loss of the beauty that had been held more dazzling than even the beauty of Nefertiti of the cursed name and memory. Because of this, there had been a period of months now during which her pity for herself had become an obsession. Who would ever know the agony of the long, dark nights when time stretched out for ever, and when alternately she wept and prayed? And what of the hours she spent with unguents, salves, creams, medications and magic preparations, and with obscene spells directed at the whore goddesses of Kadash and Arzawa and other distant and savage places? Who was to be pitied more than herself? When her doctor bad come, earlier this very day, she said to him, more pleadingly than bitterly,

"Look at me! Look at my skin, my arms! And my face! Black pouches under my eyes—lines, wrinkles, bags! Please . . . Please," she begged him. "Help me!"

The doctor, who was a fat little man with spindly legs, with Seti for his name—a king's name for a pompous little man—a commonplace man out of village mud and only the good fortune that his mother in her young and attractive years had been seduced by a priest and thereby gained her son a sponsor toward a well-paid profession—this doctor reflected that after all they were out of the same cloth, priest and peasant, royal princess and village harlot, all of them fashioned out of the same corrupt and decaying

4

flesh—the princess who would have spices, sarcophagus and life everlasting, and his own mother who went to her simple extinction and burial in a wooden box and without wrappings or embalming—the one as weak and plaintive and helpless as the other.

These were his thoughts—thoughts which in the olden times a man like himself would never have dared think, for in those days a princess was a goddess and even thoughts are not safe from goddesses; but the olden times were gone forever and few enough people, much less a physician, considered Enckhas-Amon a goddess. He gave her a purge to loosen her bowels and he told her to eat grapes, which are good for fatigue. About her skin, his science provided no competent knowledge, but knowing that she was buying creams and salves from various priestly fakers who peddled their wares at a good price to the royal family, he promised a miraculous salve of his own on his next visit.

She was lying on her couch eating grapes when Moses was summoned to her, and even through her veil of self-concern she could not help noticing how long-legged and straight the boy was growing. With his black hair cut straight across his brow and long and square at the back, he stood like a rod, the way a prince was taught to stand; and with his flat shoulders and brown skin he looked very much an Egyptian. Even his high-bridged nose was typical of the people of Upper Egypt, although less common here on the Delta, and it was only his height and the weight and bulk of his bones that separated him from his many brothers. But his health and youth and vitality accented her own sense of malaise, and she demanded querulously,

"Why did it take you so long? You're not a good boy! You're not an obedient boy! Another boy would have run

5

to his mother lying sick and weak the way I am I But not you. You dillydally everywhere—any excuse not to come to your mother."

"I am sorry," he gasped. He had actually run all the way, through the gardens, through the endless, high-pillared halls of the palace, and now he was panting for breath. "I came as soon as I could, my mother. Please don't be angry with me, my mother. Please love me, my mother. I came as soon as I heard you had summoned me."

"Silly boy." He knew how to flatter her and he somehow sensed how much she needed flattery. "I wasn't angry, only a little provoked. Illness makes one short-tempered and nasty, I suppose. But that can't mean anything to you. All you know is play and laughter and sunshine, so why should you have sympathy for a sick and ugly old lady?"

Her plea was so pathetic and transparent that even the little boy saw through it, and told her that, far from being ugly and old, she was young and beautiful. And to him, in a measure, she was, for he was no exacting judge of beauty; and as she lay there, her limbs brown and full under a throw of transparent gauze, her round breasts hardly hidden by a netlike jewelled brassière, with her earrings and necklaces and bracelets of gold all sparkling and shimmering in the sunlight that blazed down through the open roof of her chamber, she seemed as beautiful as any woman he had ever seen. So he would remember her. His praise and adulation were the praise and adulation of a child, but at this bleak moment she gloried in it, and at the same moment, suddenly and for the first time in his life, he saw her sexually as a woman, consciously as a naked woman and an object of excitement and desire. The thought sobered him, and when she asked him to come to her and kiss her, he held back as if afraid.

Enekhas-Amon recognized his moment of manhood without particular awareness of her recognition; but it was in her voice as she said archly, "Silly boy, come to your mother and kiss her." She embraced him as he kissed her. "Your mother has wonderful news for you. Can you guess? Surely you can?"

But he couldn't guess, and what would there be that a prince would want? Being a prince was not to want. Others wanted but not the princesses and the princes. He was already old enough to sense how much some men wanted— the greed and avarice of so many of the swarm of priests and clerks and stewards and physicians who were a living part of the vast palace; but with a prince it was different— or so it still seemed to him.

He was and yet he was not *the* prince. For although it was never said, certainly never proclaimed, he could not help but know that more than any of the others, he was *the* prince, the legendary and godlike result of a union between a royal brother and sister—between the God-King Ramses and his own mother. But this was something he knew only as a part of doubt, knowledge that was no more confirmed than the gossip which hinted that he was no son of Ramses at all. The palace housed at least a hundred more of his brothers and sisters—or cousins—of all ages, and it seemed that every week or so another squalling infant joined their ranks. Yet in spite of their numbers, each of them was princely and royal.

Like the others, what could he possibly want, unless it was that blasphemous notion that occasionally wrenched his heart—the notion that he would want not to be a prince? How often would he and his royal brothers hang over the wall of the great terrace swept by the Nile itself and there watch the ships poling up from the wide sea and the great rafts of tied bulrushes drifting down from Upper Egypt, down from the distant mystery of cataracts and mountain, the carefree—as it seemed—families that lived upon the rafts, and the naked brown children as wild and free as the birds in the sky! Little enough awe of royalty these children had, for when a raft drifted near to the terrace wall, they would shout a familiar greeting to the royal progeny, a shrill, unmannerly greeting not unmixed with contempt, and they would shout about the wonders they had seen—the painted black men of the South, the lions and the leopards and the giant elephants next to which a man was no larger than an ant, and the monkeys and the bright waterfowl and the endless herds of antelope—and much more that was a mixture of truth and fancies and lies concocted out of envy and frustration. But this Moses and the others did not know.

"No, my mother, tell me your news."

She sucked the juice from a grape and then delicately removed the skin and seeds from her lips and dropped them into a dish on the little table beside her couch.

"Tomorrow, my son, the God-Emperor will receive us and he will look upon you with his own eyes and talk to you, and—who knows?—perhaps give you his blessing." It was then that his fear aroused her impatience rather than her sympathy. Afraid of Ramses!I Her own father, Seti-Mer-ne-Pteh, was a man to fear. Even so recently as her own youth the times had been different and the customs had been different, and while there had been many children, there was no such teeming throng as now peopled the palace. Her father was a cold and bitter man who regarded himself as the angry arm of the god whose name he bore. He had little use for Egyptian women except to plant his royal seed in, and little time to spare from his frenetic conquering and building. Not love but fear was responsible for the thousands of Egyptian children who were eagerly given his name by their parents. Not so was his son, Ramses, her brother; here was a bull, a cock of the walk who could not see a woman without desiring her. He boasted that he could populate a land with his own seed and, often enough, when Enekhas-Amon saw the children pouring like a noisy river through the palace corridors, she believed his boast.

These were the companions of Moses, and little enough his mother knew of their endless discussion of a hundred forbidden matters—including the question of Ramses' divinity, which they tended to equate with immortality. In this they both believed and disbelieved, feared it and mocked it, prayed to it and blasphemed against it—and clung to it, because each of them—the short and the tall, the fat and the skinny, the runny-nosed brats and the strutting bullies—each of them believed that he or she carried a part of the divinity. Except Moses; he walked among them as an interloper; he blasphemed less than they did, and accepted the divinity of the great emperor more out of fear than faith. His mother had never sensed how deep and unshakeable this fear was; nor would she have been able to comprehend it if he had explained. She had behind her two thousand years of divinity, and with it the practical knowledge that it brought neither surcease from illness nor any particular happiness. The sickness that was robbing her of health and beauty was in no contradiction to the fact that she was in some measure immortal; but in the thoughts of her son Moses life and death, divinity and immortality, were tangled with all the uncertain threads of his short life.

When he said, "No, no, please, my mother, no. I don't want to. Please..." she could not know how vivid in his memory was the recollection of something that had happened only a few weeks before. It was in one of their playtimes, between teachers or priests or military instructors, and they wound through the palace with increasing relaxation and louder and louder bravado. In the mighty pillared corridor that connected the two enormous wings of the great structure, two of the princes challenged each other to climb the side hangings. These linen draperies, painted and decorated with bright colours, hung from rings slid on to poles laid from pillar to pillar, on top of each. The stone columns were forty feet high, and to Moses and the other children they were even higher than their massive reality. Moses was not the only one among them whose bravado gave way to fear as the children scrambled aloft. But they climbed like monkeys, with the agility of monkeys, each one clutching one end of the huge drapery, hand over hand, and each fighting to be the first. And he who was first, a skinny lad of eleven years, a Ramses of the true blood and divinity, had just reached the top, barely visible in the high, deep-shadowed ceilings, when the drapery at his end tore loose from the bronze ring, breaking his hold and casting him down to the floor. Over and over he turned in what seemed to Moses an endless length of time before he struck, screaming with fear; and then he struck on his head in a ghastly, bloody mess that made the children take up his screams as they looked at the horrible little heap that remained of divine immortality.

This is what Moses thought of as he pleaded with his mother, bringing back her petulance and annoyance.

"Well, I don't know what to say! I don't know what has come over you."

"Please, my mother."

"Foolish boy!" she snapped at him. "Hurt me! Cut my heart out! That will satisfy you, won't it?"

"No . . . no, my mother."

His dark eyes filled with tears, and she was somewhat mollified by that. It wasn't many boys who, in these loose times, cared that much about their mothers. "And if I died and went to lie at the feet of Seti, would you weep for me? Don't you understand? If the God Ramses commands me, and I say to him, 'Oh, no, my brother, oh, not at all. You wish to see my son, Moses, but he doesn't wish to see you'? What then? Am I not dead? And whose hand struck me down?"

"Not mine, my mother. Please don't say that." Now he wept in earnest, the tears rolling down his flat cheeks, and he looked so beautiful and tall and compassionate that, in spite of herself, her heart went out to him and she opened her arms and cradled his head against her bosom, tenderly wiping away his tears.

"Come now," she whispered, "no more of that. You will come with me tomorrow, and receive the god's blessing. No one in the palace is as handsome as you are and I can hardly wait. Tomorrow morning I will send Rea, my own hairdresser, to dress your hair and powder your curls with gold dust. On both arms you will wear the sacred bracelets of Amon, my own from my mother—and now I give them to you, my only child. They will always be yours; they are not to go in my tomb. You will wear only a loincloth, for I want him to see your whole body in its nakedness, to see how fine and perfect you are; but on your feet, your silver sandals. I am having them polished for you. You will also wear my golden neckpiece, for we are now of a size. Then you will be a prince such as this palace has not seen before, and the god will recognize that. Let him be a god, he's still my brother and he won't forget that so soon—not while I live. There, my son. Will you be afraid on such a glorious moment? What on earth is there to be afraid of?"

He drew away from her and stood up and said slowly but desperately and seriously, "He will cast me back into the water."

"*What!*"

He saw the doubt, the fear, the anguish that had suddenly seized her face, but his own fear forced him to repeat what he had said. "He will cast me back into the water."

"Who told you that?" she whispered hoarsely.

He shook his head.

"Moses, tell me!" she almost shrieked. "I command you to."

Again he shook his head. "I pledged my word, my *justice.*"

"And my own justice?"

"My *justice,*" he repeated miserably.

"A priest? Some dirty priest of common, jealous blood. I know. They're everywhere now—listening, plotting, conniving. Well, I still know the difference between a priest and a princess of Egypt! I'll cut his throat with my own hands!"

"Not a priest," he begged her, terrified now at this unprecedented outburst.

"Then one of those miserable whores' brats that my royal bull of a brother sires every night!"

"I can't tell you."

She suddenly reached out and grasped his arm so tightly that he cried aloud with the pain, and she said, with the coldest anger he had ever heard in her voice,

"Well, it's a lie, my son—a vicious, filthy lie. You will learn some day how much and how easily they lie. So wipe it out of your mind for ever. You will grow up now—your childhood had to end some day. Listen to me. I have never told you who your father was. I am not telling you now. For this I have my own reasons. But I will tell you this. The God Ramses is a man like any other man. I know it. I am his sister. I lay in bed with him. Do you understand what I mean, my son?"

Moses nodded miserably.

"But the one thing I insist upon—you must not fear Ramses. In the old days," she went on, with a sort of desperate intensity, "they would have believed that he was born a god. Some still believe that he will die a god and go to sit on Seti's throne with him. That may be, but who has come back to bear witness? And remember: he has more to fear from me than I have from him, be assured, more than you have. Now go and play—and leave me."

Still he stood there, gripped and held there by his own torment, and when she questioned him, he managed to ask, with a desperation that equalled hers,

"Is the god—the king—is he my father?"

Her face was tired and haggard as she said with a calm

that completed his terror, "I've said all I am going to say. Never again ask me that, my son. I am your mother, but I am also a princess royal of the Great House and no one, not my son, not any man on this holy soil of Egypt, shall dare ask me a question to provoke me. Now go away and play. I am tired of you, foolish boy. Leave me alone."

Then he fled, bursting through the hanging, leaving doors swinging behind him, racing past the rows of looming columns out into the sweet air and the sunshine; and behind him, his mother wept. She wept for the way fate had dealt with her, for herself, for her lost youth and beauty, for her ever barren loins. She wept out of jealousy and hatred for her brother, for the concubines who so eagerly graced her brother's bed, out of hatred and resentment against every living person in the great palace except the one child who now exacted the total small measure of love that was hers to give.

[2]

ALMOST AT THE sunlight, with the bright gardens spread before him, the voice caught him, soft, silky, "Moses, Moses—whither so fast and furious? Look behind you, boy." He swung around and saw the priest sitting on a little stool in the pleasant shade of a column, a white robe over his fat jelly-like bulk, a thin, mocking smile on his moon-shaped face. "Oh, come over here, boy, and stop jittering like a mare that smells stud. What could frighten you that wouldn't frighten me? If I ran twenty like that, I'd drop dead and there'd be something for the embalmers to tackle. Eh, Moses? Do you want me to call you the prince who was afraid?"

"No—no, your holiness, please don't."

The priest found this amusing, for he began to chuckle, sending waves of mirth rolling over the layers of his flesh. His robe fell open, and Moses forgot his fear in the fascination of the great heaving stomach that was revealed.

"And don't call me 'holiness,'" he chuckled. "Only the dead are holy, and it takes a thousand tons of rock to keep them that way. You know my name, which is Amon-Teph, and your own foolish name is Moses. I knew your mother, the goddess Enekhas-Amon, before you were born, when she was young and beautiful and I was young enough and slim enough to look twice at a beautiful woman, even a princess. Yes. You see, I remember names and you don't, because I am a priest of Amon and you are an empty-headed boy—as empty-headed as all boys. Now what frightened you, Prince of Egypt?" He stopped chuckling and looked keenly at Moses, a gleam of warmth and liking in his tiny eyes.

"Nothing," Moses answered, almost absently.

"Nothing?" the priest repeated, watching the boy shrewdly. "A wild nothing? A horned nothing? Boy, listen to me—I am a good friend to you, and if you weren't just an empty-headed young wastrel, you'd put a value on a friend like old, fat Amon-Teph."

His words had no meaning to Moses, who had enough sophistication to suspect a household priest trying to curry favour with a prince. For the first time, he was aware of a sense of his own cleverness and he asked the priest as casually as he could,

"Then, Amon-Teph, you must have known my mother when she was in birth with me?"

Mirth and warmth went out of the fat face and suddenly

the priest was cold and indifferent. In the voice of a stranger, he said, "The palace teems with brats. What am I, Moses, a midwife, to remember every cub that was whelped? Go and play, boy!" But when Moses had taken a dozen steps, the priest called after him,

"Prince of Egypt, when do you think you will be a man?"

"I'm a man now," Moses answered angrily, thinking, "More of a man than you, you fat old fool."

"You're a snivelling, empty-headed boy," the priest said cuttingly. "When you think you're a man, look for me, and I'll have something to say to you."

[3]

AT THIS TIME, although he was only forty-three years old, Ramses was in the twenty-sixth year of his kingship, and already the plain folk, the peasants who tilled their little plots of rich alluvial soil up and down the River Nile, were saying that no god like Ramses had ever graced the throne of Egypt before. Unlike his father, Seti, who had exercised his *justice*—that ancient sense of conscience which was the most precious character-description an Egyptian could refer to—with cold fury and merciless judgment, Ramses was a man simple people could understand and love, perhaps because kingly insensitivity was misread as kindly simplicity. Along with that, he expressed human qualities which were always reassuring in a god. He bragged and lied without shame. He was a large, powerful, good-looking man, who did things hugely and lustily. He ate enormously, with gusto and relish, drank vast quantities without ever losing his head, and engaged his manhood in a manner that more than anything else convinced his subjects that his divinity was founded in fact. If his apparently inexhaustible virility—or lust, as some would say—had been laced with sadism, a quality not unknown among former kings of Egypt, or had been petty and sick in its manifestations, the people would have simply tolerated it and accepted it as they accepted the inevitable aberrations of godhood on the throne; but here it was, so vast, so unprecedented, so all-encompassing that they took pride in a reputation already recognized all over the known world.

This pride had to include an acceptance of Ramses' broad and catholic taste. It was true that the old order of things, the everlasting and unchanging stability of Egypt which extended back into the cloudy mists of time, was passing away; nevertheless, it was not in the manner of Egyptian god-kings to haunt the city docks where the ships from far places tied up and to dicker personally for new bedmates. It was one thing to set a pattern where no attractive Egyptian woman he laid eyes on could escape his bed; it was another for Ramses to take as his concubines the women of every nation—strange, heathen women, black and white and brown, women of such far and little-known places as Philistia, Dardania, Hatti, Sicily, Crete and Sardinia, Kush and Babylon, Pedesia and Arzawa, Ugarit and Megiddo and twenty other cities and tribes and nations—and to honour the royalty of every brat these strangers dropped. But whatever Ramses did was mixed with the knowledge that he did more of it and more splendidly than any of his royal ancestors.

He was not content to take the ancient title he bore—Pharaoh, which means *great house*—figuratively, as others before him had done. If he was to be known as the lord of a great house, then such a house would come into being; and he took the city of Tanis in the Delta, renamed it Ramses for himself, and set about making it a place such as the world had not known before. In the midst of it he built his own palace, a literal *great house*, a structure so vast and of so many rooms, apartments, corridors, terraces and gardens that it was held that one could live in it for a decade and still not know all of it. No palace like this had ever been in Egypt before, or anywhere else for that matter, nor was there another city like Ramses. The king built docks and warehouses that became focal points for the world's commerce, and to Ramses, from near and far, came the ships of every people that trafficked over the seas. The king also built great monuments and tombs and commissioned stone sculpture that dwarfed anything in Egypt.

Indeed, stone and stone structures became a driving passion with the king. The connection between the immortality of stone and the immortality of man was old and deep in the Egyptian consciousness, and with Ramses, nothing was enough, not was there ever enough labour to build what he desired to build. Everything, finished, was belittled in his eyes. Even the great throne room where he held court and passed judgment now seemed insufficient to house a god; although to Moses, who saw it this day for the first time, it was a chamber of such size and overwhelming splendour as to make him feel like a frog dropped into the River Nile, lost and unnoticed.

Actually, the royal chamber was about a hundred feet in length and about sixty feet broad—by no means the largest room in the palace. The floor was of black basaltes, the beautiful hard marble that Moses had seen so often floating slowly down the Nile on great rafts of cane, from the distant land of Kush where it was quarried; the throne platform was of white limestone inlaid with silver and gold, and the throne where Ramses sat was in the old style, a large carved block of the palest alabaster with a back only six inches high. The side hangings of the room were of white linen, suspended between granite columns thirty feet high and embroidered with a hieroglyphic and far from truthful account of the glories of the king's reign—and including a remarkable description of the great war with Hatti. Behind the king himself there was a brick wall covered over with a bright mosaic, which depicted him in his chariot, laying about him with his mace, his horses rearing on a field carpeted with Hittite dead.

The king himself sat in the attire of the sun-god Re—a dress which he affected increasingly, and one which in its simplicity well suited his strong, muscled body. His complete lack of adornment—not a necklace on his shoulders, not a bracelet on his arms, not a ring on his fingers—was a telling contrast to the ostentatious and glittering display made by everyone else in the throne room. As with Re, what jewel could enhance his glory?—And he, the master of all jewels, made the effective point that he need burden himself with none. On his head he wore the golden crown of Re, a simple and undecorated band of gold which circled his head just above the brows and flared out to a height of five inches—very much like a truncated, inverted fez; and in his right hand, lying in his lap, he held the traditional golden sickle. For clothing, he wore only a plain, pleated, knee-length kilt of white linen. His feet were bare, his legs bare of covering or adornment.

Moses, who had seen the king from a distance a number of times but never so close as now, was both disappointed and puzzled by the drabness of his costume. Everyone in the throne room—priests and stewards and royal attendants and various ladies of unstated position and relationship, and captains and administrators and royal progeny grown to manhood, and foreigners who fascinated Moses with their strange hairdress and clothing, and the Princess Enekhas-Amon, and indeed Moses himself—everyone was dressed more richly and ornately than the king; but Moses could not comprehend that only one powerful and kingly could dispense with ornamentation. For the first time he had doubts about the omnipotence of the living god of Egypt, and this helped him keep his fears under control; also, his absorption in the pageantry and colour of the scene, the perfumes and spices that tickled his nostrils, the tale the hieroglyphs unfolded to his well-trained eyes, and particularly the huge, bright picture behind the throne—the romantic scene of battle, the dead Hittites, the champing, rearing horses—helped take his mind away from his rapidly ebbing fears of the king.

As time passed, he was able to look at the king steadily and notice the resemblance to Enekhas-Amon—the wide jaw, the full, fleshy mouth, the arched brows, and the small, thin nose. It was incongruous to see the familiar head set on the heavy, muscular shoulders. Even as his mother whispered to him, "Moses, don't stare like that!" the king's eyes met his and then lifted to recognize Enekhas-Amon. Without any of the manner of the god that Moses had imagined, he smiled thinly and nodded for her to come to him, and then said a word or two to dismiss the priest who was talking to him. As the priest backed away, Moses noticed that no one came closer than twenty feet from the throne platform without the king's beckoning nod—and he also heard his mother whisper quickly.

"Remember, at the platform, prostrate yourself—and then crawl forward slowly until you can put your cheek against the god's feet. Flat on the ground then, and you remain there until he tells you to rise."

Walking stiffly, as he had learned was the proper way for a prince to walk in ceremonial circumstances, Moses gave no indication of hearing her. He was conscious that the babble of voices had stopped, and though he dared not look behind him, he was certain that every eye in the place was fixed on him and his mother. Even the guards who stood behind the throne platform were watching him curiously, and when he ventured to glance at the king, he felt that the black, deep-set eyes held the same curious interest. As he knelt down and crawled up the cold steps of the throne platform, he saw his mother's legs marching firmly forward; but for his part he was glad that he had to lie flat on the floor and wriggle pronely toward the god. Not only did it provide—to his trembling soul—a sort of protection, but it relieved him of the necessity of seeing the god's face. Yet, as he crawled, he could hear them greeting each other.

"Well, my sister—as young and beautiful as ever. Welcome."

"That's nonsense, and you know it. I am neither young nor beautiful, and I lie in a corner of this palace sick and suffering. I'm as lonely and as forgotten as a woman can be."

"If I had only known..."

"That's neither here nor there, my brother, and I have

a notion that no illness of mine would bring any pain to you. But I didn't come here to quarrel with you. We've done enough quarrelling, and for my part I want to forget it. I came here because you promised me five years ago that on the day of my son's tenth year you would look at him and give him the god's blessing."

"Did I really?"

"It's a small matter to you, my brother, but it's a large matter to me. You did, and I remember quite well."

"You always had a good memory, Enekhas-Amon, and my own is rather poor. So this is your son?"

Moses lay before him shivering, his cheek pressed against the god's bare foot, his breath choking on the heavy fragrance of perfume, saying to himself, "Please, please, dear god, let me crawl away, but don't make me stand in front of you."

But the god was otherwise disposed, and he said, not unkindly, "Get up, boy, and let me look at you."

Moses tried to rise, but strangely enough the will to motion was somehow not communicated to his limbs and he lay there paralysed, begging himself, his legs and his arms to respond to the occasion. Ramses nudged his face gently with his foot.

"Come, boy. Get up! No one's going to harm you and there's nothing to be afraid of." And to Enekhas-Amon he said,

"How old did you say the lad is?"

"Ten years, and you know it, my brother. Now, Moses, get up!"

His mother's tone released him from his paralysis and, blushing with shame, Moses managed to get to his feet, to see Ramses chuckling with more amusement than the sight of a frightened boy would seem to warrant. He hung his head in mortification as Ramses said to Enekhas-Amon,

"My dear sister, accept an apology. I do remember. The name brings it all back—the name, of course. Who else but my own dear sister would defy a thousand years of revered practice? Moses indeed! Now, boy," he said to Moses, who took his only comfort in the fact that Ramses kept his voice low so that he could not possibly be heard by any except those on the platform, "stop hanging your head like a silly, blushing girl. Straighten up and let everyone see that we have a prince of Egypt here with us. I'm not going to eat you, boy!"

"Yes, your holiness."

"And don't call me 'holiness,' " he said, almost precisely as the fat priest had. "That name's in great favour in Egypt these days, but not among our family. It doesn't sit right, and I'm far from holy; I'm a licentious old goat, as your mother will tell you if you give her half a chance."

It was some sort of contest between Ramses and his mother which Moses could not comprehend but only feel in terms of death winging down on them. Surely after what had been said neither he nor Enekhas-Amon had any hope of leaving the throne room alive, and his whole heart pleaded silently with his mother to take heed and bridle her tongue. But far from reading his thoughts, she replied indignantly,

"Never, and you have no right to say that, brother! Where is your *justice*, your heart? I have taught him only reverence and devotion to the god who sits on Egypt's throne."

"My dear sister, I was only amused by his name, and now you're making me out to have all sorts of evil notions.

Never have I seen a sick woman as full of vinegar as you. Put your hand in mine."

More confused than ever, Moses saw his mother take Ramses' hand, all the while smiling at him with a mixture of contempt and respect—or so it seemed to Moses, who had seen his mother smile so rarely of late. In any case, it gave him back enough of his courage for him to ask,

"And what is the matter with my name, Lord Ramses, my father?"

"See, Enekhas-Amon," he said, waving his golden sickle, "the lad has a tongue and uses it smartly, if I may say so." And to Moses, "Nothing is wrong with your name as a name, sir, but it's only part of a name, and where is the other part, we ask ourselves? I am amused, not at you, but at my royal sister who does things that no one ever thought of doing—a disturbing quality in a woman, Moses. As for your name—what it says is fine—a child is given." He turned to the woman now, "But where is the rest of it, my sister?" a note of gentle mockery in his voice. "In all Egypt—there is no other Moses—because Moses is not a name at all. It is a question, my sister—and a rather insolent one, at that."

Enekhas-Amon shook her head, her eyes narrowing dangerously. If Moses had been watching her now, all of his fear would have returned, but he was staring fascinatedly at the king, who shrugged and said,

"I'm just making a little jest, lad. If you were Tut-Moses, Amon-Moses, Anubus-Moses or any one of twenty other Moses, no one would raise a brow. As a matter of fact, I like Moses—as it is. A child is given, and that's enough. Stop looking at me that way, my sister—because I had the feeling that we had both cleansed our hearts of that sort of thing. Kneel down, Moses, and I will give you the blessing of the gods of Egypt. They will look kindly upon you, and they will turn arrows from your neck and knives from your heart. And perhaps they will even fear you a bit, so that when you cross over into their land they will not deny you the life everlasting which is the heritage of a prince of Egypt."

As Moses knelt and felt the king's hand on his head, he could only sigh inwardly with profound relief that it had ended as well as this. He was too young to be concerned about life everlasting, but old enough to want to live at least until he got out of this unpredictable man's presence.

[4]

IT WAS SURPRISING how quickly he forgot his fears. A boy, even in the palace of a god, remains a boy, and for Moses there was more happiness than unhappiness. His life then was a full one, and if at times from the walls of the great palace he saw and envied the peasant lads, the street urchins, the river waifs who ran as wild as leaves tossed in the wind, who went as they pleased and slept where and when they pleased, he also had enough wit to sense that their abandon was short lived and that his own lot, whatsoever lay behind it, was a lucky one. And even for the royal progeny there were hours of abandon and aimless play, though there were more hours of school, of endless instruction in the use of the tools of war, of rigid instruction in the art of making and using hieroglyphs, of composing poems according to the classical style, of memorizing those spells and rituals from the *Book of the Dead* considered necessary for the cultural equipment of a prince of Egypt; of likewise committing to memory the psalms and prayers considered most salutary, of learning the process of mathematics and the elements of astronomy, or practising the measured precision of five dances, of becoming expert in the hundred rituals of manners that would always reveal in an instant who was highborn and who was lowborn—and finally, of instruction in the development of that strange and jealously held property of Egyptians, their *macaat*, which Egyptians would hesitate to render into other languages, holding that the quality existed only in Egypt and was therefore unintelligible to foreigners, but which Moses would translate in later life as the word "justice" although, growing into it, he felt it sometimes as "truth", sometimes as "order", and sometimes as a hunger to be a little better than he or any other man was.

It was a full life, and if the days did not lag, neither were they counted. Afterward for Moses this time would have no beginning, although it ended, as so much of childhood does, with the first pain and grief of maturity. Each day blended into the next, and the day past was blurred into the timelessness of the present. It was a land where the sun shone everlastingly, where all that was always had been and always would be—and when, with his royal brothers, he was taken up the Nile in one of the splendid palace barges to view the shining Pyramids of Giza, the incredible mountains built in the ancient past by kings half-forgotten, and still standing so bright and clean with their surface of coloured and glazed tile undisturbed—the absolute of Egypt was proven to him beyond the power of words. Even more strongly than when a teacher-priest read to them, in the ritual singsong, passages from the *Book of the Beginning* telling how the gods created Egypt and Egyptians so that their own godly selves might endure. Yet when his pride rode too high and free, the maggot of his own doubt sucked at his insides.

The innuendos and thrusts of his brothers he could possibly explain away as normal envy of the son of the god's sister, the only son; for the complexity of the God Ramses' marital and extramarital existence made for difference and distinction among the royal children. There was a strange streak of devotion in the king that would not permit the disenfranchisement of any product of his loins, but as the condition of his mates was varied, so was the status of his sons. The children of the virgin slaves whom Ramses took to bed lived together in a single dormitory, for more often than not their mothers were soon sold into foreign places. As for the concubines, they lived in the royal harem, and while their sons might remain with them even up to the age of seven or eight, they were then given over to the palace priests to live with them and to be raised by them.

Only the few who were actual wives of the God-King had apartments of their own in the Great House, slaves of their own, and households of their own—and of these, few if any possessed either the wealth or independence of Enekhas-Amon.

So, envy and pique and bitterness Moses might well expect, but the half of a name which he bore—and which became the target of so many taunts—this he could not escape from, Even in the child there were two persons—the prince of Egypt and the Moses, a child given, not as other children are given, but through some mystery, which to a child spells horror and foreboding—and thus the one rode on the shoulders of the other.

Yet not so heavily that the boy didn't laugh and play with the fullness and fortune of his youth. Circumstance declared him a prince, and as the sun-drenched days became weeks and then months, he grew with the strength and bearing of a prince—a tall, full-muscled boy, supple of movement and with a promise of great power in the wide spread of his shoulders. His face began to change, and bit by bit the comforting resemblance to the people of Upper Egypt left him. His high-bridged nose, so typical of the families of Thebes and Karnak, became thinner, more hawklike, and his nostrils widened, began to curl slightly. The baby flesh fell away from his high, prominent cheekbones and his chin hardened and sharpened, with none of the gentle, soft beauty that the royal family prided itself upon. But the change came slowly, as slowly as his growth and maturation.

[5]

AT THE HOUR of noon, when the sun stood highest overhead and would therefore not glare in their eyes, the princely children were exercised in the use of arms. Afterward they would clean their steaming bodies in one of the many pools and fountains that graced the gardens, frolicking naked in the pleasure of their health and their youth, and after that they would anoint themselves with scented oil and eat their midday meal—figs, grapes, crisp, flat biscuits of fresh-baked bread and goblets of water. In a manner, it was the best time of their day, the time when they felt most manly and most conscious of the admiration of their sisters, who watched them from the broad balcony which encircled the war-court.

But for this they had first to pay a price, and the grim, scarred war captains who trained the children of Ramses showed them no mercy for, as they pointed out, the spear cast in battle cannot distinguish between royal and common blood, and even gods who live in this world die and leave it as easily as the poor mortals who serve them.

The princes were divided into groups according to age, and every day each group practised with one or another of the weapons—the dagger; the sword and shield; the spear or the long, black Kushite stave, polished ebony, and as long as the man who carried it. But as the boys grew older, there was more and more practice with the bow, which was the weapon Ramses loved best.

There was a time once, as Moses and the others had been told, when the Egyptian weapon had been a light bow of cedarwood, a bow that a woman could draw; and for ages it had served to hold back the black men of the Land of Kush and the savages of the Libyan desert. But when the war with Hatti began, more than two centuries before, the Egyptians faced a mighty, five-foot war bow made of layers of laminated horn and with enough force to drive through a wooden shield as if it were paper—or through a man and into the heart of the man behind him. With this bow and with their terrible war chariots, Hatti conquered the sacred Land of Egypt and even for a space sat upon the god's throne. But when the craftsmen of Egypt learned to make the laminated war bows and turn them against the conqueror, it was short shrift for Hatti—who was driven back across the desert and penned like an animal in his walled cities in the Land of Canaan.

So the war bow became the walls of Egypt, but the royal children had little cause to love it, for every day their arms and backs ached and practice with it was relentless and unending. Yet as they moved toward manhood, the bow began to bend to them instead of they to the bow, and more and more they felt the elation of their arrows driving truly into the target.

As on this day, when the shooting was good, and when old Seti-Hop, their instructor, gave less grudgingly of his praise than ever before. The boys stood in one long line facing the courtyard wall before which their row of straw targets was placed, a target for each of them and each target bristling with arrows. Next to Moses stood Ramses-em-Seti, one of the few boys as tall as himself, strong and ripening in the arrogance that was already replacing the childhood good will of the princelings. He was a skilled bowman, perhaps the best in the group and with each shot he whispered some carefully insulting challenge to Moses. "Watch that, crow-nose," or "Dry your fingers before you shoot," or "Your arrows fly heavy, my lad—wet feathers?"

The insults, from others as well, were not new. Moses lived with them; and he was now old enough to tell himself that if the insinuations were untrue, they were beyond the notice of one whose blood was as high as any god's who had sat on the throne of Egypt; if they were true, he would only hasten the inevitable by responding to them. Himself, he shot calmly, easily, with a natural feel for the spring of the bow and the line of the arrow, ignoring the boy next to him. He was able to judge his target by the feel of the bow braced against his stiff arm, the curve of the parabola already instinctively gauged and calculated by his brain. The same awareness extended to the bows of the boys on either side of him and, noticing a slight upward shift in the point of Ramses-em-Seti's arrowhead, Moses wondered

why he planned to top his target. In that moment he saw
a little child of five or so, the naked brat of one of the war-
court slaves, hidden in the shrubbery at the base of the
war-court wall, only his round face visible and smiling
with delight at the sight of so much royalty bending the
tools of war.

Action coincided with recognition, and as Ramses-em-
Seti loosed, Moses thrust him forward so that he went
sprawling, his arrow quivering in the ground a dozen
paces ahead of him. Livid with rage, the boy sprang to
his feet and demanded who had touched him. The shooting stopped; a deadly, tangible silence spread among the
princes; and in that moment the child leaped from the
bushes and ran howling from the court. Old Seti-Hop
watched the slave brat with a thoughtful eye and then
walked toward Moses, his face sad and serious—and Moses
in turn dropped his bow to the ground and nodded to his
royal cousin.

"You then—you profaned me! You struck my flesh!" the
angry boy cried.

For the first time in his life Moses experienced the dead
frustration of a just but unprovable position, and he knew
how futile and self-defeating it would be to try to explain.
He had struck divine flesh without cause or reason, and
the dishonour of his act was not lessened by his own divinity. He had behaved not like a prince but like any lowborn
waif of the street or the river; and when Ramses-em-Sed
walked up to him and expectorated full in his face, his body
became as rigid as forged iron, unmoving and unbending.
But in his heart a red flame of anger burned and grew into
such a murderous hatred that he had to close his eyes and
pray to all the gods he remembered that he should be given

control of himself—and not act to stain himself and his mother and all of his godly ancestors with an act of fratricide.

When at last he opened his eyes, he was alone except for Seti-Hop and he turned his head away so that the old bowman would not see his tears of rage. Seti-Hop put his hand on Moses' shoulder and said with curious warmth and almost in pity,

"Go now and forget all this, Prince. A man commands himself before be commands others, and if I am not mistaken, you are beginning to be a man—and something of a bowman, too. I only wish that at your age I had the eye to judge your brother's target as keenly as you did. As for what you did, some will say a slave's life is worthless, and others say different. You will have to find your own answer, Moses."

[6]

MONTHS LATER, MOSES was reminded of the incident—a memory he would as soon do without—when, returning to his mother's quarters, he encountered Amon-Teph, the fat priest.

It was at twilight, when the setting sun grasped the tops of the giant roofless columns in its rosy clutch, bathing the pale granite in an unearthly radiance that only Egypt in all the world knows—and only Egypt at sundown. Moses was standing in the dark forest of stone, staring up at the beauty above him, the black pillars turning bloody and then rose-red against the blue lavender sky, and then the great strokes of rich purple to herald darkness, and the blood colour creeping up the pillars as rose-pink became crimson and then black. Moses never saw this—and it was never the same for two nights—without experiencing a mixture of rapture and melancholy, rapture beyond expression, and melancholy to make him feel that in himself he knew and measured all of the world's joy and sorrow since time began. Adolescence had only recently begun for the boy, but it was a land where fruit ripens easily—and perhaps perishes early too. As Moses watched the darkness deepen, a knowing, rasping voice spoke out of the deep shadow and said,

"Well, Prince, what do you think of such beauty? For my part, I think the gods put it there to delude us and to make us envious—and if we look too hard, to make us sick."

Startled at first, the boy realized it was the priest, Amon-Teph, and was able to relax and recall that a long time ago he, Moses, had come off second best in an exchange of words. So he answered now with youthful but firm authority, attempting to hold his voice low,

"I don't think, Amon-Teph—or at least it doesn't seem to me—that beauty can ever make a man sick. I have heard that it is one of the seven fruitful blessings; and since the gods have wished it so, it brings comfort and peace."

"Ha! So that's what you heard, is it?" the old priest snorted from the darkness. "Where did you learn that kind of talk, Moses? Are you trying to prove that the language is dead—dead as all the mummies that stink up the desert?"

"Oh!" cried Moses.

"Oh, what? If you mean blasphemy, say blasphemy. Not *oh*. I told you to come and talk to me when you were a man, but you sound like a snivelling schoolgirl. You don't even sound the man you were when you knocked a god on his holy face and saved a very unholy slave brat—"

"How did you know that?" Moses gasped.

The priest came out of the darkness, a formless shape that took Moses by the hand and said, "Walk along with me, boy, and keep an old man company." He drew Moses along with him, walking with a step so sure and definite that it seemed to the boy the old man's feet had owl's eyes of their own, and explaining meanwhile that little went on in the Great House that he did not know. If you kept an ear to the ground, he pointed out to Moses, you could even hear the locusts rustling their wings; and the thing he had meant to ask Moses was whether he, Moses, considered a slave brat's life worth a blow on divine flesh and all that might follow from that.

"I didn't consider," Moses replied. "I did it before I had a chance to think."

"And you truly felt that just by noticing his arrow point you knew where he was aiming?"

"Yes, Amon-Teph—that isn't so hard once you get the feel of the bow."

The old man sniffed and acknowledged Moses' future as a bowman. He then added that he was more troubled about the prince's future in other directions, and he ventured that common sense might also be useful equipment.

Not knowing whether to take this as an insult or not, Moses protested that his mother would be looking for him and that he would have to be going.

"You're a funny lad," the priest said, and from his voice Moses guessed that he was smiling. "You have the arrogance of a prince, but not the assurance—which I prefer to the stupid snobbery of your brothers. Your mother is not looking for you, Moses. I left her on the river terrace, and she will remain there until the moon comes up over old Mother Nile, who is neither hateful nor arrogant but has enough love and compassion for everyone, myself and you and Enekhas-Amon too."

"Why do you . . . why do you say such things?" Moses asked.

"You mean the terrible blasphemies and insults to the living gods—why, Moses, those are silly words that a priest comes to at one point or another. Otherwise, he cuts his throat and goes to see with his own eyes what is true and what is false in the *Book of the Dead*—which I am not quite ready for yet. You see, Prince of Egypt, when you marry a woman and lie with her, many of the romantic illusions you felt about her pass away—perhaps for ever. It's not too different when you marry the gods."

"Was my mother weeping again tonight?" Moses inquired.

"No—not when I was with her. Be patient with your mother, Moses. It is hard to remember that you were once the most beautiful and desirable woman in Egypt when so few others remember it. A great many men loved your mother, and some of them would kneel down and touch the ground she walked upon."

They had come out now into a broad inner court, where already the darkness was diffused and lessened by the first starlight—reflected and increased by the polished white limestone of the courtyard floor. "Don't look at me," the priest went on. "I am too old and fat to contemplate any such foolish memory in personal terms. I'm going to the observatory now, Moses. Have you been there?"

Moses said that he had—was there a corner of the palace where he had not been?—but never at night; and the priest remarked that an observatory had little significance except at night. They crossed the courtyard and mounted the stone stairs that ran up the farther wall, the priest walking slowly and breathing hard with the effort.

The stone platform of the observatory was about twenty feet square, railed in by a marble balustrade, with Isis and her husband Osiris cut in stone and guarding it from opposite corners. In the starlight the two immortals, one the moon and the other her husband, lord of the dead and the lands of the dead, looked amazingly alive. Four white-robed priests stood as a bias line between the two gods, and their soft, lilting chant, the "Psalm to Night", filled Moses with awe and not a little wonder—for as often as he had heard this sound drifting over the palace as darkness gathered, he had never known either its source or meaning.

Now, Amon-Teph stopped Moses, with only the boy's head above the last stair, whispering to him, "Wait until the Psalm is finished, for the music is sweet to the gods of the night, and from it they know that we are here to learn and acknowledge, not to bring harm to the heavenly bodies." When the psalm was finished, they mounted to the platform, and when one of the priests looked at Moses inquiringly, Amon-Teph said, "Don't you recognize him? Moses, the son of Enekhas-Amon."

"Prince of Egypt," they greeted him gently. One of them, a small old man, came over and peered into Moses' face, but without hostility. "You will learn things here," he said, "that your teachers are too ignorant or too frightened to teach you if you wish to learn."

Moses nodded, not trusting himself to speak, and sensing that here was mystery that few were permitted to share.

"With respect. There is no learning without respect, boy. In the old, old times, there was respect for learning and honour for those who knew. Not today. Today the young gods are filled with arrogance and blood lust, and what else do your brothers want but to go forth to war? Is that what you want, Prince?"

Perhaps it was a combination of the circumstances that went with the question—the silver starlight, the sweet, clean desert air, the stone platform hanging so high in the night, the highest pinnacle of the palace, the white-robed priests—reminding Moses of the ancient meaning of the word *priest, pure* in the old Egyptian—the music with which they greeted Isis, the moon, making him feel that these old men who served Isis and her kindred in the night sky were different from the plotting, conniving clericals he knew so well; or maybe it was a moment he had been awaiting this long, long time. Howsoever it was, when asked if he wanted what his royal brothers wanted—war and glory and power—he had his sense of the answer, a new feeling in his life, for never before had his whole soul and being yearned for the plain accomplishment of knowing, of unlocking mysteries unending, of knowing the whole reply and solution. But this he could not put into words or even into thoughts that made sense; he could only experience the feeling in a flush of blood and passion that made his heart beat faster and his whole body tremble as he shook his head.

"Not that? Gold and silver and precious jewels, Prince?"

Still he shook his head.

"No tongue, boy? Come now, Prince of Egypt, speak up!"

"Ah, let the boy be," Amon-Teph said. "I brought him here. Can't you see that he is frightened, as who wouldn't be, with such a set of old rascals as you gathered around him, ready to steal the clothes off his back? Let him be," Amon-Teph laughed, and the others joined him, and then, still giggling, they walked across the observatory leaving Moses alone, then put their heads together and began to whisper.

For his part, Moses was relieved not to be the object of their attention, and he began to drift along the rail, elated by the height at which he stood and by the wonderful view of the fitfully lit palace, the gleaming Nile spreading southward into the Delta, and the whole sprawling City of Ramses, the finer buildings and minor palaces with lamps to light their windows and courts, the poorer dwellings merged into the darkness. "How splendid," he thought, "to have a place like this for your own and to be able to mount here each evening to such a height that you could almost reach up and touch the moon-goddess"; and with this thought he stretched out his arm and heard Amon-Teph grunt behind him,

"You'd need a long arm to reach her, Moses."

The boy turned, surprising the priest with the glow of excitement on his long, aquiline face; and the fat man asked Moses whether he liked the stars so much?

"I feel happy," Moses said, uncertain of cause or source.

The priest nodded and placed one arm over the boy's shoulder, gesturing toward the sky with the other. "A great, strange mystery, Moses, and one of the innumerable factors that make it difficult for a priest to live up to his name. In the old days, they say, we were honoured and honourable, perhaps because we were less greedy and more credulous—or more devout. I am still very devout, mind you, but I permit myself the luxury of bewilderment, which my own teacher—when I was a boy like you—told me is more of a pitfall than gold, women or power. But I only share the bewilderment of an Egypt that snivels over ancient glories and compensates itself with the unbelievable luxury and power that the great God Seti and the God Ramses, his son and your uncle, brought to us. For that, we give humble thanks to our mother Isis, whom you can now see rising over the reedy wilderness of the Delta."

"I don't understand that," Moses said, feeling a strange sense of freedom and the right to speak anything that might come into his thoughts.

"No. I don't suppose you do," Amon-Teph said. "While you suspect that I am being blasphemous, you can't quite put your finger on the core of it. But you see, Prince, all of us who spend our hours up here watching the stars become a little blasphemous, because the stars and the sun make man humble, and I am afraid that humility and blasphemy are not as far apart as you might imagine. Were you thinking that I praise Isis for less than virtue?"

Thoroughly bewildered now, Moses shook his head, and the priest said gravely, "The moon is Isis or Isis is the moon—yes, Moses? And lovers look at the moon after they embrace; but the peasant who tills his field and brings forth the ears of wheat that keep you and me alive—as well as the lovers—and put spring and strength in your long limbs and warm my old, tired bones—he wants to feel the sun on his brown back, and when he feels its heat, he knows that life stirs everywhere. Tell me, young Moses, you who are a prince of Egypt and were educated so well that, as a lord of the Nile, you might be the equal if not the greater than equal of any man on earth—tell me, what is the name of the bright fire that warms our days?"

This returned the boy to reality, and thankful that now he grappled with what he understood, he answered, "*That* anyone knows, Amon-Teph, for the blessed Re stands with Osiris cheek to cheek, the lord of death and the god of the sun, together!"

"The cold and the warm, Moses?"

"Precisely," Moses nodded eagerly, "for alone, each would fade into no substance, but together——"

"Ah, Moses," the priest sighed, "don't argue matters theological with me, for I can only promise you the short end. I see that you were well taught, and I am sure you can recite more paragraphs from the *Book of the Dead* than I can, the way my memory serves me. As a matter of fact, your answer shows devotion to your studies. He is the god of the sun, is he not? Sun-god, river-god, heavenly-god, flood-god—oh so many of him from so far back. Did it ever occur to you, Moses, to wonder why the ancient folk built those stone mountains at Giza so high?"

Moses shook his head. The pyramids were high; why they were high had never occurred to him, and who on earth would ever think of asking such a question?

"They were more simple in the olden times," the priest smiled. "Each king considered that he would build a platform to set him on a level with the god Re. They were simple, and Re was simple, too. Do you know, Moses, people grow wiser and their gods grow a little wiser too?"

"I don't understand you, Amon-Teph."

"No. But you will begin to—because understanding

comes slowly, Moses. You have told me the name of the sun-god, but the name of the sun, this you haven't spoken at all."

"The sun is the sun," Moses said slowly, half as a question. "It has no name."

"And you are the son of Enekhas-Amon, the daughter of Seti the god, and yet you have a name—perhaps a bit unusual, perhaps only half a name—still, it serves. Is the sun less, Moses?"

"I don't know."

"Even I, fat old Amon-Teph, have a name, and my pet cat has a name—but the sun? Moses, have you ever heard the word *Aton*?"

"I don't remember," slowly and half-afraid, he answered. The night was closing in on Moses; and now the moon, the silver disc of Isis, the mother, the sister of life and death, was up over the horizon, gazing full upon him, challenging his *justice*, searching his soul for what horrible thoughts he might think in the next moment. Looking about him, almost wildly, almost like a trapped animal, he saw that the other priests had forgotten him or were deliberately ignoring him, bent on their own business. They had long brazen rods, with a loop at either end, and through these loops they seemed to be tracing the course of the stars. Sometimes they laid down their rods to make notations on strips of papyrus, and again they put their heads together for whispered consultations.

"Magic," Moses whispered.

"Nonsense, boy!" Amon-Teph snorted. "We have no truck with this new fad of magic here! We are doing our work—and at the moment mine is to open your dark eyes a little."

"Why?" Moses asked in half a whimper.

"Why? You want to know all at once. You will know soon enough. For the time being—I can tell you no more than your mother will permit me to tell you. But rest assured, my child, that you have a vital place in our dreams—and they are not always to remain dreams. Now think no more about it, let the future rest. For you, Prince, there is only tomorrow, but my tomorrows are far, far away. Are you afraid?"

"I don't want to be."

"But when I said *Aton*, your heart turned over. I am an old man, Moses, and not fit to frighten any child, much less a prince of Egypt. And you—are you enough of a man yet to know a beautiful woman when she passes by, or is beauty still a word?"

"I'm not a child," Moses answered sullenly.

"And perhaps not a man either. But if you saw all the beautiful women in Egypt today, you would never see one so fair and lovely as the Queen Nefertiti. Does her name frighten you too? And what of the god who shared her throne, the King Akh-en-Aton?"

"Cursed be his name," Moses whispered.

"Ah boy, boy," the old man sighed, placing a hand on the prince's shoulder and touching his cheek lightly with the other. "So quick to curse. And if they taught you to curse our mother, the River Nile, you would do that too—or the sweet morning wind? Curse it? No—no, Moses," he said gently, softly, winningly, "we will come closer than curses, and we will learn something, you and I. You're not too young, and I'm not too old. Do you think it is lightly that I place my life in your hands? Old, I am, and fat and ugly, but still life is sweet and the life of my brothers here—

that is also sweet. And what will happen if you go to your godly uncle and tell him that here I spoke the name of Akh-en-Aton?"

"I won't tell," Moses pleaded, feeling that this was the most awful moment of his life. "I won't tell."

"But if you should tell?"

"You will die, Amon-Teph," the boy stammered, his eyes filling with tears. "But I won't tell."

"I think you won't," the priest murmured. "Either because I am a fool, or because I am a good judge of men, even when they are young men. Do you think I would tell you evil things, Moses, and lead you in evil paths?"

Moses shook his head.

"No, you are very dear to me; and only the cause is worth the risk. Akh-en-Aton was a good and gentle man—and even as we look at the stars, so did he look at the sun and feel its warmth and goodness; and he said to himself—'The sun's name is Aton; and did he not look kindly upon us and give us so generously of his warm blood, then we would all perish and die in the everlasting night. What other god is like him?' "

"Akh-en-Aton wanted to kill the gods—"

"No, no, boy! What lies they tell you! Do you think that gods die so easily? Believe me, it was with no thought of killing the gods that Akh-en-Aton turned to the sun—but to make the gods what they must be, to bring them together with he-who-created-all, who shines down on us every day. We are all children of Aton, our father, and is it wrong for children to know their father as he truly is? Is it wrong for children to know that their father is good and that he gives them everlastingly of his warm gold? Why must we call him by many names and give him many

43

aspects? He has only one that is meaningful—his great, golden heart."

The priest was silent then and he remained silent for a long while, his eyes looking out past the marble balustrade; and as Moses watched him, the boy's fear went away. Finally, Moses said,

"But that was a long, long time ago, wasn't it, Amon-Teph?"

"For you, yes," the priest nodded. "For me—only yesterday. My own grandfather was a priest of Aton under Akh-en-Aton. So, you see, it was not so long ago. But now it's late, Moses. Go to your mother." He took the prince's hand and kissed it; the other priests turned to Moses and nodded their heads; and Moses, full of a strange, overwhelming gladness, left the platform and walked slowly down the stone stairs.

[7]

MANHOOD PECKED AT him; he was gaining his height, and the first soft, dark down began to show on his upper lip. His limbs lengthened, and his round muscles became flat and hard. Inside him strange new juices stirred him to restless, aching, longing that was without definition and beyond his understanding, Suddenly, the world was created anew and a hundred things were singular.

Often enough the children of Ramses swam in the River Nile now. This was frowned on if not wholly forbidden, but they were yearlings who had to test their stride and strength constantly—and bolster their defiance too. When night fell, they would slip down the outside stairs of the palace to the stone quays where the royal barges were docked, drop noiselessly into the warm water, and swim out—the moment tingling with the possibility that they might encounter a crocodile that had come up out of the wild marshes of the Delta.

Sometimes the bolder among their sisters joined them, and it was thus that one night a girl called Neftu-Isis, round and ripe and budding in her womanhood, swam next to Moses. Something real or fancied frightened her and she threw her arms around him, the two of them sinking beneath the water; and he, returning her embrace, finding it like no other touch of a woman's hands, new and wonderful and causing his whole body to tremble, held on to her even when they rose above the water again, reassuring her that there was nothing to fear—and anyway here he was, Moses, and a match for anything.

"You're so strong," she said, as if those words were never spoken by a woman before, and he replied, treading water with calculated ease,

"Oh, I don't know. I suppose I swim fairly well."

She herself swam like a fish, having been raised in and out of the palace pools and fountains, but she hastened to declare, "And I swim badly, Prince of Egypt, don't I? And I tire so easily."

He thought her modest and enchanting, her long black hair spreading fanwise around her head in the water, and for the first time the sight of a girl's breasts excited him. He begged her to rest on him, and with long, easy strokes he swam back to the quays. He was not sure that chance brought him to a different quay than they had embarked from. It was closer, in any case, and as the night air was cooling, he put his arms around her to warm her. They lay side by side on the stone floor of the quay, the rocks be-

neath them still warm from the sun, and it never occurred
to Moses that she knew so much more of making love than
he did. Yet she was not backward with her knowledge and,
since he knew practically nothing to speak of, he was filled
with worship and adoration. Though he was younger than
she—she was past fourteen, some nine months from the age
of marriage—he took her to his heart, decided that she was
the only woman he would ever love, and lived for at least
a week in a transport of joy.

It was not long before he overheard some of his royal
cousins talking about her, and heard too that she had been
betrothed some six months to a duke of Philistia—for
Ramses used his daughters, as he did so many other people,
to build political bridges. His broken heart somehow
healed, but not without aid from one or another of the
many princesses; and since in their code of living no store
was set on virginity and because so much love had been
pent up inside him, he loved generously and easily.

But he loved without being in love, and the singular
wonder of the first moment was not repeated. Yet he was
not like some of his royal cousins who drove themselves
after women—perhaps in imitation of or perhaps in com-
petition with their godly sire; Moses was an anomaly in
the Great House of the king, a prince with a very small
store of arrogance; and perhaps for that very reason,
women turned to him with a regard his age hardly war-
ranted.

But this modesty—which won him not only the love of
women but also the friendship of some of the gentler, if usually younger, of his royal brothers—did not spring full-
grown; it was helped to develop by the princely astronomers
who had, in a measure, made him their ward. Whatever the

ultimate goal they planned—the ultimate destination they chose for Moses and for themselves—it remained unrevealed to the boy; and as circumstances developed, it would so remain for many years. He accepted their apparent love for him or the strange reverence they bore him because they were gentle people and the creed they taught him was a gentle creed.

They never lured him to the tower or urged him there. When he came by himself they welcomed him gladly, and when a week or ten days went by without his coming, they didn't reproach him. Amon-Teph remained his teacher, and step by step there was unfolded for him the story of Aton.

He learned how for untold generations the lord and creator of all things had looked with compassion and pity upon the Land of Egypt—for while Aton, the sun, was the father and maker of all, he had chosen the Land of Egypt for his special blessing, and had given to Egyptians the sacred knowledge of truth and justice. Yet, in spite of this, the Egyptians turned their faces from him and worshipped many strange and cold gods, turning more and more to death and the shadow-world of death. So little did they comprehend Aton that they built mountains of stone that lesser gods might mount to the level of Aton—never knowing that to approach Aton would be to invite destruction, even as he who looks at Aton too long will find that the god has taken his sight away for ever.

For this Aton pitied them and often discussed their folly and wickness with his son, who dwelt within his bosom. The name of the sacred son of Aton was Shay, which meant *destiny*, or the ultimate realization of all things. Finally, Aton decided that he must send his holy son to mankind, to redeem them and to make them conscious of their ultimate destiny; and even though it meant leaving the everlasting beauty of his father, Shay agreed. Whereupon, Shay descended to earth and entered the body of the most godlike man he could find—Amen-Hotep, the ruler over Egypt. This occurred in the sixth year of the reign of this holy king; and when it happened, he knew that it had happened and he changed his name to Akh-en-Aton, declaring by this name that he was consecrated to Aton and that he would war against all gods other than the one true god.

Yet in the end the gods of darkness and hate returned to the Land of Egypt. Akh-en-Aton died, and his son was a weakling and without the spirit of Shay within him. All who were evil and rapacious and hungry for power turned against Aton and, led by the dark plotter, the god Osiris, they triumphed; and those who served Aton died by the thousands. That was less than a century ago, yet today the faith of Aton was kept alive only by a handful and only at the risk of their own lives.

"So you see, Moses," Amon-Teph said to him, "not all priests are as alike inside as they are outside, even as not all princes are cut out of the same cloth. This palace swarms with priests who came to power when they murdered the old priesthood of Aton; and because they could destroy whom they liked by charging them with the heresy of Aton, they have ever spread and increased their power. So long as the God Ramses rules, they will be held in some check, for he has an iron hand and jealousy of his own power. But god help us all if a weakling comes after him! Then the priests will pluck Egypt clean as a bone."

IN THE MIDDLE of his fourteenth year, six months past his thirteenth birthday, Moses left the war-court where the children were trained, never to return; for it was the end of his training in arms and the end of his formal education and schooling as well. From this time on he was to be considered a man with many of the rights of a man and a prince of the Great House.

He would now have the right to purchase and own slaves—men and women—for his first princely legacy of gold would come to him from Ramses. He would have the right to ask for a woman in marriage, provided that a marriage was not arranged by his mother or by the God-King. He would have the right to his own quarters, if he desired to leave his mother's apartment. He would have the right to come and go as he pleased, to hunt in the desert or in the marshes of the Delta, to bear arms, and even—provided Ramses granted his permission—to go out with one of the many punitive expeditions that ranged the borders and flung back the constant barbarian inroads. He would have many other rights, but that most important privilege of all did not come with the simple chronological acquisition of manhood: that was the right to wear upon his finger the sacred cartouche inscribed with one of the godly attributes of royalty that a prince might own—the *whu*, which was the divine right of command. Only Ramses himself could grant this right to a prince, and only by naming him in the line to the throne.

Yet, notwithstanding, the glory of manhood was a great deal, and he came to his mother straight from the war-court, burdened proudly with all the panoply of war—dagger and sword and oxhide buckler, laminated bow and quiver of arrows, Kushite stave and javelin—such a weight that he could hardly walk, but trying to indicate that it was merely a feather, nothing at all—and what prince of Egypt was not capable of carrying an armoury on his back?

With Enekhas-Amon, the years dealt ever less kindly, and more and more she had become a recluse in her chambers. For the past year she had attended none of the fêtes or spectacles or formal courts, avoiding almost all of the few friends who remained to her. Aside from three women slaves of long service and Moses, she saw only Seti, her physician, and Amon-Teph, who had fallen into the habit of calling upon her every week or so. Her headaches came more and more frequently, each attack making her weaker and lessening her powers of recovery; and in the process of languishing and self-pity, the last remnants of her beauty disappeared, leaving her haggard and thin.

But today she was all pride, as close to happiness as she had been in a long time; and rather than a long-limbed, sunburned boy, bowed down with a ridiculous weight of weapons, she saw a man of passion and strength and vengeance, who with his mighty right arm would beat any and all opposition.

Moses recognized the rare glow on her features, and as she stood up, he laid down the arms and embraced her. Already he was a full head taller than she, and as he held her and felt her head against his bare breast and the wetness of her tears of pride, he was deeply touched and by no means without guilt for the days when he had wasted the endless hours of play with never a care for her. He told himself that now it would be different, that now he had a degree of understanding that was no part of childhood.

She apologized for her foolish tears, and wondered what he could think of her behaving this way?

"I could think only the best of you, my mother."

She wanted him to stand back, away from her, so that she could look at him again; and she feasted with her eyes as if she were hungrily consuming food—food enough to make her whole and well again. "What a fine, strong man he is!" she thought to herself; and indeed he was handsome enough for all her pride, his legs lean and strong, his back straight and wide, and his shoulders the powerful shoulders of the man he was becoming.

"You are all that I ever dreamed, my son, and only one thing is missing."

"And what is that?" he smiled.

"The divine cartouche on your finger," she whispered.

"Mother, my mother," he said, feeling older and wiser and more free from passion than she could ever be, "who am I to think about the throne of Egypt?"

"Who? The only one. Who else can stand beside you as the Prince of Egypt?"

Moses shook his head. "My mother, the God Ramses has a hundred sons and more—and how many daughters? As for me, I am not even sure I am his son."

"Why do you say that?" she snapped suddenly. "Have I ever told you that? Who has?"

"Gossip."

"And you believe gossip—common gossip?"

"How could I live in this house and not believe gossip?"

Enekhas-Amon sighed and lay down upon her couch

again. "It tires me to fight you, my son. Perhaps you are right, and he isn't your father. But suppose a greater god had fathered you?" She asked this wistfully as she lay there, the last bit of youth and hope flickering across her worn face; and Moses felt weighed down with pity for her and yet a little angry at such childishness. He was old enough to know that no god had sired him, if indeed—as Amon-Teph sometimes wondered—any god had ever sired a mortal man.

He shook his head, looking at her gently and compassionately.

"Is it because you are a man that you know everything now, my son? Or is it because you are a man that you have decided I am just a foolish woman who knows nothing of any consequence?"

"Please, my mother," he begged her, "don't accuse me of such things. If I am a man now, it's because you gave me the means of manhood. And perhaps because I am a man, or the beginning of a man at least, I know now that there is a smell of something awful here—which I never knew before—and I don't think that you and I, my mother, will ever sleep easily under the same roof as the God Ramses. I have been thinking that now it is time for us to leave this palace. I never asked you whether we have wealth of our own, but if we have even a little, we can go away. I have heard that Luxor in Upper Egypt is a good place to live, and it is such a distance that the God Ramses will forget us——"

"He doesn't forget so easily," Enekhas-Amon smiled, amused to hear her son, who only yesterday was a little boy, speaking with such grave and earnest conviction, "and I'm not at all sure that he would allow us to leave. He likes bothersome things to remain close at hand where he can watch them, and I think, Moses, that it is a little childish to talk of a smell of something awful here. This Great House is just what it is—a very large house. There are still some things you don't understand—and that is my fault more than yours. As for wealth, you will be one of the richest men in Egypt, and I could hardly give you an accounting out of my poor memory of the copper mines, the gold mines, the herds of cattle and the fields of wheat that belong to me. I don't think about them because they brought me little enough in the way of happincss—just as I don't think of the ships that are mine that sail the great sea from end to end, bringing us the wealth of a hundred lands. Of all that, Amon-Teph has an accounting, and all of it will be yours. Don't urge me to travel to places that are only fables to you, my son. I am a sick woman, and here I will die—and in not too long a time, I'm afraid. And yet I am not afraid. You are the only one I will leave with regret."

"Don't talk like that, my mother!" Moses cried. "I wish my tongue had withered before I spoke to give you grief!"

"Boy, boy," she soothed him, "nothing you said gave me grief. My grief is all inside me, where it has always been. How can you understand, with your youth and health? Every day the pain in my head is worse—and only this morning, Seti urged me to let them open my skull so that the foul vapours can escape and give me some peace."

A look of bare terror came over Moses face and he fell on his knees before her couch, taking her hand and pressing it to his cheek, begging her, "No, no—please, my mother, don't do it! Don't let them! They will kill you just as they always kill with trepanning! Amon-Teph told me and he swore he would die before he let anyone open his skull! And he said that Seti isn't a doctor, not a real doctor, but a puffed-up fool and a magician too! Don't let them!"

Enekhas-Amon was pleased rather than disturbed by this outburst; it helped her to know that the boy cared so deeply, for she was so uncertain and mistrustful of love that even Moses had to prove his devotion over and over. She stroked his hair lovingly, reassuring him that not Seti but the finest surgeons in Egypt would perform the operation—if, indeed, it had to be undertaken. That was still in the future and, as for Amon-Teph, he, too, knew a little less than everything. Yet he was a good man, she hastened to say, turning the boy's tearful face up to her and looking into his eyes.

"A man doesn't weep, my son; and as for Amon-Teph, heed him well when he teaches you. He will teach you to be the kind of man Egypt has forgotten. There are few such teachers left in Egypt."

"You know?" Moses whispered. "You know the things he teaches me?"

"How could I help knowing? Even if Amon-Teph had not told me? Night after night—well, Moses, we have out dreams for you. I know little about the gods, but a great deal about politics, and the two go hand in hand. Do you think it was for want of a god to stand sponsor for you that I called you Moses and only Moses? I am sure that the God Ramses himself suspects the meaning of the strange name you bear, which is only half a name, and which foolish people laugh at. Let them laugh, my son. Let the God Ramses laugh, for he knows too much and too little of who you truly are—and perhaps it was wrong for me to keep the truth from you for so long. Well, just a little longer now. You are a man already, but there is still height and strength and knowledge—another year, another two years. Meanwhile, bear yourself like a god, my son—not simply as a prince of Egypt but *the* Prince of Egypt. Let all who see you know that—not by word, but by the way you walk, by your abiding truth and *justice*, by your look and your bearing. It will not be long now."

The lengthy speech tired her, and though Moses pressed her, she lay silently on her couch, her eyes closed; and not a word more would she say.

[9]

THERE WAS A sense of balance and reality in Moses that made him less vulnerable to wild dreams and heady illusions; and to his way of thinking there was less reason to bear himself as a god—which was a highly speculative and confusing notion at best—than there was to bear himself like a man—which was a factual condition and one that offered untold advantages and excitements.

Like his royal cousins who had come into the same estate, he soon tired of the novelty of carrying forty or fifty pounds of war equipment through the day and, like them, he pared it down to a bronze dagger. While even this constituted braggadocio in so peaceful and orderly a place as the Great House of Ramses, it bolstered his new status to feel the cold scabbard against his thigh. With gold in his pouch, he shopped the teeming market place of the city, savouring, along with his delicious sense of freedom, the colour and excitement of life in a busy international bazaar; for here, only a hundred yards or so from the water front and the immense docking facilities that Ramses had built for his beloved city, were the merchants and the products of all the world—silks from the legendary land of China where, it was said, people were yellow of skin with slanting cat's eyes; beautiful ivory carvings from the equally legendary Ganges cities; dried fish and black wool from Troy; regal purple wool and linen from Phoenicia; fat figs and worked silver from Philistia; hard smoked sausage and willow bark from Sardinia; cedar from the hills of Lebanon; salt from the sea people—the pirates of Myrmidia, Locria and Argos; wrought gold and wine from Crete; pepper and cloves from the merchants of Hatti, who brought it from the very ends of the earth; pottery from Achaea and Salamis; feathers and hides from the land of Kush; caged lions and leopards from unnamed lands to the south of Kush; khat and dates from the Bedouins of Arabia; and succulent dried fruit from the gardens of Babylon.

And even more fascinating than the wonderful display of goods were the men who sold them; for the Egypt of Ramses was no longer the hidden land, walled in by desert and sea. Quite the contrary, it was the hub and market place of the whole world—the land of knowledge, tolerance for all strangers, and worldly sophistication. Here Moses saw painted barbarian Caucasians pleading for someone to trade them iron, bits of iron, any iron—the magic metal which the Egyptians were now beginning to work—for their beautiful furs, so unnecessary in this land of everlasting sunshine; here were the merchant lords of Mesopotamia with their long woollen robes, their conical hats, their greased, curled hair and beards, their round faces and their curling nostrils; here were the Sea Rovers, with their ten-foot spears and their huge, circular and brightly painted shields; here were desert Bedouins, in their dirty, torn robes, haughty suspicious and reserved; here were men of Kush, coal-black and deep-voiced; Philistines, superior and disdainful; hard-handed, hard-muscled sea captains and supercargoes of Phoenicia; Hittites; Canaanites; painted, half-savage traders from Shekelesh and Sherden; and even the haughty, bronzed-clad princes of distant Etruria.

And here, too, was the slave mart, where only Egyptians were the sellers; for this was a family and hereditary monopoly in Lower Egypt and all foreign dealers were forced to deal with them and through them. Here Moses would stand in fascination—not in moral judgment, for this was as much a part of his life as the sand and the sky—but held by a feeling that was not without moral content and guilt; watching the huddles of poor, naked, chained wretches, the children, the babes drinking their mothers' milk of servitude, the boys and girls, the maidens and young men, the old and the sick and the stricken—and it was a new feeling that Moses experienced when, with the twilight and end of a market day, he saw the servants of the slave-dealers thrust knives into the hearts of the unsaleable, the weak and diseased beyond repair, so as to save the cost of feeding them through future markets.

It was an awakening feeling of horror and disgust, without logic or social condemnation to support it, and therefore it was no more than an emotional current in the boy—and not a very deep one at that. But it was also part of his growth and part of the effect upon him of the strange and dangerous religion of Aton. His emotional response was fed by other impressions as well. For the first time in his life) he consciously reflected on the fact that few people in Egypt were like the inhabitants of the Great House, tall and full-fleshed and healthy. The Egyptians he saw in the city were smaller and thinner; unperfumed, strong with the odour of body and filth; often toothless, diseased; often skinny, with bloated bellies. The children ran naked like animals in the market—a jungle in which they fought for scraps, for crusts of bread; in which they begged and pleaded and stole.

But not from Moses or his cousins did they beg; they fled his path and covered their faces; and their elders bowed deeply or effaced themselves in one way or another. Where a prince of Egypt walked, a path was clear, and if by some accident one of the peasants touched one of the royal brothers, he would fling himself down and plead for forgiveness.

At first Moses enjoyed this, but he was unable to be habitually disdainful, as his cousins were. Very well for his mother, in her impassioned speech, to tell him to bear himself like a god; the notion sat poorly with him and in time the obeisance of the market place came to bore and even to irritate him. Then he went there only to buy. But buying was a great pleasure. Manhood called for something more than a boy's loincloth; and one of his first purchases was a dozen pleated linen kilts—the garment sacred to Egyptian nobility. Sandals followed, and then his fancy was caught by golden collars, with bracelet and belt to match. He bought a headband with a sphinx as a frontlet and a ring set with rubies.

In regard to his mother, he learned for the first time how to purchase release from guilt. He bought her bouquets of the brightest flowers he could find, red and black and yellow poppies, Kushite *nogus* which were like huge white orchids, roses, and the magnificent lilies, pink and pale yellow, that were cultivated in the morass of the Delta.

He selected the choicest fruit for her—the magnificent melons for which Lower Egypt was justly famous; sweet grapes; pomegranates, picked fresh on the plains of Sharon and brought at all speed in the Philistine galleys; apricots and luscious plums; and for sweets, he sought out the best golden wine molasses from Canaan and the honey that the bees made from the flower gardens of Crete.

She had little enough appetite, and each time he brought her a gift, wine or fruit or flowers or a golden necklace, she scolded him petulantly and hinted that he was simply trying to make her forget all she heard about his carrying on with the sluts of the Great House.

True enough, the attitude of his royal cousins who were female changed a good deal with his accolade of manhood. Now he was legitimate prey in a practical sense, and the single son of the God-King's sister was no small match. But, more than that, Moses was an extraordinarily striking young man, and at the age of fourteen stood almost six feet in height—lean and hard. If, when judged alone, his bony face was hardly handsome, he nevertheless presented a strange and interesting contrast to his cousins.

He had no inner drive for the conquest of women and no uncertainties about their liking for him. The sight of a lovely girl, her breasts round and firm above her transparent skirt, her lips and nipples rouged, pleased him, without any great excitement. He felt that someday he would see one who pleased him so that he would not be able to pass his days without her; but there was more than enough time for this.

THERE WERE PARTS of the Great House where he had not been for years, and his exploration or re-exploration of odd corners was in good part an attempt to find again the golden, dreamy days of childhood, already so far in the past—as it seemed to him. One day, he stepped into a room, the door to which stood wide open, and which was open to the Nile on the opposite side. As the walls were coated with white lime, the room was filled with light. What had caught Moses' eye was a line of wooden cubbyholes on one of the side walls, each opening containing a toll of papyrus; and as he entered the room, he saw against the opposite wall a large slanting desk of cedar, if desk it was, the lower and outer edge of its surface about four feet high, and then slanting back and upward to the wall.

A man stood at this desk, leaning over a large sheet of papyrus that was tacked on to the cedar, and working slowly and carefully with a copper quill that he frequently dipped into an inkpot suspended from the cedar surface. Also hooked on to the edge of the board were an assortment of devices strange to Moses, rules and graded curves and triangles and T-squares, all of copper. It was the first time that Moses had ever seen a work easel.

He had been there no more than a moment when the man, without turning from his work, said, "I imagine you are in the wrong place, Prince of Egypt."

"Oh?" Did the man have eyes in the back of his head? "How do you know that I am a prince of Egypt?"

"Who else enters unbidden and stays?" he answered caustically.

"I'm sorry," Moses hastened to say. "I didn't know you were working and that I would disturb you. I didn't know anyone was here. The door was open and I saw the rolls of papyrus."

Still without turning, the man snorted, "By all that is holy or unholy, what kind of a prince is this who answers politely and with deference when he is scolded? Only because I consider my talent fairly valuable do I take the liberty of insulting the divine young blood around this place, but you are the first not to threaten to have me quartered and thrown to the crocodiles—a favourite means of execution among your brothers. Who are you? What is your name, Prince of Egypt?"

Tiptoeing closer, so that he might better see what the man did, Moses answered, "My name is Moses."

"What Moses? Or do you have only half a name?"

"Only half a name, I'm afraid. I'm the son of the Princess Enekhas-Amon."

"Oh yes, of course—the prince with half a name. The mystery prince of the Great House. Let me have a look at you, boy." He carefully placed his pen in a holder and turned to Moses, revealing the lean and thoughtful countenance of a man of forty or so, grey-haired, and with a pair of dark, small eyes that seemed permanently narrowed in detached amusement. Yet he was obviously surprised to see the tall young man who stood facing him, observed him with interest, and finally smiled.

"Yes, for half a name, you hold your own. You don't look like half a man, Prince of Egypt. May I call you Moses? You don't seem as prone to vanity or anger as your brothers."

"Call me Moses, yes, and I must explain that they are

not my brothers. The God Ramses is not my father, and I am the only child of the divine Enekhas-Amon."

The man nodded with appreciation at this.

"And who are you, sir?" Moses asked.

"No one very much, and of no station, low in birth and of common blood. My only good fortune is to have a trade and a skill. I am chief engineer in construction, at the bidding of the God Ramses and responsible to him alone. I am also very good at my work, if I may say so, and since of all the gods who ever sat on the Pharaoh Throne since Egypt lives, the God Ramses is most passionately fond of building—and knows more about it than most engineers, I may add—he endures me and my work. That is why I can take liberties. I have a caustic tongue and a nasty dislike for empty vanity, even when exhibited by those of divine birth. So long as the God Ramses desires another building or road or tomb, this will be tolerated. When or if he grows tired of this particular avocation, I will have my throat cut. Until then, I shall mind my own business and keep out of palace politics and say what I please. My name, Moses, is Neph, a plain, common name that poor people bestow on their children when their children are many and when poverty has dried their sense of poetry.

"I was one of eleven children—and now I am the only one alive. None of the others lived past a thirtieth year, and my father and mother laid themselves down and died when the great banker, Seti-Kaph, who held their land in mortgage, took it because they had a bad harvest and could not make payment. I don't know why I am telling you this, except that I seem to like you, and knowing a little about you, I suppose I pity you. My own fortune came when my mother's brother, who had become one of these new priests of the new era, succumbed to her pleading and had me apprenticed to one of the engineers engaged in building this Great House. For five years I cleaned his tools, scrubbed him, flattered him, and crawled on my belly before him. Yet, before this house was finished, I was drawing and changing plans. This very room was part of my design— with the dream that I might work here some day. But since I remain a man who lives by his work as well as his wits, I must go back to it now, having told you the story of my life—and having failed, as I see, to shock you or drive you away."

"I would like to stay for a while, if you will permit me?"

"It is not mine to permit. You are the prince."

"Only with your permission, Neph, will I stay. I would like to watch you as you work."

"Very well. But I would appreciate it if you did not speak to me. I don't like to talk when I work."

Moses nodded, and the engineer returned to his drawing. From behind his back and at enough distance to be sure that he would not disturb him, Moses watched him with increasing fascination. He had never seen anything like the pen the engineer used. It had a slit down the side to the point, and each time Neph withdrew it from the ink, he wiped it clean with a piece of chamois, leaving ink only in the slit, which he kept upward as he used the pen. It left a clean, thin line on the papyrus, and mostly he used it with one or another of the guide instruments.

Equally interesting was Neph's numerical notation. Mathematics had not been the strongest part of Moses' education, and beyond the use of several types of abacus (an instrument common to all Egyptian calculation) the use of the royal cubit as a pace measure, and the notation of numbers through simple brush strokes, he had almost no mathematical knowledge. He noticed that Neph did not refer to his abacus, which hung from the wall, but used as a basic system a method of numbering Moses had never seen before—and one which puzzled him until he realized that it was numbering. It was based on a rectangle, each side counting as one, the completed square as four, crossed as five, and crossed from the opposite direction as ten. This was as far as Moses could follow it, although it extended into further and more complex forms. He was aching to ask about it, but kept his lips closed and tight. In the same way, he tried to guess how distance was measured. He knew the cubit sign for stride, foot, hand and finger, but only the sign for stride was used by Neph—that being subdivided and multiplied with numbers.

While Moses had been led into grappling with abstractions, through the teaching of Amon-Teph, his life had been such that he had never before encountered an abstract of distance, space and elevation. His involvement here became so intent that when Neph finally turned to look at him, Moses was at first unconscious of his scrutiny; and the engineer sat there, staring in his own amazement at a prince of Egypt lost in the contemplation of a building plan. He said, not unkindly,

"Well, Moses, sir, what do you see in my plans that engrosses you?"

"I don't know," the boy answered slowly, but so intensely and with his brows knit in so puzzled a frown that the engineer was able to comprehend his inner excitement, his amazement and his bewilderment—and was also moved to wonder whether this strange prince met every new aspect of life with the same intense interest. Neph, in spite of a long-standing distaste for the royal children who thronged the palace, found his own curiosity pricked; in a fashion his heart went out to the prince, and be found himself regretting that this was not some simple peasant lad of low blood whom he could befriend and perhaps apprentice to his trade. Another part of his mind warned him to stay clear of the gods' relatives, to mind his own business, and certainly not to get involved with the son of Enekhas-Amon.

"Do you know what I'm doing here?" he asked Moses, his voice sharp enough to make him regret his caution. Certainly there was no harm in treating the prince as decently as he would treat any other human being; and, more gently this time, he said, "I mean this," pointing to the papyrus. "Do you know what it is?"

"I think so," Moses nodded. "No—I'm not sure. I've never seen anything like it before. I thought first that it was some kind of a drawing of a house, but if it is, why do the walls lie flat around the open floor, and why is the roof off by itself?"

"Such is education in the royal school," Neph shrugged. "What do they teach you—that we build houses by throwing the stones in at random? Do you know that everywhere in the world Egypt is known as the land of the stones— because we have built in stone as no others have? Do you think we build at play? For every house, every tomb, every plaza, every temple—yes, for every monument or statue of fountain or pool, for the stone benches for the idle to dally on or the wharves where the ships tie up or the warehouses where they store their cargo—for all of it and for each part of it, there must be a plan like this one, a plan drawn to careful scale, with every measurement of the utmost precision. Only when the plan is complete to the last tiny detail can we calculate how much material and how many workers we will require—and then actually get to the building, which also requires the plan for every step of construction. As to why it is all open and flat—I am not one of your palace decorators, titillating the eyes of nobles. I must see all of the building at once. When it stands complete, then the roof and the walls will be where they belong."

The harshness of his voice was eased by the twinkle in his eyes; for in spite of all his interest Moses would have bridled. No one except the God Ramses had ever taken such a tone with him before, and if he was an unusual prince among the princes of Egypt, he was still one of them, bred and trained in the acknowledgment of his own divine origin.

"And what kind of a house is it?" Moses wanted to know.

"A granary," Neph said.

"The first one you've built?"

Neph snorted. "No. Prince of Egypt, I am not building my first granary. I have built at least ten—but I built them in the dry desert, where common sense would suggest grain should be stored. But since the war with the Sea Rovers and since their attempt to invade from Libya, your uncle, the God Ramses, has felt that the desert granaries could be destroyed. Whereupon, he has instructed me to build granaries on the mud islands in the Delta, where they will be secure against attack."

"In the slime out there?" Moses wondered. "In the morass? is it possible?"

"It is impossible," Neph answered sourly, and faced back to his work. "But I am doing it," he added. "When the

God Ramses instructs, you do it, and whether it is possible becomes incidental." He resumed his work, Moses watching him again, and after a few minutes of silence, Neph asked,

"Moses, would you like to see how we do the impossible?"

"I would, please, Neph," Moses said eagerly.

"Then be at the palace quay before sunrise tomorrow. Be there on time, because we depart in the hour before sunrise. Now, please leave me alone. I cannot work with anyone in the room."

[11]

IN THE MIDDLE of the night he was awake, his heart pounding with the notion that he had overslept and that Neph had left without him. He rolled out of his couch, fastened on his loincloth, thrust his feet into a pair of sandals and buckled on his silver dagger belt. Without stopping to cleanse himself or make his libation, he ran softly from his chamber and then plunged through the darkness of the palace, letting his feet find the way they knew so well. The corridors, except where they were open to the sky, or fitfully lit by the passing torch of a night guard, were like pools of black ink; and though ordinarily be would not have been at ease in the great warren at night, now he thought only of getting to the quay in time. When be reached the river terrace, he ran full into the arms of one of the guards—who drew back in surprise at the sight of a prince plunging along through the night.

"Tell me," Moses gasped, "when will it be dawn?"

"Prince of Egypt," said the guard, "there are four watches through the night. Mine is only the third. There are at least two hours before the light comes." He held his torch toward the prince, consumed with curiosity but not dating to ask; and thanking him, and now walking, Moses felt his way down the stone stairs to the quay.

Here the starlight, both from above and reflected from the still surface of the great river, let him see the shape of the place, the boats tied up to the bronze rings and the boatmen sprawled out asleep on the decks and curled up in the cordage. Never before had he been out at the riverside so late at night—or so early in the morning—and the silence, the stillness, the glassy surface of the water, the lack of even a breath of wind—all of it combined to give him a sense of awe mixed with a little fear and a little excitement. Keeping his hand clenched over the pommel of his dagger, he walked softly back and forth—feeling that he was the single living, thinking creature in all the world.

But presently he began to feel drowsy, and he stretched out on the quay, pillowing his head against some hempen cargo sacks that had a tantalizing smell of black cumin and coriander. He lay there looking at the brilliant spread of stars strewn through that clear, close sky, wondering whether they were the gods or the torches of the gods or perhaps the playthings of the gods—wondering whether a man might build so high that he could look upon them and touch them—wondering dreamily about this and that; watching the course of a meteor, the thin trail of fire, and speculating whether some god had cast out a star, if there were gods, and not, as Amon-Teph and his friends said, simply one mighty force contained in the fire of the living sun. He wanted to believe Amon-Teph, because he loved him and honoured him; but if he did, then the God Ramses became only a man, and all the sombre gods of the night must die—if indeed they had ever lived—and even the spark of the divine that he himself possessed as a prince of Egypt would go out, and he would be no different from any peasant.

With all these thoughts flowing through his mind, he finally closed his eyes; and in that same moment, it seemed, he heard Neph's voice "Wake up, Prince of Egypt, for now we must go!"

Startled, he sat up—in a grey world, the river gone, and the quay hanging over an endless field of white mist. Neph stood before him, a cloak over his shoulders, and as Moses shivered in the morning chill, Neph took his cloak and placed it about the boy's shoulders. Moses tried to protest, but Neph smiled with that strange tenderness that so many men have in the hour before dawn, and shook his head. "Wear it, I am warm, and soon the sun will rise. But you will be chilled, and I don't want to bring you back sick."

"Thank you, Neph," Moses said, and then the engineer led him over to the edge of the quay, asking whether he had spent the night there. "But I didn't want you to sail without me."

"Strange Prince of Egypt," Neph thought, and asked, "Could we sail without you, Moses, when I had given my word?"

Moses was puzzled and not wholly awake, glad for the warmth of the cloak and feeling gauche and foolish. The boat was drawn up at the quay, two of the oarsmen holding it to the docking rings. It was a broad galley-barge of shallow draught, eight oarsmen on each side forward, and a little deck about seven feet square in the stern, and then the usual stern outrigger for the steersman and his long oar. On this deck, three men stood, two of them holding long, leather papyrus quivers under their arms, and the third with an armful of curious equipment, angles and tripods and folded measures and hollow brace tubes.

Moses and Neph climbed into the barge and picked their way among the oarsmen to the stern deck, Moses noticing that while the towers were slaves, they were not chained to the seats as were the seagoing galley slaves; and he concluded that in this small craft their lot was not so hard as to impel them to run away.

The barge was already moving out when he reached the deck, the oarsmen skilfully pushing off and swinging the bow out to the river and then falling into the long, even stroke that they would maintain for hours. Moses stood back towards the helmsman, away from the four engineers, who were already discussing their problems—a discussion so full of technical words that Moses could not follow it with any real sense of meaning. He could see that they were all plain-looking men, lean, with knotted muscles and short-cropped hair, disdaining even the kilts of the middle class and wearing only loincloths, leather sandals, and leather belts to support their tools and pouches.

The whole adventure excited him far more than he dared reveal. He would have liked to ask the helmsman how he could possibly steer so confidently in the mist and grey half-darkness, but he did not want to display his ignorance. He stood there, silent and happy, watching the rhythm of the oars and waiting for the first edge of the sun's disc in the dawning. They passed a fishing boat making out to the sea and Moses noticed, not without envy, how casually the engineers exchanged greetings with the fishermen.

Neph joined him and said, "Watch now, Moses, in the east over yonder," pointing with his arm, "for any moment now, we will see the edge of the sun." As he spoke, the sky in that direction began to lighten rapidly and a breeze from the sea broke the mist and set it running in long streamers. Lighter and brighter grew the sky, until presently an edge of fire showed over marshy islands and many-fingered water. They were entering the marsh-delta, a world in itself, broad, still wild in places, filled with innumerable islands and a labyrinth of winding waterways, undulating with papyrus and marsh grass and bulrushes, painted here and there with large patches of lilies.

Close as it was to the City of Tanis, to which Ramses had now given not only his name but an importance beyond that of any other city in Egypt, it was still another world to Moses and an unknown world as well. He had accepted the fact that his city was in the Delta, and though the river upon which it was built was called the Mother Nile, he knew that the Nile had other branches into the Delta—but he had never been in these wild eastern reaches. He had never seen the Delta this way, so wild and strange and untouched, flooded with the fiery pink light of morning, endless, without house or human being.

"Have we come far?" he asked Neph.

"Not far, Prince, but we go further—three hours more, almost to where the floodwaters cease, almost to the Land of Goshen, where the slave people live."

"Where they live? You mean there is a nation of them there?"

"No—no, Moses," Neph said, looking at the boy with some amazement. "You mean you don't know these things?

How do you grow up, you of the divine blood—as prisoners? No, don't be angry. I'm a plain man with plain speech, and if we are to be friends, you must take me as I come."

Moses grasped Neph's arm. "I would be your friend."

"Better my son," Neph thought, feeling the twinge of pain of a man who has once had and lost a son. "If you want me for a friend," he said, "I'll be that, although I'm old enough to be your father—and you must be patient, for I have never seen a prince of Egypt before that I could tolerate, much less love."

Moses grinned at that, and Neph noticed how sweet the boy's large-boned face could become.

"We were talking," Neph said, "of the Land of Goshen, which lies to the east of here at the edge of the Delta. It is not a large land, but grassy—and rich; yet out own people never favoured it and will not live there. For one thing, it is unevenly in flood. The Delta is not like the rest of the river, but a living, changing thing, and the land around it floods unevenly. Sometimes in Goshen five years will go by without inundation, and then the soil, which is rich in good clay, becomes rocklike and cannot be ploughed, even though the grass still grows. And unless our Egyptian peasant can turn over the land and plant a crop, he will not abide in a place. Secondly, when the wild shepherd kings and later the cruel men of Hatti came down into our blessed land, there was no hope of protection for anyone in Goshen. So it is not a place where Egyptians like to live . . ." His voice trailed away. The whole sun hung above the marsh now, and he was caught and silenced by the beauty of the morning. And Moses, for once, felt with his heart instead of his head what the religion of Amon-Teph meant to those who believed. In this moment, he believed, and in the face of that warming, beneficent ball of fire and splendour, all other gods became dark and mean and insufferable. He closed his eyes and let the sun blaze upon his face, and with apprehension and wonder prayed to Aton; but his very fear overcame him, and pulling his face aside, he demanded of Neph,

"But the slave people?"

"Ah . . . yes. . . ." Neph returned to his thoughts more slowly, and for a moment Moses believed that they had both been at the same worship—a thought much too dangerous and one, therefore, which he immediately thrust away.

"The slave people," Neph said thoughtfully. "They were desert people, wild and ignorant and superstitious, many tribes of them, but all of them speaking the same language more or less, which is like the language of the Phoenicians, only cruder. They say it was about a century ago that they first appeared. There was a terrible drought that killed all the grasslands in the desert, and when their flocks were dying, and when they themselves were little more than skin and bones, they swallowed their fears and came from the desert to beg that our frontier guards would let them pasture in the Land of Goshen. Whereupon a messenger was sent to the king of Egypt—he whose name is wiped out and whose memory is cursed——"

Moses could not help himself, and with the horrible feeling that he was speaking through some direction, he asked softly, "Why is his memory cursed, Neph, when he was good and did good; when he was just and lived in justice? His name is not wiped out. His name is Akh-en-Aton."

The fear, the surprise and shock on the face of the en-

73

gineer was the last thing Moses had expected, and as
Neph's hand gripped the boy's arm, his eyes darted to the
other engineers. But they were sprawled out on the deck,
eyes closed, warming themselves in the morning sun, and
they gave no evidence of having heard. Neph shook his
head and begged Moses to forgive him the violation of
touch, to which Moses replied that since they were friends
now, there was to be no more talk of violation.

"You talk too freely," Neph sighed. "Boy, will you help
your enemies destroy you?"

"My enemies! You mean you know too!"

"All Egypt knows of the prince who is alone."

"Alone!" Suddenly, Moses grasped Neph's hand. "Do
you know why . . . if you could tell me why—"

"I would tell you if I could, Moses. I don't know. If you
were only cursed, you would not be a prince of Egypt. You
are also blessed in some way. If the God Ramses hates you,
he also fears you. You are in some kind of balance, and I
imagine it will not be long before you know. We are a
people fond of mysteries, we Egyptians, too fond, I often
think. And when you find this one out, it will be neither
terrible nor very mysterious. That I can tell you."

"How do you know?"

"Well—how does one know? One lives and sees and
thinks, and in my case I have come to the conclusion that
a man's life, like a house's structure, must obey certain
rules. Don't make your life miserable, Moses, with this kind
of fruitless speculation. But at the same time don't upset
that balance by delivering yourself to them because your
tongue wags freely."

"Not freely; only to you," Moses answered.

"Why should you trust me?"

"I don't know," Moses shrugged, "and when you come down to it, Neph, I don't much care."

"You're too young not to care, and when I tell a story, Moses, kindly let me tell it my own way." And then, as if there had been no exchange of confidence, he went on, "As I was saying, he whose name is wiped out and whose memory is cursed—he had pity for these starving beggars from the desert and he let them pasture in the Land of Goshen. So, many desert tribes made it their home and grazed their goats and sheep there. It was a good arrangement for us. These desert Bedouins had no art of metalwork, only stout knives that they made from fragments of flint, and for cheap bronze daggers and knives, they supplied us with cheese and wool. So they lived in their own ways, worshipping their own gods—but when the God Ramses came to the throne, we had to make a slave people out of them."

"Out of the stranger among us? Him whom we took in and sheltered?" Moses asked incredulously.

"Many things are not what you are taught in school, Moses. Yes, out of the stranger among us. You see, in the older times Egypt was not the land it is today. Fifteen hundred years ago, Moses, the God-Kings Khufu and Chephren and Mycerinus built the great pyramids at Giza, and I often think that never again, as long as the world lasts, will men build with such grandeur and skill. Today, people have forgotten the old science and the old knowledge, and because they are ignorant and superstitious, they say that Osiris sent his servants to build the pyramids with magic. So it is today—everywhere this cursed magic of spells and incantations, because when ignorance triumphs, people become afraid of the truth and take magic to their hearts. But we who are engineers know better, and it was no god but plain Egyptian engineers like myself, and honest Egyptian workmen, who built those stone mountains—even though two and a half million blocks of limestone were required to make the largest one.

"In those times, Moses, there were few slaves in Egypt and few priests, believe me, and the peasant was a free man who owned his own piece of land. He was not taxed for half of what he produced and he did not have to see his family die of hunger and misery. He was a proud man, who did not have to bear the priesthood and the nobility on his back. I talk like this to you because so did you talk to me a little while ago. We can trust each other and we will say what we think.

"Well, in those times when the Mother Nile was in flood and all the land lay under the water, renewing itself, the God-King called the *corvée*. And because they were like brothers to each other and to the land, the Egyptians came from the whole length of the Nile. They came by the thousands, their tools over one shoulder and a bag of bread over the other, and they laughed and sang, for here was the whole land together to do one thing. That way, in each floodtime, they raised up the pyramids and the splendid temples and monuments. But that was a long, long time ago, Moses, and if the God Ramses were to proclaim the *corvée* today, who would come? The sick and broken serfs who work for the landlords and are left scarcely enough to keep body and soul together? The healthy men, the strong men, are in the army, and even there we have all too little, and must perforce hire mercenaries wherever we can. The beggars and loafers from the city streets? And if the beggars and serfs were called, would they heed the *corvée?* How willingly would they work, with all their hate and misery? No—today we can build only with slaves, and such is the God Ramses' lust for building that there are never slaves enough. He took ten thousand slaves in the war against the Sea People in Libya, and five thousand more from the land of Kush, and still it is not enough. Thousands of our own people are sold for debt—but never enough, never enough. So it was that some twenty years ago his soldiers went into the Land of Goshen and told the desert people there that the God Ramses had taken ownership of them and now they would work for him without pay. At first some of them resisted, but when a few hundred were hanged and a few hundred whipped, the resistance came to an end. Some of them fled back into the desert, but not many—for it is a long time since they lived in the desert and they fear it and have forgotten its ways. And soon they will forget that they were ever free people and they will be content to be slaves. So it goes, Moses."

"But they were strangers and they lived among us," Moses said. "Will the gods forgive us for this?"

"The gods forgive all kinds of things, Moses, and for my part, I am a builder and I need workmen." He shrugged and smiled narrowly. "A man who broods about right and wrong will soon take leave of his own senses. The world is what it is, Moses."

But Moses, on his part, felt that he was coming to know less of what the world was; or perhaps it was the world that was taking shape before his eyes for the first time—a real world, boundless and chaotic and so far meaningless. One day in the market place had washed away his own sense of being grossly misused, and had given him a measure against a world where not all were princely; and now the slave, to whom he had never paid much attention was becoming a symbolic and constant factor in his thoughts.

Thus he passed away the hours while the barge slid through one twisting waterway and then another. So often were they lost, seemingly, in a wilderness of marsh grass and bulrushes that Moses came to think that the helmsmen steered by some magic code; yet beyond that he realized the true answer—that here he was among men of wonderful skill and knowledge whereas he, as a prince of Egypt, had only a smattering of reading, writing and arithmetic, a store of mixed history and legend, some skill with weapons, and perhaps a hundred themes committed to memory from the *Book of the Dead*—none of it of great practical use. How often he had been warned to stay out of this great marsh, where one could so easily be lost for ever; yet to these men it was as familiar as the corridors of the palace were to him.

Even Neph had forgotten him now. The four engineers had spread plans upon the deck, and their discussion of this and that problem went on endlessly. Left to himself, Moses went to the bow and curled up there, one arm hooked in the bronze mooring ring, and there he remained until Neph called him to share their morning meal of bread, figs and wine. He discovered he was very hungry and ate all they gave him, indifferent to their smiles at his wolfish appetite.

While they were eating, they came in sight of their destination, a flat island about two acres in size. The granary already thrust up its brown brick walls from six to ten feet above the land, and here and there, on rough scaffolding, bricklayers were at work. The bricklayers, Moses decided, were Egyptian; but other men, unloading bricks from a barge tied up to a makeshift dock, must have been from the slave people Neph spoke of, for not only did they wear unkempt and tangled black beards and long hair gathered by a knot of leather, not only were they lean to the point of emaciation, but here and there among them overseers stood and watched their work, overseers who carried swords in their belts and on thongs around their necks three-foot leather whips.

As the oarsmen eased their barge up to the dock, Moses noticed many other freight barges drawn up on the muddy shore of the island, and from these more bearded slaves were unloading crushed stone and additional bricks. Each man had on his back a wooden rack, an open box that he grasped by two handles which extended over his shoulders. His fellow slaves would fill the box to capacity with bricks or stone or bags of mortar and, barely able to walk, every muscle rigid and tight, the man would make his way over the plank that extended from the boat to the shore—bricks and mortar to the bricklayers, the crushed stone to be emptied into a deep ditch that circled the entire island.

Moses followed Neph and the other engineers ashore, and since they became immediately concerned with their own business, talking to the overseers and the bricklayers and examining the work in progress, he decided to wander about by himself and see what he could see.

The slaves interested him because he had never before heard of the people of Goshen whom Ramses had taken as his servants. If he saw his own high-boned face among these slaves, it was not with any recognition or understanding; he walked slowly around the island, watching them at their work and wondering whether they could continue to work like that as the hot day wore on, or whether they would fall to the earth and die.

They, in turn, paid no attention to him, if indeed they saw him at all; and when he gazed straight into their bloodshot, sweat-filmed eyes, he felt that there—was a veil they used to thrust the world away from them. Indeed, they were not to be admired—unkempt, unshaven, naked and barefoot and stinking with their perspiration, filthy with the caked mud of the morass, a string for a belt and only a dirty piece of cloth or leather to keep their parts from the shamelessness of exposure. When they spoke to each other they were stingy of words, having little breath to spare from their labour, and then they spoke in their own tongue—strange and hard to Moses' ear, a curious consonantal language that cut the words sharply and lacked the soft flow and flavour of Egyptian. Yet they also spoke Egyptian, as Moses noticed when the overseers addressed them, an Egyptian that was accented and hardened into what seemed and sounded like a translation of their own language.

When Moses felt Neph's tread at his side and heard his grunt of greeting, he said,

"Why, Neph, do they live on? Isn't it better to be dead, to die quickly and with some honour than to be worked and beaten to death like a beast?"

"No," Neph answered shortly.

"I don't understand. I would die and welcome the dark lord Osiris."

"No, you wouldn't," Neph said.

"But I tell you I would!"

"Ah, yes, you tell me that. When life is full and sweet and young, as it is with a prince of the Great House, then the thought of surrendering it becomes an easy abstraction. You have so much life that you can be prodigal with it, Moses. But when life hangs by a thread, then by all the gods that be, it is nothing you give up easily! Life is the reason for life, as you will some day learn, and reason enough, you may be sure."

"I don't understand you," Moses replied.

"No. Better that you don't, I think. Come now, Moses, and I will tell you something of houses and how we do the impossible. First of all—you see how hard the ground under your feet is, and it will be harder still when we pave it with limestone."

Moses nodded.

"And yet a year ago, it was the same soft, oozing mud that you will find on any of these swamp islands. That is why we dug this ditch all around. The first problem was to drain the ground. We do that by ditching and letting the water seek its level, and we leave the ground high, after which it is baked hard by the sun. Now we are filling the bottom of the ditch with crushed stone, so that it will act as a dry well and not silt up. We will line the sides with slabs of rough stone, lead run-offs into it, and roof it with stone. Since we have already raised the ground level at least two spans, we can be assured of permanent dryness."

"All that just to dry the land?" Moses said unbelievingly.

"That was not a problem, Moses, but a matter-of-fact business that Egyptians have been practising for two thousand years. That is why Mother Nile is our servant and not our master. The problem was to build a warehouse in this damp swamp that would not sweat and rot the wheat." As they talked, Neph led Moses to the building and inside the walls, where slaves mixed mortar in flat troughs and carried it up the scaffolding to the bricklayers. "You see, Moses," Neph went on, "in our land, where the public granaries mean the difference between famine and survival, we have always built these storehouses of stone. Since they were built in the desert, they not only stayed cool, but dry as well. But when you build in stone here in this morass, the inside or cooler surface of the stone will sweat—that is, the dampness in the morning air will turn into water and rot whatever grain you have inside. Even if we lined the stone with cedar planks this would still happen, for the wood then turns wet and sour. So, after thinking the matter through, we decided that we would build with brick and we set the slave people in Goshen to making bricks out of the clay pits there, mixing the clay with chopped straw, which gives it great firmness and lasting quality.

"First we had to experiment with a small structure to see whether the brick would sweat in this climate. It did not sweat. Brick is a marvellous building material, as the Babylonians learned long ago; for while stone is dead, so to speak, brick lives and breathes and adjusts. Well, first we drove piles into the ground while it was still wet; then on the piles we laid a limestone foundation, bringing the dressed stones here on barges and fitting them into place. Then, on the limestone, we laid a floor of mortar to seal it, and on the mortar a second floor of brick. The brick walls will rise twenty feet high, after which we will line the walls in a veneer of cedar. We will roof the granary with cedar beams and planks and then weatherproof it with pitch, which we must bring from the bitter Sea of Canaan, even as we must bring the cedar from the mountains of Lebanon. So, Moses, you will know that it is easier to look at a house than make one, and while the God Ramses waves his hand and says, 'Let it be done', there are others who must do it. If you are ever the god-king, I hope you will remember this day," he finished lightly.

"Why do you say that, Neph?" Moses asked, his face tight with annoyance and misery too.

"I'm sorry. I didn't mean to give you hurt."

"Don't say it again."

"Then I will never say it again, Moses. I told you that I have a provoking tongue. Don't let it come between us."

"I won't," Moses agreed, less upset at Neph than at himself and the depression into which he had been cast through watching the slave people of Goshen at work.

[12]

YET MOSES WAS as little given to depression as he was to fancied slight or insult. Life and health burned too strongly, and if his cousins made no friend of him, they did not exclude him from their pack-like testing of manhood. With a dozen of them he took the long journey across the Delta to the ancient city of Buto, which was once, long ago, the capital of Lower Egypt, but now a poor and provincial place given over in great part to the breeding and sale of horses. There was also in Buto, to entertain the horse merchants and buyers, a great house of prostitution, known throughout Egypt for the variety and beauty of its women, who were purchased by special agents in the slave markets of Philistia, as well as in those of Egypt.

There, for the first time, Moses chewed the famous khat of Arabia, drank wine with it, and spent the hours of darkness in a nightmare of wild debauchery, drugged dreams and drugged lovemaking. His recollections the following morning, filtering through a splitting headache, filled him with shame and despair. The young man he saw, staggering through the night with his divine relatives, treating women with brutal, even sadistic lechery, firing himself with aphrodisiacs and wine, proving his manhood with blows and foul oaths—this young man was himself, seen now with hatred and disgust. He crawled out of there in the light of morning, hiding his face from the disc of Aton. Staggering, pitching drunkenly, he found a patch of white sand and lay face-down until at last he fell asleep. But while he slept, he dreamed, and in his dreams, his godhood left—and he shaped his dreams to provide the worse penance and torture he knew: to be cast down and turned into one of the slave people of Goshen, to work in the festering swamp under the blazing sun till at last, racked with pain, he collapsed from a fatigue too compelling for even the overseer's whip. It was only then that the burning rays of Aton became soothing and beneficent—and he, in turn, still in his pain, repeated the psalms of Aton that Amon-Teph had taught him. And when he repeated the most sacred psalm to Aton, the hymn to the god of all gods, then gently and lovingly his pain disappeared. He woke with his lips moving and speaking,

"Oh, Aton, how manifold are thy works,
    Though some are hidden from the sight of man,
    Though art the single god, no other like thee,
    And thou hast created earth as thou desired."

It was past midday, and a tall monument cast its shade upon Moses. He rose, stiff and sore in every limb, and went to the barber, who washed him, anointed him and combed his hair clean. Then the barber shaved him, for already his down was turning into dark beard; and while shaving him, the barber commented upon the fact that so many of royal and godly blood had been his customers this day. "Such an honour is rarely done me, O Prince of Egypt," he prattled. "I have a little wealth set aside, and perhaps if I pay for an embalming and good linen wrapping and a modest tomb, this divine contract will act as a spell to put off the wicked and jealous gods of that other place and give my soul sanctuary. Do you think so, Prince of Egypt? I cannot tell you how I have dreamed of immortality—which, of course, is something that you who are godly take for granted. But as a simple barber, it is another matter entirely, and I cannot tell you how often I have lain awake at night trembling with the fear of death and extinction. A poor man must accept such things and, believe me, I tried to. But now—now—well, tell me, what do you think, O holy one, O Prince of Egypt?"

"I think you are an idiot," Moses said petulantly, "and your talk makes me sick." But the moment it was out, Moses felt ashamed, and he despised himself for taking out his own misery on this pathetic little man—who, in fear that he had angered one of the young gods, hastened to say,

"You have said the truth, O Prince of Egypt. I am a fool and an idiot. So my wife tells me each day. Even my children say so. Thank you, O lord, for telling me the truth out of your own unselfish sense of profound justice. When you leave here, I will do obeisance and prostrate myself and kiss the ground where you walked. Only forgive me my presumptuous insolence."

Moses' eyes became wet and his stomach tightened as he listened to the barber, who pressed the point out of increasing fear,

"Will you forgive me, God-Prince?"

"I forgive you," Moses forced himself to say.

"I thank you and seven generations of my blood will venerate you, O God-Prince." His gratitude continued, as verbose and flatulent as all else he had said, and Moses escaped from him and his shop with relief.

From there he went to the corrals, where he found the others of the royal party. They appeared to have made a better recovery than he, for they were hungrily munching bread and dried fish even while they argued on the good and bad points of the horses in loud, boastful terms. The only other customers present were a party of landed noblemen from Upper Egypt, who, Moses noticed, looked upon the princes with distaste and no little contempt; whether because of their bad manners, or their obvious ignorance of horses, or a still strong and bitter hatred by most of Upper Egypt for the dynasty of Seti, Moses did not know. But as he chewed the bread and fish his cousins gave him he watched these hard-faced lords of the Upper Nile with interest and curiosity, for it was in their land that Aton had come to power over all the gods. They wore the wide and heavy golden collars of the South, bright-red linen kilts that fell to below their knees, and high-laced sandals; and they carried iron swords and wore polished iron bracelets as a sign of their power. Their physical resemblance to himself was immediately apparent to Moses, though it was less precise a resemblance than that of the slave people of Goshen, for while they were similar in the long cast of head and the thin, high-bridged nose, they had none of the hawk look, the flaring nostrils and wide mouth that made Moses' face so unusual in Egypt.

Then Moses forgot them, for one of the slaves of Seti-Pash, the owner of this breeding farm, brought into the corral a yellow horse that took Moses' heart so quickly and complete that he knew he would have no peace until he owned it. It was large horse, much larger than any of the Egyptian breed, broad of girth and with a long, cream-coloured mane of hair that swayed like a banner as the horse pranced and reared in the full excitement of life and strength. It had no sooner appeared than Moses vaulted the fence and ran to it, that he might claim it first. But he was alone, and he saw his cousins watching him with smiles of derision for desiring so unorthodox a beast.

But Seti-Pash also ran to welcome the sale and bowed low to Moses, telling him not to heed the sneers of those who did not know the difference between a horse and a donkey; for here was such a horse as came rarely into the hands of an Egyptian dealer, a three-year-old bought by a Phoenician trader from breeders on the island of Crete, whose horses were legendary the world over. Yet its price was only a little more than the price of a fine Egyptian animal.

"I want it," Moses said shortly, opening his pouch and taking out a handful of plain rings. "These are pure gold, made to a measure of six to an iron sword. How many for the horse?"

"O godly one, I should give it to you out of my reverence for the Great House, but I am a poor man who some-how must always sell for less than he buys. I ask only twenty rings." He looked up into Moses' angry eyes, still full of the bitterness the prince felt over the night before, and began to plead a justification of his price. Sick at the man's deceit, Moses took a handful more from his pouch, more than the twenty requested, and threw them down on the dirt and horse dung. As he led the horse away, he snapped,

"I will not haggle with you. Clean the dung off twenty and give the rest to your whores!"

As he took the horse through the corral gate, he saw the lords of Upper Egypt approaching him, and they asked him if they could examine the horse. He nodded, and they walked around it, noting its points and discussing it. Then one of them said to Moses,

"It's a strange but fine horse, O Prince of Egypt, yet I wonder that you took him. Your godly brothers seem amused at your choice."

"They are not my brothers but my cousins, and I care little whether or not they are amused."

"Oh? You seem an angry man, O Prince of Egypt. We are noblemen of the city of Karnak, so we have had some dealings with angry men, and we are here in the Delta to buy horses and iron bars for forge work—and we noticed you, if I may say so, O Prince of Egypt, not only because of your height and godly bearing, but for your appearance. We do not see many faces like yours in Lower Egypt. Is it then that the God Ramses is not your father?"

"I am the son of his divine sister, the Princess Enekhas-Amon," Moses replied, seeing no reason not to tell them who he was, since they were courteous enough and interested in his horse, now tugging at the halter and champing at the ground.

"Oh?" again. "You will forgive me, O Prince of Egypt, but the name of your godly mother surprises me. Amon is a name of Upper Egypt, indeed of my own region, and I have been led to believe, perhaps falsely, that such names were forbidden in the Great House."

"They are not forbidden," Moses answered slowly, wondering what the man was driving at, "but I suppose they are frowned upon. There is no other name like it in the royal family, but a few people are named from Amon. I am sure you know that here on the Delta, our god of the sun is Re—not Amon, as in your land—and my divine grandfather, Seti, is a god of power and worship in our land."

"Yes, of course," the man nodded, looking at Moses with additional interest. "My name, O Prince of Egypt, is Amon-Moses, so you can understand my curiosity. Would it be your own divine pleasure to tell us your name?"

Moses shrugged. "My name is Moses."

"Yes—the child is given—but of what god, if I may ask?"

Moses smiled without humour. "My name is Moses, man of Karnak—no name or half a name, as one pleases. It is my name and enough for me. If you would make more of it, I am at your disposal, and perhaps you will find that here on the Delta we are not inferior to the men of your land in settling a quarrel."

"All the gods forbid that I should seek a quarrel with you, O Prince of Egypt. If I have said anything that I should not have said, then I beg your forgiveness, and I will abase myself before you if you should desire."

"It is for me to beg your forgiveness," Moses said unhappily. "I am so filled with anger at myself today that I turn it on anyone and everyone I meet. Let us part in love and justice."

"So let us part," the men of Upper Egypt said, bowing before him.

Then he led the yellow horse around the corral to where his cousins were still buying and bickering. They began to snicker as he approached, and they exchanged what they considered to be clever remarks about Moses and the horse, pointing out that since both had strange qualities, to put it gently, they would make an interesting and compatible pair on the streets of the city of Ramses. Thin-lipped, his nostrils quivering with rage, Moses led the horse up to them and said quietly but coldly,

"Go on then, you royal bastards, and I'll kill the next one of you who makes a remark about me or my horse!"

They became silent and still—the slur so incredible, so utterly blasphemous, that at first no reaction was possible. At last one of them, the same Ramses-em-Seti whom Moses had laid hands on in the war-court so long ago, found his voice and said,

"A strange insult to come from you, nameless one. We have tolerated you a long time, but that time is over. Get away from us now before we shed blood."

Leading the horse, Moses walked away—walked on and on, like a man in a dream, seeing nothing, hearing nothing, his mind blank and thoughtless. When he came to himself he was on the outskirts of the city and the sun was dropping into the horizon. From a peasant he bought four loaves of bread and a sack of clean water. The bread of that time, baked in flat, hard cakes about eight inches in diameter, was pierced in the middle and strung on a rope of braided grass. As did the peasants, Moses slung the bread and the water from his neck, mounted his horse, and, bareback, rode on into the night. He stroked the horse as he rode—and the horse appeared to respond to his need for friendship and comfort. When it became too dark to see,

Moses dismounted, tethered the horse to a scrubby tree, ate a piece of bread and drank some water, and then found a dry spot of warm sand, where he lay down and fell asleep.

So in two days he made his way across the Delta, sometimes in mud, sometimes on the dry, baked surface of the king's road, forded branches of the Nile that were mere trickles in the dry season, had himself and his horse ferried across the wider branches, and finally arrived home in the City of Ramses.

[13]

HE SOMETIMES THOUGHT, in the afteryears of recollection, that the year which followed his purchase of the yellow horse was the lonely year of his life, an empty year; but in that, he was wrong, for this year which brought Moses to his seventeenth birthday was a year of transition and change in a manner Moses hardly knew.

He was isolated as never before, even the girls turning from him, friendless except for Amon-Teph and Neph, the builder—but they were two good friends, and he spent many long hours with one or the other, hours on the observatory listening to the tales and legends and dogma of Aton—the one god who was all gods. From Neph he soaked in other lore, though he would not return with the engineer to the island of the morass and the slave people of Goshen—and in time he spoke to Neph of Aton.

Neph was hardly surprised, and indicated that he had anticipated something of the sort. He told Moses that many men in Egypt held a part of their hearts for Aton—the gods of the night being easier to destroy than the great, golden orb of Aton. Moses, however, argued in the theological terms of his training that after all, even the mighty Aton died each night, to be reborn the following morning and, such being the case, who ruled during the hours of night?

"Moses," Neph smiled, "do you know how Aton dies?"

Of course he did—as who in Egypt did not?—and he proceeded to repeat to Neph, in the same schoolboy fashion in which he had memorized it, the story of the goddess Nut, whose body arched from horizon to horizon and formed the sky, her mouth in the west, her groin in the east; and each night at sunset she swallowed the sun, which rolled down her body into her womb, from whence it was born in labour each and every morning.

"It's a pretty story," Neph admitted, "and I liked it when I was a child; but truly, Moses, do you believe this foolish legend?"

"I don't suppose I do. But I don't know any more what to believe."

Neph said that a good way was to believe what your eyes told you, and if practical men did not do that, there would be neither engineers nor builders. He asked Moses whether he had been at the seashore, and Moses nodded.

"And have you ever seen a ship put out to sea?"

"Many times," said Moses.

"Then you have noticed that after the ship has disappeared, the masts and banners and sails still show?"

Puzzled, Moses nodded, a strange, wild idea forming in his mind.

"Why?"

"Does the sea bend?" Moses whispered.

"Ah! Then why doesn't the water flow downhill away from our shores? And Moses, if your goddess Nut keeps her face on the horizon, then why does the horizon move away from us—no matter how far we go? I have been to Hatti and Canaan—yes, even to Babylon, which is an un-imaginable distance from here, and yet, wherever I go, the horizon goes away before me. Have you seen the hills at Giza and Memphis?"

Moses nodded cautiously.

"And you see them as far off as you are. First you see the top—then more and more as you approach. Now, Moses, consider, could there be a horizon if the land were flat?"

Moses stared at him, wide-eyed and bewildered, and then said, "But if the land is curved, why don't the rivers and seas run off?"

Neph smiled with the satisfaction of one who makes a simple but extraordinary revelation. "Because all the world is a ball, Moses, a ball that floats in the sky—bigger than you could imagine—but still a ball; and if you travelled to the west or the east and went on and on, in time you would return to your starting place. Here in Egypt, among engi-neers, builders and men of science, this has been known for centuries—as even the Chaldeans have known it for many years. We keep our peace because the priests will have none of it—and how many people would believe?"

"I can't believe it," Moses said. "If the earth was a ball, we would fall off, our houses and rivers and soil—all of it."

"So we would," Neph nodded, "were it not for the glory and goodness of Aton. He made this earth, and all the days of mankind he circles it from east to west. It is his breath, his desire, that holds us to his earth. Never does he sleep or rest, since time began, and always he watches and sees, for we are his children. This is the true glory of Aton, Moses, and there are no other gods, because there was only he at first, and all that is or was or will be, he made. So I tell you, but keep this counsel. Don't even tell the priest, Amon-Teph. I have put my life in your hands now."

Belief or disbelief—he didn't know. It was better to be out with his yellow horse, whom he had named Karie, the Egyptian name for the legendary land of the yellow men, where all silk was made. It was better to race across the hard clay of the river flats, to course over the endless sand hills; to seek out the forgotten and beautiful monuments of antiquity, half-covered with the drifting sand, yet still beautiful; to ride curiously through the endless peasant villages in the rich flood valley; to journey south to the always wonderful pyramids; to run free and unattended, dreaming all his dreams.

He was more with his mother, too. It was only in this year that he began to understand the strange and woeful complex that was Enekhas-Amon, the courage mixed with her pathos, the gorgeous plans and fancies that existed side by side with her pettiness and selfishness—and the single-mindedness of her love for him. Now Moses had tasted enough of young manhood to begin to comprehend the tragedy of a woman so revered, so beautiful, so courted that her whole life pivoted around the fact of her beauty— and the loss felt by such a woman when her beauty vanishes and with it all that beauty brought her. There was still much about Enekhas-Amon and himself that he did not know—the dream which she hinted at so mysteriously— but here and there a piece of the puzzle would fall into place; and the very fact that he himself could only unravel ends and bits made him comprehend how widespread and desperate the plot of which he, Moses, was the pivot actually had become. But for all that, he had no faith in it or its outcome.

He tried to pay court to the ageing, sick and tortured woman who was his mother—to satisfy a little of her half-forgotten need for attention and adulation. He persuaded her to walk with him on the lovely balconies that overhung the river, to sit in the gardens with him, to watch the evening homage to Osiris with its procession of white-robed, shaven priests and veiled virgins; and even if she hated Osiris and all he stood for, the pageant and the music were rewarding. Yet always he was conscious that she lived—not merely for him—but for the intricate plot and web she was spinning.

So the year went and came to its end, as all things must, and sometimes, when Enekhas-Amon looked at the tall, broad-shouldered young man who was her son, she would turn away quickly to hide the tears in her eyes—for to her hungry eyes, never had a prince of Egypt been so much a prince.

[14]

AMON-TEPH TOLD MOSES that his mother, Enekhas-Amon, had decided to submit to trepanning. The priest was becoming an old man now; the flesh on his face dropped in heavy folds, and his hands trembled. His reddened eyes were wet with emotion.

"I'll soon put an end to that," Moses said.

"No——" The priest shook his head. "All our plans have come to nothing. We have played out our game, my son, and when that happens, old people like ourselves have the

right to make our own decisions. It's not for youth to decide, because the last thing youth can comprehend is what
it means to be old and defeated."

"Isn't it high time you told me about this game you've
played?" Moses demanded angrily.

"Be patient, my son," the priest said, smiling wryly.
"We've made it a mystery where there really isn't any, but
only to protect you. Soon enough you'll know everything,
but not yet. Trust me. And as for your mother—that too,
all of it."

"But she's not going to be trepanned!"

"Why, Moses? Is life so sweet that she should cling to
it? Do you know the pain she lives in? Anyway, I'm afraid
the choice is not hers, for a few days ago the God Ramses
called her to him and spoke to her. He said that he had
heard about the severe headaches she suffers, and he noted
that such was frequently the case when people had too
much pent up in themselves—adding that he felt it was time
to let the foul vapours escape. In all of this he was talking
figuratively, but she understood him completely; and when
he said that he had decided to ask for a trepanning, what
could she do? She asked only one thing—that the God-
King's hand would not be raised against you, and to this
he agreed. I believe him, my son, and for this I am happy;
for I tell you, Moses, you will be such a man as is made
for great destiny—whatever our beloved Aton decides that
our destiny should be. And never misjudge Ramses; he is
a strange and terrible man, but also one of the most remarkable men Egypt has ever known. I say this because it
may well be that your life eventually will be pitted against
his and your wit against his wit. Respect him, Moses."

Yet Moses scarcely heard the priest, for his mind was

racing and planning, and finally he burst out, "Tonight, Amon-Teph, the three of us will leave this place. I'll buy a chariot today, and we'll head for Upper Egypt, perhaps for Karnak, where we may find shelter. I know horses now, and weapons, too—"

Amon-Teph interrupted him with the same wry little smile. "Moses, Moses, what a lot you have to learn about people, You can never run away from yourself, and such adventures belong only to storytellers. Nothing you say can make your mother change her mind, and if you talk in such a fashion, you will only disturb her. Now you must be a pillar of strength to her. Be gentle, be wise and understanding. All these past seventeen years of her life were dedicated to fearing a great prince. That is all she wanted, and from that she believed all else would flow. Show her that she was not wrong and that she did not fail."

Moses stared at the priest, the tears running down his cheeks; and Amon-Teph wiped away the tears with a corner of his robe. "I never saw you weep before, Moses," he said softly. "Tears are for children, and you are a man, and a great prince of a great nation. Recall, how often I have told you about the *ka*, the soul of a human being—which like a mirror of truth reflects man as be really is. You know that we of the priesthood of Aton have learned, perhaps from our suffering, to put little trust in this mummery of embalming and entombing—yet for that very reason we have come to know the truth about the *ka*. Perhaps in some dream Enekhas-Amon has looked at her own *ka*, looking into a mirror that showed the past and the future at once. The *ka* is deathless, my son, and if you wonder that I talk this way, then consider—many men loved your mother, too many men and the God Ramses loved her, perhaps the only woman he ever truly loved, but no one loved her the way I did. The ground she walked on was holy, her smile was a benediction, and for a kind word from her I would have gone to my death. It may be that only Aton should call such love forth from a man, and it may be that I am paying a price for this; however, I am not sorry, and this love never changed. She changed, but to me she remains the divine and perfect princess of the Great House. Sometimes I think I see something of the *ka*, but again this can be the meandering of an ageing man. Let it be, but be kind to her, Moses, and if god is willing, she will survive the trepanning."

Unable to speak, Moses nodded and went to his mother.

[15]

ONE OF THE many pictures of this time that was imprinted upon the mind of Moses indelibly, to be remembered clearly in a future when so much of life in the Great House had become confused and blurred, was that of the royal surgery when he brought his mother there.

Since the lamps of the time were so poor, surgery, like other important work, was performed only in daylight; and now, as Moses and his mother and Amon-Teph walked through the long corridors of the palace, it was just past the noon hour. They had to traverse a central hall of some four hundred feet, which connected the various wings of the enormous palace, the hall of the towering pillars, where Moses had long ago seen his childhood companion dashed to his death; and since there was no slave or cook or sweeper in the Great House who did not know that this was the day Enekhas-Amon's skull would be opened, hundreds of eyes were fixed upon them.

The mother walked like her son, straight, head up and eyes fixed ahead—eyes which moved only to glance occasionally at her son, upon whose arm her hand rested. She had scorned to cloak herself, but walked dressed as a royal princess, wearing a sheer skirt that just touched the ground, a belt of gold bars set with pearls, and a great collar of thin gold plates that fell to the edge of her bare breasts. Her shoulders were held firmly back that her breasts might not sag, and her face was the result of a whole morning with the finest cosmetic artists in the land. With creams and rouge and putty and little bits of tape, they had filled in the wrinkles of her skin, shored up the loose folds of flesh, covered the black circles under her eyes, used drops that made her eyes shine like a girl's. They had fixed long lashes to her puffy eyelids, so that the curve and shadow hid the flesh itself, and had rouged her mouth and delicately blended colour into her cheeks. Her hair was covered by a magnificent wig, dressed in the royal fashion, with the stiff, barlike wedges on each side; and not by prerogative but because she knew that now, still alive, she walked in her own funerary procession, she wore the thin circle of gold that is worn only by those who rule Egypt as gods.

The effrontery brought forth gasps of shocked surprise from the onlookers, and Moses could hear the angry whispers from the clusters of priests and magicians who watched them from the shadow of the columns; but even if it meant his own death during the next few minutes, he would not have had it otherwise; and he had to struggle within himself to keep from weeping with sorrow, joy and pride for this strange, many-sided woman who all his life had been a sickly and petulant mother, but was now more the queen of Egypt than any of Ramses' wives and concubines.

As for Amon-Teph, like Enekhas-Amon, he was walking in his own funerary procession. He had taken his leave of life and also of fear. A lifetime of dreaming and plotting bad come to nothing, but now it seemed to him that he had lost little and perhaps gained a great deal; and as he walked along, feeling inside like a young groom and lover with his bride, he reflected that perhaps it was so with all men—unable to judge the importance of anything until the goal has been reached or lost for ever.

So they walked to the royal surgery—a broad, high-roofed room, open entirely on one side to the gardens below and with the long curtains drawn back on the other side. Here were many court functionaries, priests and magicians to support the doctors with their spells—and nearly the entire medical staff of the Great House; for the trepanning of a member of the royal family was no small matter. To Moses, the whole aspect of the occasion was macabre and hateful, the marble operating tables covered with white sheets, the stone basins to catch the flow of blood, the rows of bronze instruments, scalpels and knives and drill-bits, the laminated bows for drilling, the hundreds of flasks of drugs and medicines, the mortars and pestles for grinding herbs—and of course the surgeons with their priest-like shaven heads, gathered in learned intimacy and talking their important mumbo jumbo—the endlessly reiterated and distorted fragments remaining from the long-past time when medicine had been a living, groping science in Egypt.

Seti, his paunch greater than ever, his legs more spindly than ever, rushed forward in his capacity as personal physician, but a glance from Moses kept him at his distance; and Re-Kophar, the priest who was chief and overlord of all medical matters in the realm, made his obeisance to Enekhas-Amon, and said,

"Divine sister of the God-King, all is ready, and in a moment the chief surgeon will be here." He was a tall, sour-visaged man, and he made his face even longer and more dour as he said, "Compose yourself, for not only will you be in the hands of skilled physicians, but even at this moment, the gods are being informed of your troubles. I myself will watch every step of the operation—"

"I am composed," Enekhas-Amon smiled. At this point her head was a furnace of pain, and her whole body ached and throbbed from the strain of the walk; but she was determined, since all else was lost, that her son should retain a memory of her that would recompense him at least a little for the years of complaint and petulance. Seeing that in spite of himself the prince's eyes were fixed on the silent insult of the golden crown, she removed it carefully and handed it to him, saying lightly,

"It is only a piece of metal. But when I wore it men like yourself could not take their eyes from it and therefore looked less keenly at my face, which, for all that cosmetics can do, is still the face of an old and sick woman. Take it. It won't burn you, Re-Kophar."

Then, still smiling, she said, "If this must be good-bye, Moses, my son, bear yourself well and proudly." She did not trust herself to say any more, and all the carefully composed sentences that she had prepared for this occasion melted away. She saw that Moses was at the end of his control, so she simply raised herself on her toes, kissed his lips, and touched his cheek with her fingertips. Then she turned and walked into the surgery, where the barbers were waiting to wash her and shave her head.

Moses remained motionless, a person in a trance, until Amon-Teph took his arm and led him a little distance away. "You can watch the operation, my son," Amon-Teph said. "Do you wish to?"

He shook his head.

"I will watch it," the priest murmured. "I don't want to leave her now."

"Watch over her, Amon-Teph."

"You will wait here?"

"Yes, I'll wait here. Will it hurt her?"

"No. They will give her a potion to put her to sleep, and if she feels pain, she won't remember."

"Go to her, please," Moses said.

When the royal surgeon entered, the hangings were closed behind him, and then the curiosity seekers, the gossips and the idlers drifted away. The hours of the operation were too long to wait, and Moses was left alone in the corridor with his thoughts and the hum of voices from the surgery as his only companions. His thoughts moved slowly—disjointed memories and fancies. The corridor was lit by open vents to the roof, and down through these vents came bars of sunshine, a line of golden bars in the distance; and near Moses—was one of those pillars of sunshine, the yellow light filled with dancing motes of dust. He remembered afterwards the way the dust motes danced and eddied in the sunlight, but little else that went through his mind then could he remember.

And when at last they brought Enekhas-Amon out on a great wooden stretcher carried by six slaves, her eyes closed, her head swathed in bandages, Moses felt completely drained of all emotion. Next to Amon-Teph, he followed the slaves back to the apartment where he and his mother lived, and when they had set down the stretcher in her bedroom, he told the slaves that they might go.

"She must be kept very quiet," Amon-Teph said, "and always someone must be at her side." The three old slaves who tended her were fluttering around and Moses told them,

"I'll remain with her. Leave us now."

It was late afternoon, and through the broad window of the chamber Moses could see the shadow of the Great House creeping out over the Nile. The boats of the fishermen were pushing slowly upstream, back with their day's catch, and across the river the bent figures of the peasants were scraping at the soil. Another day was ending in the endless march of the days of Egypt.

He turned back to Amon-Teph, who was holding Enekhas-Amon's wrist, feeling for the pulse. Moses felt strangely unmoved as he looked at the waxlike sunken face of his mother. He felt no recognition. He would only remember the women who had smiled as she took off the crown.

"I can't feel her pulse," Amon-Teph said.

Moses took a silver hand-mirror from her dressing table, wiped it on his kilt and then held it in front of her open mouth. He put it carefully back where he had taken it from and said hopelessly yet calmly to the priest,

"My mother is dead, Amon-Teph."

The priest drew the sheet up over her face. Moses walked to the window and stood looking out and as he stood there he heard the old man pleadingly intoning,

"Which thou, oh god, seek the western horizon,
  the land lies in darkness, in death,
  and the lion stalks forth from his den,
  the creeping beasts strike.

"Day comes and you light the horizon
  and drive away the beasts of darkness,
  so that men may awake and stand on their feet
  the world over, they do their work.

"Oh, Aton, how manifold are thy works—"

[16]

TOGETHER MOSES AND Amon-Teph left the bedchamber of Enekhas-Amon and walked through the darkening corridors to one of the many balconies that looked out upon the river. They were alone on the terrace and they stood at the stone balustrade looking out into the night.

"I had thought to go to the observatory," the priest said, "but I am afraid that death came there first. Since I have despised Osiris during most of my life, I should have no great fear of him afterwards; and I am impatient to be with your mother. All that notwithstanding, I cling to life and I am afraid to die. God praise your youth, Moses, for the older we become, the more jealous we are of our little spark of life."

Out of his own thoughts, Moses sighed and wondered why the God Ramses should stoop to trepanning. "Why didn't he kill her and be done with it?" he asked Amon-Teph, his voice so cold and awful that Amon-Teph shuddered.

"When you have loved a woman once, Moses, and have taken her to bed with you, are you ever rid of her?"

"He's rid of her."

"Yes—possibly, I don't know. We are a strange, tortured people, Moses, and the mind of the simplest peasant is a maze that you would lose yourself in. Your mother was in constant pain. Of their own accord people have their skulls opened to relieve the pain, and often enough they live."

"Are you defending Ramses, Amon-Teph?"

"I'm defending you, my son," the priest answered sadly. "Why don't you weep and let the hatred out of your heart?"

Moses shrugged. "No more tears, as you said. And don't be afraid for me. I will bide my time. I begin to find qualities in myself that I never suspected. I think I can be patient. But now we are going to talk, Amon-Teph, and no more mysteries. Look where you have come with your foolish mysteries."

In something close to a whimper, the old priest said, "I can stand all that awaits me, but not your contempt, my son."

Moses turned suddenly and clasped the old man to his bosom, telling him, "No, my father—not contempt." His voice choked, and he shook his head. "Not contempt, my father, my teacher. I am trying to be a man. It is hard."

"I know."

The first edge of the moon arose now about the dark

flat edge of the Delta. They remained silent for a time, each struggling with his own emotion, until Amon-Teph was able to say,

"Ask what you wish, and I will answer you the best I can though I think you know most of it. You bore half a name because the other half waited. You would have been Aton-Moses."

"I suspected as much. But I think I'll remain Moses. There is little point in strutting and posturing now, and I haven't enough vanity to take a name that means my death. There are many reasons why I want to live, Amon-Teph, not only because life is good and sweet, but because I have a score to settle. To tell the truth, I am tired of the gods. You destroyed my fears of Osiris and his creatures of the night—and for that I will be everlastingly grateful—and if Aton is the only god, just and loving, he will not need me to carry his name. I know that you and my mother and perhaps some others dreamed for many years of seating me on the throne of Egypt—well, who am I to judge, as you have made plain to me? But the choice was a poor one, my dear friend. I am not an Egyptian, am I?"

"No—you are not," Amon-Teph admitted. "But Aton warms more places than the River Nile."

"Be that as it may, who am I?"

The priest stared long and thoughtfully at the moon before he answered, and then he turned to Moses and asked him searchingly, "Are you sure you want to know? Can I judge whether you should know?"

Moses cried, "I must know! Can I live in emptiness—out of nothing, no past, no memory?"

"You have the memory of Egypt."

"No! No longer! I want my own! Let me be the judge!"

"Very well," the priest sighed. "But to understand it, you must understand what it meant when the holy Ahk-en-Aton proclaimed Aton as the one living god. He, Ahk-en-Aton, lifted Egypt out of despair and defeat, and brought in a brief age of light and hope—of art and science and fearless inquiry—as in the ancient times when Egypt shone for the whole world like a light in the darkness. And it was his son who raised to the throne beside him Enekhas-Aton, his sister, in the old way of the god-kings. But Tut-ankh-Aton was not the man his father was, and even while he sat on the throne, the glory was fading. The whole great tribe of priests who lived like leeches on the back of the people and who were cast out when Aton triumphed—they were already at work planning and organizing the revolt that overturned the kings of Aton and finally placed Seti on the throne. That you know, and you know how mercilessly Seti destroyed every vestige of Aton worship. Before Seti, Tutankh-Aton succumbed to fear and changed his name to Amon—his wife's to Enekhas-Amon, and some bitter whim of Seti gave that name to your mother.

"So think of her, Moses, a girl of great beauty, great birth, the sister of Ramses—I will not call him god again—and beloved of Ramses. He wanted to make her his queen, but she could bear him no children and she bore children to no man. The soothsayers and magicians told him that this was the curse of Aton, and that if she would change her name, she would become fertile and bear him a son. But this, for some reason, for some streak of iron inside her, she could not do. They had terrible, violent battles and he came close to killing her—and her own love for him turned into a malignant hatred. It was at that time she found me out and came to be instructed in the worship of

Aton—and because I loved her and had adored her face from the first time I saw her, I could refuse her nothing, and embarked on this venture that ends here.

"In those days, she began the retreat that ended in her seclusion, and very often she would take her barge and go out for days into the endless waterways of the Delta; and sometimes, perhaps because she pitied my doglike devotion, she would allow me to come with her. Thus it was that we went, one day, along this channel and that one, almost to the Land of Goshen, which lies, as you know, on the eastern edge of the Delta. We were drifting along, the slaves dipping their oars just enough to give us headway in a channel so narrow that the oars brushed the marsh grass, your mother curled up on a mass of pillows in the bow, singing softly—she still sang then—and I standing beside her, when we saw something floating in the water ahead of us. Understand, Moses, there were only the two of us in the boat, and the slaves at the oars, and the helmsman, who was both a slave and a Delta pilot. The thing in the water was a basket, smeared inside with hard clay mixed with bits of cloth, with a child inside it—a child no more than two weeks old. When we picked up the child, the basket was already sodden and beginning to sink. You were that child."

Moses said nothing. He simply nodded and waited for the priest to continue.

"It doesn't disturb you more than this?" Amon-Teph asked gently.

"It has disturbed me since I can remember. I feel better now. Now that I know, I can think about it without being afraid. Where did the child come from, Amon-Teph?"

The old priest spoke slowly, for he had to tell it in his

own way now, as if he were compelled to make all of it alive and present; the royal barge lying there in the reeds; the princess under her canopy clutching the child to her bosom; the baby, red-faced from its exposure to the sun, wailing in discomfort and hunger; the princess snapping at him,

"Don't stand there watching, Amon-Teph—find someone to give the child suck before it dies of hunger!"

"But where? Where, in this wilderness?"

"Where the child came from, you fool! Take off that foolish robe of yours and find out where the child came from!"

Amon-Teph nodded as he recalled it for Moses. "I thought I would sink and perish in the morass, but as she willed, I did. Naked in a loincloth, thigh-deep in mud, I waded perhaps a hundred yards along the side of the channel, and then the ground became firmer. The reeds were seven or eight feet high above the water, so I could not see where I was going; but suddenly I was through the reeds on dry ground and there before me were perhaps a hundred men and women and children—who scattered in panic when they saw me and began to run away, leaving behind them the remains of a little fire in which they had burned some incense and leaving behind them, too, a carved cedar box."

It was the carved cedar box, Amon-Teph made clear, that brought them back; for when they realized that they had left it behind, they stopped running and began to return. They had been surprised, but the sight of one muddy Egyptian, a priest, by his shaven head, did not serve to sustain their fear.

"All of you come back!" Amon-Teph shouted. "I'm not

going to burn you! I'm a priest of the Great House and I want to talk with you!"

So they returned, warily, and two of them leaped forward and seized the box and dragged it within their ranks. Afterwards, Amon-Teph told Moses, they let him see what was in the box. It was a large, black water snake.

"Their god," Amon-Teph told Moses now. "The snake of fertility, to which they made the sacrifice of the child. A very ancient and common practice—even among our own people two thousand years ago. The same snake that you will see curled around the legs of Isis—a superstitious and ignorant cult."

"Who were these people?" Moses whispered.

"One of the slave peoples of the Land of Goshen," Amon-Teph shrugged. "They are all much the same, Bedouin wanderers from Sinai and Canaan who received sanctuary in the grasslands during the great droughts of a century ago—and whom Ramses enslaved. These called themselves the children of Levi, who was one of the children of Israel, for they keep an endless record of their ancestry. This was part of the tribe—I imagine there were six or seven hundred in the whole tribe—and they said they were related to other tribes who also came from the children of Israel and who had remained in Canaan and Sinai when these went to Egypt. They spoke Egyptian of a sort, as well as their own tongue, for you must remember they have lived long among us. I learned a good deal about them; it was some time before we left there."

"Tell me what they looked like, Amon-Teph."

The old priest was tiring, and he seemed annoyed that the story must still continue. "Dirty, bearded, ragged— maybe they would have looked like you, Moses, had they been raised in the Great House; but they were skinny, dirty slaves, ignorant and superstitious."

He wanted the story to end; perhaps he, Amon-Teph, was now impatient for the end of many things. He was tired, and he wanted to lie down and be alone with his sorrow. The rest he told briefly, and his listener, dulled with too much emotion, sorrow and heart-sickness—and the death of pride in birth and blood; for who could grow up among the lords of the Great House without such pride?—and the heart-hurting knowledge that he was a waif, a nobody, a nameless offspring of slaves, thrown by these slaves in their blind ignorance and superstition as a sacrifice to a water snake—yes, his listener also desired the story to end. He heard how Amon-Teph had challenged these people to produce the mother; and when they lied and denied that it was their babe, he told them that a royal barge of the Great House lay a stone's throw away, and that if they insisted upon provoking him, he would return the following day with a squadron of soldiers. Then he went among them until he found a woman whose full breasts were so wet they stained the front of her gown, and he ordered her to come with him.

"My mother," Moses said dully.

"Enekhas-Amon was your mother," the priest answered him harshly. "All your life I refused to tell you this, and I could have died with it as easily. Not because you were born a slave, but because you have in all truth become a prince of Egypt, have you forced this out of me. I made this woman come with me on to the boat, where she gave suck to the child—to you."

Then came the rest of it—how a pavilion was set up on the shore for Enekhas-Amon, the mother and the child;

how two slaves of the house were left to guard her while Amon-Teph went back for supplies and to make arrangements; how they remained there at the edge of the morass for five days, until Amon-Teph found an Egyptian wet nurse whom he could trust; how all of the slaves who were with the barge were sold in the markets of Hatti—for, as Enekhas-Amon said when she returned to the City of Ramses, after four months of quiet hiding in Memphis, the child was hers; and how, with a full measure of wit, gold and threat, the secret was kept.

"But not entirely kept, Moses, my son. No secret is—and while you had a mother, the question of a father remained. Enekhas-Amon would never name a father—she could have—myself, or others of better blood and station who loved her—but she would not. She held that Aton was your father."

"And she believed it?" Moses asked.

"I think so," the old man sighed. "We all believe what we want to believe or what we have to believe. just as I think that Ramses, the God-King"—his scorn was mixed with fatigue and disinterest—"believes that you are his son."

"No!" Moses cried. "Spare me that!"

Amon-Teph shrugged. "There is much that I would have spared you, but this is the way things are. Ramses, from all I could gather, believes that Enekhas-Amon was waiting for the moment when it would be ripe to proclaim you. Ramses did not wait. . . .

"Well, there it is, all of it; and as for you, my dear son, my dear son"—he had to fight to control his voice; the tears were running from his eyes now, falling strangely upon his loose, pouchy cheeks—"live." His voice was a hoarse whisper. "Live and be strong and good and just. You have been all the life that your mother left to me, and you two gave me what to love and what to live for. You are as noble as any man in Egypt, and when it's finished, as it is now for me, you realize that we are all brothers, all of the same wit and folly—slave and freeman, noble and peasant. You are what we who loved you desired you should be, and it is the poor, foolish pride of Ramses that makes him claim you for his seed. Let him think so, Moses, and he will not stain his hands with your blood; for whether he faces Osiris or Aton, such a stain would destroy him. Live," the old man gasped, "so that your mother and I can live in you."

Then he kissed Moses and left him; and Moses stood there watching the priest walk slowly and uncertainly into the night.

[17]

"SO I AM the son of slaves, of the dirty, dying wretches who live in the Land of Goshen," went through him, hour after hour, day after day, cutting apart his grief, filling him with anger and frustration and hatred of himself—and building resentment against his dead mother. Yet there was something in him, a core of solidity that allowed him to fight this resentment, to cling to the image of his mother as his mother—and not to turn against her the corroding humiliation that was eating out his heart.

He wanted to retreat into himself, into a cave, into shelter against the whole world. However, there was too much to be done. The woman who died was his mother to the world, and he lived in the world. To him they came—and he had to talk to them. The business of death was not a simple matter in his land, and the higher one's station, the more complicated did death become. Sulking, hurt, filled with pity and grief and self-pity, reverting to the boy who was still so much a part of him now, at seventeen and a half, he would imagine himself raging at them, "I am a slave, and such matters don't concern me! Do what you wish!" This he left in his mind; he remained a prince of Egypt, and he did what he had to do.

All of the hours during the days after his mother's death were filled with the funerary proceedings. He had to discuss with the royal embalmer the details of the process—a procedure which, if normally consoling, was now disturbing and distasteful to him. A dutiful son was expected, in the way of lasting love and concern, to observe some of the steps of funerary preservation; but to Moses the thought of seeing his mother's body disembowelled, the skull empty, floating in the stinking tanks of subcarbonate of soda deep under the Great House, the place of horror and frightened whispers in his childhood, was more than he could tolerate. Let the ghouls, of which there were always a sufficient number, exhibit the preoccupation with the soaking and washing and stuffing and binding that went under the name of piety. When the royal embalmer suggested eight weeks of soaking and then began to enumerate the various herbs he would use—the myrrh, cassia, balsams, peppers—brought from the Ganges Valley at such cost and trouble, as he pointed out—the seven salts from Arabia, Kush, Libya, and on and on, like a lessons in geography— Moses told him coldly to do what had to be done.

"But the arteries," he insisted. "There are three methods of injecting the arteries. I never fail to discuss the advantages of one method, the disadvantages of another, with those responsible for the deceased. Forgive me, Prince of Egypt, but the responsibilities of those beloved of the deceased do not end with death; rather, as our holy scribe and teacher, Kafu-Re, put it in the time of Amon-em-Het, the deceased finishes one trial to be ordained into another. My own *justice* forces me to put it to you thus. Now, the injection of the arteries——"

So Moses bowed his head and listened to the discourse on the manners of injecting the arteries of a corpse. There was no escape; and more and more he was beginning to realize what Amon-Teph meant when he spoke of the prisons men build for themselves—from which a key or a door provides no exit.

With the master sculptor, he had to discuss the finish of the stone sarcophagus which Enekhas-Amon had ordered ten years before. It bore her likeness, but the final finish remained to be completed. Did he, the divine prince of Egypt—and may the gods will that he never be troubled with such details in his grief—desire a natural finish of unsurpassed smoothness? And with or without a worked plate of bronze? On the other hand, some in the Great House preferred enamel with the stone? Further, would the body be placed in the sarcophagus here or at the tomb?

Vaguely Moses knew that the tomb of his mother was in Upper Egypt, somewhere near Karnak. He would have to discuss that, too. Meanwhile the sculptor would have to meet with him and the coffin-maker. The chief of the staff of royal artists would also be concerned—and of course, one Seti-Moses, the major-domo of the Great House.

He was a relative by blood—a first cousin two or three times removed—to the God Ramses, and it was often said that while Ramses was God-King of Egypt and the Empire,

Seti-Moses was god-king of the Great House; and himself, Seti-Moses was wont to describe as the busiest man in all of Egypt. Which perhaps he was, for with a staff of almost a hundred scribes and clerks, he kept the famous papyrus rolls upon which were listed not only the nobility and priesthood of Egypt, but their wealth, their land-holdings, their estates and mines in foreign places, their slaves, their horses, their cows and sheep and goats, their gold and silver and bronze and iron and linen, their sons and daughters and wives and concubines, and—as some wits held—their performance in bed and out of it and their innermost thoughts as well. All this was kept up-to-date with an incredible number of entries and deletions each year—and even a scribe in the service of Seti-Moses was a man to be feared and reckoned with.

Moses did not doubt the industry of the pig-eyed, enormously fat man who waddled into his chambers and confronted him after the death of Enekhas-Amon, for in all his life he had never before spoken to Seti-Moses and he had seen him closely only once, on an occasion when the major-domo was leaving their apartment. To Moses' eyes, he had not changed; time left him untouched, and as he entered, a scribe and clerk following, his huge face fixed in an expression of influential condolence but devoid of sorrow—as if he, so close to the gods, would see that things went well—his huge body swathed in transparent linen, Moses experienced a final capitulation to pomp and circumstance.

Seti-Moses settled himself in a chair that swayed uneasily under Ms weight, and the clerk and the scribe squatted on footstools. Always a diplomat, knowing that kings are mortal in this world if not in the next, well-aware of the conflicting rumours of the origin of Moses, and not unaware of the one which held him to be the son of the God Ramses, he opened by reciting his praise of Moses, of the prince's bearing, intelligence and nobility—and then he explained his appreciation of a son's grief.

"Yet, even as one steps into life eternal," he pointed out, "those unfortunates who remain behind must deal with practical matters. Ah. yes, practical matters, Prince of Egypt, which we would gladly dispense with, but which stand between ourselves and chaos. The barbarian eats and drinks for the day; a civilized person lays aside a little of his substance, so that those loved ones who remain may not know want and sorrow. I suppose you know you are a very rich man?"

"I know that my mother had enough for her wants. As to my own wealth, I care little."

"There speaks inexperience," Sed-Moses chided him, wagging a fat finger in front of Moses. "The fly dies with the cold weather, but the bee waxes fat and happy in its own honey." He was a man fond of maxims. "One hundred and fifth verse, *Book of Horus*. Fortunately you are a rich man, for your mother was wise in her overseers. I have here a full accounting of your holdings, which I shall read you. All accounted for. No cheats. Your blessed grandfather, the God Seti, cleansed us of administrative cheats." He ran a pudgy finger through a fold of his neck. "Then we shall discuss the apartment—which you may use freely if you desire. Being precise in my methods, I like to prepare an enumeration of the effects you will place in your godly mother's tomb; also, what animals you see fit to slaughter.

There is also the question of approval or disapproval of the management of your property. Also, your own needs in gold reckoning—"

His authoritative, rasping voice droned on and on, on and on, as the hours passed, on and on until darkness came, and then he made an appointment to see Moses the following morning.

There was Neph, too, to make it plain and simple that he remained a friend, come what would.

"The trouble is," Moses said, "that I don't care very much what comes."

"All right. Now you're shocked and bitter and hurt. That will pass, Moses. You're young and strong—and wealthy," he added. "And you're a prince of Egypt."

"And your God-King murdered my mother!"

"So long as you say such things only to me," Neph told him, "you are simply being impetuous. If you talk like that to others, it will be more unfortunate. But I didn't come here to scold you. I came to tell you that I have a leave from the major-domo to go to Karnak and prepare your mother's tomb. I found the location and the plans in the funerary hall, and there doesn't seem to be too much to do. In any case, I can take that burden off your mind, and you can rest assured that when I finish and when Enekhas-Amon is entombed, no one will ever find her resting place. I think it's best that way. I am taking a hundred workmen, and if you want me to take her household effects, I will prepare a barge for that."

Moses seized his hands and pleaded, "Let me go with you, Neph! Let me go with you and out of this cursed house—even for a few weeks!"

"Gladly—and then what would you have, Moses? That

your mother should go up the river alone? That all Egypt should talk about it? That what is already bad enough should become even worse? Moses—for the sake of those of us who love you, put your head up! Be a prince of Egypt! That is your only hope!"

So more hurt was added to hurt, and now he told himself that Neph, the only friend who remained, had also turned against him. For Amon-Teph came no more, and when Moses walked through the corridors of the Great House, those who saw him stood back silent and uncommitted.

As long as he could, he bore this; and then, half-mad with the bursting, tangled emotions inside him, he took his yellow horse and rode him into a staggering lather—himself exhausted, aching, but with the guilt of mistreatment of a dumb beast he loved added to the rest.

It came about finally that his mother's embalmed body was placed on a funerary boat; and, leading a procession of five other barges, it began the long, seemingly endless journey south on the Nile to Karnak. It was not as Moses had dreamt of going to Karnak—and when he came there he had no other desire than to see his mother entombed, and then to be done with the place. In any case, the God Ramses had just left Thebes to return to his name city, and the great men of Karnak were wary about pushing forth into the funerary proceedings of a sister of Ramses whose burial he specifically marked with his absence; and while Moses felt the eddy of those forces in Egypt—and specifically in Upper Egypt—that still kept alive some hope of the return of Aton, the whole god and only god, he also nourished his own contempt for their fears. In his present mood, he saw little choice between life and death; and his youth prevented any sound judgment of forces or any other distinction between foolhardiness and courage. Where he could once readily comprehend how idealistic and impractical were the plans of his mother and Amon-Teph and the other priests of Aton, his present hatred of Ramses made him feel that golden opportunities to dethrone the king had been passed over and lost. In these moods he would forget that he was the waif of a wretched slave people who lived in Goshen, and begin to believe the unfounded rumours concerning himself; and then, sliding back into the reality—the reality that became ever more marked as he matured into large-boned, long-muscled and hawk-faced manhood, he would fall prey to the black depression that had taken hold of him on the day of his mother's death. In such case, he returned down the Nile in a great retinue of boats, slaves, priests and soldiers—but with only one friend, Neph, the builder. Yet for that he was fortunate, even though he did not know it; and talking hour after hour, night after night with this plain, practical man who built what the kings would be remembered for, he not only gathered a store of knowledge and at least a little wisdom, but he began the process of calming his soul and learning the manner of acceptance and forbearance that would be so necessary in all the future years of his life. The gentle downstream journey, the soft lapping of the water in the river that had always been for him and others in the land the mother of life, the moonlit nights when the boundary ridges of the valley stood so black and beautiful, the sight again of the pyramids at Giza—all of this healed and rested him. But the dams of his soul were only fully opened after he had returned to the Great House.

It happened the day after he arrived there, when a slave

came and set down in his chamber a large basket. Moses opened it, and there in a copper bowl was the head of his teacher, Amon-Teph.

Then Moses put his head in his hands and wept, opened all the dams of restraint and control, and wept, sobbing and aching—with all the grief of a boy orphaned and bereft. But when the weeping finished, he was whole again, and his anger was clear and cold and precise. He walked again like a prince of Egypt when he bore the basket in his own arms to the embalmer and told him that he must find the body and embalm both in a manner fitting, or not live long upon this earth. And when the corpse was found, Moses and Neph put the body of the old priest to its rest in a deep, rock-lined chamber in the sand, just the two of them by night.

[18]

RAMSES WAS BACK in his city and in his Great House, and once again it was the centre of the civilized world. The life of the Great House renewed itself, as it had with the end of summer so long as Moses could remember; and here again came the petty kings and lords and desert sheiks to pay homage and curry favour; the ambassadors and the diplomats of Hatti and Phoenicia and Babylon, of Philistia, and twenty other minor nations; the merchant-pirate-princes of Crete and the sea-islands, the factions over-thrown by palace revolt and beseeching the God-King's aid; and the factions who desired to overthrow and also sought aid. All the indescribable colour and pageantry of the Great House resumed: the beating of the drums; the music of the pipes; the array of the finest Egyptian soldiery; the barges and sea-boats at the royal quays—the hustle and bustle and whispering and conniving of the great ones of the world assembled at the heart of the world; the white linen of the Egyptians; the leopard skins of the men of Kush; the plumed brass helmets of the Sea People waving their fans of yellow and red; the purple gowns of the Phoenicians; the tall black hats of the Hittites, cone-shaped and flattened on top; the striped robes of Meso-potamia; the fringed kilts of Philistia; and the striped woollen cloaks of the Bedouins.

All this Moses saw, and yet it moved him less than it ever had. He maintained the insular superiority of the Egyptian to whom all others were barbarians; yet where Egypt had been inside him, there was now an emptiness. He who had been the least prideful of all the palace children now walked with an unconscious hauteur which would have repelled people even had they not recognized a prince from his clothes, headband and golden collar; and many a curious glance was cast at him as he strode through the palace and its gardens. Foreigners would ask who the tall, lean and bitter-faced prince was; as often as not they received no satisfactory answer. A wise man felt it was a part of wisdom, and prudence, too, not to discuss the son of Enekhas-Amon with anyone.

It was on one such occasion, walking through the gardens, that Moses found his way barred by three of the sons of Ramses. He knew them well, and one in particular he knew even better; but even concerning Ramses-em-Seti, his indifference overcame his distaste, and he made to walk around them. They shifted their position to bar his way again, and one of them said,

"Who walks so proudly must have other areas of pride as well."

"Not necessarily," Ramses-em-Seti pointed out, "for I have thrown my spittle in his face without wounding his pride."

"Your spittle," said the third, "is probably sweeter than what he is used to. Do you perfume your mouth, my brother?"

"Always."

"I wonder whether his mother did?" the first one said.

All of this Moses listened to stolidly, only a trifle puzzled that his own irritation did not give way to anger. They had insulted him and now they were insulting his mother. He found himself unmoved.

"His mother was powerful," Ramses-em-Sed observed. "He was a prince of Egypt while his mother lived."

"But he's still a prince of Egypt. Notice his clothes, his bearing, his pride."

"And his *justice*?"

"Ah, his *justice*. A quality I can't see. But his pride is apparent."

"Do you think so?"

"Obviously."

Ramses-em-Seti leaned forward and expectorated full in Moses' face, angry himself now and crying out, "Does your pride survive that?"

Wiping his face with the back of his hand, Moses answered coolly, "You're not very inventive in your insults. What do you expect from all this, divine cousin?"

"I expect to fight you and kill you."

"I don't particularly care to fight you," Moses shrugged,

"and though I despise you more than you could possibly understand, I have no desire to kill any of you."

"I don't see that your desire has much to do with it now," said the first one, Re-em-Opet by name, the short, stout, squint-eyed result of the God Ramses' brief passion for a Libyan dwarf. "The act is done. My brother has only to tell it, and we witness it. You can hide in your chamber then, but no more walk in the palace or the gardens or the streets of the city."

Ramses-em-Seti nodded. "Gossip has it that you were dragged out of the water. Being wet in any case, we'll call you Spittle-Moses. It will last."

"We have appointed the place and time," said the third one. "The old pyramid in the date palms. Do you know where it is?"

"Of course he knows, said the first one.

"At moonrise tonight. Choose any hand weapons," said the third.

"Armour, if you wish," the second.

They were deeply serious now, and having said this, they turned and marched away. For a while Moses stood where he was, and then he went to a bench in the shade of a fig tree and seated himself, staring moodily at the blazing, sun-drenched colours of the garden. But as he sat there his mood changed, and the more he recalled the pompous manner of Re-em-Opet, the more amused he became. Suddenly, for the first time since his mother's death, he found himself chuckling with laughter; and chuckling, reaching and picking figs and eating them, he considered the matter. When he had considered enough, he got up and went to seek Seti-Hop.

Moses found him finally in a little sunken garden,

where the old man lay naked in the blazing sun, trying to soak the arthritis out of his aching joints. It was more than a year, perhaps two years, since Moses had seen the old warrior, and the prince was startled to see how small and shrivelled the man looked. In Moses' childhood, when Seti-Hop had taught him and his cousins the art of war, he had seemed a large man—larger for his bronze helmet that he wore so often as a mark of his authority. Now he was so skinny and small that Moses could have taken him up in his arms without difficulty.

When Moses appeared, it seemed that Seti-Hop was asleep, and so he sat on a bench to wait. But then the old man opened his eyes, squinted, shaded them to peer at Moses, and rolled over.

"Don't get up, please, Seti-Hop," Moses said.

"Eh?" The old man lay on one elbow, watching Moses. "Greetings, Prince of Egypt. I mourn your loss. I should have come to call, but I don't interfere with palace politics, and anyway, I'm nobody."

"You're my friend, Seti-Hop," Moses said. "I count my friends on the fingers of one hand."

"Oh, am I?"

"I think so. I need a friend now. The Prince Ramses-em-Seti insulted me, my mother and my origin. He also spat in my face."

Now Seti-Hop sat up and looked at Moses shrewdly. "He did that once before, as I remember. Does he make a habit of spitting at his betters?"

"Evidently. This time, he has a purpose. He challenged me to fight him and announced he will kill me. He set the time tonight at moonrise at the old pyramid in the grove."

"Fight you? The damned fool," Seti-Hop yawned.

"Well, that's what he has his heart set on."

"Tell him to go and lick a sacred cat's ass, Prince of Egypt."

"I suppose I could, but then he'll make life in Egypt difficult. He can't go on spitting in my face and insulting me, can he?"

"I don't know," the old soldier shrugged. "I'm not of noble blood, so I've never had those problems. Anyway, the God Ramses won't have fratricide among his sons. Buy the bastard off, you're rich enough." And when Moses smiled, he added, "I talk as I please, Prince of Egypt. I'm old enough and dry enough to be a mummy now. I suppose you're going to fight him?"

"I don't see what else I can do."

"What weapons?"

"Hand arms, he said. I imagine he'll use that long, iron sword of Hatti that he makes so much of."

"And you, Prince of Egypt?"

"I'll use the Kushite stave, Seti-Hop. And I won't kill him." Moses reached over and touched the old man's arm. "And incidentally, I am not one of the God Ramses' sons— remember that. Now will you come with me tonight?"

"No doubt I'll pay for it." Seti-Hop grinned. "And I'll get worse from my wife than you'll ever get from the prince. But I'll come. Don't let him spit at you again, Prince of Egypt. It's a nasty habit."

[19]

THE FIGHT WAS shorter even than Moses expected.

When he and Seti-Hop arrived on horseback at the old pyramid, a broken ruin no more than twenty feet high, with a clear space on flat ground in front of it, a considerable company were already present. Apparently, the sons of the God Ramses had no compunctions about the business, nor did they appear concerned over the consequences. At least a dozen brothers of various ages had come to witness the fight, bringing with them bread and wine and fruit, as well as their current ladies and sisters of favour. They lay about on linen coverlets, spread at the foot of the pyramid, and some of the younger ones had climbed the pyramid for better position. Slaves held torches to add to the moonlight, and a slave was completing the arming of Ramses-em-Seti, strapping on a bronze breastplate. Then he stood in breast-plate, helm and armplates, a round bronze shield on one arm, his long iron sword in hand.

Moses and Seti-Hop dismounted, the old soldier thrust-ing the six-foot-long, black-ebony stave into the soft ground, while he and Moses dropped their cloaks. Grinning at Ramses-em-Seti, the old man muttered,

"Look at that, Moses, a prudent, carefully-protected man, to carve your gizzard."

And he continued to grin as they walked forward, Moses naked to a loincloth, contemptuous in his manner as well as in his dress and arms. It was not only for agility and ease that he had come without arms, but very much because he expected that his cousin would be armed from head to foot. He had been nervous but not afraid, and now, seeing the sprawling representation of regal blood, stuffing their mouths with food or making love or drinking wine, sharpening their wit with clever aphorisms that they un-derlined with significant glances in his direction, his un-easiness turned to disdain. Until now he had regarded his cousins with the same objective acceptance of existence that he exercised toward the palace. They were there—as they had always been. But now, suddenly, his mood changed to profound disgust. Better to be of the blood of the slave people, he told himself; and, as he looked at them, he understood that he had never seen them before. His face, from contempt and amusement, set in anger and bitterness; and Seti-Hop, seeing this, nodded with relief. He knew of no substitute for hatred in a death fight. Seti-Hop then handed Moses the black stave, which he hefted and then let rest against his neck while he spat on his hands and rubbed them dry.

Meanwhile, Seti-Hop walked forward and cried out, "Now see me, O Princes of Egypt, for you know me. I am old Seti-Hop, master-at-arms, and I trained the God Ramses to use a sword and chariot before any of you sucked your mother's milk. This is a fight of godly blood, and it's a cursed shame that such a thing should be. But things were done that can't be recalled, so fight you must. If blood is drawn, it will be no fight to the death—but end there!" And when the brothers began to shout in protest, his hard, cold voice quieted them.

"Not with me, young sirs—not with me. There isn't one of you I don't remember from when he crawled, and it was I who taught you to fight. I'll have no murder done here tonight—and by all the gods in Egypt, go to the God-King if you dare!"

"Then if you want no murder done, Seti-Hop," one of the older brothers called out, "tell that nameless dirt to put away his stick and arm himself!"

"I tell the prince of Egypt nothing. He chose his weapon, as your brother did, and if he chooses to die, that is his affair and so much the sooner an end to this nonsense.

And let no one interfere, for if I am armed only with a dagger, I've used it for half a century and used it well. I give you my word that, princes of Egypt or no, I'll hamstring anyone who dares enter this fight after it begins. If you want to limp your life through, disregard me." He looked questioningly from face to face, but no one challenged him. The moon was above the trees now, and the little glade turned to silver, the silver rippling over the vine- and moss-covered pyramid—giving the scene an unearthly and gripping enchantment that even the royal brothers felt, quelling and quieting them. They were caught too by the picturesque and momentary immobility of the fighters—Ramses-em-Seti, broad-shouldered; his hunched, tense back bound over with great layers of muscle, like the broad back of his father, his armour glistening with moonlight and throwing off the leaping reflection of the torches—and Moses, taller, leaner; his strength hidden in the linear growth of bone and muscle; his brown body alert without tension; both his hands holding the stave at arm's length and loosely in front of him.

"I whistle to fight," said, Seti-Hop, "and I whistle to stop. May the gods help either of you if you disobey me. Ready now!"

He put his fingers to his mouth and blew a wild, piercing whistle. Moses crouched just a little, balancing on the balls of his feet, one foot forward and both spread wide. Ramses-em-Seti swung his long Hittite sword high, put his shield in guard, and leaped at Moses, quick to end the fight in one clean blow that would cleave his seemingly defenceless cousin's skull in two. As he came in, Moses crouched a little more deeply, threw up the ebony stave— ten pounds of wood as thick as his wrist—and caught and parried the sword stroke upon it. The same motion allowed him to strike Ramses-em-Seti a glancing blow on the side that threw the prince off balance and gave Moses an instant in which to shorten his grasp on the stave and use it as a pole-axe. The great weight of the stave speeded Moses in the arc, a continuation of the first motion, a round, terrible blow in which he put all his strength and which sent the stave whipping into the other's bronze shield. The shield folded in like a thin copper plate, and above the crash of wood on metal came the clean, ugly sound of the prince's arm snapping. He screamed as he staggered back, spun, and then fell headlong on the ground; but he had kept his sword in his grasp, and as he attempted to rise with it, Moses brought down his stave again, crushing hand and wrist in one awful blow. Through the wild-animal-like screaming of Ramses-em-Seti, the piercing whistle of Seti-Hop sounded, for the second blow was given even as he raised his hand to his mouth, and the whole fight had lasted no more than a few seconds.

Dragging his stave, Moses deliberately turned his back and went to where he had dropped his cloak. As he did so, Re-em-Opet leaped to the screaming prince, scooped up his sword, and swung it over his head. At Seti-Hop's roar of anger, Moses spun around, saw the sword and swung at it with his stave, breaking the blow and knocking it out of Rem-em-Opet's hand. His fury exploded in him, like a spring released, and dropping the stave, he seized the prince by his fat neck and thigh, swung him overhead with a demonic surge of strength, and cast him across the glade like a sack of wheat. Re-em-Opet landed on his broad behind, howled with indignation and pain, and rolled over on hands and knees to rise. As he did so, Seti-Hop, dagger in hand, leaped at him and slashed both buttocks open. Then he wiped his knife on the cool grass, slipped it into its scabbard, and walked over to Moses. Then they put on their cloaks and Seti-Hop turned to face the royal brothers. Not one of them had moved; they sat frozen in silence and horror, while the glade rang with the anguished screams of the prince whose arm and hand were broken and the whining pain of the other prince, who had been hamstrung.

Seti-Hop and Moses went to where a slave held their horses, mounted and rode off. For a time they rode in silence, but then Seti-Hop said, with some admiration,

"You're a quick man and a terrible one, O Prince of Egypt. It comes as a shock in a quiet lad."

"Did you think he would kill me?" Moses asked, still trembling with the effort and anger, his robe soaked with sweat.

"Who knew? One doesn't know in a fight. He thought he would. Anyway, it made a good night's work and I think you wiped out the insult. However, one of your cousins will never be able to use his hand again, and the other will limp through his life. He deserved that."

"I'll survive it somehow," Moses muttered. "But what about you, Seti-Hop?"

"What about me? Do you think me an utter fool, Prince of Egypt?"

"No. And I didn't say so."

"Of course not, and you don't live to my age in a place like the Great House without common sense. I went to the God Ramses tonight before I came here, and he specified the rules of the fight. I explained that the odds were long against your dying, but he took them. And don't look at me as if I betrayed you, Prince of Egypt. I think I saved your life."

[20]

STRANGELY—OR PERHAPS not so strangely—the fight at the pyramid remained a secret. Moses confided in no one, for aside from Neph, there was no one for him to confide in, and Neph was away at this time; Seti-Hop had long experience in keeping his silence, and evidently the royal brothers and sisters had decided that the affair brought them no credit and the less said about it, the better. The two wounded princes were confined to their chambers under the care of physicians—who were equally adept at silence—and so for three days, Moses moved about as if nothing had happened.

There was, however, a difference of degree; for now no member of the royal family spoke to him, nodded mat him, or smiled at him; they went out of their way to avoid him, so he was forced to conclude that at least some inkling of what had happened at the pyramid had seeped out. And at the end of the three days, he was summoned to the throne room at the order of the God Ramses.

Eight years had passed since the God-King last had spoken to him, and for a child growing to manhood, eight years are an incredibly long time. During those eight years he had seen Ramses many times, but never closely, never to speak to him, never to be noticed by him. It struck Moses as strange indeed that while he himself had grown to manhood, the God Ramses seemed changed not at all.

Once again, as eight years ago, Moses was dressed in

the best that a prince, of Egypt might wear—golden collars and golden bracelets, jewelled bracelets and jewelled head-bands. Once again the pomp and ceremony, the blaze of colour and people, of mosaic and tapestry impressed him; once again he lay upon his breast, his check against the God-King's foot until he was bidden to rise; and once again, all others in the great chamber stood away so that Ramses might not be overheard.

Yet it was different. The mighty audience chamber had become merely a large room. The decorations seemed to verge on the garish and tasteless. The hieroglyphic tale of Ramses' mighty feats in the war against Hatti was studded with obvious lies. And the god was only a man—a man whom Moses hated, and feared, too.

Yet Ramses was no less at ease, and he smiled as he told Moses to step back, the better to look at him. His look was keen and searching, and his dark eyes fixed themselves upon Moses' so intently that the young man had to drop his own gaze. Then Ramses nodded and told Moses to come close to him, observing that this had become necessary since a good many priests had taken to practicing hearing the way an archer practises with his bow. Then he said,

"Well, Moses, you are a likely-looking young man. How old are you now?"

"Eighteen years, sacred god."

"Don't call me by that ridiculous title. Call me father. And stop thinking that I killed your mother and get the murder out of your heart."

"Yes, my father," Moses answered flatly.

"A little more warmth, Moses, and a little more wit and understanding. A fool doesn't rule an empire like mine as long as I have, and the worst mistake you can make is to consider me a fool. Your mother was sick, very sick, and the pain she suffered is not to be understood by anyone so free of pain as you. Try to understand that I loved your mother."

"Yes, my father."

" 'Yes, my father,' " Ramses mimicked him. "Is that all you are going to say to me?"

"I will answer any questions you put to me, my father, as best I may."

Ramses threw back his head and roared with laughter— so that all in the throne room turned to look at him curiously and wonderingly. His whole body shook with laughter, until finally he subsided, rubbing his knuckles into his wet eyes. "By all that is holy, Moses, you are a strange man and a brave one. A foolhardy one and without much sense as yet, but that may come. You remind me of the great ancient lords of Upper Egypt who fill our olden sagas, and you have the same knifelike look as the sculptures of them. I confess I half like you, but you are too stimulating for our quiet life on the Delta, and it seems that where you are trouble gathers. Why didn't you kill that wretched product of one of my less profitable nights in bed when he fought you?"

"I had no reason to kill him, my father," Moses shrugged. "He had only insulted me, and that didn't seem to measure up to his life."

"And your honour? Your pride?"

"My honour will survive. And as for my pride, my father, it died with my mother, the holy Enekhas-Amon, who gave it to me."

"Now what do you mean by that?" Ramses snorted. "Don't talk in riddles, boy. I hate riddles. Yet I think you're right. You're not cut to the cloth of murder, for which, be sure, I am grateful—since Seti-Hop seems to think that when you are angry, no man in this palace could stand against you. War is something else. Seti-Hop considers that you will make a good soldier, and I am inclined to agree. Here you will bring only sorrow and trouble, Moses, for I think you were born to sorrow and trouble—but on our borders you can give much to Egypt. Also, it will be good for you to go away from here until tempers cool and fancied wrongs are forgotten. In ten days from now a punitive expedition of some fifteen thousand men leaves for the Land of Kush, where the black men have forgotten that while my patience is long, my forbearance is short. You will go along with them as a captain of chariots and you will remain away for three years. You will learn a good deal, I imagine, in three years; and after that time, you can return here to this city of mine."

"Yes, my father," Moses said, still flatly.

"A wiser man, I hope," Ramses concluded, his voice as humourless as Moses' now.

So ended the audience with the God Ramses, and the childhood and youth of Moses as well.

PART TWO

The Captain of Kush

[1]

OLD WAS THE Land of Egypt, but the Land of Kush was also old, and though there were a thousand of nations, cities and peoples the world over, there was only one Kush, and like the Kushite were no others. In the olden times, the Egyptian guarded one end of the world and the black man of Kush guarded the other; from Egypt's Delta, the blue sea tolled away, endless and boundless until it poured over the rocky edge of the world—to run underground and bubble anew from the dark and unknowable mystery of Kush. That was in the olden times, but long before the time of Moses, men had grown wiser and and had learned the art of shipbuilding, and the great ships of Egypt had sailed all over the blue Mediterranean—so that the edge of the world was no longer the edge of the world. So the Delta and the great City of Ramses became a gateway to the whole world beyond Egypt; but to the world beyond Kush, there were no gateways.

And as the world opened and unfolded, the armies of Egypt marched forth to conquer. If they were defeated now and again, it was the way a river is defeated by a log and brush jam; the block breaks eventually, and the river rolls on—and so did the armies of Egypt toll over the world. Nothing could resist them, seemingly, for with Egypt came organization, order, and planned lines of battle, and against these organized lines of spears and columns of chariots, neither the heroes of Philistia nor the warriors of Hatti could persist. The Babylonian fled in terror and the heroic Sea Rover cast his spear and ran back to his ships. But the men of Kush only returned to Kush—for Kush was as boundless as it was distant, and who had ever conquered it?

"*There* is a man of Kush," Moses had been told once, long ago, by Amon-Teph as they walked in the market place of Tanis. "There is a man from far away, and with the things of far away, one should always be concerned, O Prince of Egypt—"

But more than with Amon-Teph's words was Moses held and entranced by the great black man who was occupied in trading a thick, hammered-gold bracelet for sacks of wheat and barley. To Moses, who was then still a boy, the man seemed a giant, and his towering headdress of red and yellow feathers made him appear even taller. Many brown men of all shades had Moses seen, but this man of Kush was black as ebony, so black that the sunlight danced and sparkled on the sheen of his skin; and the sight of his great frame with its broad shoulders and mighty muscles made the boy realize why the people of Kush were spoken of for their beauty as well as their valour. This man had a long, narrow head, a small, tilted nose, and a heavy-lipped, wide mouth. The bones of his face were large and strange, so that it was hard to tell at first whether he was more beautiful than he was ugly or more ugly than he was beautiful; but from the way the Egyptian women could hardly take their eyes from him, it did not seem to matter. He stood like a prince himself, not willing to bend his spine even a trifle to the bargaining, and his broken Egyptian came in deep, resonant tones from his great chest.

His feathers were fixed in a copper band that circled his brow, and Moses could see that he did not have hair as he knew hair, but what looked like tight-curled wool. Down the length of his back, its tail sweeping to his heels, he wore a leopard skin, and the two front paws were fixed around his neck with a gold buckle. Beneath this, in front, he wore a necklace of three rows of enormous claws, each claw separated from the next by a white ivory bead. Around each calf, just below the knee, was a bracelet identically made, and similar bracelets circled each arm above the elbow. On each wrist, he wore a hammered-gold bracelet like the one he was trying to sell, and around his waist he wore a short woollen kilt, striped yellow and red. instead of sandals, he wore low boots of some soft skin, embroidered all over with yellow and white beads, and he wore a belt of white leather, from which many pouches as well as a long bronze dagger hung. He wore a round shield of bullhide, three feet in diameter, and a great spear, eight feet long and tipped with metal.

Colorful and tall and strange and barbaric he was, yet for all his erect and proud manner, his attitude was somehow pervaded with an air of amusement and easy good humour that robbed his presence of any threat. This, above all, Moses was to remember in reference to the strange and distant Land of Kush, and some of Amon-Teph's words too; for the priest said, as Moses watched,

"O Prince of Egypt, it is not merely that Kush is far away, it is also the fact that Kush is Kush, which is something you must understand. It keeps itself so, for many men believe that they have been to Kush, but few have been there. I talk not of the land beyond the Sixth Cataract, not of the desert highlands, but of the actual and elusive Land of Kush, from where this man comes—and few like him will you see here upon the Delta. So look well. The world is filled with wonders and with people who do not pray to the dark gods of Egypt's night. This man, when he dies, will be wrapped in his cloak and put bare and unembalmed into the ground, his shield under him, his spear upon his breast, yet he fears death as little as you and I fear a stray gull from the sea——"

Meanwhile. a crowd of dirty, naked street-urchins had gathered around the tall black man, and they pressed closer and closer, in spite of the efforts of the merchant to drive them away with an intermittent outpouring of abuse and threat. They goggled with such awe and interest at his colourful headdress that finally he took it off and placed it on the ground in front of them. A few of them gathered enough courage to touch it, and then one bold child of eight or so lifted it and placed it on his head—but it was so large that it slipped down to rest on his shoulders. At this, the black man burst into deep roars of mirth—mirth so contagious that in a moment the children were laughing with him, and even Moses and the old priest were smiling in delight.

So it was when Moses saw for the first time a man from the Land of Kush.

AND SO HE thought and recollected now, the spirit and vigour of his youth putting grief and depression aside. It was not his nature to cling to pity of himself, and after all, the God-King Ramses had treated him not too badly. The Great House and all the City of Ramses were sour to him, and of the three people he had loved, two were dead and the third had to be avoided, if only out of simple forbearance and consideration. He had always yearned for the South, for the mysterious, legendary world of Central Africa, whose northern boundary was Kush—just as he had always admired the men of Upper Egypt, who held the border marches against the wild black men.

And there he was going, after all. He was eighteen years old, tall and strong, and it never entered his mind that the war of Egypt against barbarians could be anything but exciting and glorious. It was true, he reflected, that he might have come off better in his exchange with Ramses. Facing the man he regarded as his mother's executioner, he had held back all the bitter words that were in his heart, but on the other hand—as he told himself—he had been put off by the obvious lack of hatred or even anger on the part of the God-King. At worst, Ramses was annoyed with him, at best, amused; and this not only puzzled Moses, but frustrated his desire to nurse his own hatred. The truth of the matter was that Moses hated poorly—which was hardly surprising, since nothing tempers passion so well as knowledge, and Moses had not only absorbed the fruits of Amon-Teph's tutelage but the scepticism of Neph, the engineer, as well.

Whereby, he was content to transfer his vengeance to the distant future three years away. At eighteen, three years is a lifetime.

These thoughts were in his mind as he walked across the old City of Tanis a few days after Ramses had pronounced judgment. He was bound for the chariot stables and the parade ground, where, he knew, he would find Seti-Keph, the Captain of Hosts who would lead the expedition to Kush—and where he, Moses would present himself for service. As he walked through the old, twisting streets, past the little houses of sundried mud brick, he hardly noticed the naked children scampering out of his way, the men and women touching their brows at the holy sight of a prince of Egypt, for his thoughts were full of the adventure and excitement that would be his. He pictured himself balanced on a swaying chariot in the wild mêlée of battle, shouting his war cry and striking down the enemy. So much did his imagination occupy him that he arrived at the parade ground with no sense of how he had come there, and stood surprised, staring over the great spread of hardpacked mud at the long building, the famous stable of Ramses, where ten thousand horses were housed and fed.

The parade ground, however, linked reality to his thoughts, for at least a hundred chariots were being exercised, and the drumming of the horses' hoofs, the cries of the drivers, the grinding and shrilling of the wheels, and the great clouds of dust that hung over man, horse and chariot made it very easy to imagine this the field of battle. All this Moses had seen before, but always as a detached spectacle; now he was of it and in it, and as he circled the field toward the barracks and stables, he felt trepidation mixed with anticipation.

Nor did Seti-Keph lessen the reality. A short, broad, hard-muscled, flat-faced man of fifty or so, Moses found him standing in front of the stables, a handful of his officers around him, watching the chariot exercises with a sour and exasperated expression. Barefoot, he wore a loin-cloth, no ornaments, no weapons, no mark of his rank and distinction except the network of scars and the patches of scar tissue that covered his whole body, even his face and his balding head. But that in itself, Moses knew, was his distinction, and who in all Egypt would not recognize this son of a nameless peasant who had gone to the wars in Canaan as a weapon-bearer at the age of ten, and who had never known or desired a year of peace since?

Similar badges of scars were worn by the men around him, and they were alike with the alikeness of occupation, just as one sailor is like another sailor, one carpenter like another carpenter. So were these men similar in the brown, dry quality of their skin, the hardness of their faces, and the tight squint of their eyes as they gazed across the sunlit field. Like Seti-Keph, their master, they wore only loin-cloths and, at the most, a leather-hung dagger low on the hip. But what struck Moses about them, seeing them here in their own habitat and not in the palace with all its gaudy trappings, was an awful lack of any suggestion of human-ness. It was not that they appeared cruel or bestial—but simply non-human; yet if he had been asked concerning this, Moses would have been hard put to explain why or how the impression came to him.

Then, abruptly, Seti-Keph flung out one arm and cried,

"Enough of that and be damned with it! There are no char- iot men in Egypt! Give me the worst lout of Hatti, and he'll do more with a team and a wagon than those peasant dolts you pretend are charioteers! Am I a fool?" he roared at his captains, and when they met his furious gaze in silence, he shouted,

"Then do it yourselves, the god's curse on you! The God-King says—Take two thousand chariots to Kush! Two thousand! Ha! Where? How? All right—all right! Now leave me alone!" And he stamped past them and came face to face with Moses.

For a moment, Moses thought the Captain of Hosts would swell up and explode with sheer, frustrated rage, Arms akimbo, he stood staring speechlessly at the prince, at the stiff, white pleated-linen kilt, at the belt of golden bars, each bar inlaid with rubies and pearls; at the great golden collar, with its sphinx-head pendant; at the silver- trimmed sandals, and the gem-set silver scabbard that held the prince's dagger. But sanity and sagacity overcame rage, and Seti-Keph drew a deep breath, swallowed, and man- aged to say,

"Are you looking for me or another, Prince of Egypt? I am Seti-Keph, Captain of Hosts." His voice was cold and flat, a statement of duty that could ill afford emotion.

"I come to you, Seti-Keph," Moses answered unhappily, conscious of the unflattering and unfriendly look of the lieutenants of Seti-Keph. Evidently, they had no high opin- ion of the children of Ramses, and perhaps a little expe- rience to back up their judgment. Moses had not expected to be welcomed with open arms, but as a matter of course he had anticipated the same deference accorded every- where to his rank and birth.

"And why, may I ask, O Prince of Egypt?"

"Because the God-King would have me with you to Kush, as a captain of chariots."

"Oh?" Seti-Keph nodded his head ominously now. "I remember. Moses—the prince of the half-name. Indeed, and as a captain of chariots! Yes, indeed! It has been whispered, O prince, that you have made something of a name for yourself in your palace brawls. Therefore, you are fit to be a captain of chariots. This is something I don't deny. I don't deny any decision of the God-King. No doubt you are a practised charioteer?"

"No. Seti-Keph, I am not."

"You are not. But a captain of chariots you are! Ah!" he spat out, shaking his head and clenching his fists as he strode past Moses toward the barracks. The chariots were coming in from the field now to the stables, and slaves came running to meet them and handle the bridles, and the officers of Seti-Keph drifted off, some after the Captain of Hosts, some towards the chariots. Moses was left standing alone, ill at ease, not a little disturbed at his introduction to the next three years of his life. "What now?" he wondered. "If it means so little to be a prince of Egypt here at the parade ground, what will it mean in Kush? And whom do I turn to?"

As if in answer to his question, one of the officers who had gone to the chariots turned back to him now, a tall, rather good-looking man with a long white scar running from temple to cheekbone on the right side of his face, just touching the corner of his lips and giving him permanently the expression of a derisive grin. He smiled at Moses, saluted by touching both hands to his forehead, and said without ceremony,

"My name, Prince of Egypt, is Hetep-Re, Captain of Chariots under the Captain of Hosts. It would seem to me that at this moment you require a friend and advisor. I place myself at your disposal. Without someone like myself, things will go from bad to worse with you. Not because Seti-Keph is a cruel man, but because he is a completely frustrated man at the moment. I can help you. I will be happy to help you."

Moses' immediate reaction of relief and gratitude was tempered with caution. This was a new world, as he had begun to learn, and instead of accepting Hetep-Re at his word, he asked to know why.

"Why indeed, Prince of Egypt? If I said it was because I honour the godhead of the Great House, it would take us for ever to get to the point. Let me be both blunt and honest. I am a poor man, as most soldiers are. There's precious little truth in the stories of the fortunes in spoil a soldier brings home with him. He takes what he can carry, and the tavernkeepers and the whores get most of it before he ever reaches home. I have a wife and three children in the city, and who knows whether one returns from Kush or anywhere else? You are a prince of Egypt. My friendship is for sale at a price."

Moses smiled. "I see. So are things done in the army. And suppose I were to regard your words as an insult and kill you here on the spot? I am a prince of Egypt."

"Agreed. But I am an old soldier, and I don't kill easily. Take my advice, young man, and learn something about the horse before you ride him. A spear or an arrow is ill trained on questions of royalty, and only a prince out of favour and twice cursed goes for three years to the Land of Kush, where every manner of heat and hell prosper.

Don't threaten men so easily. I made you an offer. Take it or leave it."

"How much?" Moses said shortly.

"Twenty minas of pure gold."

Moses whistled. "What do you propose for your wife while you're gone, soldier? A palace?"

"Take it or leave it, O Prince of Egypt."

"I take it."

"Good. Now we are friends, and if you buy me, nevertheless you buy a man. Now let us find some shade and a cold drink and talk about tomorrow. There's a winehouse behind the stables where the soldiers go, and god or no, you had might as well begin to be a soldier now."

[3]

THEY SAT ON a bench outside of the winehouse, in the shade of a *pelph*, a variety of thorn tree with shiny copper-green leaves that grew profusely on the Delta; for try as he would, Moses could not bring himself to enter the dark, strong-smelling tavern where a crowd of soldiers drank wine and talked colourfully and obscenely about sex and war. He found now, and he would find later, that it was not easy to soften and bend the iron rods of royalty and godhead that had been forged in him during the years of his youth; and while it was one thing to unbend to anyone who shared the clean white splendour of the palace, prince or priest or scribe or slave, it was something else entirely to rub shoulders with these sweaty, dust-covered and foul-mouthed soldiers.

A prince who cannot at all times be a prince will likely enough be a defenceless and worried creature, and Moses was not yet old enough to cover his feelings successfully. He saw how appraisingly Hetep-Re watched him, and he felt that the soldier saw through him and into him.

"Well," he told himself, "it will not always be this way. I made my way in the palace and I'll make my way in this army too." Hetep-Re was saying that this was a new world, and if one were to live in it, one had to accept it. Soldiers had virtues, he supposed, but their trade was killing, and they were a dirty, foul-mouthed and hard lot. It was more likely that they would end up in the desert, their bones picked clean by the vultures, than in any embalmer's tank. He himself, he pointed out, had never seen the inside of the Great House of Ramses, but from all he had heard, things were a little different there.

"Yes, I would say so," Moses nodded.

"Well. Prince, so it goes, and our trade has its compensations as well as its burden. We see odd parts of the world, which is a good deal bigger than the priests say, and we have our moments of wealth even if we don't hold on to it. We get sufficient taste of women and power to glut our appetites, and if we are lucky we live. Kush is a hard place, hot and very far away, and the men of Kush are wild and terrible on the battlefield. But I would rather fight against Kush than against Hatti or Philistia."

"Why so?" Moses asked, and then apologized, lest he be revealed for an utter fool, "I know nothing of war, I'm afraid."

"And I know nothing of manners or culture," Hetep-Re responded generously, cocking his head at Moses and inquiring, "You can read and write, can't you?"

Moses nodded. "I began to read at the age of eight, and I've been reading and writing ever since."

For the first time, a look of awe and respect came over the face of Hetep-Re, and he nodded sagely. "A prince of Egypt indeed. I think ours will be a profitable association. Seti-Keph does not read or write. Neither do I, for that matter. It's a better weapon than an iron sword, Prince of Egypt—and therefore to be kept under your kilt with other excellent weapons until the time you use it."

Moses was amused and more at ease in a world he recognized, a world of plotting and counterplotting, lies and deceit, a world not unlike, in this respect, the Great House.

As they spoke, a knot of chariot-drivers was gathering around them, stating at the jewels and finery of the tall prince of Egypt. With a look and a wave of his hand, Hetep-Re dispersed them, snarling a few obscene words about their parentage. "Dogs," he said to Moses. "There's the first lesson of military life. Your soldier is a dog. Throw him a bone but crack the whip too. One officer holds power over a hundred men. They would tear him to shreds if they didn't fear him."

Moses looked after the retreating men and then took up the conversation again. "You said you would rather fight against Kush than against Hatti or Philistia—?"

"Did I? It's true. For one thing, they have no chariots in Kush. For another, little metal—copper, some bronze, but almost no iron. They have much gold and they work it well, but to work bronze, they must buy their tin from us. They are brave and savage men in battle, but they fight as the Sea Rovers fight, each man for himself, and they can't stand against disciplined foot-soldiers or chariots. The danger from Kush is that our order of battle may break, and then if they come into us with their battle madness, all the gods in Egypt cannot help us. But there's time for that. It's

151

a great distance to the Land of Kush—and from here in the Delta, we will be on the march and on the river for better than seventy days before we reach even the northernmost outposts of Kush. Right now, the advice you are paying for is of a more practical kind. Have you had much experience in a chariot, Prince of Egypt?"

"A little."

"A little—well, better than none, I suppose. You will learn a lot on the march. Until then, you must not make an enemy out of Seti-Keph. Keep out of his way. You are a prince of Egypt, but in the wilderness of the South, a prince is nothing and Seti-Keph is all. That is hard for you to understand, but you must."

"I will try," Moses nodded.

"You are also, by the God-King's appointment, a captain of chariots. But Seti-Keph will give you no host to lead, and he would be a fool if he did. If you insist, he will give you lip-service so long as we are on the Delta, and after that he will hate you."

"It seems he hates me already."

"Oh, no—no. That's his way. There's no milk of kindness in him. He's a hard and shrewd man—how else would a peasant-boy become Captain of Hosts? But he doesn't hate until he has a reason to hate. He has a wild bellow, like a bull in heat, but underneath he is as cold and calculating as any man in Egypt. I lead a host of a hundred chariots. My advice is for you to remain with me and let the situation develop. After our first battle, Seti-Keph will be looking for captains of chariots to replace those who have been killed. Now, do you have a chariot?"

Moses shook his head.

"All right—you're a prince of Egypt, and you're not

poor. Let me take care of the chariot. I don't know how to read or write, but I know chariots. Now, do you have horses?"

"Only one horse—but he's a fine beast and strong and full of spirit."

"Now by all that is holy," Hetep-Re demanded disdainfully, "how do you harness a chariot with one horse?"

"I don't," Moses smiled. "I ride him astraddle, as the Libyans do."

"Do you?" asked Hetep-Re, not without a note of contempt in his voice. "Do you find it pleasant? I'm afraid I like things the Egyptian way, the horse in front of a chariot and not under a man, but every man to his own taste. I heard it was a vogue at the Great House, but they have their ways at the palace and we have ours. For the campaign, you will want two teams of broken chariot-mounts, for horses are hard to come by in Kush and you'll need replacements. And when you learn enough about a chariot to feel that you were born in one, you can harness four horses, two on the tree and two wing beasts on leather harness. But right now you want two matched teams. The best are from Hatti, trained and broken there, but they come high?" He ended on a note of questioning. Evidently, he was uncertain of the resources of even a prince of Egypt.

"Whatever they cost, buy them," Moses shrugged. "I am very rich, if that is what you want to know. I have more wealth than I know or care what to do with, so there is one less secret between us."

Hetep-Re smiled warmly and nodded. "I am a poor man, but I like wealth. I am told that the rich are indifferent to it sometimes, and when that is the case it makes them very admirable and you can take pleasure in their breeding. You might not think it to look at me, but I have the greatest respect for breeding, culture and the better things in life. Unfortunately, the circumstances of my birth denied me full access to them. Now that the situation is clear, I'll buy the best—the very best of everything. Nothing else is fitting. Do you agree with me, O Prince of Egypt?"

"I agree with you," Moses said coldly, attempting to hide his distaste for the officer, arguing to himself that this was the reality and that he might just as well make his peace with it. A man with wealth was a fool not to use it— and in the same mood, he asked the officer curiously,

"Tell me, Hetep-Re, now that we have discovered that we can be of use to each other, is there anything in this army that wealth can't buy?"

The Captain of Chariots took the question seriously and considered it carefully. "One thing," he finally admitted, "but that is worth thinking about. Seti-Keph, the Captain of Hosts.

"But this kind of discussion can wait. For the moment, O prince of Egypt, there is one thing more you require—a chariot-driver. I will undertake to train him myself, to give him my personal attention, providing you buy a young, strong and brave man."

"Buy?"

"Yes. You want a slave. For one thing, you will not find a free Egyptian in the Delta, a healthy man with strength and courage, who will go with us of his own accord. If you buy a peasant out of debt, he will probably be a clod and a dolt. For another, it is the custom among us. A captain of chariots does not ride body to body with a free man— much less so a prince of Egypt. And this purchase, I feel, should be yours. Find a driver of your own choice, for often enough your life will depend on him."

"Very well," Moses shrugged. "I will buy a chariot-driver. Anything else?"

"A delicate matter, but unavoidable. If I am to buy, I need gold."

"You do indeed," Moses nodded. "Come tonight to the gateway of the Great House and ask for Moses, son of Enekhas-Amon. I will have the gold for you."

"Moses?"

"Moses, Prince of Egypt."

"Very well, godly one," said Hetep-Re, rising and bowing low. "I come tonight."

[4]

NEPH HAD RETURNED. In the last hour of the sun, Moses found the engineer in his chamber, standing before the large window and watching the twilight fall upon the pink and purple Nile. It occurred to Moses that the engineer recognized his tread, for he did not turn even when Moses stood alongside of him, but nodded and greeted him without looking at him.

"Are you at prayer?" Moses asked.

"Prayer? I burn no flesh, Prince of Egypt, no incense, no spices, and the little I knew from the *Book of the Dead*, I have forgotten. How shall I pray?"

"The heart prays to Aton. You need only feel and think."

"Oh? Is that something old Amon-Teph taught you?"

"Yes—"

"I wonder whether after a day of observing the greed and folly of this world, Aton doesn't have a bellyful, and is more content to get away in peace than to be bothered by the whining of pious hypocrites."

"Why is it, O Neph, that so many who believe for so long in Aton—and at such risk of their lives and fortunes, end up by becoming cynical and bitter?"

"Do they? Then I would imagine, Prince of Egypt, that you should look into the meaning of what you call cynicism. Your cynic begins his career by renouncing the gods and believing in people. Not because he loves people, but because he hates the gods. But he becomes disillusioned because in the end plain human beings don't stand up very well as gods. The gods are noble because they lack the power to be ignoble. That's an interesting concept, isn't it? The gods are immortal, not because they lack the curse of death, but because they lack the blessing of life. But your cynic fails to appreciate this. He wants a god who has at least the modest virtues of men, but because men are not godlike at all, he ends up by despising all people."

"I thought you didn't believe in the gods, Neph?"

"Let me put it a little differently. Since I am an Egyptian, I do believe in them, but I dislike them intensely."

"Now I don't understand anything you are saying," Moses said with some annoyance. "Are you laughing at me?"

"Have I ever laughed at you, Moses?" Neph sighed. "I have been away because the God-King sent me to Giza to draw up a plan for repairing the great pyramids. This is the fourth time he has done this, and the plans were prepared five years ago and are collecting dust here in this room.

He periodically dreams that the gods of old are warning him not to neglect the pyramids, but he is also torn by the thought that they overshadow his own stone monuments. But my thoughts didn't leave you, Moses. I heard of what happened, and you shouldn't be angry at me because I wasn't here when you needed me."

"I'm not angry!" Moses snapped, knowing that he was— and that he had felt totally abandoned by the one man who had given him some feeling of what it meant to have a father; and knowing too that now he was lonely and afraid, his heart pleading with Neph to reassure him, to tell him that his life had some sense and meaning and purpose, to give him spells and knowledge that would be a shield against fear.

"Of course you were angry and hurt," Neph said softly, "but what can I do for you, my poor Prince of Egypt? You can't lean on me—only on yourself from here. We all look for ourselves and our answers in this folly that we call our glorious Egyptian birthright. In the old books, it says that once people lived here in peace and contentment, but I wonder? Man is what he is; accept that, Moses, or you'll break your heart looking for something more than he is. This strange search you are embarking on is fruitless and without any answer or end."

"You know what I came for and you know what you're giving me," Moses said wretchedly.

"I would be a liar to give you anything else. Three days ago, at the Assembly of the Lights, I stood on the terrace of the Great House and watched the lights dancing and waving all over the city. I felt youth or the illusion of youth come back to me, and I went out into the streets and drank the wine held out to me and put a sprig of myrtle in my ear and danced and laughed and sang and then took a girl half my age to bed with me on the riverbank—"

"It sounds like a good night," Moses shrugged.

"As good as any, I suppose. But when you eat bread, you should feel your belly full, not empty. Enough of that now. Ramses, they tell me, has made you a soldier. Are you pleased, Moses?"

"Why not?" Moses said lightly, trying to give the impression that Neph had misjudged him, that if he had not found, neither had he sought, and that he desired neither pity nor affection. "My head is still on my neck, and as for the Land of Kush, well, I would go anywhere to get out of this vile House and out of the City of Ramses."

"All right then," Neph nodded. "I also think it is better for you to go away than to remain here, although my life will be the emptier for that."

"You have your work."

"Well—have it that way, if you will." He smiled without any happiness, and Moses wished that he himself were dead before he had hurt the one person in the Great House who was his friend. "I do have my work, and next to love, work is the best thing I know. I'll look for you to come back, Moses."

"I go for three years."

"So long? But not so long for me as for you, Moses, for as the years pass, they pass always more quickly. You are going away to war, my son, and what do you think war is?"

"I know it's not like the life here. Men die. I know that," Moses argued, on the defensive and already feeling a loyalty to the dust-covered men on the parade ground—special in his sense of being consecrated to a specific adventure and pledge, to something that the run-of-the-mill, workaday citizen could neither comprehend nor share. "I know it's not all pleasure, but it is excitement and adventure and glory and a chance for something more than the gossip and conniving of this House. Something you can dream about, at least——"

"Yes, you can dream about it," Neph nodded.

"Then why don't you tell me what you think?"

"It would do no good to tell you, Moses. I want to help you in any way I can. If there's anything you need?"

"Yes—I need a slave for a chariot-driver, Neph," Moses said almost arrogantly. "What kind of a slave should I buy?"

Quite seriously, Neph replied, "A Bedouin, I think."

"A Bedouin?"

"Yes. They're stringy and hard, and they can take a lot of punishment and they know the desert. You'll be in desert a good deal, and I think that's the kind of a man for you."

Suddenly, Moses could not speak, feeling that his heart had swelled out to choke him. The sun had set, and it was quite dark in the chamber now. Moses stood at the window, bent forward, his hands gripping the sill, and when Neph asked him if he felt ill, he shook his head and managed to say,

"I'm sorry, Neph."

"You have nothing to be sorry for, O Prince of Egypt."

"I asked you never again to call me Prince of Egypt, Neph."

"I understand."

Now bits of time flowed by, and they stood there in the darkness, neither of them speaking. More time and deeper darkness—and then the first silver trickle of moonlight laced itself upon the river. It was Moses who finally broke the silence.

"Neph?"

"Yes, Moses."

"I want you to tell me from your heart, and not to think I am a boy asking you. I'm no more a boy; I'm a man, Neph. Will you tell me?"

"If I can."

"Is Aton god?" Moses whispered. "Is he the only god? Will he look down upon me wherever I go?"

"Wherever you go, the sun will be there, Moses," Neph answered sadly, so sadly that it seemed to Moses to be the voice of another man speaking.

"And is Aton god?"

"I don't really know, Moses."

"But what do you think? What do you believe?"

"I don't know. I'm an engineer, Moses, only that. If I build a house, I will put a lamp in it to light it. And what is holy—the lamp or the craftsman who made the lamp? It's hard to think, Moses, when the whole world is afraid of thought or truth. If I went out into the streets and said aloud what I say to you here, they would tear me to pieces. And as for this thing that we call god, Moses, how long a road will you travel if you look for him? Other men have tried, and instead of god, they find hunger and misery and greed and selfishness, and in the end, death. Let the priests have it their own way. Akh-en-Aton thought he could fight the priests, but even though he was God-King of Egypt, they defeated him in the end, and the streets ran with the blood of those who worshipped Aton. This is a dirty business, this business of the gods. Let it be, Moses."

"But if it doesn't leave me alone?"

Neph shook his head and said nothing.

[5]

IT WAS STILL the world's morning, that time when Moses walked in the old streets of the old City of Tanis, which in his day had been renamed Ramses; and in many places it was a time of coming alive after a long sleep. It was the time of the merchant, and the whole Mediterranean world was quick with the knowledge that what you had to sell, another would buy. It is true that the caravan merchants of old Akkad and of far-distant China had crossed desert and mountains with their wonderful wares, but that was only a trickle. It needed the inland sea and men of ships, and ships and more ships to turn the trickle into a mighty torrent; and so quickly did these merchants smash the barriers of fear and superstition, sailing through the Pillars of Hercules to Britain and Ireland and even Norway, and through the Hellespont into the Black Sea and up the great rivers of the wild land of the Caucasians—so quickly did this come about that there was not time for someone to invent money.

Yet a sort of money there had to be, and among the Phoenicians pearls and precious stones became the units of trade and measure. The Sea Rovers of the Achaean Islands used balls of tin and gold and silver, and the people of Hatti used the most precious metal man had ever found, iron, in cubit-long bars. Among the Egyptians, yardage of linen and sacks of wheat had become too cumbersome for the ever growing commerce of the City of Ramses, and finger-rings and bracelets of copper, tin and gold were becoming set units of value. Nowhere on all the known earth was there a place where the Egyptian ring had not found its way, and there was no movable product of the earth that had not been unloaded at the stone docks of Ramses.

Thus it was that Moses went to the slave market with a leather pouch of gold rings hanging from his belt, and a good deal of uncertainty as to how one buys a chariot-driver. The slave mart was at the far end of the water front, where the cries of pain and fear, the stench and the horror that was matter-of-fact in slave markets could not disturb the people of the Great House. Here, where the stone quays ended, the river edge was mud and muck, protected from the flood-water to some extent by wooden piles and horizontal palm trunks, but never dry, and used by the fishermen as a place to clean and scale their daily catch.

A long, brick-walled, thatched-roof shed had been built and lately improved by the slave-dealers, who worked in a loose association of some forty families and had a monopoly throughout the Delta of slave purchase and sale. Slaves taken captive in war belonged to the God-King by right; but slaves brought by merchants from other lands, and Egyptians sold into slavery for debt were bought and sold in the main market. Until the time of sale, the slaves were kept in chains in the long shed, men, women and children indiscriminately bound together, except for the virgins, who were kept separate. Once each day, they were fed a meal of dry bread and salt fish, and now and then a little fruit to ward off sickness. They made their toilet in the river muck behind the shed, and each morning, to clean them for the day's market, they were dragged through the river bottom by the servants of the dealers. Since the dealers stinted on food, every mealtime was fight and fury and screams and recriminations, and since the floor of the shed was damp, packed mud, there was a good deal of sickness. Very often, half in pity and half in contempt, the fishermen would throw the ravenous slaves the entrails and heads of the fish they cleaned. Some of the slaves disdained to go near the foul scrapings, but others ate them eagerly, and sometimes mothers would plead with their children to eat the raw and ugly stuff, knowing out of their own distant tribal experience that it had the ingredients to ward off diseases.

But the bad went with the good, and often enough the quick decay of such rotten food would set some slave to screaming with pain, while others joined in sympathetic keening and moaning, recalling memories of home and family and weeping in hopeless frustration. When this happened, the servants of the dealers would invade the sheds, plying their bullwhips to the left and to the right, and thereby bringing quiet and peace of a sort.

This was not entirely cruelty; slaves were slaves; they were a part of life, and even a young man as sensitive and thoughtful as Moses could not actually imagine a functioning society without slaves. Nevertheless, he felt distaste and annoyance at having to go to the slave market.

He told himself that he hated the place because it stank so, and his discomfort at having to look at people whose lives were so miserable was not without arrogance. He differed from his brothers and sisters, the cousins of the palace tribe—and more so since he had discovered the secret of his birth—in that he could not be indifferent to creatures of low degree. However, he condemned the dealers in human flesh, not because they bought and sold mankind, but because they were greedy and avaricious in driving their bargains. Like so many people who had access to inexhaustible stores of wealth, the anxiety that produced greed and miserliness was not part of Moses' understanding. Because the necessity had never faced him, he considered the craving for the goods of life to be mean and despicable.

Yet, for all their meanness, there was little that went on in the City of Ramses that these dealers did not know. They knew the truth that was sacred and the truth that was profane. They knew the mother, abandoned by a feckless husband, who came to sell herself that her children might eat. They also knew the scribe who sold them his son that he might buy jewels for a noblewoman he was enamoured of. They knew the high priest who purchased virgins of a particular physical structure of which he was pathologically fond, and they knew precisely what type of woman Ramses would pay any price to take to bed with him. They knew the secret of the religious fanatic who, in pursuit of a custom done away with centuries in the past, had bought four slaves to kill in his wife's tomb, that his dead spouse might be well served as she entered the afterworld; and they knew not only who purchased slaves for the houses of prostitution, but who patronized these houses.

They also knew Moses, the prince of the half-name, and they knew the rumours concerning his being sired by the great God-King. They knew why Ramses had banished Moses for three years. They knew the wealth of Moses almost as well and in as much detail as Seti-Moses, steward of the Great House. They knew that Moses came to purchase a driver, for Hetep-Re had come himself to explain and to demand a commission—a commission that the dealers indignantly refused. They knew that the prince would pay well for the best, and therefore they had delegated one of their number, known for his delicate manners and his ability to deal with godliness without giving too much offence, to act as agent for all of them—all of them to profit, whatever slave was selected.

The name of this dealer was Kotophar, and he was standing at the end of the row of large granite auction blocks, apart from the crowd of shrilling traders, when he saw Moses approach. He had never seen the son of Enekhas-Amon before, and like many others who saw Moses for the first time, he was struck by the singular quality of the prince, the large-boned yet not ungraceful frame, the high-ridged face, and the wide shock of black hair. The arrogance of his bearing, his palpable distaste for his surroundings, and the lack of friendliness in his greeting to the polite and amiable dealer made Kotophar increase the price immediately, even above the previously agreed-upon figures.

Kotophar greeted him with many bows, many self-deprecating observations, and with the assurance that he had no other purpose in life than to serve him. He then demonstrated his slyness by dwelling on the beautiful maidens in stock—it being understood that such an errand would most usually bring royal blood to this ill-favoured corner of the city.

"Where, alas, we are forced to pursue our livelihood," Kotophar sighed.

"I want a man, not a woman," Moses said shortly.

"Ah? A body-servant? A bearer? A cook?—we have two cooks from far-off Edfu, men of distinction and talent. Or perhaps a eunuch? We have a number——"

"You needn't go into all that," Moses stopped him. "I want a man to take with me to Kush as a chariot-driver. I want a man of my age, more or less. I want a strong man, without disease, with all his teeth—and one who is not submissive but hates the fate that made him a slave. Preferably, a man who can drive horses and knows how to care for them, but give me the other qualities and he will learn that."

The slave-dealer nodded sagely, his face creasing in a troubled frown. He continued to nod through long moments of silence before he sighed and announced,

"You ask a good deal, O Prince of Egypt."

"I am not in the mood for games or bickering—your name is Kotophar?"

"Your holiness, your godliness, my name is Kotophar. I am dirt under your feet, nothing and less than nothing, so I have a name of no distinction, O Prince of Egypt. Yet it is ennobled on your lips, so I thank you."

"Then you know who I am, and if the price is within reason, I will pay it. Show me the slave and spare me the rest of it."

"Ah—believe me, godliness, I would lay down my life to spare you the pain of a pinprick. But what you ask requires some thought. It requires some thought. If you would be good enough to come this way, O Prince of Egypt." He led him past the crowd to the other end of the sheds, all the while explaining that the best and strongest slaves were the prisoners-of-war, and they were reserved for the God-King—not for any purpose that required such fine flesh, but to dig ditches, pump water and drag stones. Of course, that did not mean that there were no unusual and often exquisite items to be found here in the greatest slave market of any civilized nation. There were indeed. But chariot-drivers?

They had walked the length of the noisy crowd, buyers not only from Egypt but from Philistia and Hatti as well, driving their bargains at the top of their lungs, each one trying to outshout the others and the dealers attempting to roar over the noise of all of them. How anything in the way of purchase or sale could come out of such chaos, Moses did not know; and to make things worse, donkeys and camels and pack horses made their own noise on the outskirts, and slaves unloaded piles of goods that would have to be measured or weighed before being bargained and fought over to arrive at the proper price-exchange for the slaves purchased.

But none of this appeared to trouble Kotophar, who shrugged and commented that they were lucky that today was an off-day. "It gets a little out of hand," he said, "when the men of Upper Egypt come down to replenish their beds or their pantries. I was thinking, O Prince of Egypt, that the Hittites have a way with horses universally admired, and it comes to mind that we have an excellent young man from Hatti, strong and healthy, who was sold out of the king's guard because he had the misfortune to pick a quarrel with the lover of the queen's sister-in-law. There is also, if my memory serves me, a giant of a fellow from Kush, but whether he knows horses or not, I can't say."

"And you would give me a Kushite to fight against his own people? Let me see the man from Hatti!"

Now they were at the end of the long shed, far enough from the crowd to converse in normal tones. Even in the warm sunlight, the interior of the shed was dark. Moses had the impression of many men, chained to posts or rails at the back of the shed, some of them sprawling on the floor, some standing, some crouched. Two Egyptian slaves, wearing the bright-red loincloths of the dealers and branded across the face, squatted on a granite slab—and then leaped to do Kotophar's bidding when he told them to bring the Hittite.

Moses had seen men of Hatti before, but his impressions had been formed by rich traders and diplomats at the court of the Great House. They were not at all like the bearded, tattered and gaunt young man they dragged before him now.

He crouched like an animal, his small blue eyes squinting to keep out the bright light of the sun, his long, tangled, honey-coloured hair like an animal's pelt over head and face. He still wore the Hittite trousers, ragged and dirty now, but from the waist up he was bare, and Moses drew back in disgust from the network of half-healed whip scars that encased him like a shirt.

"I assure you, Prince of Egypt," the slave-dealer said, "that he is strong and young. Look at the muscles, not at the scars. Scars heal."

"His spirit is broken. What would you sell me, a whipped dog to go to war?"

"He's a chariot man, through and through——"

Moses did not know that this was a programme of contrasts, that Kotophar had already decided which slave he would buy and was merely laying a proper groundwork for his price. The transgressor from Hatti was taken away and another Hittite appeared, a man of about thirty, well-dressed in the stained but still impressive robes of a courtier, his hair combed under his felted hat. When Moses turned on Kotophar in anger, the second Hittite was replaced by an Egyptian criminal, redeemed from a death sentence by the slavers, a short barrel of a man whose

pig-eyes gleamed in murderous hatred. He was quickly removed for a brown-skinned Libyan who swaggered defiantly but whose face wore the dull mask of an idiot. This
brought them to Kotophar's choice, a Sea Rover from My-
cenae, who was the sole survivor of a ship that had foun-
dered off the Delta, and who was found by the fishermen
and sold to the slavers.

He was a tall, well-built and handsome man, his long
brown hair hanging in two thick braids down his back, his
face covered with a curly brown beard, his hands large and
capable. Almost convinced that he had found what he was
looking for, Moses asked,

"Can he talk our language?"

"Holiness, he was only taken three days ago."

"Slaver, what do you take me for—a fool?" Moses cried.
"We march for Kush in a few days and you would sell me
a man I cannot speak to! I am tired of all this!"

Kotophar apologized with a mixture of frustration and
sorrow. He begged Moses to forgive him and begged him
to understand that it was not as easy as it might seem to
furnish what he desired at a moment's notice. If the Prince
of Egypt could only wait a day or two, then the request
could be satisfied to the last detail.

"I have no time to wait," Moses answered sharply.
"Have you Bedouin slaves?"

"Bedouins?" Kotophar repeated in amazement.

"Yes. We will be going through desert much of the way,
and they know the desert, don't they?"

"Forgive me, Prince of Egypt, but you are a young man
and you have lived most of your life in the Great House. I
have lived mine where mercy ends and knowledge begins.
I tell you—you cannot trust a Bedouin. He will smile at you

while he plots your death, and sooner or later, he will put a knife in your side——"

"Spare me a lecture on personal mannerisms and tell me whether you have a Bedouin slave who will suit me?"

A strange expression came over the face of the slave-dealer, and he nodded slowly, almost with pleasure. "Perhaps I have, but as to whether he will suit you, O Prince of Egypt, that is for you to say."

"What do you mean by that?" Moses wondered.

"What could I mean, holiness? This Bedouin is young and strong and his spirit is not broken. He comes from a slave gang engaged upon public works at the edge of the Delta, and they have capable overseers, believe me. If they could not break his spirit—well, see for yourself." And he called to the two slaves and gave them their instructions. At first, they did not move but looked at him in fear—until he shouted, "What are you afraid of, you dogs! The man is bound and hobbled!" And then apologized to Moses, explaining that their own slaves here at the mart were without spirit. The Prince of Egypt put such a store on spirit; and like a well-fed, sleek cat, Kotophar watched them drag a twisting, struggling slave up to the stone, and then when he would not mount it, attempt to drag him on to it. This was beyond their strength. It was not only that the slave was strong—Moses had seen strong men before—but he moved like a whip being cracked; and as if in answer to Moses' unspoken thought, Kotophar said,

"The amazing thing is his reserve of energy. Nothing destroys that. He is like an animal. He has been whipped more than that Hittite you saw before, but you won't see him cringe. And his strength!"

Suddenly, the Bedouin stopped struggling and leaped

on to the stone, flinging off the two slaves as if they were children. He stood there, his hobbled legs spread, stating at Moses—at the prince's golden trappings and glittering jewels. He was not a tall man, at least a head shorter than Moses, but he was very broad, his trunk barrel-like, his arms and legs wrapped in mighty casings of muscle. His neck was so heavy that it made his head seem smaller than it actually was. His face was flat and broad, covered with the curling beard of a young man, and his long black hair hung behind him in a single thick but tangled braid. Like many of the Bedouins, he had a short, thick nose, and his dark eyes, deep-set under a broad brow, watched Moses with a mixture of contempt and amusement. Suddenly, he said to Kotophar in a strangely accented, nasal Egyptian,

"Who is this gilded popinjay—a customer? Tell him he'll be cheated if he buys me!"

"This is a prince of Egypt, you dirty cur!" Kotophar shouted. "You stinking, filthy desert scum—this is a god you face! To be bought by him would be the greatest honour ever done you in your rotten life!"

Moses, all the while, was watching the Bedouin with fascination. He was naked and barefoot, a bit of rag serving as a loincloth. His trunk and legs were hairy—more so than with any Egyptian Moses had ever seen—but even through the hair Moses could see the whip scars that latticed his flesh. And for all his dirt and savageness, he had a certain winning quality, making Moses feel that here was a man other men would follow willingly and love greatly.

When Kotophar finished swearing at him, the slave broke into deep bellows of laughter.

"By all the gods in the world of death, I will kill you yet, you whore's bastard!"

"And lose a sale? Oh, no—Kotophar."

"Well, there you are," the slaver shrugged, turning to Moses. "You wanted a man of spirit, O Prince of Egypt."

"How old is he?" Moses asked.

"Who knows? He answers no questions unless it pleases him. I would say no more than twenty years. His teeth are good and his beard is soft and new. He's no good for work. He breaks tools and incites his fellow slaves. He's afraid of nothing on earth. You feed him slop that would kill another, and he thrives on it."

To all this, the slave was listening with interest, an expression of amused contempt upon his face.

"What is his name?"

"Nun."

"Nun? An Egyptian name."

"He's no Egyptian, holiness. These Bedouins have lived outside the Delta for generations. They speak a sort of Egyptian and most of them have Egyptian names. They are a filthy, skulking lot. I've never seen one like him before."

"Nun, can you drive horses?" Moses demanded.

The slave cocked his head thoughtfully, as if considering whether to answer or not. Then he grinned and said, "I have been driven, but driving is more in your way than mine, popinjay."

"Men have died for saying less to a prince of Egypt," Moses pointed out.

"But I am dead, popinjay, and if not one day, then it's the next. So I spit on your kind."

"I am not angry," Moses thought. "I have never been talked to this way before except by my cousins, but I will not be angry." He wanted the man. There had been two men in his life to whom his heart went out, Amon-Teph and Neph—and here was a third; but strangely so, for what he actually felt was that if he could win the respect and loyalty of such a man as this, he would win a new and necessary belief in himself. Kotophar was watching him keenly, attempting to decide what his own role in the matter should be, whether he should let this bitter jest of his run its course, or whether he should prove his own regard for the god-kings of Egypt by calling the guards and having them run this miserable Bedouin through. All his knowledge of quality in slaves cried out against such destruction, but meanwhile he was feeding a man who would never find a master.

Moses decided for him. saying, "You, Nun—I go to the wars in the Land of Kush as a captain of chariots. I want a chariot driver and a man who will fight when he has to fight. Are you my man?"

"Grow up before you talk of wars, popinjay!"

"I will buy him," Moses said quietly. "Untie his arms."

Kotophar's face fell, for to take the price he and his companions had decided upon for this wild creature would be both outrageous and fraudulent. "But the price, Prince of Egypt?" he protested weakly.

"Whatever your price is, go to Seti-Moses, and he will pay you. Now untie his arms."

"Now he is yours, O Prince of Egypt, so please untie his arms yourself."

"I said, untie his arms, slaver!" Moses snapped.

Kotophar shrugged. His hand on the hilt of his knife, he approached the stone slab cautiously and warily, and when he came within three feet of the slave, Nun stepped forward and spat in his face. Enraged, Kotophar drew his knife and flung back his arm, but Moses shouted,

"He is mine, Kotophar! You kill him—so help me, I will kill you!"

Trembling with frustrated anger, and rage at the prince as well as the slave, Kotophar withdrew, knowing that Seti-Moses, the palace steward, would take all excess profit from the deal, and also knowing that he could do nothing about it. He told the slaves in attendance to untie Nun, and this they did, the Bedouin remaining rigid. The moment his arms were free, legs still hobbled, he made a mighty leap from the stone, his arms outstretched for Kotophar's throat. The slave-dealer, trying frantically to get away, tripped and sprawled on the ground, where he lay screaming for the guards. Meanwhile, Moses, in a motion as quick as the Bedouin's, stepped in, caught one outstretched wrist, and met the charging Nun with a lowered shoulder. He heaved and jerked the man's arm, and with the force of Nun's charge, flung him like a sack, head over heels, so that he hit the ground on his back with a mighty crash that knocked the breath out of him.

The guards came running with their long spears lowered to stick the slave like a wounded animal, where he lay, but Moses stopped them with a roar of warning.

"He's mine! Hands off!"

Nun staggered to his feet now and advanced on Moses as fast as his hobbles would permit, and already they were ringed by a crowd of buyers, dealers, slaves and loiterers. Head down, shouting hatred at Moses in his own tongue, they closed, and Moses felt the grip of that awful strength. He drew his dagger and slammed the weighted hilt against Nun's head. The slave staggered and lost his grip, and Moses flung him off and struck him on the side of the face

with his clenched fist. The blow was a hard one; it was like
striking a post; yet the slave only reeled, and once again
Moses seized his wrist, braced, and flung him over his
shoulder on to his back. Moses stood over him this time,
and when Nun attempted to rise, Moses drove his heel into
the man's face. Again, Nun tried to fling himself erect, his
face covered with blood, and this time Moses seized the
chain that hobbled him and pulled it out, sending the slave
crashing back on the ground, where the man lay, not trying
to rise again, but watching Moses with a new look of war-
iness and respect on his bloody face.

For the first time, Moses became conscious of the fren-
zied screaming of the crowd. It was applause. He was being
applauded for the triumph of subduing a hobbled and unarmed Bedouin slave—and they were all too fogged with
the chance to cheer one of the godly inhabitants of the
palace to realize that the victory was sheer luck, abetted
by a dagger hilt and a bronze chain. Suddenly Moses felt
sick to his soul, sick with the memory of the viciousness
he had displayed towards the slave, sick with the knowledge that they all feared any slave who could not be broken
by the whip, sick with the spectacle he had made of himself
in a bloody hand-to-hand fight at the slave mart.

Then Moses did something that was unthinkable for
any prince of Egypt, something that was remembered by
the people of old Tanis when most else about him was
forgotten—something that changed him in a moment from
a hero of the crowd to the complete opposite, for those
who cheer heroes on the street. He became a prince who
was unprincely in this manner: He tore off his linen kilt,
leaving himself naked to his loincloth; he walked over to

the fallen slave and went down on one knee beside him; and with the holy linen cloth, he wiped the blood and dirt from the man's face and neck and body.

The crowd fell silent, and Moses heard the silence as he had heard the cheering. Better, he thought, and told himself that never again in all his life would he want to hear cheering over anything he did. He called to Kotophar to open the hobble.

"He is your man, O Prince of Egypt," sneered Kotophar, throwing him the key. It fell close to Nun, but Moses did not move to pick it up. Instead he rose and looked at Kotophar— a look that Amon-Teph or Neph or his mother would have remarked upon as something in Moses that they had never seen, something frightening and hard as a diamond and implacable too. Nun saw the look and so did Kotophat and so did those in the crowd, and if they had any notion of playing with insult, they gave that up. Kotophar stared back for only a moment; then he picked up the key and unlocked the hobble—and Nun smiled thinly at him, a smile as humourless as his master's expression.

When the hobble was off, Moses said, "Get up and follow me, Nun."

The slave rose and walked after his master out of the slave mart. Thus it was that Moses came by a man and servant, whose name was Nun.

[6]

WHEN MOSES CAME to the parade ground with Nun the following day for the slave to receive his first instructions in the management of a chariot team, Seti-Keph, the Captain of Hosts, motioned for him to wait. As before, Seti-

Keph stood in a little crowd of his captains; now he left them and walked over to Moses, where he observed both the prince and the slave thoughtfully. Then he told Moses to send the slave to the stables, but to remain a moment himself, so that they might talk.

Nun went in silence. He had not spoken a dozen words since the day before. He had taken what was given to him, a hot bath, his hair freshly dressed in the same heavy braid—for Moses knew how sacred hair and beard were to the people of the desert—clean loincloth, kilt and sandals, salve for his bruises, and a heavy leather belt with loops for weapons; but he asked for nothing. He had been given a room to sleep in and the door was left unlocked; and Moses, his own room close by, had lain awake for hours, fearing he knew not what—that Nun might try to kill him, that he would run away; but when he finally rose and walked softly to Nun's room, he saw the Bedouin sleeping soundly in the moonlight that streamed through the open casement, sleeping loosely and easily as a child sleeps.

In silence, he ate his breakfast; in silence, he went to the stables now; and there was a new expression on Seti-Keph's face as he watched the slave obey Moses' command. When Nun had gone, Seti-Keph indicated that Moses follow him, and they walked over to the shade of an olive tree, far enough from the officers not to be overheard. The Captain of Hosts reached no higher than Moses' shoulder, yet Moses did not think of him as a small man. In the shade, Seti-Keph squatted on his heels and motioned for Moses to do likewise.

"Well, Prince of Egypt," he said, "you are one of the young gods of the Great House, if temporarily out of favour, and I am just a peasant who has butchered his way to success; but if you are to ride a chariot under me, you must acknowledge my command."

"I know that, Seti-Keph."

"Good. I see you are not one of those young bloods who chew a grudge and can only smooth it out with blood. Neither am I, so maybe we will get along. I am a plain-spoken man, as your godly father knows only too well——"

"The God-King is not my father, Seti-Keph," Moses interrupted.

"Be that as it may, I am still a blunt man and I say my piece, for better or worse. I was upset yesterday, and if ever in the future you should be unfortunate enough to be shouldered with the responsibility of assembling and pro-visioning and arming and marching two thousand chariot and ten thousand foot to the end of the earth, then you will know why I was upset."

"Please don't apologize, Seti-Keph," Moses said uneasily.

"By all the gods, I am not apologizing! I am explaining. I spoke to you harshly, Prince of Egypt, but it was not because I bore you animosity or because you are out of favour with the God-King. I would have spoken that way to any of your brothers. I blow hot, but the heat cools quickly. That's the sort of a man I am. Now you are with me, and perhaps you will be more of a soldier than a bur-den?" The last was half a question. Seti-Keph had been tracing lines in the powdery earth with a twig as he spoke; his keen black eyes peered at Moses from under his shaggy brows.

"I will try," Moses said.

"I heard you won a slave."

"I've had slaves before, Seti-Keph."

"Not like this one. I don't like brawlers, prince or peasant. War is something else. You don't fight with your bare hands——"

Once again, he peered questioningly at Moses, who said nothing. "I spit at them," he went on, "with their talk of your holy kilt. You can wipe your behind with your kilt, for all that it matters to me. The gods are holy, not a kilt that a prince sits on, and I revere the gods and worship them wherever I am. You were right to comfort your man when he was hurt, and if your kilt was all the cloth you had—well, you used it. You tamed a beast and now he's your beast. But when your enemy is hurt and bleeding, I expect you to put a knife to his throat——"

Again the inquiring look from under the brows.

"——War is a butcher's business, O Prince of Egypt. It is not like life in the Great House, nor is it as good as the warmth of the mud hut where I lived as a child. It stinks, O Prince of Egypt, but like other things that stink, it is necessary. There was never a time without war and there never will be such a time. I tell you that he who makes war well and wisely has power and wealth; and he who loses, vomits in the blood of his wife and child. So we will make war well and wisely, and you may believe me that there is a lot to learn about war. I know. War served me well and I serve the God-King well; both together. In our land today, there are two orders, the high and the low—and the low live like the beasts in the field, only worse. I know, for I have lived both ways. And among the high, unless you are born of the Great House, what else is there but to be a priest, a scribe or a soldier? Out trade is a hard one and it calls for hard men. Not now, but remember my words a year from today, O Prince of Egypt, and you will find their meaning. Meanwhile, I see that you have fallen in with Hetep-Re. He knows his trade, but he is a dirty snake, so watch him."

"I have not fallen in with Hetep-Re. He helps me, and I pay him for his help."

"You will find that whatever you pay him, you don't pay him enough. As for driving horses and a chariot, you and your slave will learn that in time or break your necks. Now tell me, O Prince of Egypt, have you a mind for war and killing?"

"It is what the God-King wanted, so here I am, Seti-Keph. I will tell you what I have a mind for—to get away from the palace and the whole conniving stink of the City of Ramses."

Now Seti-Keph slapped his thigh and laughed heartily. He was a peasant now; there was no gloss over the man, no manners, no veneer—and perhaps for this as well as other things, Moses found himself liking him. He was to learn later that no one becomes Captain of Hosts out of his own wit and skill without having the power to make other men like him.

"Fight like you brawl, and fight with sense and without fear," grinned Seti-Keph, "and I will put you over a host before you are through with the black men of Kush."

[7]

SINCE THE TEN thousand foot-soldiers would come together at Karnak, on the upper Nile, they had been marshalled and dispatched from the various cities of Egypt for better than sixty days now. Each host and there could be a hundred to three hundred men in a host was the responsibility of its own captain in terms of leadership; but the manner of raising a host and equipping it varied. Karnak and Tanis were a long distance apart, and if the Kushites or the Libyans took a sudden notion to raid the rich and beautiful cities of Upper Egypt, it fell to the powerful lords of the border marches to meet their attack and thrust them back. For this reason, they traditionally built and fostered their own armed strength—and, traditionally, they were feared and watched suspiciously by the god-kings of the Delta.

Yet niggardly as these lords of the South were when it came to lending their men to Ramses for his marauding sorties into Hatti and Philistia and Canaan and Mesopotamia, they did not hold back when it came to war against Kush. They had no other enemies to compare with the dark menace of Kush; and other enemies could be defeated and broken, whereas Kush poured out of the eternal and endless forest and jungle and wasteland of Central Africa, where no man had even been and where the power of the gods of Egypt was as nothing.

So their hosts would assemble at Karnak, and also to Karnak would come levies from Giza and Memphis and Lisht and other cities of Middle Egypt. In the Delta itself, soldiers were and had been recruited from the once vigorous and numerous peasantry who tilled the thousands of acres of black and fertile soil; but of late the harvest had been thin indeed, for the peasants who came out of the army were of no disposition to go back to digging the muck, and without too much urging, they sold their land to the speculators and rich priests—who in turn set up broad plantations worked by slaves.

For this reason, Ramses had been forced increasingly to

rely upon mercenaries for his foot-soldiers, and was thus trapped in a vicious circle, mercenaries to make war and more war and more war to find the gold to pay the mercenaries. For this particular expedition, Seti-Keph had been forced to hire three and a half thousand foot-soldiers of foreign origin, a thousand spearmen from Hatti, five hundred from Philistia, some hundreds from Libya and some hundreds of the Sea Rovers, who had magic ears when it was on the wind that war and loot were in the offing. The King of Babylon, who had sent Ramses slave women and two of his plentiful stock of daughters as princely gifts, now sent him six hundred archers at a tidy price.

So it was that from here, there and everywhere, the army was recruited and put together. It was one thing for the God-King to lift his sacred sickle and say, "My patience with Kush is finished. Now, with sword and flame, we will teach him that the gods of Egypt are not to be despised in the South." It was another thing entirely for Seti-Keph to carry out Ramses' anger and lust for wealth in practical terms.

Full seven months before, three of the most trusted captains of Seti-Keph had been dispatched to Karnak, there to begin the organization of supply wagons, work horses and pack donkeys—and to begin to collect and store the tens of thousands of pounds of grain that would be required to feed the expedition in its march through the desert. Water was not a problem, for they would follow the course of the River Nile, but hundreds of boats had to be found or built. Nor was it possible to use any of the great fleet of river boats that plied the Nile between Karnak and the Delta, for only ten days' journey above Karnak was the First Cataract, and from there on, the boats would have to be dragged upriver as well as overland. A thousand more details would go into the expedition before it was ready for war, and all of these Seti-Keph had to decide. If victory came out of his planning, it would be known far and wide that the mighty God-King of the holy Land of Egypt, Ramses II, beloved of Re, had smitten the pagans of Kush with his hard hand; but if defeat came, it would only be known that a peasant dog named Seti-Keph had betrayed his master.

So it was that the last of the foot-soldiers had taken ship for Upper Egypt before the chariots were ready to march. Whatever else was necessary to an army, in the time of Ramses, the chariot had become the weapon of Egypt— and all else was conceived only as support for the chariots. Never before had the world seen such a weapon—and indeed when the Egyptian foot soldiers first encountered it, in the time when they tried to bar the way of the Hittites, they fled in screaming fear and disorder; for it took a hardened man to stand up to a line of these thundering wooden carts with their massive four-foot wheels and their spinning, flashing axle-knives. And when the power and the productivity of mighty Egypt was combined with the inventiveness of Hatti, then the individual chariots of the hero-warriors became masses of wheeled death that nothing on earth could resist.

On the fourth day after he had spoken with Moses under the olive tree, Seti-Keph gave the order for the march to begin. He had by now assembled twenty-two hundred chariots with driver and fighter, and fourteen hundred reserve horses, which would serve as pack animals until needed for replacement.

MANY TIMES HAD Moses sailed south from the Delta into the main body of the River Nile. Like all Egyptians, he had from his earliest childhood heard reference to the river as "the good mother", "the holy river", "the sacred mother of Egypt". and it was difficult for him, in spite of the teaching of Amon-Teph, not to approach any journey upon the river with superstitious awe as well as excitement. He had been to Giza on the river several times, and once beyond there to Memphis and Lisht—and recently all the great distance upriver to Karnak in his mother's funerary procession.

But now he was leaving the City of Ramses and the Great House and all the memories and associations of his childhood, good and evil, for ever; for, as he told himself, who knew that he would return? He was young enough and healthy enough—and enough in love with life to think lightly of death, and the thought that he might be struck down in battle and die in far-off Kush troubled him not at all.

It must be admitted that he felt cocky about the way he had handled himself. Let the city gossip that he had blasphemed by wiping his slave's blood and dirt with his holy kilt; the fact was that he had subdued a beast of a man and tamed him, when no one else could—and if he knew men so little as to think so simply of the silence and brooding obedience of his slave, that bit of ignorance did not trouble him either. He had also, he told himself, won respect from the Captain of Hosts—and all in all, he was more anticipative and more pleased with himself than ever before in his young manhood.

The Nile was like a golden road beckoning into his future, and all the deep sorrow and pensive complexity of the past few months had been cast off. The very fact of being a part of the expedition was giving him a sense of membership, of belonging to a social unit of power and importance; and this was a feeling he had never experienced in the Great House, never so long as his memory went back. He felt— and quite wrongly—that here in this great army, it would matter little if his fellow officers knew that he was no prince of godly blood but a cast-off of a wretched slave-tribe in Goshen.

Now that he felt in the process of belonging, he also sensed a driving need to belong, and he no longer fostered and cherished his own singularity. To the contrary, he was resentful of singularity and all manner of separateness—as he now felt—that had been imposed upon him; and when, the night before the morning of departure, sacrifices were held and the gods were invoked for the fortunes of the army, Moses participated eagerly, with only a twinge of conscience over Aton and those good priests he had known who had given their lives in the service of Aton. Like a boy, he would not permit himself to think about such matters, and when Amon-Teph took form in his mind's eye, Moses said to himself petulantly,

"I did not ask for his teaching. Who was he to turn me away from everything my own people hold sacred?"

My own people remained, like a bone in his throat. More and more had he been coming to dream of the knowledge of his birth revealed, the whole world mocking him and himself in chains and whipped. No prince, no prince! they screamed at him. Or in the dream, the skinny, dirty Bedouins would gather about him to claim him.

So he walked in the shelter of the chanting of the priests, his eyes fixed upon the hundreds of golden torches that exercised a hypnotic effect upon him, his body sheltered under the thin shroud of linen that was his holy garment. All about him were the chariot captains, each shrouded like himself; and he thought of them as men of strength and power and dignity, very different from the spoiled royal progeny of the palace. When the priests lifted their voices in the "Hymn to Set", the god of the Great House, Moses joined in the singing of the banal words, forgetting how he and Amon-Teph had smiled so sadly over the superstitious obscenities the hymn contained. And when he was disrobed and stood naked under the moon for purification, he invoked Isis and Osiris as did the others. . . .

And in the morning, in the grey light of morning's beginning, be came with Nun to the parade ground, Nun leading Katie, the yellow horse, which was carrying not only his share of baggage but extra weapons, bundles of arrows and an extra shield and iron sword, these to be stored in the chariot itself. Nun dragged out the chariot and harnessed the horses to the chariot-trace, as Hetep-Re had taught him to—and Moses could not but remark on how easily and well he learned. Katie, bewildered with the weight of inert baggage he carried, was transferred to the reserve herd. Moses and Nun guided their chariot into position behind Hetep-Re, who led his host.

Almost every soul in Old Tanis turned out to watch the chariots move through the city to the docks; the procession was a gallant and wonderful sight. The clashing of cymbals, the shrilling of silver pipes and the beating of the big bullhide war drums infected man and beast with the excitement of the moment, and the horses pranced and reared, sending the crowds in the narrow streets into gales of laughter and surges of pretended panic. The horses wore headbands of gay, bright feathers, and colourful ribbons streamed from the spears of the warriors and the bronze handrails of the chariots. Many of the hosts had painted the spokes of the huge chariot wheels a common colour, bright yellow in one case, crimson in another, black and white and purple, and both driver and warrior wore their best of armour and ornament.

And all along, women ran with the chariots, wives and mothers and sisters and sweethearts and prostitutes, weaving a mixture of endearments, accusations, tears, pleading and lusty talk to a point where many a man would have leaped from his chariot, had he not known that the savage and iron hand of Seti-Keph was already over the Host— and that from here on any infringement of discipline would be punished without mercy.

And among these chariots, Moses and his slave Nun went to war with Kush, went down to the stone docks where chariots, men and horses were loaded on to great, broad barges—to be rowed upstream by thousands of slaves to Abydos, where they would disembark and go overland to the assembly point at Karnak.

So war began for the shining-faced and eager prince of Egypt—who had yet to learn that war is many things, but mostly waiting and boredom.

[9]

IT IS SAID of man that when he grows old, his recollection of the settled course of his life is less well remembered than its interruption by crisis and journeying; yet in years after,

Moses would recollect only two incidents during that long, apparently endless journey up the river from Tanis in the Delta to Abydos, which was just below Karnak, and not far from the assembly area of the army, ten miles to the south of Karnak.

The first concerned a conversation with Seti-Keph, Captain of Hosts, and it came about this way, out of the sense of belonging that Moses wanted so desperately from the chariot captains. . . .

For some dozen days they had been moving upriver: that mighty fleet of almost a thousand barges, the motion of the tens of thousands of oars making a sound like a giant waterfall, the talk and laughter of the men, the endless days—so quickly lost to counting—under the timeless yellow sun of Egypt, the immediate bazaar atmosphere of the little river towns where they tied up to buy fresh fruit and fresh meat and drink every drop of wine the peasants had put by, the tough soldiers swaggering drunkenly in the streets and debauching in each place a whole population of girls who had come to growth since the last army came by on its way to Kush.

But Moses was bored and restless. They tied to shore at the little city of Em-Akad, actually no more than a village, but containing a rather imposing temple sacred to Mut, the mother and fertility goddess. Long since had the fertility cults, in any overt form, been abandoned in the Delta, where the priesthood was powerful enough to overcome any female domination of the major rites; and in the more important temples of Tanis and Sais arid Busiris, women were tolerated only for certain rituals sacred to Isis—and then under the seal of silence. But upriver, where the cosmopolitanism of the Delta hardly touched the changeless peasant life, the old gods were still revered; and when the ebb of the flood laid its new black coat of rich mud and fertility on the fields, the peasants came to worship the gods of creation—and above all, the fertility mother, Mut.

It was the time now. The fleet poured its unexpected thousands on to the muddy, oozing shore, and the alluvial strip of rich land, a day's journey up and down the river, poured its maidens across the land to the temple. The priests had set up phallic symbols of carved wood, and a naked matron wearing the brazen snake of Mut around her loins led the worship. The maidens were naked too, except for snake symbols painted around their bodies in the raw red-earth pigment that these people ground out of desert stone and mixed in an olive-oil base; and the young men who accompanied them wore red loincloths, dyed with the same raw pigment, and carried wooden wands, light strips of cedarwood that were roughly painted in imitation of a serpent's scales.

Night was close on when the soldiers of the fleet came ashore—the slaves were not permitted to leave the boats— and the priests were now handing the maidens twisted torches of oil-soaked papyrus. The girls and young men, already caught up in the slow, hypnotic rhythm of their dance, only smiled or laughed at the soldiers; but the priests, half in fear and half with greed of potential profit, made them welcome, begged them to partake of the worship, and sent the temple slaves to fetch goatskin sacks of wine.

As night fell, the papyrus torches were lit, the rhythm of the dance quickened, and the chant shrilled higher and higher, led by the wild, screaming voice of the naked matron who stood on a stone pedestal before the temple. The maidens danced past her, into the temple, lighting the long corridors between the massive pillars—and the young men pursued them, striking them with the cedar wands, lightly at first, and then harder and harder.

To Moses, standing together with a group of captains, taking great gulps of the wine whenever it was passed to him, this was a strange, barbaric and fascinating sight. He had heard of the Fertility Assemblies, as they were called, but he had hardly believed that they were practised in any part of Egypt in this enlightened age. The sight of the temple lit with hundreds of waving torches, the naked maidens being beaten by the young men—the screams of pain mixed with rapture—and the sound of the now almost unbearable chant heated his own emotions to a fever pitch. He was also rapidly becoming drunk on the strong, sour, peasant wine.

The night was hot and humid, for all day long the alluvial mud had been steaming, and now this mixed with the scent of the incense being burned in the temple. It was as if a cloak of hot, palpable sexuality had filled the place, and as the screaming maidens ran from the temple, the youths beating them, the soldiers broke loose, forgetting religious devotion in their suddenly aroused frenzy. Where the village youths stood in their way, they were flung aside, and the night was filled with screams of laughter and real fear and simulated fear as the soldiers seized the not-unwilling girls. A group of the maidens, waving their arms in mock terror, fled laughing to the protection of the chariot captains, who received them with no hesitation.

So the night began for Moses, a wild, drunken night and not unlike a previous night that brought him sorrow afterwards. In the hour before dawn, Hetep-Re and another captain dragged his sodden, mud- and vomit-covered carcass back on to the barge, where they let him fall on deck and sleep there until the hot sun awakened him. The fleet was already under way when he woke up, opened his eyes and saw Nun standing by him, observing him with an expression half of disgust, half of hatred. . . .

Of this Seti-Keph spoke, having called Moses the next day to his barge, the lead barge of the fleet, and the largest. The front third of this barge was built up with quarters for Seti-Keph and his staff, roofed over with a deck from which he could observe and command the entire fleet. Now he had sent away his officers, so that he might talk alone with Moses; and when Moses appeared, the Captain of Hosts was sitting glumly on a little three-legged stool. He rose to greet the prince, and nodded for him to be seated on another similar stool.

For a while they sat in silence, Seti-Keph studying the fleet which trailed for almost a mile behind him, and Moses unwilling and unable to start the conversation, knowing only too well what the subject would be, and filled with dread and shame and misery.

Where, he asked himself, was his joy and pride of only a few days before? Was he to be an object of contempt and mockery here too, as well as in the Great House?

As he sat there, Seti-Keph glanced at him occasionally, wrinkling his brow uneasily. He had difficulty in saying what he felt he had to say. Seti-Keph had dragged a king of Hatti in chains from the tailboard of his chariot; he had executed a prince of Phoenicia with his own dagger; and he had forced into his bed, with blows and oaths, the sister of a king of Babylon; yet for all that, he remained in his innermost being an Egyptian peasant—and to an Egyptian peasant of that time, the royal blood was godly. He found himself thinking—"And suppose I am spared to die in bed and be embalmed, and this young fool of a prince opens the doors of the other world to me? How then?" He bent his head characteristically, peering at Moses from under his heavy brows and said, surlily,

"Among my own folk, one was a man at twelve and tilling the soil—and at fourteen one took a wife. How is it with the folk at the Great House?"

Moses stated at the deck in silence.

"Suppose you were a soldier, O Prince of Egypt," Seti-Keph shrugged, "and suppose you had scar marks all over you out of five campaigns. Then I might say, he has earned his right to play the fool." He straightened up suddenly and shouted, "No! I wouldn't even say it then!"

"I was with the other captains," Moses muttered.

"Ah—the other captains. And what are they?" he snapped. "Pigs, scum of the earth! A lot of dirty butchers who can think no further ahead than a whore or a gold bracelet they'll cut off the hand of a Kushite! Are they men because they can bend a bow or cast a spear? Is that what you want, Prince of Egypt, who came from the gods of the Great House?" His voice softened now, and Moses raised his head to see that a strange and lonely expression had come on the flat, ugly face of the Captain of Hosts. "Well, Moses," he sighed, "what am I to say to you? We are all drunken wanderers, when you come down to it, and each one does his butchery in his own way. I sucked my mother's milk, but had no heart when my men slew the mothers of Canaan—and now I will show them in Kush what the anger of the God-King is. Huh? I have no pride, so I look for pride in you, because you are noble, born with the blood of the gods in your veins. And at night," he went on slowly, the agony of his thinking twisting his mouth and tightening it, "when I can't sleep for fear I will die before morning, I am sick with the heresy that there are no gods at all. Heresy—who is free from this heresy, except fools who have seen nothing of life or the world? But in the morning, I make libations to Re and I believe again. I must believe. Otherwise, what is the sense of life that is only a moment—as you will see, some day, O Prince of Egypt—a moment between the awakening and the final sleep? What sense, unless a man cherishes the gods? And when a god becomes drunk and dirty and rolls in the river mud with some stinking, painted peasant girl——"

"As the others did," Moses attempted.

"You're not the others! Do you think, because I'm a hard old butcher with no manners and no graces, that I know so little of men? Do you know what a leader is? A real leader, who has to win it himself? To know men and to make them respect you! I know men. I know you, O Prince of Egypt, and I know what a man you will be—if you want to find manhood? Do you?"

Unable to face him, Moses stared over the river hopelessly.

"Do you know what you want, O Prince of Egypt? Of wealth, you have enough. Then what do you want? Power? Glory?"

Moses shook his head.

"Then what?"

Striving desperately to keep back the emotion that was choking him and the tears that were pressing his eyelids,

Moses managed to say haltingly, "I don't know, I don't know—except if it be to find out who I am, and why I am—"

"You are too young to want to chew the most bitter cud of all," Seti-Keph said, not unkindly, "for there is a desire that is never fulfilled. Go back to your barge now, for we have talked enough, and it is possible that I have talked too much. In time, we will make war, and there you'll find a bloody linen cloth to wipe your mind free."

The second remembered incident of the water journey took place a few days after this, when Moses turned to Nun—the silent, waiting Nun—and asked him,

"Why do you hate me so? Have I been cruel to you?"

"No."

"Did I enslave you?"

"No."

"I gave you clothes for your back and sandals for your feet."

"Yes, you gave me that, O Prince of Egypt," Nun agreed, his voice level, his eyes empty as they regarded Moses.

"And you eat the same rations the free men eat, all the bread you want and meat and fruit when we have fruit. Do I feed you slop and filth, as Kotophar did?"

"You feed me well, O Prince of Egypt."

"Then do I come between you and your gods, Nun? When you make the serpent of clay and the little figures that the Canaanites worship, do I forbid them? Do I tell you to worship the gods of Egypt?"

Nun smiled without humour and without joy. "I have seen enough of the gods of Egypt. It would not matter what you told me."

"You are not just a slave," Moses argued.

"What then?"

"We go up against Kush. We will stand side by side in a chariot and fight side by side—and if such is to be our fate, we'll die side by side."

"If such is to be out fate, O Prince of Egypt," Nun shrugged, his smile thin and evil, his eyes narrow, thoughtful and calculating—so that a chill of fear came over Moses, a sense of being trapped beyond help or hope. No more could he say, and still Nun looked at him and smiled——

But a few days later, Hetep-Re said to Moses, "If you will forgive me, O Prince of Egypt, some of us were talking about that slave of yours whom you call Nun, and it is our opinion—for what it is worth—that you would do well to slip a dagger between his ribs and give him to Mother Nile. If the task is distasteful to you, we will gladly see to it for you."

If Hetep-Re had expected some violent reaction from Moses, he was disappointed; for the prince only studied him long and thoughtfully, and then asked,

"Why?"

"Because if you don't kill him, as surely as the Nile flows, he will kill you the first chance he has."

Instead of denying this, Moses said, "I will need a driver."

"Seti-Keph favours you. Ask him for a foot-soldier, and I'll train him to drive a team—just as I trained this one."

"For what price?" Moses could not forbear asking.

"Now you do me an injustice, O Prince of Egypt," Hetep-Re replied. "Who spoke of a price? Am I not to be permitted to serve you—or am I to be treated like a dog and kicked every time I come to lick your hand?"

"You are no dog, Hetep-Re," Moses said tiredly. "I behaved badly. I am sorry."

"Never apologize to me, godliness. Never, I say. In my small way, I desire to serve you. Only that. Shall I kill him?"

"No," Moses said.

"You know that he will kill you, O Prince of Egypt."

Moses nodded indifferently. "I suppose he will try," he said, and he left it there, turning away from Hetep-Re with the detached and thoughtless arrogance that only a lifetime in the Great House could give an Egyptian of that time, leaving Hetep-Re cursing silently and thinking, "I've warned you—you stupid young sot; and if there weren't some profit to be had out of you yet, I wouldn't have done that."

[10]

IF ON OCCASION Moses recalled Ramses' light reference to a punitive expedition against Kush, it was hard to balance the reference with the vast force that came together below Karnak. Seeing the masses of foot-soldiers, the spears stacked like wheat in a broad field, the herds of horses and donkeys, and the seemingly endless ranks of chariots, Moses tried to comprehend the great campaigns he had read about, where a hundred and fifty thousand men had comprised the army. It was difficult to believe that any army could be larger than this.

The river trip, so slow and changeless, disappeared into his past; and once the chariots and horses had been landed at Abydos, Seti-Keph made it plain that he would brook no further delay. He forced a march for a day and a half to the assembly area, where foot-soldiers and supplies had been marshalled for months now; and then, in an angry scene with his captains, denied them the right to a day's pleasure in Karnak. He knew full well that such a day, after the boredom of the long, river journey, could end only in violence between the men of the Delta and the half-hostile nobles of Karnak, and he had no desire to turn his campaign into fratricide before it had even begun. Instead, he laid out a programme of work and organization that would permit them to begin the march against Kush early the following day.

Moses, with little to do, once he and Nun had seen to the horses, spent the hours before sunset wandering through the encampment of the foot-soldiers, excited at this assembly of so many warriors from so many strange and distant places. He gaped at the golden-haired Achaeans with their splendid beards, their plumed bronze helmets, and their mighty nine-foot spears—and grinned mutely as they crowded around him to examine his iron sword and dagger. He listened to the guttural, consonantal speech of the Babylonians, picking out a word here and there that he could understand, and fingered their fine woollen cloaks, softer than the finest linen and dyed colourfully with stripes of yellow and red and black. When he came to the men of Hatti, they laughed and poked fun at him in their strange tongue, so soft and musical and so different from either Egyptian or Babylonian. From his golden ornaments, they recognized him as noble and they doffed their high, truncated hats to him. With gestures, Moses praised their marvellous laminated bows, and in return, they made him drink a cup of their heavy fig wine. Strangest of all were these carefree men of Hatti, with their tight trousers, their high boots, and their sparkling blue eyes.

So he wandered among the mercenaries of the nations, swaggering a little in the company of soldiers, and tasting the freedom of a young man far from home and bound for adventures at the unknown ends of the earth. just before night fell the thin notes of the silver chariot trumpets called the soldiers to their places, and Moses ran to join the press of warriors and drivers around the chariot of one Sokar-Moses, second in command under the Captain of Hosts. A giant of a man, muscled and scarred and barbaric in the dress he affected, heavy gold ear-rings in the style of the Sea Rovers and a helm of shining silver, he had a voice as thunderous as his appearance; and clapping his hands to make his points, he named the order of march. Hetep-Re—in whose guard was Moses—and a dozen other captains were to lead with their hosts and act as scouts and body-guards for Seti-Keph if the need should arise, while the remainder of the chariots brought up the rear.

Moses ordered Nun to sleep near the chariot, to which their horses were tethered; and he himself spread his cloak on the warm sand directly behind the chariot. But sleep would not come. All night long, the motion and sound of the camp continued, the muffled tones of men, the heavier tread of horses, and sometimes the hard shout of an officer. Hetep-Re came by once, saw that Moses was awake, and said, "Not every night like this, Prince of Egypt. When we match, they'll treasure sleep and fight for it." And once, having dozed fitfully, Moses opened his eyes and saw Nun standing by the chariot. "The horses were restless," Nun said. "I saw to them." And Moses lay back, his heart tight in the pinch of fear—yet wondering whether Nun could kill a man who slept, kill him in cold blood. He thought not, but they said that you never knew a Bedouin or the blackness in his heart. Moses lay stretched out, looking at the brilliant canopy of stars over his head, recalling how the companions of Amon-Teph studied them and measured them, wondering what they were and what they meant, his fear mixed with the thrill of wonder, the starry heavens turning his young heart and plucking at his dreams. Thus, in the gleaming face of the heavens his fear of Nun was forgotten.

Then the stars began to dull; the black sky greyed itself—and suddenly, the drums beat. So it was that the army came awake, to begin the march upon Kush.

[11]

THEY MARCHED ON the western bank of the Nile, with the river between them and Karnak. The road—packed sand with the larger rocks removed, it was a road by grace of name only—ran for the most part under the desert escarpment; but since the river had not yet reached its full ebb, they would find themselves plodding in mud—when the river canyon narrowed; and then it would be drivers and warriors out to put their shoulders to the wheels of the chariots—and often enough a call back for the foot-soldiers to come forward and help the mired chariots. This was the occasion for the hostility between the man on foot and the mounted man, and with the heat and the mud and the swarms of black mud-flies, it was often enough that Sokar-Moses came running to break up a fight with his heavy, undiscriminating bullwhip.

Moses was fortunate, for there were no situations beyond the strength of himself and Nun; yet soon enough he had abandoned his kilt and weapons and harness, and marched naked in a loincloth. They were still below the First Cataract, so they envied the slaves who paddled the little supply boats; but later, the situation would be reversed, and the slaves would toil like beasts in the water, waist-deep, fighting the boats upstream.

The first night, as Hetep-Re had predicted, the tired army slept well and deeply, but as the days wore on, the march became the rhythm and reason of their being—and their bodies hardened to the task. There were stretches where the escarpment narrowed cliff-like over the water, and then ropes were rigged to haul the chariots aloft to the desert, while the horses were led up narrow paths. In other places, the escarpment receded, and the river valley between the cliffs was ten, fifteen and even twenty miles wide; and in such places it was not uncommon for the army to make a march of thirty and even thirty-five miles between dawn and dusk. Here sunset and sunrise took on qualities that Moses had never seen before; there were certain minerals, streaks of quartz and striated rock in the cliffs on the east bank of the Nile that turned them into shimmering walls of beauty each night, such beauty that no slave or foot-soldier could look at unmoved.

Between Karnak and the First Cataract, a matter of two hundred miles as the river flowed, the drab little peasant villages with their plain squat huts of sun-baked mud brick and their hard-working, insular and superstitious peasants became fewer and fewer. When the army was sighted in the distance, the mothers and maidens of the family climbed the escarpment and hid in the desert. The men worked stolidly, clearing their irrigation ditches of the fertile alluvial deposit and preparing their fields for planting, and only the children came to stand open-mouthed and awe-stricken as the army marched by. The once glorious city of Edfu, far south of Karnak, was little more than an abandoned ruin, its still-splendid temples served by priests without worshippers, its population reduced to a dozen landed families—and their slaves; for today more and more of Upper Egypt was perishing as the poor peasants sought better fortune in the Delta country.

The march itself was savage and unrelenting—and it would become more so as Egypt was left to the north. If slave or foot-soldier fell sick or broke a leg or suffered some other disabling injury, he was left behind at the wayside to fare for himself as best he could; but Moses noticed how few fell sick or suffered injury. Their feet developed hide like a bullock's, so that even a whole day with only thin sandals between foot and burning sand did not bother them; their skins tanned to a deep burnished brown, and with the short, measured rations, every man in the army became lean and hard as whipcord. Constantly dehydrated and in need of saline, they ate the dry, tough salt meat and salt fish as if they were the most delectable fruit, and the River Nile gave them all the water they needed. Now the air of Kush blew to them from the south, and they did not lag. Mercenaries, professional soldiers and the dregs of the Delta ports all licked their lips for the still distant reward of the soldier—gold and women.

As they neared the First Cataract, Seti-Keph sent word for Moses to bring his chariot up alongside. This was the first time since the march began at Abydos that Seti-Keph had sent for Moses; but on many occasions Moses had seen his glittering, brass-veneered chariot dash down the column, and every evening he saw the lamps lit in the linen tent, where Seti-Keph and his high captains pored over maps and made their plans for the campaign. Seti-Keph was no bureaucrat in the field; every detail of the army came under his own eye, and if he didn't interfere with the prestige of his captains in their exercise of command and discipline, he nevertheless saw and filed in his memory their methods of command. Day by day, Moses' respect, for the qualities of this strange, hard little man, in whom compassion and brutality were so curiously mixed, increased— and day by day he set more store on the indications of liking that Seti-Keph had expressed for him. Now, he welcomed the invitation as a pleasant break in the monotony of the march, and he felt pleased and honoured as Nun drove the chariot up the column to where Seti-Keph and his staff led. Seeing him approach, Seti-Keph pulled ahead so that Moses could drive alongside him, and then, as the two chariots slowed to a walk that matched the pace of the foot-soldiers, the Captain of Hosts cried out good-naturedly,

"A good welcome to you, Moses of the half-name, and how do you like campaigning?"

"I like it well," Moses grinned.

"Ah, now, and I believe you do, O Prince of Egypt. What would your godly father say if he could see you like this, naked to a loincloth and dirty and muddy as any foot-soldier or porter?"

"He's not my father, Seti-Keph, and I don't give a fig for what he would say. But this is a better life than I've lived until now, I tell you that, sir!"

"Wait until you see blood run before you decide that. Anyway I like the look of you. A soldier dresses as a soldier should. I also like a shaven face. When an Egyptian grows careless in his shaving, I feel something is breaking inside of him. Do you shave each morning, Moses?"

"I do, Seti-Keph."

"And who shaves you—that sullen bull who drives your chariot?"

"I shave myself," Moses said, and Nun smiled thinly without looking at either man.

"You'll find that not so easy when the work is blood and death. Teach the Bedouin to shave you, lad. A servant is made and not born, and if he can handle a chariot axe as he does the reins, you have a man worth holding on to. He cares for it well, too, and a good chariot is life and death here in the South. Grease your axles three times a day, and watch your tires. I'd give a hundred of the chariots, few as I command, to have the iron tires the Hittites use. The gods themselves can't split an iron tire when it's well forged. But a little crack in these bronze hoops will send them off when you most need them—and then the gods can't help you, no, sir—and the wheel goes next. Watch your tires the way you watch your horses' feet. Well—I didn't call you up here to lecture you on chariot care. And sometimes I think that the gods decide when we are to be born and when we are to die, and iron tires won't change that, eh?"

"No, I suppose not, Seti-Keph," Moses answered.

"The fact is that this afternoon we'll break out march early, for I have a social call to make. Sokar-Moses will come with me; but I would think it a grave discourtesy to the man we will visit to have a prince of the Great House among my captains and not do him the honour of asking you to cross his threshold. So will you come, Moses? It will be for the evening, and I can promise you that you will not be bored."

"I don't understand," Moses said.

"How then? Will you not come? I know there are no others of godly blood here, but I am not well enough versed in manners to think that it would belittle you, O Prince of Egypt, to break bread with plain people. You do so on the march. Does crossing a man's threshold make the difference?"

"No, no—please, Seti-Keph, I will be honoured."

The sour face of the Captain of Hosts broke into a smile. His temperament was almost childlike in its mercurial quality. "What then, boy, speak up?"

"Only—who lives here? Even the peasant villages are behind us now. These are the marches where Kush and Libya raid as they please——"

"Oh, no—no, not as they please, Prince of Egypt. If you doubt the long, hard hand of the God-King, only look behind you!"

"Still, for one man it must be dangerous. Who is he?"

Seti-Keph laughed with pleasure. "The one man for whom it is not dangerous. He's a physician, Moses, and some say he is the best in the world—and even the angriest men do not harm a doctor. We are none of us exempt from the need, and he treats all who come to him. Thus he lives in peace where perhaps another could not. His house is on the escarpment, within sight of the First Cataract."

"How do you know him, Seti-Keph, and why does he live here alone?"

"Not alone, Moses, for he has his wife and daughter with him, and slaves too. As to how I know him—well, I have been this way before and Kush has felt my fist before;

but I also knew of him when he lived in Karnak and men came to him for treatment from all the world. But, you see, his father was with the evil ones, and this man's name is Aton-Moses, and he will not change his name. For my part, I have my religion and I was born with it and I will die with it. I don't hold with dabbling in the affairs of the gods, and the politics of this earth are dangerous enough for me to want no part of the politics of the next world. But a time came when the priests would brook this situation no more, and they told him to change his name and reveal the tomb of his father, so that they might burn the mummy and consign his father to the blind darkness of un-being forever—or else himself face death without embalming."

"What did he do?" Moses asked slowly.

"He laughed at them, as I have the story. To one priest, he said—You have pains in your belly now. Within thirty days, you will need an operation or face death. Who else can operate on you? Then, to another priest, be said—You have headaches, and they will open your head. What then? I can cure your headaches without trepanning. Who else can? And to a third priest—Who will prepare your medicine when I am dead?

"So you see, Moses, one does not kill a doctor so easily. Then they sent their complaint to the God-King, and he said to exile this physician to the southern edge of the land, but not to kill him. That was more than twenty years ago, and he has lived here since. Nor do I think he would ever leave this place, and later you will see why. So when we break march, cleanse yourself and dress yourself as a prince of Egypt, for it would not be seemly that we go to him in the dirt and cloth of our journey."

Never had Moses heard Seti-Keph speak with such respect and deference of any man—not even of Ramses him-self—and he was eager for the march to end. Early in the afternoon, they broke for camping, not yet within sight of the legendary cataract, but already at a place where the river plunged and tumbled over large rocks, the water churning and foaming as it roared north—and already the slave-porters were fighting their life and death struggle with the supply boats.

Moses let Nun unharness and curry the horses, while he himself bounded down the bank and into the churning river. When he was clean, he had Nun break out the bag-gage, and while a circle of curious soldiers looked on re-spectfully, he combed out his thick black hair, put a gold circlet on his brow, and clad himself in the spotless white linen and shining gold insignia of a prince of Egypt.

[12]

AS THEY APPROACHED the house, Sokar-Moses driving Seti-Keph's chariot, in which the three of them rode, the thunder of the cataract became louder and louder—and then, by some freak of acoustics, muffled itself as they came over the ridge. It was a fine sight, the River Nile visible far in either direction, the foaming, tumbling rapids beneath them, and the round, blazing sun dropping into the western desert. But when the house appeared, Moses had eyes for nothing else; for he knew immediately that in all his life he had not seen such a house, nor would he likely see one such again.

Not that it was so different from other Egyptian houses, but there was something so graceful, so complete in its proportions as to have a deep effect on the observer—who

afterwards would admit its beauty because there was nothing discordant about it. Like many noble houses in Karnak,
it was a simple rectangle in shape, the flat roof supported
by stone walls; but unlike the houses of Karnak, it had no
wall around it to hide its grace, and it was built not of
sandstone but of white limestone that glowed pink and
purple in the late sunlight, and in the side walls it had great
windows to let in the light—windows curtained by hangings of bright yellow and black. Its entire shape was a natural outgrowth of the upcropping escarpment, and it stood
apart from the slave quarters and the stables, so that no
unnatural influence might mar its simple beauty. As they
drove up to the front, Moses saw that it was entirely open
to the river, its verandah framed with the ancient reed-
shaped columns, marble cut to simulate bundles of tied
river-reeds—a type of column that had not been used for
more than a century. The limestone verandah stretched in
front of the columns to the escarpment edge, and then led
down in steps of curved terrace that narrowed finally to a
little staircase cut out of the cliff rock itself. And placed
here and there on the terrace were reclining cats and one
marvellously carved sphinx—all of them in black volcanic
basalt—with three large, white, house cats moving sinu-
ously among the carvings.

As slaves ran up to take the horses, three people moved
across the terrace, one a small, round-cheeked and obviously good-humoured Egyptian who welcomed them with
such warmth that it would seem he had been waiting their
arrival all the years he lived there, the second a slight,
timid-appearing woman, past middle age, apparently his
wife, and the third a young woman of poise and beauty,
the daughter—Moses guessed—clad in a thin, transparent

gown that left one rich, round breast bare and lovely, in the manner of the southern folk.

It was many a week since Moses had seen an attractive woman, and forgetting his manners, he gaped foolishly; but in the excitement of the meeting, no one noticed. Seti-Keph and Aton-Moses embraced warmly, both of them bubbling with pleasure, while Sokar-Moses and Moses stood waiting to be introduced. Aton-Moses named his family with easy formality that demonstrated his breeding, his "beloved wife and companion", the Lady Setep-Aton, smiling at Seti-Keph to show that he understood and regretted this constant use of "Aton" in the family names; and then the "jewel and comfort of my declining years", his daughter, the Lady Merit-Aton. But even as he spoke, his eye fixed on Moses, and his manner became suddenly wary and dubious. This was noticed by Seti-Keph, who quickly said,

"No, no, my dear friend—I bring no disturbing guests to you. My messenger mentioned Sokar-Moses, this giant beside me, who is my right arm and first under me in command of the hosts. And this young man, I took the liberty to bring with me; for I know you would have been hurt had I neglected to. He is what he seems to be—the blood of the Great House of the God-King and a prince of Egypt; but he is a good lad, and I think you know that I am no poor judge of men."

There, in front of Moses and the rest of them, Seti-Keph rambled on with his explanation, as if he knew that there could be no welcome and ease in the lovely white house until he had made their position clear.

"I know that you have heard a good deal about the sons of the God-King in the Great House, but this young man is something else indeed—and mind you, I make no comments on what happens in the Great House. I am an old soldier, and an ignorant one, too. But this man was sent into exile for three years by the God-King, and for many a day now I have watched him. He is an Egyptian, and without mean pride—and he travels with a single servant who drives his chariot, without retainers, without embalmers and women and priests and scribes, and he is a truthful man, Aton-Moses. For many a day I debated whether to bring him here, and then I decided, knowing him, that your house would be honoured by his presence. His name is Moses."

The family, the three of them, mother, father and daughter, regarded Moses gravely; then the father bowed from the waist, covering both eyes with the tips of his fingers. The mother and daughter did likewise. Then, when they had uncovered their eyes, Aton-Moses said,

"Never before has a person from the Great House entered my home, and surely this has a meaning beyond honour, though we are honoured beyond the ability of words to express. If I was slow in my response, O Prince of Egypt, it is because for these many years I have played a careful game with our lives and happiness as the stake—as good Seti-Keph has no doubt told you; and I would just as well that no one at the Great House be reminded of my existence. Here and about, the people cherish my little skill and weave their own wall about me—but the Great House and the City of Ramses are a long distance away. Enough of explanations. We welcome and honour you, O Prince of Egypt—for my own hospitality stands in doubt now." His eyes twinkled as he finished speaking, and his welcome was so direct and warm that Moses' heart went out to him.

The woman of the house nodded uncertainly, but the lovely Merit-Aton smiled at Moses with delight and admiration.

Aton-Moses clapped his hands, and slaves appeared with stools for them to sit on and with perfumed water to wash their feet and with wine to quench their thirst. They sat in a half-circle on the verandah, the house shading them from the last heat of the sun, and small bronze tables were set before them. Bowls of ripe grapes and figs were put down and simple clay dishes full of sliced melon and goat-flesh, the meat cooked in a savoury sauce of honey that Moses had never tasted before. Wicker baskets of hot bread were constantly presented to them, and for each person, a high-necked clay flask was provided, each one holding about two quarts of liquid. These were placed on the floor, and a long hollow reed allowed the diner to drink without disturbing the heavy bottle. The drink was a cold, slightly-fermented fruit juice, and Moses thought that in all his life he had never tasted anything so delicious and stimulating. He saw the others accept the dinner as nothing very extraordinary—and he realized how little of the life and custom of his own land had reached him through the walls of the Great House. He also recognized something that he had heard a good deal about—the very different status of women here in Upper Egypt. Whereas in the Delta the men would have dined alone, here the women participated on a basis of easy equality, something that Seti-Keph and Sokar-Moses were apparently well acquainted with, for they fell into it as a matter of course.

For the first hour, Moses said nothing. He nibbled at his food—for the excitement and pleasure of the occasion had taken away his appetite—and listened to the conversation, which was mainly between Seti-Keph and Aton-Moses.

How little of the news and politics of Lower Egypt reached here Moses realized as he heard the Captain of Hosts review the history of the past five years—and he also realized how little of those politics he had really understood. He heard the long war between Hatti and Egypt analysed as a power struggle for the riches of Canaan and for control of the iron mines in Lebanon and the vast wealth of Mesopotamia, and he saw war and conquest in a new perspective, as he had never seen them before. He listened to Seti-Keph's account of the expedition to Kush, why it was undertaken and what Ramses hoped to accomplish by it. And he realized that Seti-Keph was a man who exercised neither judgment nor ethical attitudes toward his own profession. Once, not too long ago, Moses would thereby have dismissed the man as a brute; but he was learning that the question of who is and who is not a brute is none too simple—even as the nature of man constituted a maze he had never dreamed of.

Aton-Moses shook his head seriously and unhappily. "Wars should not be fought because a few bands of wild young men came down and crossed the frontier."

"They also killed and burned and looted," Seti-Keph pointed out, but with no passion.

"Will a war bring back the dead? The truth is, my friend, and you know it as well as I do, that the lust of the God-King for slaves and gold is insatiable. When the Libyans come out of the western desert and do the same thing, he takes no umbrage, for the Libyans are as poor as Bedouins, eh?"

"If I went looking for a just war," Seti-Keph growled, "I would still be a peasant in the Delta."

"And perhaps a good deal happier."

"I doubt that. There are no happy peasants in the Delta today. But since I am a soldier, I do as I am told."

"We enslave ourselves with people who do as they are told," the doctor sighed. "And like all great nations, we Egyptians take such cursed comfort in it. We know so surely that nowhere but in Egypt is there culture and beauty and proper reverence for the gods, and we make a lovely cradle for what used to be called our conscience. For a thousand years we have been boasting to the world that only we possess the holy *macaat*, that peculiar Egyptian word which we claim can be translated into no other tongue. Is it conscience, the knowledge of right and wrong? In part, we admit loftily. Is it justice—yes, we admit elements of justice, don't we? Mercy? That too, and of course an element of innate nobility. But those are only indications of *macaat*, which is all of them and more. *Macaat* is Egypt, the noble, the divine." There was such bitter irony in his voice that Moses looked to Seti-Keph and Sokar-Moses to take offence. But they only smiled with the sort of tolerance that assured the doctor that nothing he could say would offend them.

"But do you know what this *macaat* really is ?" the little physician demanded.

"You failed to mention honour and courage," Sokar-Moses said with some defence, not eager to pit himself against wit and intellect; and actually admiring the crackling speech of the physician. He had said very little until now, and his self-deprecating smile was at odds with his great bulk and ferocious appearance. "I mean, a soldier would have small *macaat* without those—don't you think?"

"I don't think! Honour—courage—those are war words, and they mean one thing to the professional butcher and something else entirely to normal folk. As a physician, I tell you they are your medicine; otherwise, how would you brigands sleep nights?"

Now, surely, Moses expected the company to explode, but the two women sat calmly, their hands properly folded on their laps; Sokar-Moses was taken somewhat aback; and Seti-Keph burst into roars of laughter, rocking with laughter until the tears ran down his cheeks. "All my life," he spluttered, "I have been trying to say something like that. Rest easy, Sokar-Moses—the truth is always demanding and bitter. And you, Prince of Egypt," turning to Moses, "can put this all down to the ranting of old men. He is not yet nineteen years," he explained to Aton-Moses, "so all your lonely wit that you spin in the empty nights here seems damn' foolishness to him!"

"Oh, no—no," protested Moses, speaking for the first time.

"And you think it blasphemous and treasonable, my son?" the doctor asked gently.

"I think it wonderful," Moses managed to say.

"Well!" cried Seti-Keph. "There you are. But what *macaat*? You were going to tell us, weren't you?"

"Yes, if you want to hear?"

"Go ahead."

"*Macaat* is righteousness, which is the curse the gods bestow on a people they desire to destroy."

Moses understood this not at all, but he didn't dare to say so and catching the grave eyes of Merit-Aton, he felt that above all things he must not reveal his own narrow horizons, his own great limitations. For the first time in his remembered life, he had lost all consciousness of being a prince of Egypt—and all consciousness of his princely fraudulence as well. In the Great House, he had heard contemptuous remarks concerning the "over-educated" and "over-sophisticated" barons of the Upper Nile, of their plotting against the gods, of the treasonable scepticism they had imbibed with their worship of Aton, and the way in which they undermined all that was truly Egyptian and holy. But never had he dreamed that there actually were people who thought and conversed in this manner. A part of him was experiencing that sudden discovery of vast horizons that comes to some young men once in their lifetime; another part of him was afraid, for in what he remembered as closest to this, his best talks with Amon-Teph and Neph, there was always the secrecy that admitted the action as punishable sin. Here it was open, without any conspiratorial overtones, and filled with laughter and innuendo.

Seti-Keph said, "So you think the gods plan to destroy us."

"Unless we destroy ourselves first."

"With our *macaat*?" Seti-Keph asked mockingly.

"With out cursed righteousness. What do we know of people? We have lost all sense of them. What do your lords on the Delta know of Kush?"

"I know nothing of Kush, where I have never been," Sokar-Moses said bluntly, "and I've met few who do."

"I respect an honest man," Aton-Moses nodded. "There is no Kush. I see our young prince doubts me. I'm not being facetious, as Seti-Keph knows. Kush is a name for all of Africa to the south of us. Civilizations have come and gone in that strange land to the south, but always we Egyptians speak of Kush. The black skin is Kush. Bah! Our Egypt's wars are as empty as our *macaat*. Right now, there is a new life, a new kingdom, a new civilization coming into being in what we call Kush. Not the tribes of cattle-raiders whom you smashed in the battle at the Sixth Cataract seven years ago, Seti-Keph. They are gone. They never recovered from that battle. These are black people who live far to the south of the Sixth Cataract, weeks of marching up the Blue Nile. A long journey, if you are to reach them with the cruel hand of your master. They have built a city, and they herd their cattle and till their fields in peace. The few wild raiders whom you will practise justice against were driven out, and came down here for want of a better place to go. But now you will punish the innocent for the guilty."

"And how do you know all this?" Seti-Keph wondered.

"I have long ears," Aton-Moses scowled. "There is little goes on hearabout that I don't hear this or that concerning it. It may be that they have forgotten I exist, on the Delta— as I hope—but a hundred days' journey to the south, the name of Aton-Moses is known, I assure you, and I have had patients from places you never dreamed existed."

"Aton-Moses," the prince asked, "you said a hundred days' journey to the south?"

"And why not?"

"We have come so far," Moses said unbelievingly. "I never knew such distances were in this world——"

"You will know better than half of a hundred days' journey by your own sweat and sorrow," the Captain of Hosts chuckled, "for after we leave here, there is that much and more before ever we set foot in Kush."

Abashed and feeling that he had wholly exposed his youth and ignorance, Moses nodded silently; but he met the warm brown eyes of Merit-Aton, and they were sympathetic rather than derisive. Aton-Moses, noticing his embarrassment, hastened to change the subject, and he said,

"Tell me, O Prince of Egypt, what are your impressions of out backward—and lonely 'Upper Land'?" giving it the old name.

"I don't think it's backward," Moses answered eagerly. "I like it. I feel good here—and I think I love the desert and these escarpments."

"Yes—the desert is something you love or hate, no in-between; and I have heard that nowhere on earth is there anything to match the colours of our escarpments. Look!" He pointed eastward, across the gorge of the Nile, to where the setting sun was beginning to display its nightly flow and ebb of colour upon the escarpment. "So it is, each night, and each night different. In the tales we tell our children it is Mother Mut herself who comes each evening to clothe her beloved cliffs and keep the chill night air from them. Do you remember, Merit-Aton?"

"I remember," she nodded, her voice low and musical, and said to Moses, "but why the cliffs needed protection from the cold, I never knew and no one could ever tell me, not even my father, who knows almost everything."

The teasing was very gentle, and Moses realized that it was a part of their relationship—a relationship between parent and child that he could hardly comprehend, for it was outside his own experience or anything he could imagine.

"Almost everything," her father said. "I suppose all this would be strange to you, Prince of Egypt—just as the Great House would be most strange to me. I have never seen it. Is it as wonderful as they say?"

"Wonderful? I never thought of it that way. It was there, the place where I lived."

"Was it a happy place to live?" the girl asked.

Slowly, Moses said, "I think—that no palace is a happy place to live. This is just a very large house—some say the largest house in the world; but it is full of fear and super-stition and every kind of hatred——"

"A court is a court," Seti-Keph shrugged.

"Yet it must have parts of beauty," Aton-Moses pressed, "since at least part of it was built by the same man who built this house for me twelve years ago."

"The same man?" Moses whispered excitedly.

"Yes—a wonderful man. A plain Egyptian peasant boy, like Seti-Keph here, but when they win through, they are our best, I sometimes think. He had a vision of building a great dam across the valley where the First Cataract falls, a project like those we did in the olden times. He felt it would require as much stone as the great pyramid at Giza, but he knew it could be done. He had planned every detail of it, and he would build sluice gates to control the flood-waters, so that never again should we have havoc when the flood was too great or famine when it was too little. He fired the imagination of the God-King, who sent him here with a thousand slaves to begin the work. But no sooner was he here than the priests came, hot on his heels, with another counter-order from the God-King, whom they had convinced that such a project would be sacrilege. It would interfere with the ordained course of the Holy Nile, and in their anger the gods would visit doom upon us."

"I think he was right," Seti-Keph said solemnly.

"I would expect you to think so. Anyway, back and forth went the messengers for half a year, while the engineer fretted away the days and almost went mad with frustration. That was when I met him and we became friends, for he was an image-breaker, as I am, and we are the closest fraternity on earth, you may believe me. We lived in an old house of sun-dried brick then, and more or less to pass the time, he drew the plans for this house and had his idle slaves build it. So you see, if Egypt got no dam, I at least got a house, and a very nice one, don't you think?"

"I think it is the most wonderful house I ever saw," Moses agreed. "Was the man who built it called Neph?"

The general excitement and interest over that led to Moses' talking more than he wanted to—and after he had told them of his own experiences with Neph, the conversation died away, and they sat in silence, watching the gorgeous play of colour upon the escarpment. Yet in Moses, the turbulence of his thoughts churned parts of him unknown and untouched and the wonder of this waking dream enthralled him even more than the twilight glory of light on the cliffs. That it was Neph, his own beloved Neph, who had built this house might have seemed a far-fetched coincidence, had it not been for what the doctor said of the image-breakers—"the closest fraternity on earth". Was it that way, then—and was Amon-Teph to live for him again and again? For it was always Amon-Teph, the first of them in his life, who appeared in his mind—whether through the caustic irony of Seti-Keph or the practical wisdom of Neph or the strange and sometimes frightening philosophy of this little doctor who lived alone on the edge of Egypt. What had they in common? Was it because they doubted? But Neph had not doubted when he proposed to build a great stone wall across the valley and hold back the River Nile. How furious Neph must have been at the priests—and it was no wonder that he hated the gods so! No, it was not doubt but questioning—always questioning. He recalled now one of the many times he had spoken to Neph concerning Aton—and Neph had said impatiently, "You think too much of the gods, Moses. Why should you have to know if Aton is the only god?" "But you know, Neph——" And Neph had looked at him with such sadness that Moses became afraid. Neph said, "The only god is truth, Moses, and that is not given to any man to know." But weren't men like these aware of some of the truth? Why had Neph never told him of this plan to dam the river? Was it because they were a closed fraternity, these men, and could commune only with each other? Certainly they were so different from others that they might well be a race apart.

Aton-Moses broke the silence, saying, "I am curious, O Prince of Egypt, concerning your name—if I may be? For, unlike mine, it is only half a name."

Moses returned slowly from the maze of his own thoughts, and Seti-Keph said, to put the matter to rest, "The prince of the half-name. Why not? If he wants it so——"

Moses spoke almost dreamily, "It is half a name given to me by my beloved mother, the Princess Enekhas-Amon. The other half she would give me some day—so she thought. But she died. Ramses, who calls himself the God-King, murdered her."

There was a strained silence after he spoke, until Seti-Keph said, "Here we are good companions, O Prince of Egypt, and we talk freely and we trust each other's honour. But there are some things that should never be said." It was not a reprimand; it was simply an observation.

"And do you know the other half?" Aton-Moses asked softly.

"Yes——" to the only man he ever met or heard of who bore it himself. "But it died with my mother, and my half-name is enough. I am used to it."

Setep-Aton spoke, the first, the only time, her voice as gentle as the cool desert breeze that comes at nightfall, "But we old ones have kept these children long enough, listening to our sombre nonsense. We talk of life, but youth lives. Go now, O Prince of Egypt, and my daughter will show you the house and the terraces. There will be a moon tonight, and sweet Lady Isis will light your way."

[13]

HE FOLLOWED THE girl in silence, and she led him down a limestone path that moved snakelike along the edge of the escarpment. A balustrade protected on the river side, while a planting of pink *Anu* cactus formed the other border. Occasionally, a step dropped the level, and after about a hundred paces they came to a pocket in the escarpment where a tiny temple stood, gracefully proportioned, a black, basalt floor some twenty feet square, surrounded by pillars of pale pink sandstone. The columns were roofless, and in the very centre of the floor, there was a simple altar of white limestone.

In the desert moonlight, the place had a truly unworldly quality, a haunting charm that made Moses feel he was full to overflowing with emotions he could neither identify nor control. He was aware of a sweet yet painful happiness, and he seemed to know at once all the joy and grief in the world. When Merit-Aton's bare arm or shoulder brushed against his flesh, his heart beat wildly.

"I brought you here first, O Prince of Egypt," she said, looking at him in that grave manner of hers, and perhaps thinking how strange it was that this tall and handsome young prince should be with her at all, "because it is the most beautiful place we have. My mother wanted it. She is very religious in the old way—which I suppose is different from the Delta way. Your gods are very magnificent and powerful and they have humbled our gods, but we have not cast our old gods out. Where could they go? We love them and pity them for the glory they brought us in the olden times."

"Why does the temple have no roof?"

"Always, in the olden times, our temples had no roofs, O Prince of Egypt."

"Will you always call me Prince of Egypt, Merit-Aton?"

"Always? You are here tonight, and tomorrow you go away. That isn't always, is it?"

"Will you call me Moses tonight?"

"If you wish me to," smiling slightly but not looking at him. "Shall we go into the temple? It is a holy place—Moses—and peaceful."

"Then you too worship the gods?"

She turned and faced him, looking long and keenly into his brown, high-boned face. Then she said, in a way that reminded him of her father,

"How shall I know you, Moses? You are a prince of Egypt. Never before have I seen one who wore the holy neckpiece upon his breast, the golden and jewelled emblems of kinship with the gods, and upon his head the royal circle. But I know this. From the House of Seti and the House of Ramses, we of Upper Egypt have had only misery and death. You came upon our land like locusts and your priests were like locusts, and you ate up all that was fine and beautiful. And because we had dared to think, to reach out, to break through old and ugly superstition, you destroyed us. You killed and killed until the blood ran ankle-deep in the streets of Karnak, and in beautiful, wonderful Amarna—the city our fathers built as an offering to truth and brotherhood—there you made a waste and devastation that put even the Hittites to shame, so that not even the memory of good and gentle people and their work should remain. When your army marched up the Nile, between here and Karnak, it was like going through an empty land, wasn't it?"

Moses nodded dumbly.

"Yet once there were hundreds of prosperous villages there. But Seti and Ramses needed slaves and more slaves, and since we were marked evil—as you no doubt heard from your childhood—you dragged our people away to work on your monuments to butchers, and to dig in your mines. And then you ask me, so slyly, do I worship the gods?" She stood panting and trembling as she finished, something unspoken working inside her.

"But believe me, I did not mean that," Moses protested. "How can you think that I wanted to trap you into some admission? Do I look like that sort of person? Do you think I hate you, Merit-Aton?"

"I don't know what to think. I think one thing, and then another. You are a guest in our house. I never spoke to a guest like this before. Any guest."

"And does your father think of me so?" Moses asked desperately.

"My father is old. He says—Let the dead past rest. He says—Here in this house is sanctuary and understanding for men of all races. He says that they leave evil and shame behind them when they cross a physician's threshold. I honour my father. But I am not he, Moses."

"Yet you heard me say that Ramses murdered my mother."

"Your mother was his sister. So they do things on the Delta. But you are the blood of Ramses."

"I am not!" Moses cried harshly. "And if you would not drive me away from you for ever, Merit-Aton, never again say that I am the blood of Ramses!"

She was taken aback by his sudden fierce anger. He had stepped into the shadow of one of the sandstone columns, and he had become a tall black silhouette, his sharp face showing its strong and strange profile.

"But your mother—and it was Seti-Keph himself who whispered that the God-King is your father——"

"Say no more of that," Moses sighed. "Believe me, we were taught many things in the Great House, but not to lie. I have half a name, and if my poor mother had lived to see her unhappy dreams come true, I would have been called Aton-Moses, the name your father bears. I was trained and tutored by a holy priest of Aton, a man both wise and good, who was the closest thing to a father I ever knew. And when Ramses discovered that Aton was worshipped in the Great House, he cut off this priest's head and sent it to me as I sat mourning my mother—the better for me to reflect on the folly of belittling the gods. So if you thought, Merit-Aton, that I was some wretched spy who came to trap you into placing your life and your father's and mother's lives in my hands—well, here is my own life in yours. For only the God-King of Egypt could bear the name of Aton-Moses in the Great House, and whatever Ramses may have suspected, he never fully knew how my mother plotted to place me on his throne. So you need only tell that to Seti-Keph, and all his liking for me will not stop him from sending me back to the Great House in chains."

She was weeping now. "No—no—why did you tell me?"

"Because my life is not mine any more," Moses blurted out. "It is yours. And if you can't trust me, I don't want to live."

"I forced you to tell me. I am wicked and deceitful!"

"I told you because I wanted to tell you, Merit-Aton. My whole life is yours. Do what you wish with it."

Then he took her in his arms and he wondered how it could be that when all his life he had looked at women, he had never truly seen one before. He was at an age when love is pure and wonderful, a sweet well of limitless strength and a guarantee of power beyond death and life everlasting. The miracle of his being alive struck him like a revelation, and for the first time he felt that he wholly understood the meaning of all existence. His emotion was so true and singular, so far as he knew, that he firmly believed that, in all of man's existence, no one else than perhaps the woman held in his arms had ever experienced its like. The two dark mirrors of her eyes, filled with her own tears of delight and apprehension, told him his own thoughts; and their communion was that instantaneous merging of self that occurs in the moment two people conquer and surrender simultaneously—and which can only happen wholly to the young in years. For the essence of it is a simplicity that no one carries into his later life, as Moses would come to know.

After the first embrace and the first touch of their lips, they took their purity gently in hand, carrying it like a fragile object between them. With only their hands touching, they went to the edge of the escarpment and stood there in silence, staring at the star-swept desert sky and the glittering black ribbon of the Nile in the valley below—and reviewing the wonder of their very existence.

For a long time, they remained in their silence, until Merit-Aton whispered, "Moses, my beloved Prince of Egypt, when did you know?"

"The moment I saw you."

"Truly?"

"Truly, I think," he replied. "I am so filled with something like truth that I couldn't lie to you."

"And it happens that way. I thought it was only in the old tales that such things could happen. My mother would read such stories to me when I was a little girl, but when I became older I learned that her marriage to my father was arranged before they ever saw each other. They have been happy, I suppose, but could they understand what happened to us tonight?"

"No one could understand it," Moses said softly. "I have told you nothing of myself, yet you understood me—and I know you, Merit-Aton, as I know my own soul." Then, with a sudden note of fear, he cried, "You are not promised?"

"I? No—no, who would betroth a son to the daughter of the evil Aton-Moses? And my name, will I lay it aside?"

"Not for me, never, my beloved—never. And I have no

father or mother to give my hand away——" He held out his broad, long-fingered, sunburned hand. "It is mine to give as I please. Will you have it, Merit-Aton?"

She took his hand and pressed it to her lips. "Thus we are betrothed," she said, smiling at him.

"It is still for your father to say? It is."

"My father," she said gravely, "loves me so, he would give me his own life, if I asked it. Shall he deny me a prince of Egypt who is so tall and pure and beautiful?"

"I am not pure," Moses cried, ready to bare every indignity of his life and to demonstrate how wretched his soul really was; but she put her fingers to his lips.

"No—how could you know your own purity? Would you be a man if you did? It shines on you and from you, like the golden collars and the red rubies you wear. I saw it the moment you appeared——"

"And yet you accused me?"

"I was afraid. Oh, my beloved, think of me here, and a golden prince rides up in a burnished chariot. Is it any wonder that I was afraid?"

Her way of speaking, peculiar to Upper Egypt, and strange and antique to Moses, caused him—under the spell of the moonlight and his own emotion—to look upon her with a reverence and delight that was quite obvious. She touched his cheek with a little gesture of pleasure, the matching of his delight with hers. . . .

So did a moment of indescribable glory touch him. Who is to say that any truer knowledge ever comes to a man? And if the secret of man that makes him man is love, then the single complete knowledge of it is never forgotten. In the warm balm of the wind blowing from the south, they wandered in each other's hearts and through all time. There

was so much that they had to say and exchange, and however much their separation from the reality, they could not
lose the knowledge that the army marched the following
day. She told him of her life, her dreams and innermost
thoughts, of the strange people of so many lands who
sought out her father here in his retreat, of her growing up
with a fantasy of how love would come and with the realization that it would not come. And he, in turn, told her
of his childhood and youth in the Great House, of his
mother, Enekhas-Amon, of Amon-Teph, of his going into
the marshes of the Delta with Neph, of his night-battle with
Ramses-em-Seti, of his horse, of all the adventures of
youth—and all of them were wonderful to her. Only the
truth of who he was, he could not reveal, assuring himself
that there would be time for that and putting aside the one
area of fear that he could not overcome.

So the hours passed, until suddenly the setting moon
returned to them and awareness of time. "Half the night is
gone," she said. "In a few hours, it will be morning." "But
what will you tell them?" "It is for you to explain," she
answered gently. "Talk to my father as you would to me.
He has seen so much suffering that there is no room left
in him for anger or intolerance. And he loves you for what
you are."

"You love me," Moses smiled. "How can you talk for
him?"

"I saw it in his eyes."

"But if he sleeps now?"

"He doesn't sleep. How would he sleep before his
daughter or one of his guests? If I know him, he won't
sleep at all, but he and Seti-Keph will talk the night
through. Never were there two men more different, for my

father will step aside rather than crush an insect under his foot, and Seti-Keph lives only for war and butchery—as you will, my darling. If only you could remain here!"

"If only I could," Moses nodded. "But I will come back. Nothing can touch me now and nothing can hurt me now. You understand that?" She nodded. He took from his little finger a ring of filigree gold, with a tiny scarab of jade set into it. "This was my mother's, and this is the royal scarab that a princess of the Great House wears. I set no store on that, but it was worn by the only other woman I loved deeply, with all my heart—and therefore you must wear it."

She took the ring, bowed slightly and formally, and said, "I thank you, O Prince of Egypt, and I will honour the ring with my love for you. Sleep well for what is left of the night, my beloved." She turned to go, and when he would have gone with her, said, "No—let me go alone, Moses. So my father will see us alone——" And then she was gone in the night, leaving him to awaken slowly from his own dreams. He had never known that this was what they meant when they spoke of love between man and woman, and he considered himself as someone dead who has miraculously awakened. He was filled with an awareness he had never experienced and with understanding he had never possessed before. His heart went out to his mother, for he knew her now and felt her now, and in the same way his heart went out to others who had loved him and whose love he had not been able to return.

[14]

A LITTLE AFTER THIS, as Moses approached the verandah of the house, he heard Seti-Keph and his host talking, and a momentary feeling of fear and guilt made him hesitate. Having heard the first few words, he found himself unwilling to go forward and unable to retreat out of hearing. With the moon down, he himself was evidently invisible, and he could distinguish the two men only as dark forms against the white stone.

A querulous note in his voice, Seti-Keph was saying, "All of us guess at this and that, but if you were to ask me how Hatti wars and how Babylon wars, I could tell you. I can tell you when a chariot can be used and when it is a, deathtrap. I can tell you where to put your bowmen and where to put your spearmen. I can tell you the precise number of paces to a roving shaft from a laminated bow and a roving shaft from a cedar bow. And I can tell you when a spear should be thrown and when it should be held and when it should be stocked in the ground. This is my work, and I know. I don't say—I guess, I think, I hope. I don't say that——"

"You are not a doctor," Aton-Moses sighed.

"And if I were——"

"My dear old friend," Aton-Moses interrupted gently, "if you were a doctor, you would be a better one than I. No—no, don't stop me. I know that. I know my own limitations, and I know you, Seti-Keph. You are my friend. How many friends are we granted in this little space of time we walk on this earth? And I am doubly unfortunate, for those I love come by and pause only briefly. Perhaps for that reason I must know them better and more quickly than another man—and I think I know you. That is why we open our hearts to each other and we uncover our souls almost carelessly, as it were—only such things are never done carelessly, are they? You are a very great man, my dear friend, for you walked out of the black mud and made empires bow down before you—and never did you go mad for power, as so many conquerors do. That is why I spoke to you plainly and bluntly and told you the truth. The bond between us is an ability to face the truth. And yet when I vouch for the truth, I can vouch only for what I know."

"You know more than you are willing to say," Seti-Keph's voice came petulantly.

"No. No, my dear friend. How far can I go alone in this thing called medicine? There was a time, eight hundred, a thousand years ago, when we Egyptians were beginning to evolve a study of medicine that would have made mankind's life very different had it continued. But it did not continue. Something happened to us, and for centuries no one dared shatter another image or open another closed door. The old scrolls were copied over and over and over, until they became ritual magic instead of knowledge and science. Only when the God-King whose name you on the Delta have made a curse—only when he came to the throne and when Aton was worshipped, did we begin to inquire again. My grandfather was a doctor, as was my father, and there was a brief flash of glory which is over now. The little I know—well I guess and I speculate; what else? My father was the first man in Egypt to whisper that perhaps the heart is a pump, and that endlessly it pumps the blood through our veins. I also believe that—but why the blood spurts from one vein and flows from another, I do not know, as I do not know what makes the heart beat and what stops it from beating. For thirty-five years, I have been putting my ear to the human chest and listening to the heartbeat. This, my father taught me—always the heartbeat, for there is the centre of life as we know it. So I came to know the beat, and when a man whose beat I knew died, I would go to the embalmer and examine the heart when he removed it. Later, here in my home, I set up my own operating room, and when Libyans and Kushites and poor peasants who cannot afford to be embalmed for that life eternal the priests promise us died here, I would open their bodies myself. In time, I found certain changes I could detect and connect with certain types of heartbeats—one in particular being a weakness in the great vein that leads from the heart. Under certain conditions, this will burst. You tell me of pains in your chest—and of one terrible pain that racked your whole body a year ago. And I say—all I can say without looking into your body—that the weakness is there. You must avoid excitement, stress and, of course, the awful fury of battle. If you do not——"

"I will die. You can say it. You ask a soldier to avoid battle and excitement. And if we were to go into battle tomorrow, would I die?"

"Perhaps. I don't know, but a violent effort——"

"Ah, why am I angry at you?" Seti-Keph said. "Why not at myself—and I suppose that's where my real anger is. Only, one never expects the dark gods of death so soon. One expects them to come when beckoned—and in one's own good time. After I have finished my tomb and chosen my embalmer and written my will—ah, well. Tell me, old friend, do you believe this after-life business?"

Standing in the darkness, waiting for the reply perhaps more tensely than the Captain of Hosts waited, Moses' thoughts were a turmoil of conjecture and sorrow. Death as well as love graced this beautiful house, and so it was with life and living, a meaningless labyrinth of the tragic, the comic, the ugly and the splendid.

The moments passed. Aton-Moses was not given to glib unguents, and when finally he said, "Who knows?" his voice was flat and sad.

"I don't want to live for ever," Seti-Keph mused. "It would become a bore and a damned burden. It's just another year, another floodtime, one more project finished. You don't like to stop in the middle of what you are doing, and there are always a few things you should have done that you just never got around to. Ah. well, no use brooding about it at this hour. Sleep, my friend?"

"Go ahead, Seti-Keph. You know your room?"

"Even in the dark."

"I am not tired. I'll wait for the prince of Egypt." Again, a long pause, and Moses felt the nervous anticipation of one who expects to overhear talk about himself. But if there was such talk, it bad taken place already, and Moses saw the dark shadow that was Seti-Keph lift himself tiredly from his chair. Aton-Moses also rose, and when Seti-Keph had gone, the physician walked down to the balustrade that separated the terrace from the edge of the cliff and stood there, contemplating the black river gorge. At Moses' step, without turning, he said,

"It has been a long and late night, O Prince of Egypt. For you, I think, a happy one—for me——"

"I have imposed upon your hospitality, Aton-Moses, and kept you awake as well."

"No—I don't think a guest can ever impose upon his host, for we are only whole and human when we open our doors to a stranger." Now he turned around to look at Moses, and looking at him, waited. Not knowing what else to say or how to say it better, Moses plunged to the point, telling him,

"I love your daughter, sir. I love her with all my soul and being, and she is the first I ever loved in all my life. I don't know how to describe what I feel for her. The only thing I can say is that I love her." He finished hopelessly.

"Well?" Aton-Moses asked, not unkindly yet not warmly.

"I ask you for her hand in marriage, Aton-Moses."

"Oh?" The doctor looked at Moses thoughtfully, and Moses wished he could see the man's face more clearly than the darkness permitted. "And is it thus that you woo all maidens, Prince of Egypt, in a few hours as you pause on a journey?"

The blood rushed to Moses' face, and such was his sense of outrage and injustice, the accusation breaking as it did into his transport of purity and dedication, that he could hardly reply at all and only manage to say, "It's not—no, I never wooed another—never!"

"Then I misjudged you," Aton-Moses said carefully. "You must understand, O Prince of Egypt, that the circumstances here are unusual. You come from the cosmopolitan centre of the world, from a great court and palace where all the sophistication man knows has been put into a way of life. And from what I hear, the Great House of Tanis is hardly a place where decency or integrity are the rule; quite to the contrary—I have been assured that there is no iniquity man discovered or devised that is not practised at the Great House, and that no woman, black, white or brown, is safe from the maniacal lust of its master. To you, having lived your life there, those practices may be a matter of course and hardly worth commenting upon, but we in Upper Egypt have different standards of judgment, and there are still a good many of us who feel neither love nor reverence for the God-King. Here, on the other hand, is my daughter, who lives in this lonely and forsaken place—and lonely it is, no matter how many sick find their way here for treatment—and whose best company of her age has been her dreams. Then, one evening, a tall prince rides up to her door. What would you expect, Moses? What would you expect?"

Still smarting from the challenge to his integrity, still writhing with indignation, Moses answered hotly that he had not created the Great House or the conditions there. He was in love for the first time in his life, and he was in love, purely and forthrightly.

"And is love so light a matter, Prince of Egypt, that it can flower in a few hours?"

Moses said that he was not able to put what had happened to him into words. How could he say what he felt in words? "But when I saw her, I knew," he told the physician. "Would a year, five years have increased my knowledge? Do I mean evil to you, Aton-Moses? I would lay down my life for your daughter—and for you, too; for it was here in your house that I found my life for the first time."

"How old are you, Moses?" the physician asked.

"I will be nineteen in half a year."

"Yet in the Great House, as I understand, a prince is betrothed in his childhood."

"My mother would never permit a betrothal to be pledged for me."

"May I ask why?"

The silence lengthened as Moses stood there.

"You will not tell me why, but you ask me to believe you on faith?"

Suddenly, Moses was tired, and his own life, as it seemed to him now, was a tangled skein of misuse, misdirection and misbegotten hopes and dreams. He sounded very much a boy, a frightened and troubled boy, as he said to Aton-Moses,

"It is a long story and the night is late. I told some of it to Merit-Aton. I think I must tell all of it to you."

The note in his voice touched the physician, who said, "Only if you want to, Prince of Egypt."

"I want to, and I must."

"Then come and sit and rest yourself—and if we don't sleep this night—we will sleep on other nights when we cannot talk."

The sky in the east was pearl grey, with a thin edge of pink showing above the desert rim, when Moses had finished speaking. He told the whole story now, leaving nothing out, told of his birth and who he was. Not once had the doctor interrupted him. Finished now, Moses wondered how it was that he felt calm and undisturbed; for be was not at all certain that he had not, in the telling, lost the woman he loved.

For at least ten minutes after he had finished, they sat in silence, watching the beautiful birth of the new day. When at last Aton-Moses spoke, his voice was tired and gentle.

"I have many secrets, Moses. Every physician has. No one will hear this from me—not my daughter, no one. You are a prince of Egypt, and who knows but that if your poor mother had seen her dream and you had mounted the God-Throne, we would not have light and justice in our sorry land once again? Who knows? It would be pleasant to believe that Aton, who will soon rise above the horizon, plans and orders these matters, but I am afraid the sun is as little concerned with our affairs as we are with the insects whom we thoughtlessly tread on. Or so it has seemed to me. Now, I think this, my son. You will go this morning in the next hour, for Seti-Keph is determined to depart early, and it is better that you don't see my daughter now. Three years is for ever to youth, but it passes. Yes—more quickly than you imagine. You will be a man grown then, and there is much you will have learned, good and evil. If you still feel then as you feel now, come to us, and if my daughter loves you, you can join hands in marriage."

"Three years," Moses said hopelessly.

"Yes—but it will pass. It's the only way, Moses."

[15]

THE MARCH OF the army to the south began again, and after a dozen days of the increasing heat and blazing sun, the flies and the oozing, drying mud, the rocking, bumping chariot—the white house on the cliff became as blurred and indistinct as the rest of the past. As much as Moses attempted to retain the memory in a pristine vision of all he had seen framing the lovely woman to whom he had pledged himself, it faded and became confused in retrospect. Only the flood of wonderful and pure emotion that had passed between them stayed intact—and indeed became clearer and more precious during those nights when he lay upon his back before sleep, watching the starry magnificence of the desert sky.

And yet they went on, and the dozen days became twenty and thirty, and the soft Nile mud hardened and then crumbled into a powder that rose about them in clouds, coating skin and horse and chariot, irritating the lungs and the already frayed nerves of men who began to believe that they had marched for ever, out of the world and beyond the world—into the vague nothingland of the dead. And were it not for the presence, always beside them, of the cool and familiar Nile, they might well have taken leave of their senses. They reached the Second Cataract and the Third Cataract, great stretches of jagged rock where the tranquil river became a foaming, churning torrent, and where the slaves had to remove both boats and baggage from the river and transport them overland to a point above the rapids. At each cataract, this process would require extra days, and the angry, heat-tortured foot-soldiers cursed and grumbled because they were drafted to work with the slaves.

Now the heat increased to a point where Seti-Keph ordered night marches on those nights when the moon was in the heaven—and this was better, for the men could sleep during the day in the shadow of the jagged rocks of the river valley.

Never had Moses imagined that this was the face of war, this interminable and awful marching or crawling, as it so often became, a whole day taken to move the army five miles—nor could he believe that anything worth fighting for might exist in this stark and terrifying desert, where all life ceased a dozen feet from the river gorge. As with so many others in the army and in spite of his recent exultation, he found himself becoming increasingly depressed and short-tempered with the heat, sand and monotony—given to long spells of silence and short, bitter retorts. There had been forty priests with the army, but weeks past they had decided to remain at the southernmost temple of the gods of Egypt, a small and ancient building dedicated to Amon in remote antiquity, and now the army marched in a wasteland where the gods of Egypt had no power. This sense of being forsaken combined with the heat and monotony, and tempers flared and blood was spilled daily. Sokar-Moses and his black bullwhip flayed the column like a vengeful fury, and where there were quarrels, he was merciless, not caring to hear any of the background of the dispute, but making it plain that they would fight Kush and not each other.

Perhaps more than others, the mercenaries suffered, for they had come so far that all hope of ever again seeing their homelands disappeared; they would group together and sing sad songs of the cool and lovely memories they cherished—and listening to them, Moses would reflect increasingly on the grand madness of this game of war that kings played. On his part, the situation with Nun had worsened, and he found his toleration for the slave turning to hatred. More and more implicit was the promise of murder in the looks they exchanged. If they had spoken little before, they spoke hardly at all now, Moses only to give an order, and Nun to grunt a reply.

Now the river turned north and east in a great bend, and the feeling that they must march double and triple distance increased the bitterness and depression among the men. For weeks, they had marched where there was no life except for vultures and lizards; the unvarying ration of hard, dry bread was no longer enhanced by fruit and fresh meat purchased from peasants, for there were no longer peasants or villages or fruit trees, not was there a piece of grass upon which an animal could graze. Here, instead of flooding, the river foamed and roared through a channel gouged out of the desert, and while the desert could not conquer the river, neither could the river give life any real foothold upon the desert. In the whole army, there was not an ounce of surplus flesh left; the men were hard and dry and bitter and even the horses had become skinny. When Seti-Keph took his chariot down the line of march, he nodded in grim approval, for he knew that men in such condition will fight like devils, and with the strength of devils, for little or nothing at all.

They turned south again, and when they passed the Fifth Cataract, the landscape began to change. For weeks they had been mounting slowly towards the tableland of Kush, and now the ascent increased a little. The river ran more smoothly now, and when they had passed the legendary Sixth Cataract, it seemed they had once again found the River Nile of Egypt. Slowly, almost imperceptibly, the desert landscape was changing. It was no longer the hellish, sun-seared rock-and-sand surface that they had gazed upon for weeks and weeks. Little clumps of dry grass appeared. The dawning and sunset were softened by a flow of violet and pink colour, and now and again they saw in the distance herds of delicate gazelles that bounded away like feathers on the wind. It was still dry and arid country, but the days were not so hot as they had been and the nights were cool enough for a man to wrap himself in his cloak before he slept. The prevailing wind was from the south, and it had a sweet, clean taste to it.

It was now that Seti-Keph told Moses to leave the host of Hetep-Re permanently and to join him in the vanguard. Moses was glad enough to go, for the march had removed from Hetep-Re the few graces he possessed and had turned him into a snarling and bitter man—who pressed his prerogative of intimacy with Moses to the breaking point, making remarks of envy and malice so frequently that Moses wondered whether he was not intent upon provoking a quarrel between them. The truth was that physically the march was less trying for Moses and Nun than for many others. Not only were they possessed of excellent health, but they had youth and strength beyond ordinary measure—and this was gall and wormwood to men like Hetep-Re, who suffered not only the despair of wanderers beyond the age when wandering brings any fulfilment, but physical anguish as well.

Moses was astonished to see how apparently untouched by the march Seti-Keph was. Evidently, he bad long since mastered the art of conserving his strength, and though he had shared all the rigours of the journey, including a diet in no way different from that of his men, he appeared cheerful, rested and relaxed. He greeted Moses with the royal salute, touching the fingers of both hands to his eyes, and cried out warmly,

"I find you in good case, O Prince of Egypt! Do you still like our way of life—the butcher's market of warfare, as they call it?"

"I like it well, Seti-Keph, and I have had plenty of dust and mud and heat, but I have yet to see this butchery you all talk about."

"You will have a bellyful of that, never fear. But between the two, it is the march that takes a measure of the man more than the battlefield. It is one thing to go berserk with a sword in your hand, but something else to keep your senses during the sixty days we have just seen. I like your way with dirt and monotony, Prince of Egypt, and now I want you alongside me with your chariot, as part of my own staff."

Overwhelmed with joy and pride, Moses protested that he had done nothing to earn this honour; but Seti-Keph assured him that there would be time enough. And turning to Sokar-Moses, whose chariot paced his on the other side, he asked whether his opinion was shared?

"He's young but promising," Sokar-Moses answered drily.

"How have your chariot and horses fared?" Seti-Keph asked.

"Well enough. The horses are skinny, but their feet are good."

"Tomorrow, we will encamp and rest for three days," Seti-Keph told him. "We will hold a war council, and you may join us, Prince of Egypt. The chariots will be repaired and checked and the horses will be turned out to graze— even this dry grass will be a healthy change from the small measure of grain we have been feeding them. For in so far as there is a boundary or measure to the Land of Kush, you might say that now we have entered it."

[16]

ON THE AFTERNOON of the second day of the encamp-ment, one of the sentries, who were stationed in a circle around the encampment, each of them some four hundred paces out on the plain, sounded the call to arms. Moses, running to be with Seti-Keph, saw Nun racing in from the plain with the team of chariot horses, astride of one and leading the other—and, even in the excitement of the

alarm, had to reflect upon the coolness and efficiency of
this Bedouin slave who hated him so. While Nun harnessed
the team, Moses, armed with spear and shield, took his
place alongside Seti-Keph and his staff, ready to fight on
foot and without armour if what was approaching descended upon them too quickly. The whole encampment
was in turmoil, captains gathering their hosts for action,
officers roaring orders, men shouting with sheer excitement and release from the unbroken tension of months of
journeying, horses catching the excitement, rearing, back-
ing, sending their own nasal trumpeting into the wind—
and among Seti-Keph and his staff, a calculated and cool
observation of what the sentry had sighted.

"It's no army," Sokar-Moses finally decided. "What do
you think it is, Seti-Keph?"

The Captain of Hosts, shading his eyes and squinting
over the plain, shook his head impatiently. He leaped on
to a chariot, that he might see better, and then be said, "I
know what that is. I've seen it before. It's a baggage train.
A big one, too. When a Kushite army moves, they carry
their supplies in this way, and here are their supplies, but
where is the army? I see half a hundred spearmen at most—
and there must be ten times that number of bearers in the
baggage train." He jumped to the ground, his short, muscular body throbbing with energy and excitement, and
flung his orders in staccato rapidity: "I want two hundred
chariots ready to action—fanwise, fifty on the left, fifty on
the right, the rest clear at the centre, five abreast! I raise
both arms—it signals the whole attack, centre and both
wings to kill! I raise one arm, my left—it means gather in!
My right arm for the wings to move out to circle! Let the
foot-soldiers and the rest of the chariots stand to case and

wait orders. But keep all chariots in the clear. Meanwhile, Sokar-Moses, Atepher, you—you and you"—pointing to officers—"come with me. Shields but no spears. And Sokar-Moses, take twenty archers of Hatti and have them string their bows and stand ten paces behind us. If any weapon is lifted to us, let them shoot that man down."

Moses was impressed by the speed with which Seti-Keph's orders were obeyed, the ability of the Captain of Hosts to make decisions which appeared to require almost no thought or considered judgment. For himself, he was pleased to be with the commander, and it was with pride and pleasure that he accompanied the group of officers forward to meet whatever was coming. By now, Moses could see the approaching men clearly and his pulsebeat quickened when he realized that they were truly enough the black men of Kush.

First, at the head of the long column, marching in two files, were the spearmen, tall black men with high bonnets of feathers, yellow leopard skins cast across their shoulders, carrying round shields that were painted white, and seven-foot spears. Behind them and between their files, two black men bore a litter, and upon this, under some sort of hood or shade, a child or a woman seemed to be sitting. Moses could not make out which, the distance still being great, but it seemed too small a figure to be a man. And behind this litter, seemingly to the horizon, stretched four lines of black men, each one of them carrying an enormous bundle of stuff of some kind upon his head.

Walking forward with the officers, Moses tried to guess what this might portend. All his fancies of war, as it would come on this campaign, were of a sudden, howling barbaric attack, and while he knew that his concepts of war were coloured by the panoply of lies that war breeds in all ages, he could not conceivably imagine that this was a hostile force coming to attack them. He could already make out that the porters were unarmed, and now he realized that the figure in the litter was neither woman nor child, but a small and very old man. This old man sat cross-legged under a canopy of woven feathers that was supported by four rods of gold. The litter was adorned with the short, furry tails of some animal, and the old man himself wore a bright cloak of yellow and white feathers and upon his head a thin circle of gold. A gold necklace and gold brace-lets further bedecked him, but otherwise, except for his loincloth, he was naked. Both litter-bearers were huge men, taller than Moses, and they bore the litter and the old man without effort. On either side of him walked a black man, each with a leopard skin over one shoulder, each with a circle of gold for a headdress, each unarmed except for a dagger.

When the procession was about fifty paces away, Seti-Keph and his officers halted and waited—themselves about a hundred paces in advance of the encampment, and a moment or two later, the bowmen of Hatti took their places behind them. Meanwhile, one of the two men who walked alongside the litter held up his arm, giving the signal for the procession to stop. The other unarmed man shouted a series of orders in a strange tongue. The spearmen spread out, and the porters began to lay down their bundles, one against the other, directly behind the litter. The porters were barefoot and naked except for loincloths, strong, wiry black men, and as each of them laid down his burden, he made obeisance to the old man and then went to one side to squat patiently. Moses noticed that the porters each had one ear sliced away and he concluded that they were slaves, since he had heard of similar ways of marking slaves among the barbarians.

Along with Seti-Keph, who waited in curious silence, and the other captains, Moses watched the area of bundles grow, until presently it began to give the effect of a huge quilt spreading out over the plain. The black spearmen leaned loosely upon their weapons, and the two men with the litter—they were well past middle age, Moses noticed— helped the old man to his feet. His movements were the slow, arthritic movements of old age, and he winced a bit with the pain of his joints as he stood erect. He was a very old man, past eighty years, Moses guessed, his head bald under the gold crown, his skin loose and flabby. But there was an evident and winning dignity about him as he came forward towards Seti-Keph, and his toothless smile of greeting was direct and charming. He looked from face to face with the disarming courtesy of a good host, and then he spoke in a resonant and musical voice that was at odds with his wrinkled little face.

The two men who had walked on either side of his litter had advanced with him, and now one of them said, in understandable but strangely accented Egyptian,

"He greets you with the words—peace and plenty, and may your stomachs not know the pinch of hunger. It sounds strange in your tongue, but it is our greeting, our word-embrace. I am Kudelga, a prince as you would say, and this old man is Irgebayn, King of the Baynya, who are the people you call Kush."

To this, the old man listened with a sort of astonished amusement, as if he were unable to accept the fact that his own son spoke this incredible tongue; and Moses, watching the king, was in turn amused by his mixture of courtly grace and down-to-earth intimacy. Finding the old man attractive, his reaction was to wonder whether Merit-Aton and her father would also like him—such had been his reaction to many things lately.

Meanwhile, Seti-Keph had stepped forward from the others and said, "I greet Irgebayn", but with no warmth in his voice. "I am Seti-Keph," he went on, "Captain of Hosts, commander of this army, and the hard instrument of the King above Kings, the Ruler above Rulers, the God-King of the Great House of Egypt, the god whose justice is beyond all justice, whose anger is beyond all anger, and who leaves no wrong unrighted."

The son translated and the father listened, his head cocked attentively, the mischievous glint of amusement never leaving his eyes. He nodded as the titles were spelled out, and then he replied, smiling tentatively. Moses wondered whether his son did not temper the translation, for the younger man interposed,

"If you wonder about my Egyptian, great Captain, I have traded a good deal with Karnak and once even at Tanis, but you must understand that I speak your language but poorly. Our language is different—more lowly, more intimate. My father says that he honours and reveres your great king—as who does not?—but he would be speechless were he to converse with such terrifying titles. Therefore, he asks, with due respect, whether he cannot talk to you as one man to another?"

"He talks to me as the servant of the God-King, or not at all," Seti-Keph answered harshly.

Moses was at a loss to understand Seti-Keph's attitude. This was not the man he had known or the voice of the man he had known or the spirit of the man he had known. Some impossible metamorphosis had taken place in Seti-Keph; this was a harsh and brutal man who knew neither love nor mercy. On the other hand, Moses realized, the old king was no fool and he was carefully taking the measure of the man he had pitted himself against. He bowed his head in defeat and in homage, and then he talked expressively, his voice mounting slowly to the emotional pitch of rhetoric and pleading. Not knowing the words, Moses was nevertheless impressed by the very intensity of the old man's speech, by the earnest passion of his argument—and he noticed that not only his two sons, but the litter-beaters and the spearmen, were listening intently and not unmoved. When the son began to interpret, he had to control his own voice, telling Seti-Keph huskily.

"My father addresses you as the servant of the God-King, and my father says that if any action he is capable of will move you to love instead of anger, he will perform that action—yes, he will go down on his knees and abase himself before you, if by so doing the life of one of his children can be spared. So he says. You see, I call him father because his blood runs in my veins, for he lay with my mother that I might be born. But all my people call him father. In our tongue, the word is *podya* and *podya* is also the word for king. He says he speaks as *podya* but not as king, because he is an old, old man, too old to bear any title but father. He knows that some of his people are bad and wild, and he asks—Where are there a people who do not have some who are bad and wild? It broke his heart when he learned that wild young men of the Baynya went down to Upper Egypt and killed and stole—not only because they brought suffering to you, but because they brought suffering and dishonour to him. Therefore, he banished them for ever—and among our people, that is the most awful of punishments. My father also knows that the great God-King of Egypt sees and hears all iniquity, and when he heard that an army was coming to mete out punishment for what these wild young men had done, he embarked on a long, painful journey—for he is very old and very sick—in the hope that bloodshed might be averted. Now be asks you, O Captain of Hosts, what profit will come to any if our people meet in battle? Will not the mothers of Egypt weep as bitterly as the mothers of Kush? Will not the maidens of Egypt be as bereaved as the maidens of Kush? And will it bring back your dead to inflict death upon my people? I come humbly, great Captain of Egypt, but not out of cowardice, not out of fear. Egypt has warred with Kush before, and she knows well that we black folk are not afraid. But I am afraid—afraid for the children made fatherless, afraid for my own children, whom I love! So I say, great Captain, let us embrace in love and not in hatred!"

Listening to this, unaware even of the change of subject on the part of the son and listening as if the old man himself spoke, Moses felt his throat thicken and his heart went out to the wrinkled little black man. In his youthful impulsiveness, he found the arguments of the old man irresistible, and he had a sudden buoyant hope that the campaign would end right here and now and that only a matter of weeks would see him at the white house again. But there was no youthful impulsiveness in the stony features of Seti-Keph, who said coldly,

"How is it that these men who murdered and destroyed

on the sacred soil of Egypt are not handed over to me? What is this banishment? Am I being made a fool of?"

The old man's face became grave, and the last glint of humour left his eyes; Moses had the feeling that he had anticipated this yet hoped that it would not come. Now he replied slowly and earnestly, and after he had spoken a little, he gestured towards the great blanket of bundles that were spread upon the ground and here and there heaped in mounds. He began to enumerate on his fingers, watching Seti-Keph carefully and thoughtfully as he spoke, as if he could not believe that the Egyptian was unable to understand his tongue. When he had finished, he crossed his hands over his thin, loose-skinned breast, and bowed slightly.

"Were he in Egypt," his son said reflectively, as if he were uncertain that his father had taken the right tack, "he would worship the gods of Egypt and do their bidding. Here in Kush, he must do the bidding of the gods of Kush, and they would hate him were he to hand over his people to strangers. He acknowledges the truth and beauty of Egyptian justice, but he feels that we of Kush are also just. So he begs you to forgive him. Yet he knows that your God-King has been offended, and for that reason, he brings gifts which he pleads to ease the hurt. A thousand porters and a thousand bundles have marched with us, and they lie there. These gifts he humbly lays at your feet, in the hope that they will assuage your anger and the anger of your great king. We are not a wealthy people, and perhaps all the riches of our land are less than the wealth of one of your cities; but we have tried to bring gifts worthy of the God-King's majesty. Of pure gold, cleaned and hammered into strips, we bring ten thousand shekels, to measure it by your unit. Of silver bars, we bring twenty thousand shekels. Of the finest ivory from the tusks of the wild elephant, we bring one hundred thousand shekels, and of the red and yellow and white plumes of our jungle birds—they are very light, you know—we bring a thousand shekels. We bring diamonds to the weight of a hundred shekels and rubies to the weight of a thousand shekels. Of pure, fine copper, we bring three hundred thousand shekels in weight, and of cumin and coriander, a weight of two hundred thousand shekels. Of white wool from lambs and woven as fine and light as your best linen, we bring you to the measure of two thousand of your royal cubit, and of the woven cloth from the black lamb, we bring wool to the measure of three thousand of the royal cubit. We bring you a thousand tanned leopard skins and a thousand gazelle hides, soft as butter to the touch. We bring you the honey of the wild bee to the weight of five thousand shekels—and lastly (for my father urged that this be spoken last) we lay at the feet of your God-King ten thousand pearls, in colour from pink to white, and in size from the size of a lentil to the size of the end of my thumb. These pearls are the bulk of the sacred treasures of our gods, and as insular as we are, we know that one of these pearls, one small one, will buy ten slaves or a fine iron sword of Hatti. Our priests give them to you as an offering to the gods of Egypt—in the hope that they will look kindly and with love upon our gods."

He finished the accounting and spread his hands before him, palms up. At first, Seti-Keph and his officers stood in silence; for even Moses, who from his childhood had been taught that wealth was of small matter and who had come to know that his own wealth was almost beyond measure, was amazed and astonished at the magnificence of these gifts. It gave him some inkling of how desperately they desired to avoid war—and also, for this was obvious, how far they would go to avoid meeting the Egyptian army in battle. Was the result then preordained, he wondered? Here was Seti-Keph with only fifteen thousand men—and a staggering distance from the southernmost cities of Egypt; surely a people who could provide such a gift could also do battle with an invader and drive him back! Yet it was obvious that they doubted the issue, while Seti-Keph was without doubts, for he replied harshly,

"Is this how you measure the justice of Egypt, by bribes and petty gifts? My God-King could open one store-room in his great house and reveal more than this! Do you take me for a fool that I can be bought so cheaply?"

The son translated, his voice sombre and full of defeat, and when the old king heard the verdict of Seti-Keph, his face contracted in sadness and hopelessness. His words were slow and heavy as he answered, and his son asked,

"Is not peace the measure of justice and love?"

"For a soldier," Seti-Keph said dryly, "it is honour that must be measured, not love, and we have come to teach Kush to be humble, not to be generous. Therefore, I take these things not as gifts, but as the spoils of war—and as for your father, he is my prisoner to do with as I think best!"

"No—no!" the son cried. "For myself and my brother, yes, but my father is an old man and he came to you of his free will. How can you say that he is your prisoner? You spoke of honour, which you Egyptians hold so highly——"

"Enough of that!" Seti-Keph shouted.

The other son, who had remained silent until now, dropped his hand to his dagger; and Sokar-Moses, in a single swift motion, drew his sword and cut him down. The interpreter reached for his own dagger, but Seti-Keph, moving with a speed Moses would not have believed him capable of, plunged his dagger into the black man's heart. It had happened so quickly that the spearmen had not yet reacted—but the old king stumbled forward and fell upon his son's body, caressing his face and weeping like a little child. He had not long to weep. Sokar-Moses brought his sword down and the old man's head rolled upon his son's body and then on to the sand, a wrinkled little ball grinning up at the blue sky. And then, as the spearmen sounded a wild, fearful cry of hate and anger, Seti-Keph raised both arms and the archers of Hatti began to loose their deadly shafts. Half the spearmen fell before they could move from where they stood, and the others had moved only paces when the chariots thundered upon them.

For the first time, Moses saw a war chariot of Egypt in battle, and he realized why Kush would go down before this army. The spearmen made no attempt to close their shields and form a wall. Each man fought for himself, and the horses and chariots thundered over them or tore them open with the spinning axle-blades. Meanwhile, other chariots thundered after the fleeing porters, cutting them down that none should leave there with the story of what had happened.

A single spearman broke through to the officers, and as he hurtled upon them, crying his war cry, Sokar-Moses seized the man's spear and ran the point into the earth, while a dozen swords were buried in the Kushite's flesh.

FROM NUN, THE slave, as they made their chariot ready for the match, there came a comment to break the silence, "Yes, Prince of Egypt, I have seen Egypt at war, and they fight bravely and with honour," using the word *macaat*, the expression of the soul of Egypt—and smiling at Moses as he spoke. "Kill him too?" Moses' thoughts asked, while his silence defined the coils of his own agony wrapped around him. War is death, the negation of life, the violation of civilization and hope and mercy—but this was his career, chosen by the royal god. So do the gods, on earth and elsewhere, make war. Why then was he surprised? He had lost Seti-Keph, whom he would never be able to face with an open heart again, and would he not, in the same way, lose every man in this army? Until they were joined in battle, and he himself was struck down by the hand of this hateful, mocking Bedouin? Yet so savagely had every joy of life and living been crushed and dulled within him that he cared for nothing, not for the woman he had pledged his heart to, not for life and not for death.

The army marched. Seti-Keph and Sokar-Moses, fierce and implacable men now, had put down and settled an angry situation among the officers, who wanted to parcel out this first spoil among the ranks. It would go to the God-King, Seti-Keph decided. Were they fools to dream of taking what was signed and deeded to him? Did they think that because they were so far from the Great House that the Great House had ceased to exist? Did they imagine that if they stole the fair spoil of the king that no one in the army would speak the truth to the God-King one day?

So the goods were loaded into empty supply boats and sent down the Nile. The dead of Kush were left lying on the plain, and the army advanced. But now they advanced in battle order, and from hour to hour and from day to day they looked for the hatred of Kush to appear before them. In spite of the speed of the chariots, a handful of the thousand porters had escaped, fleeing into the wild river gorge and hiding themselves in rock clefts until darkness fell. Their feet would be winged with fear and horror, and soon enough the people of Kush would learn how their king, Irgebayn, had died.

The army marched: the best spearmen first, then the archers and slingers, then the ranks of chariots, and then the bulk of the foot-soldiers—and in the rear, the slaves and the herd of extra horses. The foot-soldiers had donned the heavy armour that was dragged up the Nile in the baggage boats, and as they marched under the hot sun, their armour and weapons burned with heat. The chariots were geared for battle, a dozen javelins racked and rattling in each one, the arrows out and ready to hand, the big laminated bows waiting to be strung. The whole army became tense and silent, an ominous and oppressive mantle upon them that would be lifted only when they were released from themselves, their fears and their own dark thoughts.

So they moved southward, day after day, and day after day they ascended the slope to a great tableland. Clump grass, dry and tough that it might exist on desert fare, became greener and more abundant—and presently the clumps became patches and the patches broad stretches of rippling grass. The nights became increasingly cool, and every so often in the daytime they would see high white clouds laced across the sky. Trees began to appear, at first only an occasional twisted desert shrub, then taller single trees, and then stands of trees. They saw herds of tiny antelope in the distance and large flights of birds would appear out of the south and circle above them. They sent out a hunting party once, but the little antelope were too fleet to be approached, and once, when a lordly, black-maned lion and three sleek lionesses stepped out of a thorn thicket to observe the army, the captains pleaded with Seti-Keph to allow a lion hunt; but he would do nothing to break their ranks or halt the even progress of their march.

Moses bad never seen country like this, and in all Egypt there was nothing to approximate it—its great stretches of fertile plain, its cool winds, and its faint backdrop of purple mountains, far to the south. It broke through his depression, for it was a country to rejoice the heart and soul of man.

It also gave Moses a sense of the insularity of Egypt. They who spoke so glibly of ruling the world had only the vaguest notion of the world. Even the monstrous betrayal of Seti-Keph became petty brutality in this enormous expanse—and the sight of the mountains, still so far away, gave indication that this too was only the beginning of something far larger....

And then one morning, as the army began its march, they saw the enemy—far and small in the distance.

[18]

AFTERWARDS, MOSES TRIED to remember—but could not—who it was had told him that no one person sees or directs a battle. A general may begin it with order and precision, and after the heat and fury have begun to wane, he may, if fortunate, gather the strings of organization to-gether again; but battle itself is a hell unto itself, and no man, but fear and fury alone, rule it. Battle is a spasm, a seizure, a fit of madness sanctioned and legalized for the victor and punishable upon the vanquished as the victor sees fit. Battle is all that man is not and was never meant to be, and when he enters battle man becomes something awful, less and more than the pattern that made him man.

Kush came to battle with grief and hate. While they were still in the distance, and Seti-Keph was coolly and methodically marshalling his order of defence and counter-attack, Moses heard their cry. It was like no human sound he had ever been witness to before. It was a deep, vibrating roar of rage from thirty thousand throats, and it boomed like a terrible drum. He heard their war drums too, a low and frightful pulse, but the roar of human rage sounded above the drums and blanketed them and cried death to the skies and the distant horizon. So awful was the cry that Moses believed that if there were birds in the sky, they would have been struck dead by it. Never before had Moses heard or imagined such a sound, but on many a night to come, it would wake him from his sleep, sweating and sick with the same fear he felt when he heard it first.

Were they all afraid—these soldiers of Egypt—as he was afraid? His chariot, in the guard of Seti-Keph, was being drawn by the trotting horses to the close flank, and the other chariots, host by host, were drawing away eastward across the plain, a curving flank like a scythe flung back for the reaping. His driver, Nun, did not appear to be either afraid or disturbed, swinging his horses in position care-fully and intently, looping the long thong of his bronze chariot hammer around his neck, where it would be to hand if he was called on to beat off an attack.

Could Seti-Keph be afraid, so intent on his work as he thundered back and forth across the front in his gleaming chariot? His plan of battle was simple, direct and obvious. Two lines of heavily-armed spearmen were forming shoulder to shoulder, making a shield-wall about two hundred paces across, one end of it anchored to the edge of the rocky river-gorge, the other end reaching to the curved scythe of waiting chariots. In front of the shield-wall, the archers of Hatti and Babylon and the slingers of Canaan had taken their places, a line of them covering the shield-wall entirely. They would drive their shafts and fling their stones until the attack was upon them, and then they would fall back through the shield-wall to support it wherever it might be broken. Behind the shield-wall were the remaining foot-soldiers, each host ready under its captain. If the shield-wall held, they would wait until the Egyptians took the offensive; if the flank of the shield-wall was turned, they would extend the wall in themselves, and if the wall was broken through, they would enter the battle at the gap.

As for the chariots, they would strike the flank of Kush when the attack was joined. So Moses knew, and with Nun, he had fixed the razor-sharp cutting swords to his chariot's axles, secure in the knowledge that nothing human could stand before them. Yet he was afraid. The short, heavy javelin he held was wet in his hand and his heart hammered in his chest. He was silent, as was the whole Egyptian army, held as it were in the spell of the terrible cry of hate that came from Kush.

Kush was close now. Their front was perhaps a hundred men wide, and the black warriors had painted their faces white in their colour of mourning and death and they wore white feathers upon their heads. They advanced at a trot, their spears over their shoulders, ready to be dropped to the level when they were close enough for the final charge; and from his vantage point in the chariot, Moses could see rank upon rank of them stretching into the distance—an army so vast that it seemed to turn the show of force by the Egyptians into a pitiful mockery. And in front of the first rank, the drummers trotted, their short wooden drums slung from their necks in front, their fingers beating out a threatening tattoo. They advanced close to the gorge of the Nile, their single plan, apparently, an attempt to break the shield-wall there and go in behind it. His mouth dry, his feeling of horror and unreality ever increasing, Moses watched; and he noticed that Nun watched too, staring in silent fascination and concentration at the great river of black men.

Kush was a good three hundred paces away when the archers of Hatti began to shoot, their powerful laminated bows filling the air with a singing swarm of arrows that could be heard even above the screaming anger of Kush. The drummers fell first, and then the first rank of spearmen dropped their lances and broke into an incredibly swift run. But before they had gone twenty paces, they lay upon the ground, skewered with arrows, while the rank behind them leaped across their bodies. Now all the archers were shooting as quickly as they could lay arrows to their bows and draw and loose, and behind them, the slingers, legs spread wide, were spinning their slings and loosing a deadly hail of rocks.

The second rank of Kush went down and then the third and then the fourth; but to Moses, watching, shifting his weight as Nun struggled with the suddenly nervous and rearing horses, the charge of Kush seemed hardly interrupted, for each rank leaped over the sprawling bodies in front and each rank was coming closer. The black warriors disdained to cover themselves with their shields, swinging them by their sides to lessen the wind resistance as they ran—and now Egypt found voice and screamed back its own hate, defiance, fear and celebration of death. The two floods of voice mingled and rose to a searing crescendo, and the horses reared wildly and added their own trumpet of violent sound. The archers, loosing low and short and without aiming now, momentarily halted the charge with a squirming, bleeding breastwork of black bodies, but like a dammed river that overflows, the black men poured over their own dead and the archers threw down their bows and raced for the cover of the shield-wall. Most of them went through, but some were impaled on Egyptian spears as the shield-wall braced for the shock.

By now, Kush had lost all order; the broken lines of spearmen made no effort to form themselves; and the massive, roaring black tide hurled itself upon the spear-wall with a crash of sound that finally cemented the screaming of the soldiers into a single terrible noise.

Yet, to Moses, it retained the quality of a hideous dream, for aside from the rearing of the horses, no movement, no change, had taken place in the long half-circle of chariots that stretched from the flank for almost a mile. Apparently the black men had decided to stake all upon smashing the foot-soldiers, believing that to be central to the decision—nor could Moses imagine what might be the fate of the chariots once the footmen were destroyed.

It did not seem that anything could save them from destruction now. For just minutes, the shield-wall held— and then it bent inward like a thin sheet of copper under the hammer of the craftsman—and then it broke here and there, the screaming warriors of Kush pouring through.

That was the last impression Moses had of the battle of the foot-soldiers; for, seemingly without signal or order, the chariots were in motion. He awoke from his dream, his fear departed, the sweat on his skin was like ice. Nun was lashing the horses and shouting at them in his own Bed-ouin tongue—and far out on the plain, the whole massive line of chariots was wheeling around, using the shield-wall as a pivot, and driving in upon the army of Kush. Then Moses' area of sight narrowed. He glimpsed Seti-Keph for a moment, the little man waving a javelin above his head, and he tried to tell Nun to keep the commander in view. But no sound, no words, no meaning, could be communicated in the hellish noise of the battlefield.

His area of sight narrowed still further and his concentration mounted as the chariot thundered ahead. First, a single black man tried to spear a horse and Moses drove a javelin through his chest. Then two more, and Moses hurled his second javelin and fended the spear of the other with his shield. The man had come too close, and his howl of agony bit through all other sound as the axle-sword ripped out his guts. Nun whipped the horses, and suddenly they were within the thickness of the army of Kush with the black men on every side of them—but already the pound-ing, half-mad horses, drawing their great wooden carts, had cast their own peculiar terror before them. The black men gave back, pressed upon each other to get out of the chariot's path, and howling his own paean of excitement, Nun drove the horses over them and through them.

Hanging on to the rail of the lurching chariot with his shield arm, Moses cast his javelins into the press of bodies. He could not miss, and as they fled from the chariot, packing themselves and making themselves defenceless in their panic, he saw his heavy javelins pin two and three men together. And when another chariot sent them against him, the spinning axle-swords ripped through body, arm and leg, increasing the panic. They fled but there was no place to flee to. They fell upon the ground to avoid the terrible axle-blades, and the bronze-shod horses and the huge, bronze-bound wheels thundered over them. Some tried to fight, to spear the horses, to climb on to the tailboards of the chariots; but these men of Kush were few, and nothing to the fire of panic that raged among them. By the hundreds, they cast down their long spears, threw off their shields and tried to flee—only to come up against the thousands of their own men who had not yet reached the boundary of battle.

The chariots did not go unscathed. Moses caught glimpses of chariots turned over, of horses lying on their backs, trying to kick out of the harness—but these were few. So long as a chariot could be kept in rapid motion, it had a good chance of remaining unhurt.

As for Moses, he was without thought or fear or horror or remorse; he was without heart or soul or conscience or concern. A red flame burned in his brain, and it burned away all that he had learned and knew of love among men, all that he had learned or knew of the whole process of belonging to humankind. The words which man had made to tell his fellow man of love and hunger and need and work had disappeared, and in their place, there issued from his mouth a meaningless scream of sound that joined the other sounds of rage and anguish. He existed not to create but to kill, and every motion his lithe body made was to kill and kill and kill.

He had cast all his javelins now, thrown off his shield and seized his bow. For an instant, the chariot broke free from the crush, and lurching and jolting, raced across an open space covered with the dead and wounded of Kush. The horses, trained not to shy from the bodies of men, caught in the tension and fury, half-mad with their own fear and excitement, galloped upon living and dead alike. All around them, the chariots raced and circled and drove into the panic-mass of Kush; but for a moment, Nun drove parallel to the black men, and Moses, braced on the sway-ing chariot, loosed arrow after arrow into the dark mass. The panic reversed itself and surged toward them, and with the other chariots, they thundered through it, Moses loos-ing his arrows without aiming or thinking. Two hundred shafts were in the quivers fixed to the inside of the chariot, and Moses loosed and loosed until his arm was flayed raw, the blood running down over his bow. Both he and Nun had been wounded, but he had no memory of how and when; their bodies were coated and streaked with blood and the floor of the chariot was slippery with blood and both horses were mantled with blood and foam, but Moses felt no pain and no fear. Time had disappeared and space was shapeless and directionless. It seemed that at one mo-ment they had been in the thick of a limitless, massive and uncountable host of Kush, and then of a sudden, the great black host had broken and was fleeing in every direction, thick clumps of men at first, and then twenties and tens and then twos and threes and then a flood of panic-stricken men in flight, each for himself, spreading over the broad, grassy plain—and behind them and on them the chariots killing and killing and killing.

His arrows were gone, but the chariot thundered on to kill. The sun was overhead, so he knew fitfully, as much as he could know anything, that hours of battle had been—and motion slowed. The horses were tired. He saw a horse of another chariot go down on its knees, dying from earlier wounds, the chariot flung on its side, the men in it thrown like balls; but his thought process was unable to consider such matters. He was to kill, his long Hittite sword in hand, and Nun, his bronze hammer swinging from its bloody thong, was also to kill. They followed the men of Kush, hunting them like hares, and they killed and killed. They killed until Moses could hardly lift his arm and the horses could no longer run. They were far out on the plain now and the silence was paralysing and frightening. The battle was out of sight, and the noise of what remained of the battle came only as a murderous whisper. Here and there in the distance they saw chariots, and here and there they saw the fleeing men of Kush, but the will to kill was drain-ing out of Moses. Life and the knowledge of life was re-turning, and it welled up inside of him as sickness and nausea. . . .

The horses walked, and Nun dropped the reins and the whip and turned to face his master. He began to laugh mirthlessly, his face twitching, and without warning he swung his bloody hammer at Moses. Moses pulled away and the hammer whistled past his face, and then Moses struck with his sword, catching Nun a glancing cut on the brow, striking him full with the flat of the blade and cutting open a gash in the skin. For a moment, Nun stood there, the blood pouring down his face; then he took a step toward Moses, attempting to raise the hammer; then he stumbled, staggered and fell upon the tailboard, rolled over on to the ground and lay there. The horses continued to walk, and as the chariot moved away, Moses stared trancelike at the man he had struck down. The space between them increased. Nun attempted to raise himself, wiped the blood from his eyes and looked at Moses. Their eyes met, but Moses was without thought or reaction, empty—and bereft of hope or anger.

And then, as the chariot drew away, Moses saw a black man of Kush come staggering and running toward where Nun lay. The black man had thrown away his shield and spear, but when he saw the still-living enemy on the ground, his fear-fogged mind remembered hate and betrayal, and he drew his long dagger and raised it to kill once before he himself was killed. He saw no more than the narrow focus of fear, fatigue and hatred; he did not see the chariot or Moses—only Nun, struggling desperately to rise and defend himself.

"Let him die!" the tortured mind of Moses cried inwardly. "Let the Kushite kill him! He would have slain me, and let him die now!" What difference did it make? There was no real separation between life and death. To kill was to function. He had embraced death, and now death was a part of him. Life was worthless and cheap. Let Nun die——

So his thoughts went even as his body moved, and he sprang from the chariot and forced his weary body into a wild run. The Kushite stood over Nun, his arm lifted to strike, when Moses killed him. And then Moses let go his sword and stood weeping, while Nun watched.

[19]

MOSES TORE STRIPS from his dirty and bloody kilt and bound Nun's head to stanch the flow of blood, and the slave's eyes were puzzled and weary. "In Egypt," Nun said slowly, "the law is that when a slave raises his hand against his master, so shall the master strike off the hand; but if the slave raises his hand with a weapon in it, then the master shall strike off his head——"

"I didn't save your life to cut off your head," Moses answered in disgust.

"It doesn't matter, because Seti-Keph will do it."

"No one knows what happened here and no one will know. I thought you were clever, but you are very stupid." Nun nodded.

"Hold your head still. Why do you hate me so?"

"I don't hate you," Nun whispered. "I am cleansed of hate. It ran out of me with my blood. I hated you because you are master and I am slave, because you are prince and I am Bedouin. I hated you and envied you, but it all ran out of me with my blood. I killed for Egypt and Egypt killed for me. My heart is empty. I belong to you." And as Moses had before, he too began to weep.

Finished with the bandage, Moses sprawled back from the slave and said, speaking as he never had been able to speak before, since he too had lost blood and more than blood in the battle, "You make me sick, Nun—just to listen to that kind of rubbish makes me sick. You are a man and so am I. We have seen some awful things this day, but other men have seen worse and lived to talk sanely about it. I hate superstition and I hate your ignorant Bedouin talk. If you can't talk intelligently, as a grown man should, then keep your dirty mouth shut!"

"Why don't you kill me?" Nun muttered.

"That's just it. That's the kind of talk that makes me sick to death. It makes me want to vomit. Haven't you seen killing enough here today?" Moses pointed to the dead Kushite, who lay face-down, only a few feet from them. "Look at him—a fine, strong young man, and I killed him! Who gave me the right to kill? Who gave any man the right to kill? When I was a boy I had good teachers who taught me love and brotherhood, and they said that man was holy because god's own son came down to earth to make him holy and sacred—and look how holy and sacred he is, lying there with a sword-cut through his neck. Every vulture in Africa is here, hanging in the sky and waiting for the great feeding, and we are the dogs of the vultures. What did I have against this man, that I should kill him? Did I know him? Did I hate him? His heart was full of anger and hatred because we did a thing to his old king that even the stones and sand of Egypt will remember with shame and horror. He was right to want to kill me, for I am dirty with deceit and treachery—but why should I have killed him? How many we killed today! Can you remember? Can you count? Look at my bow-arm—how the skin is flayed off it, my string-guard whipped to shreds! Two hundred shafts I let fly today—and how many women will weep and how many children go hungry because the Prince of Egypt went to war against Kush? *Macaat* we were born with and lived with—I spit on it! And you—you ignorant, superstitious, wretched Bedouin—you lie there and whimper for me to kill you!"

Convulsively, his whole body racked with sobs, Nun wept; he wept like a little boy whipped unjustly yet uncertain of his own innocence.

"Kill you!" Moses cried. "In all my life, I had no friend of my own age—never, and I said to myself, this slave will become my comrade and we will know each other! There is my shame. A prince of Egypt said that because he was alone and afraid—and you tried to kill me! Why?"

"I don't know, master," Nun sobbed. "I don't know. I don't know. I thought I knew, but I don't know." He dragged himself over to Moses, pressing his face to Moses' foot. "Forgive me, master. Forgive me."

"Don't do that," Moses cried, suddenly full of his own guilt. "Be my friend, Nun."

"I am your slave."

"I want a man, a friend," Moses pleaded.

Nun controlled his sobbing and stared at Moses. "Do you forgive me? Do you give me back my life?"

"I forgive you," Moses sighed, utterly exhausted, unable to face the thought of further passion.

"Give me your right arm," Nun entreated.

Moses nodded and held out his arm, covered with dirt and blood, the blood still oozing from cuts. Nun lifted his own right arm and pressed his open wounds to Moses'. "Now our blood is the same," he whispered. "Now we are blood brothers and there can never be hate between us. I thank you, my master, I thank you."

ONLY A HUNDRED paces away, the chariot horses had stopped, not to graze—for the beasts like the men were trembling with emotion and fatigue—but from loss of will to move; and as Moses came up to them, he wondered how the mind—if there was one—of a dumb beast reacted to the senseless carnage of this day. Blessed were the horses, if they knew no more than the whip on their backs. They were covered with dry spume and dry blood, and their legs were up to the fetlocks with blood, even as the chariot wheels were red with blood, and the same red on the now bent and broken axle-swords and over the bronze facing of the chariot itself, as if someone had painted it imperfectly in this dark and awful crimson colour.

Moses vomited. Nun, clinging to the chariot to stay erect, said, "It is all right, master; you will vomit away the sickness." Moses had not eaten that morning, but convulsively he continued to empty his stomach, staggering from the violence of his retching, and throwing the vomit upon himself. It did not matter to him; his sense of filth within and without was complete.

"Get into the chariot and ride," he told Nun at last. "I will walk."

"I will walk too," Nun protested.

"You can barely stand. Get into the chariot!" Moses ordered him tiredly.

With Nun lying on the floor of the chariot, Moses led the horses back towards the battlefield. It was well into the afternoon now, and the chariot of Moses was not the only one returning to the place where the battle had begun. All over, to his right and to his left, ahead of him and behind him, Moses saw the chariots returning. They were alike in the slowness of pace; they were alike in their indifference to each other; and even when another chariot came near his, no greeting was exchanged. The victory was sombre and heavy and without any joy; "glory" would come later— there was no "glory" now.

As Moses walked on, he saw how the dead of Kush increased, and he wondered if even one of the black men had escaped the massacre. Some of the fallen black men were only wounded, and he noticed other chariots turning out of their way to put the wounded to death. Yet his mind made no comment, no judgment, except to direct him to avoid the wounded when he saw them.

He walked slowly for a full hour before he reached the battlefield itself, and here the dead Kushites lay so thick that often the ground was covered by the piles of their bodies, and the river of blood that had poured out of them turned the hard plain into mud. Vaguely, he wondered how large their army had been. Seen in the morning, it had appeared to be at least twice the size of the Egyptian Host— but now it seemed to Moses that more than thirty thousand dead lay upon the battlefield. The first stirring of judgment made him feel that his flesh was shrinking upon his bones. His reaction was not horror; at a point during the day, he had lost all ability to know horror; it was more of a beginning-sense of the vastness of the pain and waste that had come about here on this day. Not did he condemn in his mind the thousands of Egyptian and mercenary foot-men who prowled among the fallen, turning each over, killing those who still breathed, tearing off the gold rings and bracelets and chains, decking and loading themselves with the necklaces of ivory beads, white claws, the silver girdles, leopard skins, unable to stop or contain their greed, staggering under the weight of useless spears and bullhide shields. There was a wall between himself and them; he watched them fight and squabble over the loot, and he remained indifferent.

Yet now he could not lead the horses over the bodies of the dead, nor have the chariot grind them any more. He turned here and there to find a path, and sometimes he stopped to drag the dead aside. He came to the place where the spearmen had made their shield-wall, and he felt a certain lightening of his heart at the sight of hundreds of Egyptian and mercenary dead. In proportion to the murdered army of Kush, they were few indeed, but he had felt that he could not live if Egypt had paid no price for this.

It was there that Sokar-Moses found him, and grasped his hand, and told him how thankful they would be to know that he lived. The last they had seen of him, he was driving down on Kush like some wild god of war, sowing death around him, the more glory to the holy House of Ramses. Seti-Keph had been asking for him constantly. He must now come to the commander.

"I don't want to see Seti-Keph," Moses said dully.

"I beg you, Prince of Egypt. I know what it is after a battle, and I know that this is your first battle. But Seti-Keph is dying."

"Dying? Was he wounded?"

"Not by the hand of man. He fought like a lion until the victory was assured—and then the gods of Kush struck inside of him. There was a pain inside him like his heart breaking, and we bore him back to his pavilion, where he lies now. Come to him before he dies—I beg you, Prince of Egypt—come to him."

Moses nodded silently, told Nun that he must go to the Captain of Hosts, and then followed Sokar-Moses to the pavilion they had raised for Seti-Keph. The group of officers around the couch upon which Seti-Keph lay stepped aside when Moses appeared, and Moses stood there, looking down at Seti-Keph—who now appeared very small, very old and tired. They had washed his body and covered him with a spread of clean white linen and raised his head upon soft pillows, but his face was knit with pain and the fierce bulldog look had left him. Already, his face had taken on the waxen quality of death. But when he saw Moses, he managed to smile with a strange, ingratiating warmth, and he held out one trembling hand and said,

"Give me your hand, my son," his voice barely a whisper. "Come closer to me. Hold on to me. I managed to stay until you came, but I can't stay much longer."

All the accumulated, angry, bitter resentment he had directed towards this man, who—as Moses felt—had betrayed his entire trust, melted now. Death levels and makes atonement and forgives, and somehow Moses comprehended the pitiful and ignominious tragedy of the death of this man. All the dignity the world knew lay outside on the blood-soaked battlefield where the black men of Kush had defended their land and their gods—and perished in that defence. So they were defended in death. But this small, frightened and lonely man had no defences. Even as he tried to boast to Moses of his victory, less than a thousand dead among the Egyptians and the whole army of Kush destroyed, Moses realized that his boast was empty and pathetic. He lay there, Moses' hand pressed to his lips, trying to find in this last act of tenderness towards one he believed to be a prince of Egypt, some meaning and reason, some quick, final taste of the love his life had been empty of. Born into a world from which meaning and reason had departed, he had attempted in terms of himself to make meaning and to live out reason as he saw it. By his own force of will, he had gained prestige, power and glory such as it was; and naked and afraid, he lay here now dying on the plains of Kush.

Moses understood. He knelt by the couch, and Seti-Keph whispered to him, "I saw you no more after we met the old king with his gifts. Did the act of justice frighten you, my son?"

"It was not justice, Seti-Keph," Moses answered.

"You turned your face from me. After you had become like a son to me—the only son I ever had." His eyes pleaded with Moses.

"Don't go away from me now"—a shade of a smile lighting up his face—"Moses of the half-name."

"I won't go away."

"Until the end? It won't be long. I won't keep you long."

"I will never leave you, Seti-Keph," Moses whispered, the tears running down his face.

"They told me how bravely you bore yourself in battle. I said I knew. I always knew. I knew you, Moses, my son." His voice dropped to a faint whisper, and Moses had to bend close to his face to hear his words. "I know you're not the blood of Ramses. Who are you? What is your name? Tell me, and I'll keep it secret even from the gods."

"Aton-Moses."

"Ah—like our friend the doctor. I open my heart to men

with that name. I lived as a butcher and I die with blasphemy. Do you truly believe in your Aton, my son? We are far from the gods of Egypt. Who will greet me when I close my eyes and go away? Who will say, this is Seti-Keph who was afraid to be humble and live out his life as a peasant? Who?"

Moses shook his head and Seti-Keph closed his eyes. His body stiffened and then he lay still. Moses stood up and walked out of the pavilion, nor did any of the captains there speak to him. It was in his mind now that he would go down to the river and wash the filth and blood from his body, and there he went. There he found Nun, who was washing the horses as they drank. Naked and powerful, like the very trunk and pillar of life, the Bedouin had thrown off his hurt and fatigue—and in his youth and health, he greeted Moses smilingly.

"Seti-Keph is dead," Moses said.

"He was a great captain."

"I wept for him," Moses said. Then he lay down in the cool, rushing water of the Nile and let it wash away the pain, the memory and the dirt.

PART THREE

The Wanderer

I T WAS NOT three, but almost four years before Moses, Prince of Egypt and Captain of Kush, returned to the City of Ramses in the Delta. Boyhood and youth had passed and manhood marked him. Streaks of grey appeared in his black hair, a premature greying which was not unconnected with the service he performed as a captain in the Land of Kush, and around his eyes, narrowed against the burning desert sun, tiny wrinkles began to form. As with some men, he reached his full stature as he turned twenty, and his tall, large-boned figure filled out with great strength and commanding aspect.

Already he was a maker of legends in distant Egypt, and this and that was told of him, some true and some untrue. The legends grew in a field of their own, and long afterwards it was told that in the Land of Kush he became a mighty king of a walled city, over which he ruled for forty years. It was also said that he became captain over all the hosts of Egypt when Seti-Keph died, and that he led them to many victories.

But it was the dream of others, not his, to be Captain of Hosts; and the walled City of Kush had walls of mud brick only twenty feet high. Who was to defend them when the flower of the men of Kush had perished on the battle-field? So they took the city of Irgebayn, smashing down its wooden gates with battering-rams, and what was done there by the men of Sokar-Moses is not the sort of thing anyone remembers in detail. The gods of Egypt were half a world away and the gods of Kush were overthrown and humbled.

The chariots of Egypt were stabled in the temples of Kush, and the women of Kush wept. There was a scribe in the Host of Egypt who made a song of it, but his song was neither new nor old. "Weep, O you women of Kush," said the song, "for your men have perished and your gods are humbled. Weep, for the glory of Kush is gone, and Kush is a beggar who crawls on his knees. Weep, for all the wealth of Kush has been scooped into the bags of Egypt, and only a dry bone will you gnaw. Weep, for it will take a river of your tears to wash the blood from the streets of Kush." It was a common song and without originality, but it was expressive.

It is also told in the old legends that Moses took a black woman to wife and sat her on his throne beside him; but the truth is that the women of Kush were herded into the market place of their city like cattle until they stood shoul-der to shoulder, clinging to their babes and their children, and then each man of the Host was allotted his portion to keep or sell as he pleased—even as the God-King, so far away, was also allotted his own portion, a full thousand of black women with babe and child to fare down the Nile as slaves to Ramses. But who is to say who were most fortunate, those who went or those who remained in the ruins of Kush? The Host of Egypt made the city their quarters, and a house was given to Moses and Nun, even as houses were given to the others; and to Moses, because his blood was godly, they gave Irga, a daughter of Irgebayn, to lie with him.

[2]

IRGA HAD SEEN eighteen years, but in the way of reckoning in Kush, or Baynya, as it was called by its own people, she was almost nineteen years old; for they regarded the day of conception as the onset of age. She was the child of her father's old age, the very last child to be given the spark of life from his loins. In Kush, a man took only one wife, so it was that of seven children only Irga now lived; her brothers and sisters were dead, and also dead were her father and mother. In Egypt, the breasts of a woman were often left uncovered, and in Kush, no woman covered her breasts; for they were things of beauty and who would not look at them? The beauty of Irga was the beauty of Kush. She was taller than any Egyptian woman Moses had ever seen, just as the men of Kush were so much taller and heavier of bone and muscle than the men of Egypt, and her skin was purple-black, the colour of a ripe and sweet plum. She carried her head as a swan does, and when she walked, her whole body rippled with grace and ease. She had a small, thin nose, heavy, sensuous lips, and she wore her tight-curled hair high like a crown upon her head. As with the other women of Kush, her garment was a knee-length kilt of brightly striped wool, woven as fine and soft as pure linen, and when the weather was cool, she wore a cloak from her shoulders. It was no wonder that every man in the army envied Moses his prize.

But Irga was something else, as Moses came to realize. The most revered gods of Kush were women, and the legends of Kush were filled with a yesterday when life was golden and men lived as brothers—and in that time, five women, who were called *Mganas*, ruled Kush. In the time of the *Mganas*, there was no war and no hatred, and no man lifted his hand to another. And now, in this bad time, the legend was revived, and the women of Kush called Irga *The Mgana* and they knelt as she walked by on the street. Sokar-Moses had some of them whipped, but still they knelt when they saw her.

So Sokar-Moses said to Moses, "Keep her off the streets, because the gods of Kush are dead. Next they'll decide she is divine—and that's the last thing we need. No god of Egypt would come here, this terrible distance, where we have not even raised a temple or altar—and where we have no priest among us. The Hittite soldiers are raising an altar to their Baal, but they are fools to think that the stink of burning flesh will waft far enough to be sniffed by one of the Baalim of Canaan, of whom there are as many as there are hills in that wretched little land. The Sea Rovers are whispering that the mother-goddess in Kush is the same as their Demeter, and they want to make peace between these two mother-goddesses. I won't have it! The gods of Kush are dead. I can handle living things that I can see and talk to, but I want no trouble with gods. We are alone here, almost half a year's distance from the Delta, and we have destroyed the gods of Kush, and destroyed they must remain."

He was not like Seti-Keph, either in wit or ability, and

he had a heavy, plodding manner of approach to all problems. He still carried his bullhide chariot-whip on a thong from his right wrist, and he never hesitated to dispense discipline personally. Among the soldiers, he was respected and feared, but he inspired neither love nor excitement. His attitude towards Moses was a mixture of respect and admiration, not unmixed with resentment—the respect that anyone of low birth had for a prince of the Great House, and admiration not only for the conduct of Moses in battle but the awe of the illiterate for one who could read and write. Yet he resented the haughtiness that he chose to see in Moses, and he was firmly convinced that Moses looked down upon him. Knowing his own need for financial security, his own lust for wealth to put away against an always uncertain future, he was confused by Moses' total disinterest in spoil and booty. Unable to comprehend the attitude of a man who had always been wealthy beyond measure or thought, he took this contempt for material things as a sort of insult directed against himself.

Now, Moses listened tiredly to his lecture on the gods, feeling a sense of embarrassment and disgust that was more and more becoming his reaction to this kind of childish superstition. At such moments, he would think of Amon-Teph, of Neph and Aton-Moses—and he would experience a desperate yearning for people who used their minds and their wits. He answered,

"Why don't you send her to the God-King, Sokar-Moses? Whereby you will be rid of her, and the God-King will have new entertainment for a night."

But this Sokar-Moses feared to do, for whatever Moses said, the Captain of Hosts could not believe that he would not earn the prince's hostility by removing this magnificent woman. Yet the truth was that Moses saw no woman except the one who lived in his mind's eye. His whole being was in love with Merit-Aton, who had so strongly affected the fabric of his youth and hope; and the legend that he made a wife and queen of Irga and ruled with her upon the throne of Kush was spun of the same thin tissue as most legends. The daughter of the King of Kush sat in Moses' house and said nothing, but her eyes followed him. Day after day, her silent accusation made him increasingly ill at ease. She spoke no Egyptian, and the language of the black people of Kush was so alien to the Egyptian ear, so interminably inflected and so soft in its vowel sounds—the very opposite of the consonantal sharpness of Egyptian—that no one in the army learned more than a few nouns in the Baynya tongue. So between Moses and Irga, there was no language at all.

Nun feared her. "She is black and the black ones are evil," he told Moses certainly. And when Moses asked him how he knew this quality of black people, he replied, "Otherwise, why are they black?" an argument which, in his mind, settled the matter, and he went on to assure Moses that she would seek out an opportunity, sooner or later, to kill him.

Moses shrugged this off, although he had developed an increasing respect for Nun's judgment of people. More and more were they growing together, Nun once more the confident, sardonic and infinitely capable man Moses had met in the slave market. At peace with himself, now that his vendetta with Moses had been resolved, less a slave than the vizier of the prince and the major-domo of the house, he directed servants, purchased food, and attended to all the odds and ends of the household. He had bartered with the Babylonians for one of their fringed kilts, and with his beard cut and curled and oiled, his thick black hair dressed and braided, he looked not unlike a Babylonian. His language was similar to theirs and he had an excellent ear for other tongues, having picked up during their long journey not only a usable amount of the strange language of Hatti, but a smattering of the talk of the Sea Rovers too.

Moses might have done better to heed him, for there came a night finally when the woman of Kush crept into his bed. He had been too long without woman, and for a healthy young man of his age, dreams were not enough. She came when he was half-asleep, and the pressure of her warm flesh, the scent of her body, the necessity of her trembling eagerness—as he thought—broke down all his resistance. His hands flowed over her back and buttocks; his lips met hers, and even as he kissed he felt the entering cut of the knife in his shoulder. She had misgauged in the dark, and he flung himself away with a cry of anger. In the darkness of the room, he saw only her shadow as she threw herself upon him, and it was sheer luck that he managed to grasp her wrist. Yet even then, after he had forced her to let go the knife, she fought him like a wildcat, and when Nun came running, it took the strength of both of them to subdue her.

They bound her and Nun got a lamp lit to examine Moses' shoulder. It was a deep cut, but in the flesh, and after Nun had cauterized it and bandaged it, he asked,

"Well, master, what do we do with her? Shall I lie with her and then cut her throat?"

"Stop being a Bedouin for a little while. Let me think."

"You always call me a Bedouin when I do something or say something that doesn't fit nicely with the ideas of an Egyptian gentleman and his *macaat*."

"I call you a Bedouin when you act like a Bedouin," Moses said sharply.

"And you think, master, that she performed unlike a Bedouin tonight?"

"How would you perform if you felt that I had killed your father and murdered your brothers? Sometimes, Nun you demonstrate as much intelligence as an insect." Moses took his dagger and cut her bonds. Nun said, "I thought you had come to your senses, but this——" Moses wasn't listening. Irga rose, trembling, shivering, but staring at Moses bitterly and defiantly. He pointed to the door. She hesitated a moment, and then fled into the night.

"Sokar-Moses will be confused about this," Nun sighed.

"Then let me unconfuse him," Moses said. "Just keep silent about what went on here."

"Naturally. I don't want people to imagine I'm owned by a madman."

[3]

IT WAS A strange, close and complex relationship that came into being between Moses and Nun. For Nun to love Moses as his master was impossible, for the love of a slave for his master is not in the deep and true sense of the word *love*: it is more akin to the feeling of the animal whose spirit is broken after enough beating; it is a fusion of dependence and hate and fear, and in its deep content it is always without dignity. Love only can exist without fear, and if the human soul can be purchased and sold at whim,

fear is never quieted. Nun did not fear Moses; they had
declared a truce, master and slave, and the truce would be
a long, long one; and they had an obligation to each other
that was sealed in the primitive rite of blood.

There was no moral implication in their relationship. It
had never occurred to Nun to speculate as to whether slavery was right or wrong—some men were slave and others
were free. Indeed, Moses, who had never been enslaved,
had far more disgust for the condition than Nun. He had
the free man's horror of a condition so much more miserable than his own; and, plagued as he was by the concept
of a wise creator who in his wisdom and goodness had
created all men, and taught as he had been to inquire in a
logical sense, it was Moses, not Nun, who asked himself
why this one should be slave and that one free?

In all ways, he and Nun were different, and it brought
them peace of a sort that each saw in the other what he
lacked and desired. If Nun did not yet love Moses, he
had enormous respect for him. Of the things Nun knew,
Moses was a good deal ignorant, for one had been raised
in the filth and the other in a palace; still the knowledge
of Moses was not a set thing, but a thing in motion that
filled Nun with wonder and, often enough, with terror.
He said to Moses once, pointing to one of the great mountain peaks that ranged south from the Land of Kush, "What
would one see from that high place, master?" The gods,
the Baalim, abode on the high places, as both he and
Moses knew, but Moses answered that they would climb
the mountain and see for themselves. To this Nun reacted
with terror, and pleaded with Moses not to do so and not
to force him to do so, and Nun could not fail to note how
amused Moses was with his, Nun's, concern.

Nun was ignorant and superstitious, but in one week he knew more about the Kushites and their city than Moses would ever learn, and where Moses would have starved, he could eat well. But, at the same time, he believed that it would bring worms to gnaw a man's belly if he raised his left arm and pointed at the sun at midday; he believed that salt was holy and that one must always bury a pinch in the soil before partaking of one's food; he believed that Egyptians, because they were circumcised, were swallowed at death by a giant serpent; he believed that a woman with an eye out of focus was a witch; he believed that every hill and mountain was the abode of a god; he believed that if he put his hand on another man's sexual organs, he would for ever have to obey that man's orders; he believed that all gods were born of serpents and that all snakes were holy—and the first time he saw Moses shear off a snake's head, he trembled with terror and apprehension for days— he believed that snake blood smeared on the door of a house would protect the owner of the house from evil spirits; he believed that to know the secret, forbidden name of a man would give you the power of life and death over him, and he believed that only Nehushtan knew the names of all men, and therefore had over them the power of life and death.

These were only some of the things he believed. Nehushtan was the god he bowed to, and he once explained to Moses that Nehushtan was the lord of all serpents and all Baalim, and a great serpent himself. But as to whether the Baalim, who lived upon the high places, were serpents themselves, he was uncertain, for he had been born and raised in low, flat country where no mountains could be seen and he knew of the Baalim only by hearsay. He had a notion that a Baal was in part a snake and in part a woman, a winged creature with the face and breasts of a woman and the skin and form of a serpent; but this Moses recognized as a corrupted version of a sphinx, which was one among the very ancient and half-forgotten gods of Egypt.

It was after the affair of the Kushite woman that Moses and Nun talked a great deal about these things. The Princess Irga was found hiding in a great urn in the ruins of the Kushite temple, but Moses would not have her back and Sokar-Moses was not minded to send his master, the God-King, a woman who was so quick with a knife. So he gave her to his officers, who rolled dice for her, and she was won by Hetep-Re, who had a reputation for winning at dice more often than a man should within the normal bounds of luck. Three days after that, Hetep-Re, drunk and raging at her unwillingness to become a part of his joy, beat her to death—a matter which did not enhance his reputation with either his fellow officers or Sokar-Moses.

The Egyptians buried Irga secretly, but it got out, as such things will, and the Kushite city seethed with rage and hatred for the conquerors. Egyptians were poisoned and murdered in the night, and in return Sokar-Moses exacted punishment and death, recognizing the need to impress the population anew with his power and justice. Hetep-Re, in all this, began to whisper about that Moses was at the bottom of things, that he had deliberately freed the black princess and had incited her to revolt, so that he, with her, might rule over the Land of Kush. And more than this, for Nun said to Moses one day,

"I have heard, O Prince of Egypt, that a certain captain of chariots is saying things that shouldn't be said."

"Whenever you call me Prince of Egypt with that unc-tuous Bedouin whine in your voice," Moses replied, "I know that it is some new insolence and affront."

"Well," Nun shrugged, "that's as may be. You always choose to think the worst of a kindness from a miserable slave. But the fact is that Hetep-Re is saying it would be a good thing for all concerned if you were dead."

"I don't believe that."

"No—a Bedouin is a liar, of course. Only Egyptians tell the truth."

"Stop that, you fool! He wouldn't dare."

"No? Then did you know, master, that a courier came yesterday with letters from Egypt, and that Hetep-Re seems to know that even though we have been gone from Egypt more than a year, the God-King has not forgotten you and expressed the hope that perhaps you would not return at all? And that Hetep-Re feels there might be gold and ad-vancement in it for him to make certain you do not re-turn?"

"Where do you hear all these things?"

"Slaves talk. They even talk to each other. And women talk. I'm just a dirty Bedouin slave to you," Nun smiled, "but you would be surprised at how well I get on with women."

"I wouldn't be surprised."

"Anyway," Nun said, "I think you would do well to kill Hetep-Re before he kills you."

"You think and talk very lightly of killing, don't you?"

"No more or less than others. There is a lot of killing goes on when you come down to it. I don't hold with beat-ing a slave to death. Maybe because I am a slave. But I think no one will weep if Hetep-Re dies."

"I won't have that kind of talk about an Egyptian officer!"

Nun shrugged and spoke no more, but he determined to take the matter into his own hands. There were no compunctions to be overcome by Nun; it was simply the question of preserving one life by eliminating another. The fact that he hated Hetep-Re as a man and an Egyptian made the decision less onerous, but it would have been no different if he had not hated Hetep-Re. Moses had become more than a part of Nun's life; he was the central pivot of the slave's life.

So Nun did what he had to do in the simplest and most direct terms. Unobtrusively, he watched the coming and going of the Captain of Chariots, and then late one night he waited for him. As the Egyptian passed, Nun stepped quietly behind him, hooked an arm about his neck and, with his other hand on his wrist, closed a vice that snapped Hetep-Re's neck like a reed. Then Nun let him fall to the ground, where he was found the following morning.

Nun's dread then was that Moses would know and vent his anger—or more—upon him; but Moses gave no evidence of such knowledge to Nun. And to an extent—lacking only the proof that makes knowledge absolute—Moses did know, and knew surely that no other man in the army had the terrible strength required to kill a man in such a fashion, before the victim could either struggle or resist. It was not an easy thought for Moses; the fact that he had killed in battle with his own hands did not, strangely, lessen his horror of murder; yet that horror was balanced by the awareness of Nun's devotion—a devotion both wonderful and frightening.

Nor was Moses alone in his suspicions and conclusions.

The mantle and symbol of his godliness protected Nun; but now the two of them could not live on in the city as they had before. Thus it was that Sokar-Moses had a long and serious talk with the Prince of Egypt, getting down to the fact that when a flame of this kind of trouble started, it was hard to find enough water with which to put it out. Looking at Moses thoughtfully, his heavy face troubled with need for a solution that was beyond his wit and understanding, he tried at one and the same time to talk to a prince and god—and to a man in his command. It made an uneasy combination, for while it was quite true that Ramses was not eager to have Moses back in the Delta—which Sokar-Moses knew—it was also true that the death of Moses in any circumstance which the Captain of Hosts could have prevented might well require, as a symbolic measure of justice, the death of Sokar-Moses himself. So while, as he pointed out, he could not blame Moses for killing Hetep-Re, who was not much good for anything anyway, the dead man did have friends.

Moses replied that it was not his custom to go around killing people and that he had not killed Hetep-Re. How he despised these petty plots and counterplots! Here they were, a great army of conquerors, camped in the ruins of a city of mud-brick houses and stricken, hate-filled people, with no other occupation than to pick it clean of every thing of value it contained and cultivate boredom and discontent. He sensed well how each day there would be more plots hatched, more hostility and greed and corruption—until in time it would take all Sokar-Moses' brutal discipline to keep the soldiers from destroying each other. Day by day, parties went out to raid whatever little villages they could find, but mostly the villages were empty; the people had fled, taking with them all they could carry—and leaving precious little booty. But it was not to the God-King's way of thinking that a vast army should be dispatched so far at such expense without exploiting every possible avenue to profit.

It was the beginning of Moses' wisdom that he reflected upon his growing contempt for his own species instead of giving way to it. Yet the more he saw of them, the less able was he, in any way, to admire his own kind. Greedy, lustful, treacherous, boastful, ignorant and superstitious, they were animals without the simple and straightforward dignity of animals; they killed for the simple thrill of killing. Mercy was a word without meaning to them, and honour—it had come to a point where the very word *macaat* turned his stomach.

They held a city whose young men had been massacred, and they turned it into a slave and a whore. They took children to bed with them, and they killed women as casually as men stepped on insects. Their talk was foul and unbridled, and if they had been wild men under the gods of Egypt, they were even less of mankind now that their gods were far away and powerless. They went out of their way to urinate and drop their faeces in the temple of the mother-goddess of Kush, for had they not dragged down her image and smashed it—just as they had overthrown all the other gods of Kush?

Never before had Moses seen the gods so clearly as now. Far away they were, but their image was in these men and what they did; and alone, where he could not be heard, Moses defied the gods aloud, cursed them, and challenged them to do their worst with him. "Pay for the acts of your worshippers," he would say to them. He became what the

Egyptians and their neighbours called *leshbed*, which means an enemy of the gods, and thereby a madman. But Moses was hardly mad. And when he passed by the temple of Kush and saw the wanton wreckage and smelled the foul stink of human waste, he did not pity the gods of Kush, who, be felt, were no better or worse than the gods of Egypt, but instead told himself, "Wait, you gods of Egypt, until this is done to you."

He wrapped his princely aloofness around him like an invisible cloak, and he lived with his dream of Merit-Aton; but Sokar-Moses told him bluntly, as bluntly as he could, that they were a goodly distance from the Great House. "I suppose you want to go back," he said.

Moses shrugged. His own vision was of a white house on an escarpment overlooking the high reaches of the River Nile.

"The God-King doesn't want you back—for whatever reason he has. But I suppose you know that?"

"I know it," Moses nodded.

Sokar-Moses went into details concerning the expedition and the God-King. Ramses was disappointed at the amount of loot that had been sent back to the Delta—just as the soldiers and captains were disappointed at their own share. It would be no victory triumph to return now, nor did Ramses desire the army back. The point was—here they were, and the God-King expected gold.

"I don't know what we can do about that," Moses said. "We can't make gold."

"But we can find it," Sokar-Moses said, and then went on to specify his admiration for Moses as a man of military parts, a warrior and a killer. He reminded Moses that in the one glimpse he had had of him during the great battle where the manhood of Kush perished, he had seen a veritable god of hate and fury. "Seti-Keph knew his men," he said. "How I wish he was here with me now!"

It had to be said, and this man made his point directly and thoughtlessly; and it cut like a knife through the veneer of righteousness the young prince was building around himself. It would have taken a more sensitive man than Sokar-Moses to realize how complex and deeply confused Moses was; the commander could only grapple with simple virtues, simple defects, as he saw them, and he told Moses that he understood the other's desire to return home. He could also smell the fear Ramses might well have of a son like this, a young man so tall and commanding in presence, terrible in battle, and seemingly lonely and given to brooding upon his own inner ambitions. A man who wore half of a name in defiant mystery.

"You will go back in good time," the Captain of Hosts assured him. "You have the God-King's own sentence of exile for three years, and already half of the exile is over. And believe me, it weighs as heavily on us as on you, for your godly father is bitter enough about the small gifts we have sent him."

Moses no longer bothered to deny his parentage every time it was raised, and now he answered only that all the wealth in the world would still leave Ramses bitter and dissatisfied.

"I pass no judgments on the gods," Sokar-Moses said evenly. "The God-King, however, suggests that this City of Irgebayn is not the City of Kush at all—not the city of which our legends tell, where the walls are covered with gold and where there is a statue of the mother-goddess all of gold and silver and one hundred cubits high. And much more, as you know."

"These are stories for children," Moses said. "How can you believe them?"

"I am repeating your father's words. He holds the city to be at the source of the Nile, where no man in our time has ever been—deep in those mountains to the south of us. But if we take the army there on a long chance of finding it, how will we protect our rear? And if we lose many men in the south, how do we know that we would ever fight our way back?"

"In other words," Moses smiled, "the Lord Ramses advises you to send me to the south to find a city that never existed, and if I don't return, no one will weep?"

Sokar-Moses was a direct man, and honest according to his lights. "More or less," he agreed.

[4]

SO, IN TIME, Moses and Nun set out to find the legendary City of Kush. Lost cities and legendary cities, cities of beauty and peace and wealth beyond calculation, were an important part of men's thoughts in those days. And Moses sensed that it had to be so. Whether it was Nun or Sokar-Moses or some Hittite mercenary, there was in every man a spark that pleaded for love, companionship, understanding; a spark that, no matter how overlaid it became with brutality and hostility, could not be snuffed out. So that when men looked upon their cities and saw the slums, the filth, the misery, the hunger, it was as if they looked upon what had happened to themselves. That they compared this

reality with a dream that had no likelihood of fulfilment
was something Moses had never before considered with
any degree of thoughtfulness. Now he did, and almost to
a point where he hoped he really would find a golden city
to the south. For if honour, *justice*—the precious *macaat* of
the Egyptians—had been proved completely hollow, he
could console himself with the memory that *macaat* was a
word he had never heard from the lips of Amon-Teph and
Neph. Quite the contrary; they had accepted, as one accepts
the day and night, the fact that the man of reason dwells
in a world of unreason. But while so much of the fine edge
of Moses' youth had been hammered dull, his optimism and
eagerness remained with him. Already he had known
wholeness and infinite knowledge during his one night of
love and enchantment with Merit-Aton; somewhere, he
could believe, there was a promised land where reason
blended with unreason—where men lived without murder,
filth and deceit.

So it could be said that when he left the city of the
Kushites to journey south, he began a search and a wandering that was to be the expression of his life. Not that
his life moved thereafter in any sort of direct line. He was
still to taste the dregs and bottoms as well as the heights,
and he was yet to know degradation and true nobility.

Still, he was different, and no longer and never again
the handsome, golden child of the Great House. He who
had been the highest-born prince in all Egypt had to live
with the fact that he was no prince at all but a Bedouin
waif; and he whose life had been sheltered and guarded on
every hand had lived for almost a year and a half now
with an army of dark-minded and blood-stained men. He
had killed without reason in all the blood-madness of kill-

ing; he had sacked a city; he had made pillage and ruin; and like another beast, he had shared the thoughts and company of men who were like beasts.

Nevertheless, however he might scorn the Delta, it was his home and his memory; and to set his face away from it, perhaps forever so far as he knew, was no easy thing. He and Nun would go where no Egyptians had ever gone before, except those who were legends, and if he laughed at Nun's fear of the edge of the earth—where the fires of Gehenna, black flames sixty times as hot as any earthly fire, burned and seized all who came near—he could find no comfort in his own belief that the earth was round. Terror of the unknown swallowed him as well as Nun.

He had been like a child with Nun and now he became like a father to Nun. His own lonely terror was submerged in the responsibility of command—and as the terror dwindled, a sort of hard, cynical pride took its place.

They set out by chariot, travelling south with the Nile. "How far will we go?" Nun asked, and Moses replied, "As our lord, Sokar-Moses, the Captain of Hosts, has instructed me, we will journey south for a hundred days, and then, if we find nothing, we will return." "And if we find what we seek?" "Then we will also return and bring the Host to destroy what we have found." His flat bitterness was not encouraging, and Nun asked no more. Moses took his black Kushite staff—the same staff with which he had fought Ramses-em-Seti, and named not because it was a weapon of Kush but for its colour—and cut a tiny notch into it. So was the first day marked, and each morning thereafter he notched it.

*   *   *

For a time, they found wheel-space for the chariot, and they travelled as best they could, following the course of the Blue Nile which veered eastward from south. Each night they made camp by the riverside, lighting a roaring blaze against the highland chill and roasting fresh meat when they were able to kill a bird or an antelope. Youth and the bondage of their loneliness brought them together, and in this time they became closer and they talked a good deal. It was during these evenings that Nun began, bit by bit and almost without conscious purpose, to make Moses familiar with the tongue spoken by the desert tribes and the herders of Canaan. The language of the Kushites had defied Moses completely, but between the Semite desert tongue and Egyptian, there was a haunting and elusive relationship—as if both languages had in the long-distant past a common ancestor. Also, it was similarly inflected—which made the verb forms easy to master. The part of the two young men that clung to boyhood took pleasure in another tongue in which to cry out or berate each other, and though no one else was near, it gave them a necessary added sense of intimacy. The estrangement that had sprung up between them after Hetep-Re's murder could not persist. As the days passed, they began to smile, and then to laugh.

It was also in this time that Moses made the discovery of Nun's ancestry. It came out during one of Nun's meandering discourses on gods and ancestors—for the deeper into the mountains they went, the more Nun feared the strange gods who dwelt on the peaks. He explained to Moses that every high place had its Baal—and he reacted in fear and anger at Moses' smile of amusement. "You would do better to fear the gods," he told Moses. In his own mind, he imagined the loss and despair he would feel should strange and vengeful gods strike down the Prince of Egypt. He could no longer bear the thought of being alone. "It is not that the Baalim are fierce," he explained to Moses, trying to imitate his master's method of logical presentation. "They are sly and tricky and they are afraid of Nehushtan—all of them, that is, except Yavah, who is a fierce and terrible Baal." "And who is this Yavah?" Moses wanted to know—whereupon Nun explained that Yavah was the great Baal of Midian, a notation less than meaningful to Moses, who had never heard of either Yavah or Midian.

It was plain that Nun feared Yavah, but even a fierce and terrible god was impotent in terms of the distance that separated them from the Baal's place. Nun pricked off his ancestry. There was in the beginning Abraham, or as he said it, Av-Ram, a mighty desert chief who came into Canaan in the long, long ago; so long ago that perhaps even Egypt did not exist then.

"Yet he had an Egyptian name," Moses interrupted maliciously. "Av-Ram—could such a name be anything else but Egyptian?"

Nun snapped back that all things good and admirable were taken by the Egyptians as their own; but his desire to expound his knowledge won out over his petulance. Like all Bedouins, he liked to talk of religious dogma and complexity, a part of which was genealogy, for as with all tribes, the most distant ancestor and the god himself were hardly separable. He was not certain whether Abraham had turned into the holy serpent Nehushtan, but in any case, the next great chief was Isaac or Yitz-Hak, and the son of

Yitz-Hak, in his speech, was Ya-Kob, or Jacob, whose secret holy name was Israel, or as Nun sounded it, Yis-ra-el.

As Nun talked on, the names fascinated Moses; and like
the words of Nun's own tongue, they seemed to flutter
upon the edge of the Egyptian language. Then the image
of the serpent caught him and excited his imagination. He
plumbed his memory for what he sought, staring at the
flames of the fire, overcome suddenly with nostalgia for
the past and with desire for memories of the past to come
alive again. So reminiscing, he once again heard Amon-
Teph tell the tale of the serpent in the box—the serpent was
Nehushtan!

Moses stared at Nun as if he had never seen him before.
Nun spoke of the sons of Ya-Kob, Yo-Seph, as he said
Joseph—and now Moses did not interrupt to remark that
this too was an Egyptian name in its sound; in all truth,
he did not hear the names at all, but asked Nun softly and
desperately,

"My friend and blood brother, of what tribe are you?"

The deep and pressing formality of address startled Nun,
and suddenly he became conscious of the drawn face of
Moses, the firelight gleaming on the high, bony ridges. "I
am of the Tribe of Levi, who was a child of Israel," he said.

Moses nodded. The whole world embraced the two of
them, crouched before their fire in the wilderness. "Are we
truly brothers at that?" Moses wondered with awe.

[5]

THE THOUGHT CAME to Moses that they had been driven
out of the world of man and mankind, for day followed

day, and of man or his work or his habitation, they saw nothing. Not too long after they left the Land of Kush, they had been forced to abandon the chariot. The Nile had become a narrow, rushing mountain stream, pouring its white froth over rocks, churning through rapids, and leaping from ledge to ledge; and it was impossible any more to find wheel base for the broad axle of the chariot. They unharnessed the horses, loaded them with what supplies they could carry, and went on. After Moses had shown Nun the few simple tricks of maintaining his seat, the Levite rode well, and they made good time then on horseback. They had entered a region of grand, spectacular mountains, giants that rolled on endlessly to the south, and there they took their way, following the river through a series of deep and beautiful green valleys. It was the month after the end of the rainy season and the mountains were still green with such a richness of verdure as Moses and Nun had never seen before. The air was sharp and clean, the days pleasantly warm and the nights frequently so cold that they would build double fires and sleep close in the heat between the blazes.

It was a country of many animals who had not learned to fear man. Bands of baboons barked at them from the hillsides and followed them curiously. Families of lions watched them without fear, and spotted leopards lay upon rocky crags in the warm sun and observed them go by. Monkeys charged at them through the rocks and brush, screaming noisily and foolishly, and their cry was taken up in the bizarre lament of hyenas. Birds of bright plumage flew across the valleys, and the hillsides swarmed with game, from the tiny antelope that appeared to soar through the air as they leaped down the slopes, to beasts as big as horses with straight horns four feet long. White goats perched on the crags, and often in the distance they saw what appeared to be cattle of a sort, a wild breed that was wary of them.

They did not have to go out of their way to hunt, but chose their targets in the morning when the animals came to the river to drink. So little fear did the animals have of them that they were able to fell game with javelins, and since there was so much fresh meat to be had, they could conserve their precious store of bread. They also found berries in plenty and they speared fish in the river.

A lion killed a horse. The wild dogs would gather around their fire at night, so they tethered the horses close; but a lion leaped from the darkness one night as they slept and dragged down a horse. They were awakened by its screaming, and each of them grasping a javelin, they found their target in the moonlight, pinning the lion to earth with the force of their casts. The horse was dead, but the excitement of the lion-kill made them proud and cocksure, and next day they took the other horse, the beautiful yellow horse, Karie, that Moses had bought in Buto, loaded all their goods on to him, and set forth on foot. Moses was in high spirits now, full of a sense of boldness and daring and achievement, and Nun caught his mood and reflected it. Both of them had been reared in lands where lions were rare and invested with an aura of kingliness, and the pursuit and killing of lions was the sport and privilege of kings.

Two days later, they went out of their way to stalk a lion and they killed it with their javelins. But the third lion took both their casts without stopping and bore Nun down, before Moses clove its spine with his sword. Nun was unhurt except for claw marks on his chest that he would bear to his death, and they were both fortunate to learn proper respect for lions so cheaply and painlessly.

The yellow horse stepped into a snake-hole and broke his leg, and they had to cut his throat and leave him to die. It was not an easy thing for Moses to do. Karie had been his first freedom—together they had tasted the adventure of youth, and there had been as much love between them as may be between a man and a beast. The past was dying—but it was doubly hard to kill the thing he loved so. Forty-nine notches were marked on Moses' Kushite staff when they left the horse behind; from here on they would have to bear their burdens on their backs. To carry their war shields was out of the question, so they took each a single javelin, sword and dagger, laminated bows with thirty shafts apiece, and Moses his black stave, and Nun made a burden of all the bread left to them. The rest they buried, raising a stone cairn to mark it.

The Nile forked, and they followed the bend that took the southernmost direction—and still they saw no sign of man and his works. Day after day they went deeper and higher into the soaring mountains, which began to lose their softness and became ranges of high cliffs, rock crags and towering stone peaks. And as the Nile grew narrower and more shallow each day, there dawned on them the realization that they were approaching the mysterious and legendary source of the Nile, the fearsome place from which no traveller had ever returned; and the thought depressed their high spirits—as did the knowledge that there could be so much of the world in which no human made his dwelling. So great was the distance they had come that the very idea of retracing it terrified them. Nun pleaded with Moses that they had come far enough.

"Master, this is the end of the world," he said, pointing to the brown, forbidding peaks, their points shrouded in purple clouds. "There is the smoke of Gehenna. Must we die because your father wants us to die? Now is the time that any man of sense would turn back."

Moses had become short-tempered and irascible, and he vented his anger on Nun because there was no one else to vent it on. "I am sick to death of your whining and snivelling and of your wretched superstition! I am sick of your Gehenna and of your rotten desert gods! Don't you think I want to turn back? it's little enough you know of men like Sokar-Moses. The God-King of all Egypt said that I must travel a hundred days, and if we return sooner than two hundred days, it will be to death. There is no returning for us, and I am lost here with an ignorant, cowardly slave!"

Nun accepted the tongue-lashing and the badge of cowardice, and that night, while lightning played among the mighty peaks and thunder shook the chasms, he sat at the fire and wept openly and unashamed. Moses now understood his terrible and uncontrollable fear, and with all his heart he desired to comfort him; but his pride would not let him apologize to a slave. Instead, he was silent, and for three days they went on in silence.

Now the Nile had become a brook, flowing through a thick jungle-forest growth that lined the bottom of the chasm they followed. Moses no longer knew whether this was the source of the Nile or simply some lesser branch. Legend held that the river had its source in some great lake of marvellous beauty, but surely this sluggish stream did not mark the outlet of a great lake. In the afternoon of the third day of silence, Moses was bitten by a snake, which he killed with his sword even as it sank its fangs into his calf. Nun gave a terrible cry, drew his dagger and shouted wildly for Moses to lie down. Moses obeyed him without thought; he was going to die, and his heart was icy-cold, a receptacle for fear. He sprawled on his stomach, wincing with pain as Nun cut the skin where the snake had bitten. When Moses twisted his head to see what Nun was doing, he saw the Bedouin sprawled at right angles to him, sucking at the open cut. That was the last thing Moses remembered, and a moment later he lost consciousness.

He learned afterward that for the day and a half that followed, he lay in a delirium; and that during that time he had periods of convulsion that racked his body from head to foot and brought him to the very door of death. He also learned, in good time, that Nun knelt over him without sleep or rest, wise in the lore of the snake, keeping his body cool and wet when he had the convulsions, holding his teeth apart with a soft cloth, lest he bite off his tongue, comforting him and soothing him. In his delirium, Moses talked and talked, and there was little of great importance in his life that he did not speak of. Thus Nun learned of the truth of his birth, that Moses was the sacrifice of the Levites that a priest of Egypt had taken alive, and that he and Moses were kin by blood. This and much more Nun learned, and there were long hours while Nun pondered the strange circumstances that had thrown them together, himself the slave and Moses the Prince of Egypt, each so different from the other and so alike.

Because he felt that Moses would die, he distilled the

knowledge with his tears and sorrow. He wept for himself, but he wept more for this strange, tall, pensive and curiously sad prince—who was at one and the same time so wise and so ignorant, so sophisticated and so innocent, so gentle and so hard, so strong and yet so helpless. In all of his life and experience, Nun had never come to intimate knowledge of anyone like Moses, and even the tale told in pain and delirium could not wholly rob Nun of his conviction that the blood of gods flowed in Moses' veins. He wept also because his relationship with Moses was the one certain, safeguarded thing in his life.

But most of all, Nun wept because he knew that he would also die, for he knew that it was Nehushtan who had put the yellow horse's hoof into a snake-hole and he knew that it was Nehushtan who had struck down Moses. Moses must die because he had blasphemed against Nehushtan and killed the snake, and he, Nun, must die because he had defied Nehushtan's will in his attempts to save the life of Moses. Nor did Nun care very much, for here, without Moses, it was better not to live.

Even while he laboured to save Moses, he felt in his belly Nehushtan's fangs, cold as ice, the death fangs of the serpent-god. Nehushtan held him in pledge, so to speak; and Nun knew that it was only because Nehuhstan was away and because his, Nun's, love for Moses was so great, that death was postponed.

So he nursed Moses and saw the poisoned leg swell enormously and turn purple. He waited for Moses to die, but Moses lived, and on the following day, with the eventide, the delirium passed and Moses weakly asked Nun for water. As Moses drank the water, his hands trembling so they were unable to hold the cup which Nun had to set to his lips, Nun told him what had transpired and also bade him farewell.

"Are you going to leave me now, Nun?" Moses whispered in sudden fear.

Holding Moses' right hand, the tears running down his cheeks, Nun shook his head and cried, "I will never leave you, master, never. I had thought that you would go first and I would follow you, but now I must go alone. I am dying."

"Nun—dear brother, what a selfish fool I am. I didn't know that you were bitten."

"I was bitten," Nun said dolefully, "not by such a snake as bit you, but where it leaves no mark, inside my belly, by the god Nehushtan. Now I must die."

"What?" Moses raised up on one elbow to stare at the Levite.

"I am pledged to the god and I must die."

"And you are not pledged to me?" Moses cried. "Where was your Nehushtan when I paid out good gold for you, and sealed a bargain and bought you to serve me or to die by my hand?" The astonished and shocked expression on Nun's face assured Moses that he had taken the right path, and he continued, "Pledged to Nehushtan! I spit on Nehushtan! This is not his land and he is no god here! And anyway, what god has the right to break a sale and contract between two men, when gold crosses hands? Answer me!"

Nun shook his head in bewilderment.

"I bought you as a slave," Moses said tiredly. "Nehushtan must deal with me before he claims your life. That's the law. Now leave me alone. I want to sleep."

Moses rolled over and almost immediately fell into a

deep, healthy sleep. Exhausted, unable to cope with the direct argument Moses had hurled at him, Nun lay down beside Moses and pulled their cloaks over both of them. They slept deeply until the rising sun awakened them. Then Moses was ravenous with hunger, and Nun was so busy building a fire, softening their bread in water, and eating with an appetite to match his master's that Nehushtan's claim was postponed. They ate enormously, finishing the last of their bread, and then they lay beside the fire and Moses talked long and gently to Nun.

He told him that a snake was a snake, a very poor sort of animal, and he repeated the teachings of Amon-Teph, that in the childhood of all nations and peoples a time comes when they worship a snake as a god. There was no great mystery to it, he explained to Nun, for man did not always know that it was his sex-organ that brought life to the female womb. When he discovered that fact, it was new and wonderful, and because the sex-organ itself was in the form of a snake, if one cared to think of it thus, he made a god of the serpent. So it was even with the Egyptians in the olden times, Moses pointed out, and said to Nun,

"Tell me, Nun, how is it among your people when they make a pledge, a son to a father, let us say?"

Nun shook his head. "It is shameful to the Egyptians."

"There are Egyptians and Egyptians, and this thing our priests know about and we learned it in school as children. For a thousand years ago, it was done among the Egyptians."

"They lay hands upon his loins and take hold of the organ," Nun whispered.

Moses nodded—and then, bit by bit, he splintered the pillar of Nun's faith. He was fighting for Nun's life, as Nun had fought for his; and he recognized that this was a different, more delicate and more difficult battle than any he had known before. He had heard how, among the Bedouin tribes, there were sorcerers who could put a spell upon a man, so that he wasted away and died in the conviction of his own doom, and he had heard of Bedouin witches who could sing their victims to death. He had heard Neph say, once, that among the forces of the earth, there is nothing so powerful as an idea that has taken root, and he understood now what had been then no more than a cryptic remark.

So during the days that followed, he worked and reasoned and fought for the soul of Nun—and in the end he triumphed.

In the course of this, in the wonder of a man, a slave, a friend who would put his mouth to a poisonous wound to suck the poison, to give his own life for the life of another, he opened his heart to Nun and told him that which Nun already knew, the story of his birth and childhood. Then he asked Nun who he, Moses, was—if Nun knew?

"If you are indeed the child who was taken by the priest, then I know," Nun answered thoughtfully. "We are a small people, we Levites, and smaller since we became a slave people, and each of us knows all the others. The father of the child was Amram, but he is dead, and his wife Jochebed may be alive or dead, I don't know. Two of their children are alive—Aaron, who was once a strong man and a good worker, and his sister Miriam, who has a sharp tongue. Jochebed was a woman of the family of Sephir, but Amram is blood-cousin to my father, so if you are that child, we are kin twice——" But Nun believed nothing of what he said, in the full, deep sense of belief; and Moses shrugged

his shoulders and murmured, "Who knows!" The Delta was
another world, far, far away.

It was five more days before Moses could walk com-
fortably, and then they set out for the south once more.

They had had enough of the heavy growth around the
sluggish brook that was once the Nile or a branch of the Nile,
and filling their water bags, they struck out over the high
ground. Now it was climbing in earnest, and they moved
straight for the high barrier ridge to the south and west. It
took them three days to climb it to the pass, and then they
beheld, to the south of them, range after range of the same
awful peaks. In the distance, at the bottom of the valley,
they saw a little river sparkling in the sunlight like molten
silver. They reached it the following day and followed it
south against the current, still climbing. Moses cut fourteen
notches on his ebony stick while they followed it through
valley after valley, until it seemed that they and the churning stream must be climbing to the very roof of the world.
At last it revealed its source, a beautiful little lake nestled
against a cliff and fed by a thin tracery of silver spray that
fell from some two hundred feet above. This cliff they
skirted, climbing wherever the face was broken enough to
afford foot-space—until, late one afternoon, they reached
the top.

To the north of them, behind them, from whence they
had come, range after range of mountains rolled away into
hazy distance—so great a spread of peaks and valleys that
they could hardly comprehend that they had crossed it. To
the south of them, there was a veritable paradise, an
unending stretch of green parkland, the waving grass
waist-high and trees scattered throughout, as if some

mighty gardener had dropped them about to suit a fanciful but admirable taste. Through this parkland, the little river flowed to the cliff's edge, and in the distance there seemed to be a broad lake which was its source. All over the parkland, herds of game grazed, antelope and great horned beasts and incredible little horses striped black and white and big horned cattle like oxen and, in the distance, giant grey figures with long tusks, which Moses recognized as the fabled elephant, paintings of which he had seen but never the animal itself.

And wending across this parkland, perhaps a mile away, they saw a line of black men, carrying the spoil of the day's hunt slung from poles.

"So we come to Gehenna," Moses thought, but like Nun he was speechless and for a long while could only stand and look.

[6]

LONG AFTERWARD, WHEN Nun or Moses would tell the story, they would speak of the village of Doogana, but that was not the name of the village and neither was Doogana its ruler or chief or king, but just a witch-doctor, an old, old man, old as the hills and the rocks, wrinkled and small, with a loose, round belly hanging in front of him as he sat cross-legged upon the ground before his hut. There he sat all day long, baking his old bones in the sunshine, with his dish of the water-of-time in front of him, a broad copper dish, with his mortar and pestle on one side of him and his clay jars of herbs and unguents on the other. There he sat, small, old, black as Moses' Kushite staff, naked except for

his loincloth—and there to Doogana, the hunters brought
Moses and Nun.

For the hunters were not people of war or hatred, but
tall, easygoing men full of smiles, black people, but different from the people of Kush and speaking a different
tongue, too. They were courteous and smiling, and they
made the gestures that people make in lieu of language.
Their animated delight with Moses and Nun spoke plainly
of a people who saw few strangers and had no reason to
fear them. They carried fine throwing spears tipped with
long, slender bronze points, but no shields, and they had
bows of beautiful, polished yellow wood. They were barefoot and their loincloths were of coarse cloth woven of
grass. Some wore copper bracelets and others necklaces of
the claws of beasts. Their bronze knives were hafted with
finely carved ivory, but not all of them had knives, and
they carried no swords and no iron.

They were full of hospitality, giving the wanderers fruit
from their bags and for drink a sort of wine tasting of
berries and carried in clay flasks. Then they led them to
their village, a matter of two hours' walk through the enchanting parkland.

The village was without a wall or any other protection,
a cluster of hive-shaped, mud-and-grass huts set among
fields of waving grain, and as they neared it, women and
children as well as men came running to see who these
strangers were. But all were full of smiles and laughter and
curiosity, the adults respectful, but the children coming
close to finger the stained, torn kilts the travellers wore, to
stare at the golden neckpiece that encircled Moses' throat,
and to touch their long iron swords. They were also fas-

cinated by Nun's great black beard, for they were a clean-faced people; and they chattered among themselves, undoubtedly making highly personal remarks, and laughed deeply at what they said—but all in such simple good humour that offence was impossible.

And so they brought Nun and Moses to Doogana, who watched them approach quizzically and thoughtfully—and then motioned to them to be seated on the ground in front of him. This they did, and then water was brought to wash their feet, and more fruit and wine and flat, fresh-baked cakes of bread were set in front of them.

Many of the people, children and adults, stayed to watch, but at a distance of at least a dozen feet; it was plain that Doogana was a man well respected. Then Moses—and to a lesser extent Nun—talked with Doogana. They talked for a good while now, and again on other occasions, for Moses and Nun remained for eighty-two days with these people and Doogana was the only one they could talk to. Yet they were loath to leave, for these were a happy and contented people who lived in the most beautiful land Moses or Nun had ever known.

And this is the substance of what passed between them and Doogana; for he spoke to them in Egyptian, accented, but easier and more fluent as the conversation progressed.

[7]

DOOGANA OPENED THE conversation with a few words about language, his manner of speech verging upon the cynical, so that Moses was often puzzled as to how to take his remarks. He pointed out that only when one faced such an insuperable language barrier as lay between these two men from Egypt and his own tribe, did the importance of communication between men become fully apparent. He himself was the only person who could talk Egyptian, which he had learned as a slave in Egypt a long time ago. He smiled slightly here, but whether to indicate that he did not hold Moses responsible for his slavery or to note the fact that he recognized Nun as a slave, they did not know. The old man enjoyed ambiguities and equivocations. For the present, he said, he would talk to them in order that they might feel a little more at home, for his people were hospitable folk with many obligations toward strangers woven into their way of life. Of course, he explained, smiling again, it was their fortune that they dealt with so few strangers, and he shrugged with great knowingness. Then he went on to his own position—that he was not by any means the chief of this place but simply a doctor. More properly a witch-doctor, or magician-doctor, as it was put in Egyptian, he added modestly; and he was deprecatory of his few talents as he explained the purpose of his drugs and herbs. The copper dish, he said, grinning impishly at them, was filled with the water-of-time, which enabled him to read the past, the future, and many things of the present which were either far away or hidden by the guile of men.

And as if to give substance to his words, he said, "With all this spoken, I wish to greet you and welcome you, for it is not often that two travellers journey such a distance as you have come. You I greet first, O Prince of Egypt, Moses of the half-name; and being of a folk without nobility, commoners or slaves, I also greet your companion, Nun the Bedouin."

When he saw the open-mouthed, gaping astonishment of the two young men, be cracked his palms against his skinny thighs and shook with mirth. The people gathered around, knowing nothing of what was spoken, recognized that Doogana had scored a point, and they joined his laughter. Nun whispered, "Master, how does he know us? Is he a god of these people?" Puzzled and bewildered himself, Moses stared dumbly at the witch-doctor, who managed to say through his mirth,

"And you, O Prince of Egypt, with all your civilization and science and skills of rational thought, shall I read your very heart? Here in this water-of-time, your mind opens like a book for me to read, and I tell you that right now you are beginning to believe that I am the ghost—the *ka*, as your priests call it—of that poor old king, Irgebayn, whom you Egyptians betrayed and slew so foully."

He rocked with glee, glancing from Moses to Nun, and then he shook his head and spread his clawlike hands. "Ah, now—forgive an old man who salts his own boredom with the confusion of strangers." He trailed a finger through the water in the copper dish. "Not here, but here"—touching his forehead—"do I read things. The water-of-time is plain good water from the well, and how can we talk with open hearts if you think me a witch? Yet if we talk, we must talk that way, or to no purpose; and aside from food—I am long past the age where women mean anything to me—talk is my great pleasure. You see, my friends, no people live alone, and if travellers are few, they still come and go, and even here, so deep in Africa, the news comes. All who pass talk with me, and it would amaze you how little happens elsewhere that I do not know. A handful of those you call Kushites, but whom we call the Baynya, rested here for a space, and they told me of the Prince Moses and of his slave Nun. Things are simple when they are explained, are

they not?" He was mocking Nun gently, for Nun was grinning with relief. "And of Moses of the half-name and his
mother, Enekhas-Amon, and of the priest, Amon-Teph,
who lost his head as well as the dreams it contained—of
them I have heard this and that in the past, for it would
be both proud and foolish for you to imagine that you are
the first to come this far from Egypt. I could have beguiled
you with that knowledge, but it's a child's game after all.
You wear the royal neckpiece, Moses, and just as another
man does not walk like a prince, a prince has his own
difficulties walking like other men. So I put these simplic-
ities together, and you thought me a witch. Am I not right?"

Moses nodded. "You are right. But how did you read
my thoughts?"

"Ah, you would have all my secrets! Yet what is a
witch-doctor but a man who guesses at a little bit of the
truth, but must wrap it in every kind of superstition to
make it palatable to the ignorant? Truth is a dangerous
thing, Prince of Egypt, and even your own man Nun becomes afraid of you and flees into himself when you try
to serve him a meal of the truth. Am I right, Nun?" Nun
stared, and Doogana rubbed his hands and giggled. "So
you will learn, Moses, and if you make a wedding with the
truth, you too will become a witch-doctor, rest assured. As
to reading your thoughts—an awful guilt is always on top
of the thoughts of a good man. To you white men, black
men look all alike, for you feel that we are less than you
are, and what you lessen, you rob of its singularity. I am
an old man—so was Irgebayn. Do I need magic to read the
rest?"

"And why do you say I am a good man?" Moses asked.

"Ah—I am garrulous, in all truth, but not enough to go

into a dissertation of good and bad. Have it that I read it in your face, or have it that your slave Nun loves you, for with all his fear, he glances at you as a child glances at a father. This is not the way of slaves and I am a practical observer. But enough of this. Tell me now why you came here, so great a distance?"

"Because Ramses dreams of the city of gold that the old legends speak of."

"And he sent you to find it?"

"Or to lose myself, so that I would not return with my hatred of him who murdered my mother."

The old man nodded, his bloodshot and yellowed eyes fixed keenly upon Moses. "A strange breed, we human-kind," he reflected. "A mother dreams of her babe and a young man dreams of his maiden, but a king dreams of gold. Does the God-King fear you?"

"Someday I will kill him, and I think he knows it," Moses said.

"I think not. I think you have had enough of killing, Prince of Egypt, to seek no more of it. And tell me, have you found this golden city?"

"It doesn't exist. I knew that when we started. It is a legend and no more."

"And are legends such lies, Moses?"

Puzzled, Moses said, "I don't understand you, Doogana. Are lies and dreams the same thing?"

"No. No. they are different. I know where this golden city is, Moses——"

Nun interrupted him, "Then keep it to yourself, old man! We are sick to death with wandering! And you will curse the city you name."

"And you, O Prince of Egypt?"

"I want no more blood on my hands, and Ramses has enough gold."

"Yet you would be high in his favour——"

"I spit on his favour!"

"Nor would you have to wander," the old man smiled, baring his black gums and four yellow teeth. He pointed to the huts, their grass thatch golden in the long rays of the afternoon sun. "You are there. This is the city of gold, the golden city, the city of dreams and legends."

Nun looked at the mud huts scornfully, deciding that like many an old man's, this one's humour was as foolish as a child's; but Moses sensed that the witch-doctor was deeply serious and he watched him with interest and respect. They had reached each other. This was another of the singular fraternity of Amon-Teph and Neph and Seti-Keph and the doctor of the white house on the cliff and Merit-Aton, who was now a distant and wonderful dream clutched in his heart. This too was a demander of why and how, an image-breaker, this old, ugly black man—and did he recognize Moses as of the company? "We wear no insignia," Moses thought, "no badge, and we have no signs. Then how do we know each other?"

"The golden city," the old man repeated.

"And where do you hide your gold?" Nun asked boldly; but the old man took no offence and answered, "We find a nugget now and then, a bit here, a bit there, and whoever finds it brings it to me. In the course of a year, we have perhaps enough to fill this copper bowl. Then I send it north with ten strong young men to the land of the Bay-nya, and in exchange, they give us bronze spear-points, bronze arrowheads, and sometimes bronze knives. We have a little copper here, but no tin, and we can't make our own bronze; yet it is less for the bronze, you, Nun, who have much to learn, than to be rid of the gold. For then it is told that in our golden city, there is not enough to make it worth anyone's while to war against us—and thus we have just a little more wisdom than the Baynya, who wear gold bracelets and gold jewels and cover their gods with sheets of gold. Do you see?"

Nun shrugged, and Moses said, "I think so, but I am not sure. You were laughing at us when you called this the golden city."

"I was telling the truth," the old man snapped.

"Why?"

"Ah—in the manner of respect, ask why. The fool laughs. The wise man desires to know why. The coward is afraid of why, and he says—give me a sword—and I will cut the root of knowledge. I will kill—he says, and lo, we have a warrior! Have you killed, O Moses of the half-name? And you, Nun, black-bearded man of the desert? Are you full of the pride of killing?"

Nun did not reply; he was afraid of the tremulous anger in the little man's voice, and he said to himself that perhaps this was a powerful witch-doctor after all. But Moses, whose heart was suddenly heavy as lead, answered,

"No, I am not proud."

"Then why did you kill, Egyptian?"

"They were the enemy and it was kill or be killed," Moses answered slowly. "I did not make war. We warred with Kush, and if I had not slain Kush, then Kush would have slain me."

"And why did you war with Kush?"

"Because the God-King wished it so," Moses muttered.

"And now the God-King looks for a golden city, so that the blood can run again. Oh, what a fool you are!"

From a black man, this was too much for Nun and too much even for his fear to tolerate. "Take care, old man," he said. "You talk to a prince of Egypt."

"Oh? And will the Prince of Egypt return with an army and put us to the sword? I think not."

"To set foot in this lovely land," Moses said. "No. I would die first. Before I brought them here, I would die."

The witch-doctor gave a shout of applause and clapped his skinny hands together, and all the people and children standing about and listening to a conversation they did not understand also clapped their hands together.

"Then my medicine works," Doogana said. "There is bleeding inside of you, but it will heal, Moses, it will heal. Think then—is only the metal golden? What of the sunshine?"

"My teacher said that the golden sun is god," Moses whispered.

"Gods—what a need for gods you Egyptians have, godsick and godridden the way you are! The wheat in the field is golden for the harvest, and I have seen fish that gleamed like the purest gold. But do you know what is most golden of all?"

"What, Doogana?" asked Moses, like a child with his teacher.

"The memory of innocence. Out memories of childhood are woven with golden thread, and when a whole people recall the misty time before they learned to kill and steal and lie and squeeze each other's blood, they call it the golden time, the golden age—and this they people with golden cities. How do I know? Am I just an ignorant old man, Moses, an old man full of superstition and magic spells?"

"I think you are wiser than I will ever be," Moses answered, slowly and haltingly.

"That I do not know, for I had no teachers—and observe, you, Nun, that a teacher is not to be mocked—ever. Thus I teach the Prince of Egypt what is beyond your understanding, and in turn he will teach you. Thus I was taught by an Egyptian physician in old Giza, when your royal father had not yet seen the light of birth. Yes, I, Doogana, a poor black slave, taken first as a slave by Kush and sold to Egypt for three shekels of silver—and yet this man taught me because he had tasted the sweet pleasure of teaching, which is like no other pleasure on earth. Much did he teach me, of medicines and unguents and how to, set the broken bone and how to sew the broken flesh and how to dress a wound so that it healed clean and fresh. He taught me of the organs of the body and wherefore one man dies in youth while another lives to old age. But most precious of all, he taught me to write and to read in your hieroglyphics, and put no bar in my way when I spent a thousand hours poring over the old scrolls in his library and the old wisdom. Thus I came to know that in the legends of all folk, there is a golden age and golden cities—a time when no man coveted what another had."

Nun said, "And your own people, Master Doogana— they do not steal or kill or lie?"

Doogana grinned at Moses and observed, "If you are a dreamer, Moses of the half-name, then surely your servant is a practical person indeed. What do they say of the Bedouins—that they will cut your throat to sell the blood for pig fodder? No—no, Nun, I mean no offence, but ignorance is rash. You call these my people; would it astound you to know that they are ruled by a council of seven women—and that the word of these women is more searching and emphatic than the word of Ramses himself? These are the mothers, and—who better to say us yea or nay than the mothers? And as for stealing—the very word is not in my tongue. Murder? Yes, sometimes there is murder, but then the murderer must go away from us and never return—and for us that is worse than death. Lies? We have no need for them, for we have not yet become civilized enough for wrong and deceit to be profitable. These are not virtues we parade; these are our way of life because we have only touched the knowledge of civilization. We are not always content, but we have more of real contentment in our little village than exists in all of mighty Egypt. The golden city—well named. You fret now—this is a foolish old black man who talks to you. But stay with us for a while—and perhaps you will think otherwise."

Moses was tired. He had wandered too far and too long; the old man was not wrong; and this place was full of peace. He smelled the sweet smell of the fields and he watched the bees gathering from the wild flowers that grew among the huts. And almost dreamily, he asked Doogana, "What gods do you worship here where the whole land is so sweet? They must be good and gentle gods."

Doogana smiled and inquired as to whether Moses believed in the gods. It was a strange question, and no Egyptian would ask it.

"I believe—but I hate them, and those I do not hate I have only contempt for."

"Some day," the old man said, crooking a finger at

Moses, "you will learn to put a bridle on your tongue, young Prince, or else it will grow long enough to strangle you."

"I am not afraid of the gods," Moses shrugged.

"That is bravado. Of course you are. Every Egyptian is afraid of the gods. But it is men who strangle other men—not gods. We have no gods here, not yet. When we go to hunt the antelope, we dance magic, and in the dance we beseech the antelope to forgive us and not fear us, for he must give us flesh or we perish. The antelope clan takes him in and gives him shelter and love, to repay him for the necessary cruelty we inflict. So with the elephant and the elephant clan. So with all the beasts and the birds. When drought comes we bring water from the lake and pour it on the ground and dance the rain dance, so that the sky may take pity and see our need and pour its water on us. Of course, Prince of Egypt, all this is magic, and even though I hear that the Great House in Tanis swarms with magicians and every sort of faker these days, I know that an educated Egyptian like yourself scorns magic. Yet given a choice of gods or magic, I will take the magic and be grateful."

"And this—all this beauty," Moses murmured sleepily, "who made it, and why?"

"Your gods?" the witch doctor snorted. "They are jealous, petty, squabbling creatures who could not make a basket or a pot or anything else of use to man. Can you imagine for a moment that those wretched creatures made all this wonder and complexity—this mystery that even in a blade of grass defies the understanding of the wisest man?"

Moses was drowsy, deliciously drowsy and wonderfully

at peace with himself. Never in all his life had he felt so relaxed, so much at ease, without fear or trepidation. The old man's sarcasm was as gentle as the afternoon wind. He found himself nodding.

"And here you are far from your mummies and your foolish tombs and all your feats of death and extinction. Death is like sleep, boy, and when you are as old as I am, you will not be afraid to sleep. As you are now at the beginning of life—so must you be at the end of it, without fear of a long sleep and rest. Go now, and we will talk again."

He spoke in his own tongue to some of the people who were listening, and they led Moses and Nun through the village to an empty mud hut. It was clean, the doorway open to the wind, and the beds were skin bolsters filled with dry, sweet grass. Gratefully, Moses shed the harness and weapons he had borne so long, but Nun muttered worriedly about spells and enchantments and told Moses that in all probability they would be murdered in their sleep. Moses fell asleep to the sound of Nun's petulant complaint, and slept the easy sleep of a child into the following dawn.

[8]

WHEN NUN WOULD ask him, "Master, when will we leave this place?" Moses would say tomorrow or the day after tomorrow; there was always time; but time was different here. These were not a people who were acutely aware of time; they kept no track of hours, days, weeks, years; the calendar was a mystery to them, and unlike the Egyptians, they did not split their days into endless and specified routine. Hour blended into hour and day into day; time was imperceptible and friendly, and like a balm it eased Moses' soul. Sometimes for hours he lay on his back in the grass, watching the white, woolly clouds scudding and tumbling across the sky. There were no clouds in Egypt's sky and no cool rain such as fell here. The soreness went out of his spirit, and the hard lines in his face relaxed into youthfulness again. He stayed and dreamed—and the only tug and tie was the white house on the cliff above the cataract. But tomorrow would still be time enough.

"I promised to hunt the elephant with them," he told Nun. They had stalked lion the week before, bringing down a male and two females. The death of a lion was an occasion for rejoicing. And Nun was not hard-set against persuasion. With his acute ear, he was already managing a word or two of the language, and the young women were fascinated by his black beard and his braided hair. Where Moses was, he was content to be, and if he had anxieties at times over a place where no gods held sway, it was at the same time a relief to be away from them and not to think of his betrayal of Nehushtan, the serpent.

Any strangers would have been held holy to these people, but Moses and Nun won their hearts with their easy openness and simple delight in the black men's way of living. Only with such a people—people who could neither conceive nor understand the notion of a prince or royalty—could Moses cease to be in any part a prince. When he sat and talked with Doogana, the old man chuckled with approval and observed that this was hardly the same man who had come to them. The magic of life, he pointed out, was not the least potent magic. Birth and manners meant little here—where all folk were loved for themselves. "Stay with us," Doogana urged him. "Our women are strong for childbearing and our land is a good land. I will teach you all the secrets I know of the art of medicine and all the fakery I know of the art of witchcraft. And we will talk of all the mysteries in life." But Moses answered that tomorrow or the next day, he must leave. Thus, too, did he answer the seven mothers, old, toothless, gentle women who were all the government the tribe needed. The game herds had increased since he and Nun arrived. What totem or clan was his, that he brought them such good fortune? Doogana interpreted for them, and explained to Moses that they were simple people and very much concerned with food for the tribe. These were times of plenty, but there were also times of want.

"Tomorrow, we must go," Moses said.

He and Nun went on the elephant hunt, and both cast their war javelins in the target. When the mighty tusker went down, the javelins of the strangers had to be cut out with the butchering, for both were buried entirely in the beast's flesh. They were heroes and great hunters, and that night at the elephant dance, they bared their backs to the symbolic whip of the dancer who wore the elephant mask. Ten light strokes did each receive—and thus the high honour of the hunt—the symbolic repentance of the elephant-slayer.

"We have stayed too long," Moses began to say.

On his Kushite stave, the notches were cut from end to end, and more than one row. Eighty-two notches marked their stay with these people, and when they left, the people turned their backs so that their weeping might not be seen. Nor were Moses and Nun dry-eyed, for they knew that this leave-taking was for ever.

Doogana embraced Moses, the old man's eyes wet with

emotion. "I think," he said, "that I have been living and waiting for you, my son, and now that you are leaving, I am not long for this earth. May your cruel gods be kind to you and take pity, for you will gather wisdom and humility with the years, and neither is beloved of your kings or your gods." To Nun he gave a little bag of powder, telling him that it was to be mixed in water and drunk immediately if either of them suffered snake bite on their journey. "As for a road, follow the stream where it flows from the pool under the high cliff, and though it turn in this direction and that, never leave it, for in good time it will bring you to the River Nile and the Land of Kush. As for your master, watch over him and let his life be your life, for men like him are not many. He is full of pain and hope, and all his life these two will war inside of him. Understand this! And for all that you are an ugly, hairy Bedouin savage, I think you are not a fool. Respect his size and strength and wisdom, but do not be misled by them. He is a simple person."

"I do not like you, old man," Nun nodded, "for I was always afraid of your spells and magic, but I think that feeling will change when I am out of the reach of your witchcraft. As you somehow knew, I am blood brother to this prince of Egypt, and I will give away my own life before I see harm come to him."

So they left Doogana and his people and the beautiful table-land where they lived, and turned once more to the ravines and the wasteland. Moses marked their passage on his staff, and when the three hundred and eleventh notch was cut, they saw the walls of the City of Kush before them once again.

9

MOSES WAS PAST the time when he could wait on his homegoing with any equanimity or patience. He and Nun appeared as from the dead at a time when Sokar-Moses, who had left for Tanis some months ago, was not expected back for another sixty days. Moses would not discuss their exploration with anyone else, but Nun had a loose tongue and soon the Host was full of their adventures. Moses faced each day like an enemy, and the stagnant process of waiting for the return of the Captain of Hosts seemed to him the most difficult thing he had yet endured.

With three long years of war and exile between himself and Merit-Aton, it had been possible to make love a dream of an indefinite future; but now that he had passed his twenty-first year and the service of three years was almost finished, he felt as if he could stretch out his arms and touch her. He had lain with no woman in that time—his dream was too pure and fulfilling; now the heat of desire burned like fire and he told himself that he would wait sixty days for Sokar-Moses and no more—and then let any man stop him.

It was two days less than the sixty that Sokar-Moses had specified—he was a rigid and punctual man—and though he was surprised to see Moses alive, he passed it off with the studied air of one who considers such a journey routine. Even the fact that Nun and Moses had reached two separate sources of the River Nile did not impress him greatly, and he reminded Moses that the legendary source, the lake as wide as an ocean where the Nile was said to have its birth, had evaded them. So deliberately insolent was his manner that Moses could have exploded with rage, had he not fixed his mind on one thing—to go home. From this he would not be diverted.

"If you had discovered the golden city and could bring that knowledge to the God-King—"

"There is no golden city, which you know as well as I do," Moses said flatly. If Sokar-Moses was different from what he had been, then so was the Prince of Egypt, and the Captain of Hosts was none too certain of himself, facing this tall, dry and competent young man. It was one thing for the God-King to indicate that he would be better pleased if the prince remained in Kush; it was another matter to keep Moses there. Sokar-Moses had heard the persistent rumours that this was the issue of Ramses' seed in his own sister, Enekhas-Amon, and if that was so, then Moses was the closest heir to the throne. Ramses would not live for ever, and he, Sokar-Moses, was still young enough to think about the future. The Captain of Hosts decided to press the matter to a point and no further, and he raised with Moses the question of his term of service.

"Here is my service," Moses answered, holding out his staff with the three hundred and eleven notches of their journey. "Long before I reach the Delta, my three years and more will be done. Will you put me in chains to keep me here?"

"And if I did?" Sokar-Moses asked, feeling for his ground.

"Then my servant Nun and I would draw our swords and you would pay a price. You would also have to explain a good deal to Ramses, for the blood of the Great House is not shed so thoughtlessly."

Sokar-Moses smiled and relaxed, making it clear that a jest is a jest. He wanted Moses to have nothing but the best memories of their association; and when Moses indicated that he would leave the following day, he did not try to dissuade him. Then they talked of Moses' great journey and of the situation at the Delta. At home, nothing had changed significantly. It was a time of peace and plenty, and the engineer Neph was currently engaged in rearing a colossal stone figure of Ramses that would be one of the wonders of the world. All Egypt was talking about it. It would rival the Sphinx and, once constructed, it would stand for ever. As a matter of fact, even now Neph himself was scouring villages around Abydos to find a particular limestone without which the work could not proceed. What else? Well, a slave-trader had brought Ramses three slant-eyed, yellow-skinned women from the mysterious land at the end of the earth where silk was woven. The God-King was delighted with these new women, who were kept on a diet of aphrodisiacs and who graced his bed every night to the exclusion of all others. He, Sokar-Moses, had seen the women at a reception, and he thought them rather skinny and flat-breasted.

Listening to him, Moses was filled with nostalgia—brought on chiefly by the mention of Neph's name. He could well imagine Neph's contempt for the creation of a giant stone figure that would endure for ever. How much more rewarding must have been the white house of Aton-Moses, and he had to ask Sokar-Moses whether he had paused there either going or coming. The Captain of Hosts shook his head, putting aside the question and it was plain to Moses that without the protection of Seti-Keph, he would not pursue further acquaintance with the physician. Had he heard anything of the family of Aton-Moses? There again, nothing.

The following day, Moses and Nun left Kush to return to Egypt. Since the journey was downstream, they decided to travel in one of the dugout canoes that the Kushites used, and while this would not hasten their journey—they would have to drag the boat overland during the stretches of cataract—it would make it easier and surely no longer. Most of his baggage and clothes Moses left behind, giving away their belongings to men in the army; he kept only an extra kilt and his princely jewels and trappings—as a gift for Merit-Aton. They loaded the canoe with bread and their weapons, pushed off into the river, and swirled downstream, leaving Kush behind them.

They were both of them in high spirits, laughing like two boys on an outing, almost capsizing a dozen times until they learned the trick of balance and the use of the paddles. Nun was a child in his delight, remarking that he had never dreamed he would be this eager to see the Delta again. And Moses, throwing off all the burden of doubt and uncertainty, talked for hours about Merit-Aton, her family, and of the life they would have together.

So they went down the river—days and days of the kind of joy and freedom neither of them had known before. Time raced with them, now that they were in motion homeward, and Moses did not count the days. It came almost as a surprise one morning to see the white house on the cliff above the river, its walls shining in the light of the rising sun.

10

AS THEY STOOD in the shallow, rushing water of the river's edge, cleaning and grooming each other, they guessed at the time that had elapsed since they first left Egypt—but no matter how they tried, they could not draw it finer than thirty days or so. They knew it to be more than three years because the flood had ebbed more than on their outgoing; yet if they had wanted to find some gauge to measure themselves, they would have reckoned by change rather than time.

They had broken the barriers between them, and they knew each other now by motion and gesture, without words. They remained master and slave, but it was Nun who manipulated the distinction, sensitive to every mood and emotion that took hold of Moses. So that now, as it was fitting that the master should be princely and clean, it was necessary that the slave should be clad to serve him. Even as Nun brushed and combed the black mass of Moses' hair, so did Moses braid the heavy plaits of the Bedouin's hair. Even as Moses lay flat and motionless on the sand, that Nun might shave his face as smooth as a child's, so did Moses trim Nun's beard. It was the first time in all their association that they had meticulously groomed and dressed themselves for an occasion, and even Nun was caught up in the excitement and expectation of the moment.

The change in themselves was not anything they considered consciously, yet they were not unaware of it. Manhood in all its fullness had come to a prince and a slave in various islands of battle and wilderness and exile; now they were taking their maturity back to civilization. Moses let Nun bedeck him. For hours, Nun had polished every bit of gold and silver with a mixture of fat and ashes. The great golden collar lay high upon the massive chest of Moses and tight around his neck, and he recalled the time he had first worn it in the audience chamber, when it covered his shoulders and weighted him like the oppressive prescience of doom. This morning it lay lightly on the white scar-tissue of battle, and though all the rings and bracelets were commonplace to him, they seemed to Nun to make a wall between the two of them. The girdle of gold plates set with rubies that encircled his waist and held a tiny symbolic hammer of royalty would have bought the lives of a thousand like Nun. The Bedouin wore a striped Babylonian kilt of soft wool that Moses had purchased before they left Kush; and if as a slave he could not wear the royal colour of gold, the silver belt Moses had given him was the finest thing he had ever put on. Yet it accented rather than lessened their difference.

It was still before noon when they finished their preparations. They left the dugout high on the bank. Moses went without weapons, for even a dagger would have marred him today, and Nun wore only belt weapons, sword and dagger. Thus did they set out for the white house, high on the cliff and a good distance from where they had halted.

As they climbed the escarpment they lost sight of the house, nor did they see it again until they were almost upon it; but first they saw the little temple where Merit-Aton's mother worshipped. She would worship there no more. Stone from stone, the temple was violated and it lay as a ruin of anger and violence. Moses and Nun approached it slowly and neither spoke, but in Nun's thoughts the gods of Kush had been here. The bodies of two children who must have fled to the temple for shelter lay there, the children of the houseslaves, and on the little bodies the flesh was dry as leather.

Moses looked at Nun wildly and wordlessly, his eyes full of fear, and Nun was afraid to speak. The house was still ahead of them, but close as they were now, they saw its ruin. All the vegetation had withered for want of irrigation; there was rubble around the house; one wall had been broken down and fire had raged through the outhouses at the back. The verandah was littered with rubble and dirt, and there had been no rain to wash away the black mark of blood.

"Master, stay here and let me look," Nun pleaded, but Moses heard nothing. They found the doctor first, a body without a head; the head had been taken away to make embalming impossible, but not so with the women. Merit-Aton lay in the sand on her face, a long Kushite spear still in her back, pinning to earth the sand- and sun-dried thing that had been her body, as if still screaming, "So did ye to the women of Kush!" Thus had she lain there, even as the shrivelled remains of her mother lay huddled beside the verandah.

It was Nun who dug the sand and buried the bodies. Moses stood on the verandah without moving or speaking, and finally Nun had to take him by the hand and lead him away. "They will not change in the sand, master," he explained, "and you can make arrangements at Karnak for the embalming. More than two years do I reckon they have been dead. Let your grief out, master—let it out." But Moses remained mute and heard nothing.

11

IT WAS THE engineer Neph who, much later, out of his wisdom and sympathy said to Moses, "Did you slay her then? For life and death are a coming and going that we are never far from, and unless one can look at death, he cannot look at life either." "I slew her," Moses answered— and to that Neph said flatly that Kush had slain Aton-Moses and his family. Kush was mortally hurt. "So all that bore the name Egypt was a target for Kush, and we ride a wheel of war that we turn like terrible and foolish children." But that was nearly a month afterward, when Moses came to see Neph again.

To Karnak down the River Nile, he was silent, but Nun could see the hurt and guilt swelling and festering inside him. He spoke a word or two when he had to speak, but no more, and they made the passage in silence, divested of every joy.

Once they were in Karnak, he gave Nun some of his jewels to sell to pay for funerary services. But before Nun returned up the river, he attended to a mission of his own. He was quite insistent about this—certainly his master was in no state to pay much attention to a sudden purpose on the part of his slave—and only when he was sure it was accomplished did Nun embark with the embalmers.

Moses was not entirely clear as to his own motives for proceeding with the embalming. Long ago, it seemed to him, he had divested himself of any real belief in the mumbo jumbo of tomb and body and *ka* and afterlife, yet the ritualized memories of childhood remained. It had even occurred to him that once Nun departed with the embalmers, he would know some peace; but instead grief and anxiety and guilt filled his mind.

In the riverside tavern where they had found lodgings, he began the process of drowning his misery in wine. He sat on the common bench at the dirty wooden table and consumed mug after mug of the sour southern vintage. So far as the innkeeper and the fishermen, the boatmen and stevedores who frequented the tavern, knew, he was just another captain of chariots on his way back to Tanis from the conquered and occupied Land of Kush, and he was of such a size and appearance that no one bothered him. His white scar-traces, his stubble of beard and his great spread of shoulder invited neither companionship nor interference. He paid for his wine with the little plates of gold that he had broken off the royal neckpiece—the bulk of which he kept in his pouch—but all manner of gold came from Kush, and where gold was concerned, men were open-minded and understanding.

The prostitutes who plied their trade in the water-front taverns learned that he was not to be approached until he had soaked up sufficient wine to become amiable and free with his little plates of gold. They saw that he could be gentle and considerate or wild and terrible. A burly riverman who resented his woman's attentions to Moses drew a knife and came at Moses. The whole room heard the snap of the bones in the man's wrist as Moses twisted it and flung the man away, as one throws a sack of wheat. They were wary of him after that. His speech was the speech of a gentleman, but he was dirty and unkempt, covered with filth that was blasphemous in a land of ritual cleanliness, unshaven, his black mop of hair tangled, uncombed, full of the lice and dirt of the water front.

Nun was gone for better than three weeks, and in those three weeks Moses ate little or nothing, lived on the sour wine against which his stomach rebelled, vomited it up and filled himself with it again and again, woke from sleep in the mud of the riverbank, in brothels and hellholes, in evil dens where murderers, thieves and pimps made common cause. Bearded, stinking with his filth and drunkenness, robbed of his pouch and weapons, he was found by Nun at last in the mud under the piles of the water-front tavern where they had their lodgings—unconscious, in a stupor of alcohol and exhaustion.

Nun was not alone. With him was Neph—for that had been Nun's previous purpose. Recalling that Sokar-Moses had told them that Neph was combing the villages around Abydos to find stone, Nun had sent a messenger to the engineer with news of what had happened at the white house on the cliff. Neph bad taken his own barge and had reached the house only hours after Nun arrived.

As Nun told Moses afterwards, he would have known Neph easily enough, for Moses' life had become an actual part of his own. Nun told Neph the story of Moses' first visit to the white house more than three years before, and of the love that had come so quickly to the Prince of Egypt and Merit-Aton. Neph listened with interest and wonder, and then, when he and this heavy-muscled Bedouin who had become so intimate a part of Moses finished their work at the white house, which Neph closed up as a tomb for the family who had lived there, they returned to Karnak together.

So it was that Nun easily raised the huge figure of Moses in his arms and, tenderly as one carries a sleeping child, bore him to where Neph's barge was moored. They placed him on a sleeping pallet in the stern, and after the barge had cast off, they washed his body with olive oil and a soft mixture of ashes and talc and then with the water of the River Nile. Through all this he slept, stirring only now and again and sometimes talking in his sleep. Nun shaved him and cleaned and combed his hair, and still he slept—through all that day and the night that followed.

And all night the barge slid over the silver-black surface of the river. With nightfall, the slaves shipped their oars, ate their supper of bread, olives, figs and water, whispered for a while and then stretched out on the floorboards to sleep. So did the crew sleep and the workmen Neph had brought with him from the City of Ramses. Neph himself took the tiller-oar and stood at the helm with Nun; and Bedouin though he was, Nun could feel the warm and secure embrace of the Land of Egypt, with its endless length of sheltered river—where all was order and peace and security. For the first few hours of the night watch, they spoke little, Nun only in answer when Neph talked of Nun's master and asked the slave,

"Why is it then your 'master,' when you told me how you mixed your blood on the battlefield and swore an oath as blood brothers?"

Nun did not answer the question glibly. He thought for a good while before he replied, "We are both of us strong men." He told Neph the story of the snake bite in the river-bottom jungle. "We exchanged lives. I gave him back his, and he gave me mine. He cursed Nehushtan, who is the god of my fathers, and he showed me how to be stronger than Nehushtan. Should one ever part from such a man? But we can't be together as brothers; each one of us is too wilful. It was my headstrong will that made them take me out of the work gangs in the Land of Goshen. They tried to kill me and I was too strong for them to kill, and they broke their rods and their whips on my back while I laughed at them. But this man I love, and I will be his slave because there is no other way for us to be together. He is a prince, and I am a Bedouin, a Levite, a child of darkness and superstition, as he so often reminds me. Well, he is right."

Neph waited, but there was no more that Nun could explain, and then Neph asked, "What did he look for, there in the South? Surely, he knew there was no city of gold in that wild land."

Strangely enough, Nun answered without hesitation, "I think, Egyptian, that he looked for gods. You Egyptians are drunk with your gods, and you love them or hate them. For my part, Nehushtan was my god, but I cursed him and put him away. It was no easy thing, but once done it was done, and I can live well enough without gods. Not you— I saw the Egyptians in Kush, where the gods of Egypt were far away. They behaved like animals. But for this man, my master, all gods are hateful, and his face is against the gods."

"Did he look for gods to hate?"

"I am not sure," Nun replied slowly. "It may be that he looked for gods to love."

[12]

AT THIS TIME, it was said among the people who lived along the River Nile that if you brought your troubles to Mother Nile, she would wash them away; if you brought your fears, she would quiet them; and if you brought your hurts, she would heal them. To Moses, the long, gentle and uneventful trip to the Delta was necessary and important, for it allowed the scars inside him to heal slowly, and it took the painful edge from his great guilt. Many were the hours when he sprawled on the warm wooden deck, watched the green shores slip by, watched the play of morning and evening colour on the desert escarpments, watched the freight barges and papyrus boats go by—and was able to look into himself, and he tried to grasp the meaning of himself, a single man, as posed against the immensity of the earth, the aimlessness of human ways, and the random cruelty and meaninglessness of human existence.

At other times he talked to Neph, very often with Nun stretched on the deck, silent but listening. All three of them were interwoven in a process of change, but perhaps the change was deepest in Nun, who said the least of any. Several times, Moses told Neph the story of the terrible battle where the army of Kush was destroyed, as if Neph could explain why men destroyed each other; and once Moses picked up an insect that was crawling across the deck and crushed the life from it between his fingers. "This is what we are to the gods," Moses said thoughtfully. "Do I know or care what the hopes and dreams of this stain between my fingers were?"

"Men are not insects."

"To the gods? How do you know, Neph?"

"Because the insects did not make us. We made the gods, Moses."

"The priests say otherwise. The gods made man."

"Nehushtan ate the eggs of a tortoise," Nun interjected, "and vomited upon the tortoise's back. He saw little things moving and crawling in his vomit, and these were men. He gave them the tortoise's back for the world and he killed the tortoise and set fire to its flesh, so that the flesh would burn for ever from each end of the tortoise shell, and this was Gehenna. And when the flames of Gehenna have softened the tortoise shell enough, Nehushtan will swallow the whole thing, and that will be the end of men and the world."

Neph smiled, and Moses said, "The gods work less crudely, for, given enough time, man will destroy himself and save Nehushtan the trouble."

"We've lasted a while," Neph shrugged, "and we may last a while longer. In spite of the gods, Nun. I remember a story of the Sea Rovers, who have among their gods one called Pro-me-tus, or something of the sort. They have many gods, but he was the only one who took pity on man and learned to love man. You see, the Sea Rovers are blunt and forthright people, as becomes men who make their way through life by trading when they can't steal and stealing when they can't trade, and they are very ready to admit that the gods have nothing but contempt for mankind. Man, they hold, is a toy, and the more the gods can torture him and bewilder him, the more delighted the gods are. This is their amusement, or so the Sea Rovers say. But for some reason this god, Pro-me-tus, came to admire and love man, and he stole the sacred fire from the great mountain where the gods live and gave it to mankind—and with it, of course, warmth and knowledge and skill in working metals."

"I would imagine the gods were hardly pleased with Pro-me-tus," Moses observed.

"No—they were not pleased," Neph said thoughtfully.

"According to the Sea Rovers, they chained Pro-me-tus for ever to a rock, and there the birds tear his flesh and there the sun burns him and scars him. It's an interesting fable, since we Egyptians do very much the same to any among us who gives fire—so as to speak—to his fellow man. Yet somehow it seems to me that we are never as bad and as unrepentant as the gods we make for ourselves."

"And even my good friend Neph, who is wise and practical, believes in the gods," Moses smiled. His smile was a warm and generous thing, and here was the first time on this trip that Neph had seen it. Neph shrugged and smiled back. "Distinguish, O Prince of Egypt, between wisdom and the desire for it. First things first. You have still not told me what wisdom you sought in your long journey south and what wisdom you found."

"Precious little, except for the hocus-pocus of an old witch-doctor called Doogana."

"Who I was happy to see the last of," Nun put in. "I don't like magic, and I don't like old men who can read your mind. I have enough trouble trying to understand my own few thoughts without worrying about someone else's digging in them. But I tell you, Egyptian, your story about Pro-me-tus is not so strange. We have a tale among our own people of how at one time man was naked and happy—perhaps because he was too ignorant to be unhappy. He ate the fruit of the trees and knew no shame, but there was one succulent fruit, the fruit of knowledge, that was forbidden to him by Nehushtan. But Nehushtan came to him and tempted him to eat the forbidden fruit, and when he had eaten it, Nehushtan punished him by sending him out of the good land into the desert. Thus we children of Israel became desert-dwellers——"

"Nehushtan," Moses nodded, "is as unreasonable and as stupidly vindictive as any other god. You see, Neph, I have no more love for him than for Osiris, although I suppose I should. We have been speaking the truth here, with nothing withheld. If I am an impostor with everyone else, I can't be with you. Like Nun here, I am a Levite—who had the good or bad fortune, depending on how you look at it, to be offered as a sacrifice to this same Nehushtan at a moment when Enekhas-Amon desperately resented her childlessness. So there, once and for all, is your prince of Egypt."

"I have known all this for a long time," Neph nodded. "Amon-Teph told me; he asked me to show you the Levites in their bondage, so that you would never envy the people whose blood you carry. They were the people you saw on the island, building the granary." He paused and watched Moses' bewilderment. Then Neph said, "Whether he was right of not, I don't know, O Moses of the half-name. He and your mother dreamed that you would one day become the God-King of all Egypt, and then restore Aton to his throne above all other gods." He shook his head, an expression of sudden sadness passing over his face. "No—not Egypt or Aton for you. You are a man now, Moses, not the boy who went away. You have seen war and you have known love and loneliness and guilt. Some day you will know anger—"

"And then?" Moses whispered.

Neph shrugged. "We will see."

[13]

LONG AND SLOW and gentle as the journey down the River Nile was, it came to its end at last, and Neph's barge

shipped its oars and scraped against the stone wharves of
Old Tanis, the City of Ramses. To the dock-workers, the
sailors, riggers and fishermen, the chandlers and merchants, the spare, grey-haired figure of Neph was familiar
enough, but no one saw or recognized the Prince of Egypt
in the tall, wide-shouldered and scarred soldier who accompanied him; and as for Nun, he walked no longer like
a slave, and for all of his beard and braided hair, his striped
kilt and the firm set of his massive shoulders marked him
more as a Babylonian or Canaanite than a desert tribesman.

To Moses, leaning on his black Kushite stave and al-
lowing the emotions of this homecoming to flow through
him, the place had dwindled—it lacked the size and grandeur he remembered. Everything was less massive, less glittering, less impressive—and he was shocked by his
awareness of stench and filth. His memories had not in-
cluded the litter of fish heads and scales on the docks, the
violent motion and shouting, and the nauseating smell of
the place. Even the Great House of Ramses, its walls looming a few hundred yards up the river, was in no way so
gigantic as his memories of it—and when he remarked upon
this to Neph, the engineer nodded and said he knew the
feeling well. It was less a physical change than a mental
one, for even in the greatest of palaces the horizon is narrow and blunted, whereas the land to the south was limitless, with mountains as high as the sky. The very fact that
he was back here once again made the recollection of those
spaces and distances more awesome to Moses, and he could
not shake off the feeling that a part of himself had been
lost and left in the tangle of mountains where the Nile had
its sources. How clearly he could picture Doogana smiling
at him so knowingly. "What happens to a wanderer?"

Moses asked Neph. "Does he ever come home?" And Neph answered ruefully that wanderers were those who sought their home—not those who left it. The cryptic intent was not lost on Moses, and when Neph asked him how he felt, he replied, "I am a stranger here." Neph wondered where Moses would not be a stranger, yet there had once been a place to come home to, the white house over the cataract; but that was no more.

During the trip down the river, Moses had learned a good deal about Neph. He heard the story of the girl Neph had once married, who had died in childbirth—as Neph tried to ease the hurt of Moses with his own hurt. "You never possess," he told Moses then. "For us, as for all men, there is only change, and if something is good and beautiful and we can look at it and be with it for even a little while, then that is enough." Moses asked bitterly, "Even for a day?" "Even for a day, my son."

For years after his wife's death, Neph had lived in his studio in the Great House. His wants were few. He ate the fare of the maintenance men at their common table and he spread his sleeping pallet on the floor. More often than not, he spent his nights at the various jobs. But with Moses gone and with Amon-Teph and the other priests of Aton dead, the Great House became intolerable, and he bought a house for himself at the river's edge above the palace.

It was there that he took Moses and Nun when they left the barge. The house was a simple structure of whitewashed mud brick, containing five rooms, a porch for eating and an outhouse for a kitchen. The roof, which was reached by a staircase on the outside, was floored with fragrant cedarwood, so that it might be used for sleeping in the hot weather, and aside from a garden of olive and fig trees, the roof was the only vanity the house possessed. "You would think," he remarked to Moses, "that having built so many houses for others, I would put my experience to work and build something more elegant than this for myself. However, like yourself, I have yet to come home, and this serves my purpose." But, as he told Moses, he had hoped that some day they would share the place, and at least it contained enough rooms for the requirements of privacy. His staff was small but adequate, a cook, a houseman and a gardener. Moses would have made no moral judgments had Neph kept a slave girl or two as concubines, for the practice was common among unmarried men and not uncommon among married men; but he was pleased that this was not the case.

The day after they were installed in the house, Neph had to return to the desert, where his men were at work on the colossus of Ramses. Though Neph had assured Moses that all in the house was his, the momentary poverty of the prince placed both him and Nun in a difficult position. He could not wear Neph's clothes, and during his time at the inn, he had lost all that he and Nun carried, gold and jewels and weapons too. Not even a dagger was left to him now, not even a pair of sandals to replace the ones he wore—which were falling to pieces. He had to be shaved with Neph's razor, and unless he desired to go naked, to wear one of Neph's kilts when his was being washed. To someone who in all his life had never questioned the availability of wealth and who had never been denied the means with which to satisfy any need that gold might fulfil, it was an interesting but irritating situation.

In any case, he was indulging a fantasy to pretend that he could live here in the City of Ramses without revealing his presence, and after two days of loafing in the garden, unwilling to venture forth on the streets in his tattered condition, he decided that he would go to the palace and talk to Seti-Moses, steward of the Great House and watch-dog over half the wealth of Egypt. He went alone, without Nun, full of the bittersweet of childhood memories as he approached the gates of the enormous building—and both amused and annoyed by the reaction of the officer of the guard when he was recognized. "It is not as if you are yourself here, O Prince of Egypt," the man said wonder-ingly, "but someone like yourself and reminding me of yourself."

The officer of the guard, as Moses knew, was an un-proven bastard son of the God-King, and thereby a degree below the proven bastards, who swarmed and grew in the palace itself. His godly manner was diluted with obsequi-ousness, yet he was dubious and curious concerning this already legendary prince of the half-name, supposedly the only true son of the godly children of Seti I, father of Ramses—and, as gossip had it, hated and feared by his royal father for his great strength, his devilish skill in battle and his demonic temper. All unknown to Moses the years of his absence had created a legend and image of himself. The taming and subduing of Nun, the slave, had been em-broidered beyond recognition, even as his blasphemy of the sacred kilt had become a dangerous defiance of the gods. Rumour had it that three of his brothers had died by his own hand, that scores of his royal sisters had given birth to his bastards.

Nor did the living presence demean the legend. The Royal Guard was composed of the youngest sons of the noble houses of Egypt, and for some reason homosexuality had become the fashion among them. The pampered, plump, overfed young men were preened in a manner that had become traditional: their armour and shields were faced with gold, and under their golden helmets they rouged their faces and painted their lips. Now they stared, with a mixture of distaste and respect, at this large-boned and lean man who loomed over them. Bare of gold and jewels, they saw him as one whose social defiance was the equivalent of nakedness. His threadbare kilt and disintegrating sandals mocked their finery, and his great shock of black hair, threaded through with grey, crudely cut to length but untouched by the skill of a real barber these many years now, gave him a wild and threatening aspect, all in keeping with the stories told about him.

Moses was indifferent to them and to the officer of the guard. He said that he desired to see Seti-Moses, the steward, and that he would wait for him on the high terrace, to which he walked without another word. Was he a stranger here too, he wondered? He stood on the terrace, looking down into the courtyard where he and the royal progeny had exercised at weapons for so many years. A new generation of children were standing with rigid and trembling arms, loosing their arrows at the targets. A younger man trained them, and Moses wondered whether old Seti-Hop was dead. The memories returned like disconnected parts of a story someone had told him, rather than as events in which he himself had participated, and he found himself disturbed by the vagueness of it. Where was Amon-Teph? Where was his mother? He tried to bring Enekhas-Amon to life and being in his memory, but her face and voice and form remained nebulous.

Now he saw people in the gardens looking up at him

and pointing to him; news travels like a shout. Suddenly he was overtaken by a great and lonely nostalgia; though he stood in the sun, the sunlight of childhood was gone for ever, and he experienced a brief but overwhelming longing to be like others. Let Neph talk—Neph was Egyptian; Neph belonged; amid justice or injustice, rebellion or acceptance, Neph was of the land. He, Moses, was a pretender, a stranger, a Levite, claiming, with the pathetic pride of the landless Bedouin wanderer, to descent from some desert herder named Israel. Shame hid his origin; shame would always cloud and confuse it. Amon-Teph had advised Neph to take Moses to the slave people. Let him look at the filthy, crippled mockery of human beings that had given seed to him, and then he would never know regret for being parted from them for ever. How contemptuous of Amon-Teph and Neph, yet how hard to blame them! Where was the nation anywhere that did not spit out the word *Bedouin* like a curse. They come and they go; their home is nowhere, and the dirt of the desert is on them. They came once, long ago, begging for food, and they remained to be slaves. What is a Levite? He will put a knife in your back; he is ignorant but crafty and shrewd—and withal superstitious and degraded, with a snake for a god. Nehushtan vomited on to the back of a turtle, and lo, man appeared. And this was he, himself, Moses, the whole heart of the jest contained in the fact that not only had he been raised as a prince, but all Egypt whispered that he was the prince among princes, the child of a royal brother and sister in the ancient manner.

Lost in his thoughts, he only now realized that Seti-Moses was crossing the terrace towards him. If the chief steward had changed, it was only to increase his substance, his stomach more enormous than ever, his shanks ringed with bracelets of fat, his arms quivering with their overlay of obesity. He walked more slowly and puffed more, but his tiny eyes had lost none of their shrewdness, and it was with a calculating and thoughtful glance that he measured Moses. In the large, prominent features of the Prince of Egypt, the high forehead and deep-set eyes, the high-bridged nose more hawklike than ever, the jutting cheekbones over which the brown skin stretched so tightly, the wide, fleshy mouth and the sharp chin, Seti-Moses saw nothing of either the God-King Ramses or his sister Enekhas-Amon; and he became more convinced than ever that Ramses' delusion that this was his natural son was completely without foundation. There was little that went on in the Great House that escaped Seti-Moses, and he too had heard it whispered how this man, as a child, had been dragged from the River Nile, where he had been cast by the slave people. Yet, like others, Seti-Moses was a prisoner of his own contempt for the Bedouin tribesmen of Goshen, the wretched, inferior creatures who toiled for Ramses. More likely, as he often thought, the tall and arrogant prince of the half-name had originated in the region of Karnak and carried not a little of the blood of Akh-en-Aton, the hated of the gods. For while the physical resemblance was not with Akh-en-Aton, the face was a face of Karnak.

In any case, he approached a marked enemy, potentially powerful, but isolated and unaware of his own potential; and he reflected upon how much simpler it would have been if the prince had died in the Land of Kush. Moses, on the other hand, was full of an awareness of himself, and he looked upon Seti-Moses, as he did upon so many Egyptians, with a sense of apartness. The hard and lean feel of his own body was accentuated in the face of the other's grossness, and his poorly hidden distaste was not uninfluenced by a habit of judging men by their physical potential in war and hunt.

Seti-Moses was formal and correct. "Prince of Egypt," he said "I greet you and welcome you, and the Great House is honoured and enlarged by your presence. Your return will bring joy and happiness to all who love Egypt; for we have known that you left Kush, and we have been waiting for you these many weeks. Thus it is that my master, the God-King instructs that you be brought to him, so that he may feast his own eyes upon you, directly you appear."

"That's all very moving and heart-warming," Moses nodded, "but I did not come now for an audience with Ramses. Look at me! I came because I need gold, clothes, shoes. I am not complaining about the cost of the years in Kush, but a prince of the Great House cannot walk the streets of Tanis in rags."

Spreading his arms, the chief steward rolled his tongue in honey. He was a man of tact and presence, and he said, in the most conciliatory of tones, "Rest assured, O Prince of Egypt, that your wealth has not lessened a shekel's worth. Rather has it increased, and there is no measure to what is yours. It is yours to take. Your mother's chambers have not been disturbed, and there is gold enough for all your wants. But first you must see your father, for that is his command."

"As I am?" Moses demanded, pointing to his kilt and sandals.

"As you are. Do you think the God-King is swayed by

baubles and perfumes? You are a soldier come back from the wars. You must come with me, O Prince of Egypt."

Moses shrugged and nodded. "Very well, then." And he went with Seti-Moses into the Great House.

[14]

EACH TIME HE approached the throne of the God-King, Ramses, it was different; yet it was also the same, for he walked through the bright and glittering throne room with ghosts beside him—his mother, so bold and beautiful and defiant, himself as a youth, himself as a child—as if all the epochs of his life had been and would be marked by his approach to this man, the greatest and most powerful ruler in all the world. Moses would have had to be insensitive indeed to fail to comprehend that the contest was between himself and the man on the throne; nor did the knowledge that he was no prince at all lessen his own sense of royal importance—not would it, until he had suffered much more. Enough of the influence of the gods—so much a part of every Egyptian—remained on him for him to play with the notion that something more than fate and circumstance had arranged their opposition. That the ruler of all Egypt could still claim—and believe—him a son was no longer an irritation to Moses; but rather a cruel yet pleasant mockery—for he had neither love nor pity for Ramses, but only an account to settle. And that he would some day settle this account, he had no doubt.

But now he had learned patience; the feeling of childhood that tomorrow does not exist had left him. If out of loneliness, pain and sorrow, Moses had learned that no human being is alone, he had also learned that the chain of life was interlinked. And the blow the man on the throne had struck at Kush—out of his lust for power and wealth—reverberated for ever; and as Moses strode towards the throne of godhood, he thought, "Our score is doubled now, O Ramses, for the two women I loved most in this world died by your hand. I learned little, but I learned enough not to blame Kush for the hatred that begets hatred."

Yet he himself had ceased to hate. There had been born in him the seed of a notion—that justice does not reside in the pliable and willing *macaat* of an Egyptian's soul, but exists as a thing apart, created out of man and man's agony, and powerful beyond belief. It partook of patience, and it waited its time, and in its own good time it was ready at hand for men who loved and feared it. It did not—and would not for long to come—occur to him that he had found a god to worship, but more and more he sensed a staff to lean on, a stronger and taller staff even than the black Kushite stick of ebony, which alone of all his weapons he had brought back to Egypt with him.

So now, as he approached the king, he noted with no small pride and pleasure his own lack of fear. The little boy, Moses, the powdered, festooned and jewel-encrusted child of Enekhas-Amon, who trembled so with terror of this almighty and all-powerful personage, clung to his strong legs and was comforted—for the Captain of Kush walked across the throne room with the arrogant assurance of a barbarian who has not learned and never bowed to the rituals of power. In his own thoughts, he said to himself and yet to them, "Look at me, you fat and pampered scribes and priests and clerks of Egypt. I am Moses, the Levite, son of Amrarn the Levite, and thus you wanted me and thus I am!"

And indeed they looked at him with wonder and distaste, for his stride was too long, his shoulders too wide—and the whole aspect of him physical and threatening and without respect. Not in their memory had a man entered the audience chamber of the God-King without adornment or badge of rank, and that a prince of Egypt should come thus, naked except for a threadbare kilt and worn sandals, amounted to blasphemy. Most of the court officials who stood in the hall remembered the prince of the half-name, but the memory fitted poorly to this sunbrowned, scarred and defiant man.

Ramses, perhaps, thought otherwise, for to his way of thinking he looked at his son who was no longer a boy but a man—and if he watched with foreboding, he also watched with pride and felt that he had reared a stout adversary. It was no wonder that this Moses returned from far places that had swallowed others!

The God-King nodded at Moses, smiled thinly, and motioned for him to mount the platform and come close to him.

Ramses himself had changed less with the years than had Moses. Now in his fifty-fifth year, he had sat for thirty-eight years upon the throne of Egypt—yet his face was fleshy and youthful, his bear-like and powerful body retaining the vitality and vigour of youth. Only the older generation of Egypt remembered a time before him, the reign of his father, Seti; for the others, Ramses was as eternal as the River Nile, and the priests made little effort to destroy the legend of immortality that had sprung up around him. He had created a far-flung empire such as the world had never before seen, and his building in stone was refashioning the face of Egypt.

His restoration of the full flush of Egypt's power and glory had closed the eyes of the people to the fact of the land in itself: the enervated and impoverished peasantry, the dwindling population, the empty and abandoned cities of Upper Egypt—and the disease of mass slavery that fed on the body of the land like a swarm of insatiable maggots. The power and the glory and the glitter of gold were his, and now, as he turned his face and greeting to Moses, it was the God-King, lord of all other kings, who spoke and said,

"So the Captain of Kush returns. Is it true, as they say, that you found the source of the Nile?"

"O Lord of Egypt, I greet thee," Moses said flatly and formally.

"I am glad to see that you have retained your manners if not your jewels. However, as I told Seti-Moses, I am not impressed by baubles, and it is easier to see the man if he is not overlaid with gold plate. You've become a man, Moses of the half-name, and you have the look of a captain of Kush—or of one of those arrogant dukes of Karnak. However, you have not answered my question."

"The priests say that the Nile has its source in the fountains of the gods," Moses answered carefully.

"Be damned with what the priests say! I ask you, not them!"

Moses nodded and replied thoughtfully, "We followed one branch south, where it dwindled and became a brook, and we returned north by another branch, but neither was large enough to be the true source."

"So? And when you say we?"

"My Bedouin slave, Nun. He and I made the journey."

"The animal you tamed in the slave-market?"

"Yes, O King of Egypt."

"And you found no golden cities?"

"We found no cities at all, only a few savages who live in grass huts and hunt their food in the field."

The God-King of all Egypt looked at Moses, measuring him and putting him in the balance; and he bulked large, even in this great and colourful chamber. Three years before this, an archer had brought down a stork winging south and had taken it to the priests for augury. In the bird's crop they found a black stone, which was a warning from the gods to their own—and the priests warned Ramses to kill the man he feared. He had to ask himself now whether he feared Moses. He had more sons than he knew the names of, but none were of the breed of this tall, strange man who stood before him. In his eyes, the wild and the unfamiliar clung to Moses; if he had sired this, then he had sired an heir worthy of the throne—but one who would never wait for death to give him his turn—as Ramses thought. A wall of hatred and fear had been erected between them, and to all of the king's advisers, this dark man was an abomination, an enemy of the gods, a blasphemer and a secret worshipper of the hated one, Aton.

And Seti-Moses had said to him, "What will Egypt have of this man who hates the gods?"

So Ramses sat on his throne, his palm supporting his broad, fleshy chin, and studied Moses, and all around the great hall, the ambassadors, the priests and clerks and stewards, the captains and princes, stood in silence and at respectful distance, their eyes fixed on the lord of Egypt and his tall son, for they could comprehend the defiance of Moses only as the defiance of one of true birth and blood and right. And, at last, Ramses sighed and said, without anger,

"If you had loved and honoured me, everything would have been different."

"I loved and honoured my mother," Moses replied.

"And now you sit like a maggot in my flesh, waiting only to eat my heart."

Moses shook his head.

"Then why did you come here to the Great House?"

"Only for gold that is mine—to buy bread and clothes with. Shall I walk the streets of your city as I am?"

"I don't steal from my children!" Ramses said harshly. "The gold is yours, and Seti-Moses will give you what you need."

"Thank you, my Lord King."

"I want no thanks from your voice when there is murder in your heart."

"There is no murder in my heart," Moses told him quietly. "Of killing, I saw enough in the Land of Kush, where your army went to teach a nation justice and left it dying and bleeding, and never again in my life do I want to raise my hand to anyone, least of all to you. There are other ways in which justice works, and if I have an account to settle, I have learned to be patient."

"And you dare to say that to me!" Ramses cried.

"Yes, I dare."

Trembling, Ramses leaned forward and whispered, "What god protects you?"

"I ask nothing from the gods."

"Then ask, for there is a question as to whether you will leave this room alive."

"Would you let Egypt and the world know that as you murdered your sister, so will you murder her son?"

Ramses lay back in his chair, breathing slowly and heavily. He was quick to anger and quick to calm. He waited until the rage passed, until he had full control of himself, before he spoke. "Why do men love you, Moses of the half-name? If you were with me instead of against me, I think the whole world would lie at our feet. Is that a bad dream?"

"For me, yes."

"You speak boldly and wildly, my son," Ramses said bitterly. "You try my patience. The priests say to kill you, and you provoke me and talk to me as no man on earth ever has. How do you dare?"

"Because you are afraid of me," Moses answered simply. "I don't know why, but you are."

"How far will you go?" Ramses wondered. "You know you are safe. I would never sleep again with your blood on my hands. I would cast you into a dungeon and let you rot, and then I would lie awake thinking of what Seti-Keph wrote to me, how he would change places with the meanest peasant on the land if he could have a son like you. And Neph, my engineer, perhaps the greatest engineer in all the world, risks his life and fortune to shelter you and help you. You will accept this from them—why not from me?"

"They are not the God-King," Moses answered, for the first time feeling a sense of pity for the man who faced him.

Ramses shook his head and smiled; he was wholly in

control of himself now, and he told Moses, without ran-
cour, "You have the look of a man, but the tongue and
impulsiveness of a foolish boy. What do you know of a
throne that you cast it aside so lightly? Do you know what
it means to hold in your two hands all the power there is
on earth?" holding out his short-fingered, powerful and
broad hands, palms up, the fingers curled. "Here is the
power! Who is there on earth to deny me or say me nay?
What I want I have, and what I take it into my head to do,
I do—and the lords and the dukes and the kings kneel to
me and kiss my feet. Do you know what that means? Do
you know what power is? How sweet it tastes? No wine is
like it, no woman, no jewel—look!" He rose to his feet,
clapped his hands, and cried,

"Clear the chamber!"

Even the royal ambassadors tripped over their robes in
their haste to be gone, and in moments the great room was
empty. "So you see," Ramses nodded, "and thus could I
clear all of Egypt, if the mood took me—or people it. You
mourn too readily for Kush. Other peoples have died and
others will, for there is only one Egypt and only one God-
King sits on her throne—and the might of Egypt is the sorrow of others. Thus it was and thus it shall ever be—so
long as the pyramids stand at Giza. And this you would
throw away!"

"It was never mine to keep or throw away."

"But it could be," Ramses said, a note of pleading creeping into his voice.

"No—it could never be."

Only now that the interview was over did Moses realize
the purpose of it, and he felt ashamed and foolish and
mawkish, with his boasting and fierce defiance. He had

been allowed to peer under the curtain of loneliness that surrounded the loneliest man in Egypt, and the king of all kings had made a plea that died into a whimper. How boastful and foolish he had been to challenge Ramses with being afraid of him! The truth of the matter—which struck Moses like a sharp and ugly pain—was that this man whose children were a race in themselves desired desperately to have a son, a son like the old legends told about, a strong staff, a shield and protector. Even if there had been no reason whatever for him to believe Moses to be his child by his sister, he would have invented reasons. His last question came almost plaintively—

"You were with Seti-Keph when he died?"

"Yes, my Lord-King."

"And how did he die?"

"As all men die, I suppose."

"Was he—afraid?"

"He was afraid," Moses said softly and unhappily. "He was terribly afraid."

[15]

HIS LIFE NOW was quiet, like the still surface of the marshes at eventide. Day folded into day, and if their existence during these days after they returned to Tanis was purposeless, it was not idle. Moses had always loved the wild and far-reaching marshes of the Delta, the tang of the salt air, the endlessly different sunsets and the thick white mists of morning. Now he bought a small two-man boat, fashioned out of tightly tied bundles of papyrus, tarred against the water and lined with fragrant cedar-wood. In this boat, day after day, he and Nun would explore the marshes, hunt waterfowl, drift, when the mood took them, toward the open sea, cook their food now and then on a spit of sand—and sometimes lie under the Egyptian sun for hours, saying little or much or nothing at all to each other. Yet there was much that they taught each other. Moses learned to talk the tongue of the Levites more fluently, and Nun learned to write easily and well in the hieroglyphs. And if again and again they moved towards the Land of Goshen, it was not for Nun to press them on, and always it was Moses who turned back.

There was a time when they went out to the desert with Neph to look at the colossus of Ramses that he was constructing, the tallest piece of stone sculpture in all the world and one that was planned to last for ever. As antagonistic as Moses was to the whole concept of perpetuating the evil and lonely man who ruled the Great House, he nevertheless could not but be impressed by the scope and splendour of the project. As always when he went to one of Neph's jobs, he felt the calm air of reason, science and logic—the laws of measurements, instruments and angles, the devotion to the job truly seen and well done. The many huge blocks of stone, some of them three times the height of a man and of even greater width than height, were scattered about the desert area, being cut and shaped and scraped and polished by a veritable army of workmen—an of them directed and watched by the master sculptor, a man named Shep-Tet. The finished model from which they copied the colossus—and which Moses learned was the eleventh Shep-Tet had created before Ramses was finally satisfied—was eight feet high, and presented Ramses in the traditional position of Egypt's God-Kings, when they were portrayed in stone, seated upon his throne with the holy tools of authority in his lap. This model was mounted upon a wooden sledge and was dragged by six horses to wherever it was needed for comparison with the separate detail pieces of the colossus.

It was a fine and awe-inspiring, if traditional, piece of work, and Shep-Tet, a small, plain-looking and tired man, the son of peasants in Upper Egypt, glowed with pleasure as Neph praised it to Moses. "For you see," Neph said, "it is not simply the problem of a piece of sculpture. We are building the largest and heaviest stone figure in the world, and mortar is out of the question. The joints must bind and disappear as a matter of perfection—absolute perfection—of surface and balance, and thus we have not only an artistic but a mathematical problem. The two are not as widely separated as you might think, and my friend Shep-Tet is an excellent mathematician as well as a great artist."

"He praises me too much, O Prince of Egypt," the little man said with some embarrassment, "but I won't deny that the praise is sweet, coming as it does from Neph. He will not tell you that for all his talk of my mathematics, I could not solve the problem of projection to the ultimate size. This he did, and when praise falls from the lips of the wisest builder Egypt has ever known——" Suddenly, he was lost in confusion and fear, and begged Moses' pardon, for surely the Prince of Egypt understood that the true builder of all the current wonders of Egypt was the God-King of the Great House——

Moses noticed the mixture of contempt and pity on Nun's face, and afraid that Shep-Tet would prostrate himself before him, he said bluntly and almost roughly,

"Stop that kind of talk, Shep-Tet! I am no priest or clerk, and Neph here is like a brother to me, and a teacher as well as a brother. I know the worth of an artist or engineer, and the stud-bull whose portrait you have fashioned, giving him dignity and beauty that he never possessed, could not build a brush shelter in a forest. Stop being frightened, for I would also talk this way to his face; and I will not see a great artist crawl and belittle himself! What else but men like you is left of the glory that was Egypt?"

The confusion was compounded, and Shep-Tet made his retreat, muttering that his work needed him. Neph, not a little disturbed, told Moses that to talk as he had was more insanity than bravado, but Moses shrugged it off and answered sourly,

"I have a sickness called Egypt, and either I will die from it or heal myself. The man would have been on his belly before me in another moment."

"He would have survived that."

"But would I?" Moses smiled ruefully and shook his head. "Neph, Neph—I try you sorely, don't I? We'll talk about your work. It's the only sanity I find today in Egypt."

Neph nodded, but the dark shadow remained on his face. "I hope no other heard."

"That's done. Tell me, how will you mount those great blocks of stone? I see no scaffolding or rigging. The housing for that would have to be gigantic, wouldn't it?"

He had touched the proper point, and in a few minutes Neph was lost in the explanation of how the colossus would be reared over the desert sands. He led Nun and Moses to the place where the foundation had been dug, through the sand and down to the bedrock, where a footing of hard granite had been shaped precisely to fit the undulations in the rock below. "Since we cannot use a binder, like mortar, with blocks of such great weight, they must bind of themselves, surface against surface—which to my way of thinking is the best method of construction for oversized stonework. The two surfaces must be smooth enough to blend into one—to a point where a hair cannot be inserted between any joint. Given the proper fitting, the stones will adhere for ever—or for as much of for ever as a human being cares to contemplate—providing they are not thrown over and providing that the foundation does not sink. The first we leave to time; the second, we can see to ourselves." He went on to point out the terraces, walks and gardens that would be built around the colossus, once it was standing.

"If you can make it stand, O Engineer Neph," Nun put in, "for, as far as I am concerned, no force on earth can lift those mountains of stone into the air and set them one on top of another."

"No? Then a good thing the job is mine and not yours, Nun, for if I want my head to continue to rest on my shoulders, the colossus must be in one piece ninety days from today. As a matter of fact, raising it up is the simplest part of the whole thing, as our ancestors who built the pyramids at Giza learned, and we will raise these stones just as they raised the pyramids. No crane or rigging within our power to make could ever move such weight. Instead we will move the first layer of stone to the foundation on rollers. When this is in place, we will simply raise the desert level to the top of the first layer. When that time comes, I'll have three thousand slaves out here, and they'll raise up the desert level in just about four hours. Then I use the same men to roll the second course of stone into place, and once again we raise the desert level. All told, it will take no more than six days to raise the figure and four days more to remove the sand, and for centuries to come people like yourself will speculate on how we lifted the stones into place."

"It is very simple," Nun nodded.

"As all things are, when you understand them . . ."

Twice more they went out to the desert to watch the work in progress. Other times, they wandered through the markets, buying something only occasionally, for their needs were few. One evening there was an assembly throughout the city to the Goddess Isis and her brother, Osiris. Few indeed could hold back from the heady and wild carnival joy of an assembly, and because they felt that Moses must turn away once and for all from thoughts of the dead, Neph and Nun dragged him with them. They bought torches and paper masks from the street-vendors; they munched the delicious hot delicacies for sale on every corner, pieces of fried fish, shrimp cooked in butter, cheese, hot bread, cakes of honey and almonds, honey and raisins, savoury stews of goat meat—and again and again, they stooped under fat wineskins and let the liquid run down their throats.

As Moses ate and drank and joined in the mass singing of the high-pitched hymns, the bonds he had tied around himself broke and fell away. He returned to the sunlit memories of an Egyptian childhood, and he remembered standing on the walls of the Great House and watching the assemblies swirl through the streets—longing to be a part of them, a part of that vast and formless crowd, suddenly communal and singular under its sea of smoking torches. Now he was glad that he had removed every symbol of rank before he left the house. Tonight he would be a *kutah*, another one of the thousands of poor and landless folk who lived in the hovels of Old Tanis, and he would drink and laugh and sing like a *kutah*. Yet his tall, big-boned figure stood out, and when the procession to the temple formed, he found a girl on each arm.

Somewhere, he had lost Nun and Neph—just as well, for he had clung to misery so long that he felt it like an obligation. Everyone was a little drunk by now, and as the procession moved singing towards the temple, the lovemaking began. It was said that wives and husbands knew not each other in the assembly, but they knew others; and as the ritual proceeded, the strange blending of the old fertility rites with the sophisticated polytheism of this Egypt, the mass release from all the pressures and bleakness of living moved toward hysteria. Here, noble mingled with commoner, princess with peasant, the paper masks levelling all to their common, vaguely remembered tribal origin. Moses knew the quick, passing love of women, not for a man but for any man, and in like indiscriminateness did they know his passion.

It was a night full of passionless passion, and a night without regrets.

[16]

AND FINALLY, NUN said it, curiosity being greater, in the long run, than deference—and homesickness a quality from which not even slaves are exempt. They had been too many times on the edge of the grassy meadows known as the Land of Goshen; and one day as their boat drifted through the papyrus-walled channels, Nun said,

"I would see my birthplace again, master, for like yourself, I am becoming too much of an Egyptian without being
one at all."

"My birthplace as well," Moses said to himself, but did
not answer Nun, who claimed aggrievedly that if he said
one word out of the way nowadays, Moses became offended.

"I'm not offended and don't be such a fool! Don't you
think I've thought of the same thing?"

"If I were in your place, I would not think of it."

"No?"

"I'd put it out of my mind if I were in your place."

"Oh? And why?" Moses asked.

"It's better to be a prince than a slave." Nun shrugged.
"It's better to be an Egyptian than a Levite."

"I think a man should be what he is," Moses said slowly.

"Why, master? Is it his doing that makes him what he
is? It was Nehushtan who made me to be born out of the
Levites, a slave. And maybe it was Nehushtan who made
you to be lifted out of the river and turned into a prince.
Was it your doing or mine? You yourself turned me against
Nehushtan, and maybe some day he will kill me for that,
but until then I will give him more grief than he bargained
for."

Moses grinned, sprawling in the prow of the boat and
watching Nun deftly move it through the waterway with
his single long sweep. "There are ways," Nun nodded
sagely. "The gods are sensitive, as everyone knows. Even
to insult them causes a certain amount of discomfort."

"I don't know if a snake can be a god," Moses answered
lazily. "A snake is an animal that crawls on its belly. If
you are quick with your sword, you can cut its head off,

and that's the end of the snake. If you are not quick enough, the snake can bite you, and that may well be the end of you—as it was almost the end of me when we were in that jungle in the South. But it was not Nehushtan who did it—only a snake. Anyway, I am sick to death of the gods and I would rather talk of something else."

"The Land of Goshen? We are moving in that direction now."

"Go there if you wish," Moses nodded.

"Then please, master," Nun said, "take off your jewels and bracelets and things of gold and take off the sacred kilt. Go in a loincloth, so that even if an Egyptian comes among them, it will not be a prince."

Without replying, Moses divested himself of his royal insignia. He was suddenly subdued and afraid, and he was glad that Nun was with him. He wrapped the jewels and gold in the white linen kilt, and stuffed it all into the basket where they kept their food. Then, for the next hour as they moved towards Goshen, he sat in silence, his thoughts a turmoil of strange emotion. It seemed to him that the strong arms of Nun were a part of fate and destiny; at the same time, he knew that this was only his own fantasy, and that a single word from him would turn the papyrus boat around and send it back to Tanis. That he did not speak that word must remain his responsibility and not Nun's—and whether he charged it to curiosity or to a desperate longing to be an integral and unapologetic part of a people, a place, a time or a history, it remained a necessity which he recognized. He did not know how it would have been had deserts, mountains and great distances separated him from the people of his birth—as would have been the case had he been born a Babylonian—but no such barriers existed. His whole life had been lived only a few miles from the Land of Goshen, cheek by cheek, as it might be put, with these poor devils who in their filth, ignorance and wretchedness sought solace in their primitive worship. In a manner of speaking, he had lived upon a tower, looking down into their valley of grief.

As to what they were, he had no illusions. He had heard then, and their ways described by Amon-Teph, erudite, sophisticated and knowledgeable—the civilized man who tried to keep the loathing out of his voice and judgment. He himself, Moses, had watched them labour under the whips of Neph's overseers—the good and gentle Neph who was like his brother and father in one—yet neither to himself nor to Neph had it appeared wrong that the long whips of plaited bullhide should nag and tear at the mud-coated skin of these bearded Bedouins. For if slaves were born human, once put out to work under the sun upon the mighty creations of Egypt, they soon were divested of their human qualities.

Not yet on earth had the thought taken root that men were equal in the eyes of the gods, under the sun, or under the starry sky.

So Moses knew what they were, and a thousand times had worn the mental badge of their shame and misery on his own smooth and healthy skin. Perhaps if the course of his own life had gone differently, if he had learned to love the sheen of gold and the glitter of jewels, if he had developed a taste for power, a lust for domination—if he had been able to have contempt and anger towards Enekhas-Amon, that vain and ambitious woman who was the only mother he had ever known—if he had never come under the spell of Amon-Teph and the old priests of the high tower, if he had not one day walked into a room where an engineer planned the glories of man's civilization—perhaps if these things had not happened to him, he might have been able to wipe away the image and memory of who he was and from whence he had come.

But had the memory gone, he would not have been Moses of the half-name. This was, in good part, his own speculation and reverie as the boat was steered through the papyrus labyrinth; and he wondered, as he had so often before, what force traces and maps the paths of men. During the formative years of his life, he had been steeped all too deeply in the dualism that exists between gods and men in the Egyptian theology, not to seize, if inadvertently, upon symbolism as explanation. These waterways in the papyrus were a mysterious network in which a man could be lost for weeks, yet Nun knew his way, and every turn and twist of the canals was imprinted somewhere in his mind. Howsoever he might appear to deviate, his destination remained firm and unchanged.

So then, it appeared to Moses, that his own wanderings had led him here, not home; because he had come to believe as did Neph that there could be only search but no true destination for people like himself. In his own way and within the crippling limitations of his own time, Moses had become a rationalist—but it was a rationalism limited and stunted within the implacable framework of the gods; and now he saw himself, the enemy of the gods, as the captive of the gods too.

He realized that it might have been different, had not the men of Kush, their hearts filled with hatred and grief, destroyed the entity of the white house on the escarpment. If he had wed Merit-Aton, he would have wed Egypt—the old, proud Egypt of the Upper Nile, and then too he would no longer have been Moses of the half-name.

Yet the sorrow that remained was for the lovely woman, not for the circumstances lost. He had no resentment against the path the boat was taking towards the Land of Goshen, for the pathways had already been defined, and neither the oarsman nor the boat—as Moses thought—did anything but follow the current.

"So be it," he said to himself, almost with relief, almost with peace. "I am tired of pretending, tired of aping, tired of being a stranger in a strange land. Let it come as it may."

Yet he knew well enough that he would also be a stranger in the Land of Goshen.

[17]

HE STEPPED INTO the water to help Nun, and together they drew the light papyrus boat up on to the grassy bank. When the ebb of the river flood began, Goshen and the other lands that rimmed the Delta were as green and lovely as anything in Egypt. But these places had no canals or irrigation works to store the water and retain it, and as the ebb continued, the face of the land hardened and parched; the grass yellowed and died, and the dust gathered and rose in puffs and clouds with every breath of wind. The land was hot and the stink of the marsh blew over it. Only the waterbanks remained green and lush.

They walked, an Egyptian in a loincloth, with hunting weapons, and beside him, a bear of a bearded man whose long hair was braided in a heavy plait. They walked in a silent land, a sorrowful and hot land, and the dust eddied around their feet.

"Is it far, the city of the Levites?" Moses asked.

And Nun snorted mockingly, "Cities? Are we a people for cities? Are the mud hovels we live in houses? We lay our heads away from the weather as an animal does." He had changed; the fetid air of the place worked in him like poison; he was full of apprehension and anger, not at Moses, but at nameless things and at himself too.

"There is a city of the slave people," he laughed, pointing to a heap of rubble and mud brick, abandoned, with only a few lizards running in and out of the debris. "Is that what we seek?" Moses wanted to know, and Nun shook his head and laughed bitterly again. "There are more slaves than the Levites in Goshen." They went on. They saw a few goats chewing at the yellow grass. The goats were scrawny and sick-looking, and Nun explained that when the goats were sleek and healthy, the Egyptians took them. Moses himself was not defined; whether he came here as Egyptian or Levite, he did not know, yet he murmured, "So Egypt steals from slaves." "Their lives—so why not their goats?" "And if you ruled a land, Nun, would there be no slaves?" The Bedouin was silent, with no answer to a question he never posed for himself.

They came to an old well with a few palm trees growing around it, and there they paused to rest and shelter for a moment from the heat of the sun. Three naked children, very small and thin, perhaps six or seven years of age, played in the shade, and they looked up and saw Nun before they saw the man behind him. He spoke to them in the tongue of the Levites and their eyes widened, fixed upon the silver bracelets that circled each arm above the elbow. They did not reply, but stared at him wide-eyed and immobile, as children do when curiosity struggles against timidity. Then they saw behind him the tall figure of Moses, the clean-shaven face and the neck-length cropped hair; and their curiosity turned into panic and they fled, whimpering and running as fast as their skinny little legs could carry them.

"The Children of Israel," Nun shrugged, gloom fastening upon him like a weight on his shoulders. "Why did we come here, O master?" he asked Moses. Not unkindly, but pointedly, Moses again asked his slave, "Where is the city of the Levites?" And Nun pointed beyond the palms to a cluster of mud-brick hovels. There, the children ran, and he and Nun followed. If Nun walked slowly and uncertainly, Moses had the added uncertainty that those he approached would fear him, and in his mind begged them, "Look on me with a little kindness, for I have a particular grief." But he was too Egyptian, and Egypt was in the upright pridefulness of his walk, in the clean-shaven brown skin of his face, in the shock of black, banged hair, in the grace and health of his smooth muscles. They would be afraid of him as the children had been afraid, and he lagged behind Nun, dragging his feet. He suddenly regretted the long hunting knife that hung from his belt, his quiver of sharp arrows and the great, ominous laminated Hittite war bow. So did Egypt come, weighed down with the weapons of death, and now they were heavy as his own thoughts, which pleaded, "But look only on my Kushite stave, where the notches beyond counting are the exile Egypt imposed on me, and that is not all that Egypt did to me as well as you."

They had a well there, outside the mud hovels, with a thatch of papyrus to keep the sun off the water. A woman drew water at the well, and to her the three children ran, burying their frightened faces in the ragged, shapeless woollen dress she wore. Another woman, sitting cross-legged beside the well, climbed to her feet, and still more women and children emerged from the hovels and from the alleys between them as the two strange men approached.

The woman at the well looked up in fear, for her face had been cast and shaped by fear, not by joy or anticipation—a thin, weatherbeaten face, dark-eyed and hollow-cheeked—and she fixed her eyes on Nun, who spread his arms in a gesture of peace and called out in the speech of the Levites,

"I am not to be afraid of, Sarah, daughter of Jabed. I am Nun, the son of Ephala, the son of Zilpah, and you are kin to me by my mother and my cousin, Ephrel, so where is the need to look at me thus, as if I were strange to everything here?"

"You are not Nun, the son of Ephala, who was taken away and whipped to death because his back was proud and unbending," the woman replied with a kind of certain knowledge and haughty defiance.

"Then look at me again, woman, and call the others to look at me."

"Nun is dead. The dead do not walk with silver bangles and fat on their flesh. And who is that tall Egyptian behind you?"

"He is my master, and he allows me to come back to look at the place where I was born."

"Oh ho—such sights for an Egyptian lord to see! And what do you want of us? We have not a bit of gold or bronze or food for you to take. Leave us in peace, whoever you are."

Now the other women were coming forward, slapping their children back, squinting through the sunlight at Nun. A handful of skinny old men pushed through and past them, cackling authoritatively. Moses halted twenty paces away, watching Nun go up to them. He had been able to follow the drift of the conversation between Nun and the woman called Sarah, until it became a quick give-and-take, and then it lost him. Now, no longer speculating or wondering, but face to face with his blood and birth, he had a feeling of relief, of the breaking of a tension as old as his consciousness. He leaned upon his stave, listened and watched, but made no movement and said nothing. "Let Nun handle it", was in his mind. Nun would know what to do, and he would do what was best; and as for himself, Moses—it seemed to him that he cared very little. He had ceased to be one thing or another; he was not a prince of Egypt and neither was he a Levite. In that time when nations were still a network of clan and tribe and family, when a man who stepped from among his people stepped into chaos, Moses was alone and, as he now argued to himself, indifferent to his aloneness.

One of the old men hobbled forward and peered into Nun's face. His rheumy, red-rimmed eyes blinked painfully in the bright sunlight, but he studied Nun conscientiously and then sneered at the women with contempt. "What do you know, you clucking fools? Old hens! This is Nun, son of Ephala. His mother, Zilpah, was the daughter of Pashur, who was sister by marriage to my own mother. Her father was the Midianite Hushur, who was circumcised by the Egyptians when they took him from the Bedouin traders. He always claimed that his great-grandfather was the Sheik Jacob, holy be his name, who held great power in the Land

of Canaan, but a Midianite is a liar—who can believe them?
The truth is that Sheik Jacob had more sons than you can
count, for he was potent the way this dog on the throne
of Egypt is potent, and every miserable Bedouin tribe calls
itself the Children of Israel. It is not enough that the Mid-
ianites claim Midian was born from Abraham and Keturah
and begot Epher and Hanoch and all the rest of their
swarm, but they must weave into their swarm Reuben and
Gad, so that they too are the Children of Israel, and even
the Amelekites, those dogs who join with Midian and deny
Nehushtan, will have it that Abraham was kin by Zefra,
who had one eye but could see around objects with that
one eye, which was—"

Moses, who had, with great difficulty, caught the thread
of the words, realized that the old man had forgotten what
he had set out to prove, and also saw that his amazing
genealogical monologue could continue until his rasping
voice gave out. He was surprised that Nun made no effort
to interrupt, for Nun was always impatient and easily annoyed by too much talk and nonsense; but in this case, his
patience was more than that of the women. One of them,
who might have been younger than she appeared and even
lovely once, interrupted harshly and said,

"Enough of that, old fool! It's Nun, the son of Ephala.
We see that. He has come to good fortune and good times.
What do you want of us, Nun?"

"Call me old fool!" the old man cried, his voice rising
in a shrill whine. "I'm old enough to be your grandfather.
I held you on my knee and you wet all over me. I slapped
your bare behind, rotten brat without respect! A curse from
Nehushtan! May his slime gather over you and rot your
flesh!"

"Leave it alone, Miriam," another woman said tiredly. "The old fool is crazy. You'll start him on his curses. He'll curse us all day long."

"Time was when there was respect," the old man whined. "Respect for the old, honour from the young. Before we were slaves in Egypt. What is a slave? A slave is dirt. A slave is filth. A slave is an animal, like an ass in the field. What does a slave know of honour or respect? Before we were slaves in Egypt, it, was different. Oh, yes, I tell you it was different. A woman didn't open her mouth then—"

"Oh shut your own mouth already, old man," another woman put in.

"Go back to your hole, old man," the woman called Miriam said tartly. "There is too much sun on your head. It will make you even more foolish than you are."

Moses realized that they had forgotten him entirely, all except the children, who were losing their fear and edging towards him, their eyes fixed on his great war bow and the shining silver handle of his hunting knife. He also realized that, in some curious way, they were using this interruption in the bleak and hopeless monotony of their lives to gain a little excitement, a little variation of their unchanging daily routine. The imprecations, abuse and curses flung back and forth were without body and evoked neither fear nor anger, and Nehushtan was referred to without respect or awe—and sometimes with contempt. He realized that Nun had attempted to justify himself in terms of religion, but here was no religion in the sense that Moses knew religion, but rather a sort of magic such as Doogana practised, degraded by the pervading degradation of slavery.

Another old man now pushed his way among the

women and faced Nun, and placed his approval upon him with an embrace of his skinny arms. He was, as he explained, Nephi, brother to Ephala, the father of Nun. Ephala had died two years ago, he informed Nun; he had slipped or fallen out of sheer weariness from a scaffolding, where he was carrying bricks. His baby brother, Ephala was, the child of his mother's age—even as he, Nephi, had been the child of his mother's youth. Thus he embraced Nun, who was alone, his mother dead of worms a month later, his sister dead in childbirth, his brother dead of the fever that had swept through them the year before. "Life is burden and misery," the old man intoned with sorrow, and the women began to weep. They wept because Nun was an orphan, because his own eyes remained dry and thoughtful, and their weeping rose in a passion of grief at their own lot. They all kissed Nun and they took him back to the shade of their hovels, leaving Moses as forgotten as if he had never existed.

But the children remained with him, and since his slave had been welcomed and embraced at last, they accepted the master. They crowded around him as he walked towards the village, and when he sat down in the shade of one of the houses, his back against the mud wall and facing him a stretch of gardens where the Levites attempted to grow some crops with almost no irrigation, the children stilled the last of their fear. Skinny and scabious they were, but also beautiful, with their long brown eyes and their silken black hair. The oldest among them could have been no more than ten or eleven years old, perhaps some of the girls a little older, and Moses realized that their childhood was brief; older children were taken to work with the labour gangs. Where were the men of the tribe now, Moses

asked them? But they were vague as to work and direction;
the men would return at sunset; they were more interested
in his shining hunting knife, and when he demonstrated
that the polished iron of its blade was sharp enough to
slice a hair he plucked from his head, they looked upon
him as a magician. They had never seen iron before.

Among themselves, they chattered in their own language, but with Moses they used the same sharply accented
Egyptian that Nun spoke; and to Moses it was fascinating
and enjoyable to talk with them. The truth of the matter
was that never before had he put himself in such a relationship with a group of children. He was annoyed with
himself, that he had allowed Nun to persuade him to put
away all his trappings and jewels—they would have made
gifts for the children; and he told one little girl that he
would bring her a necklace of pearls to put around her
neck. She did not know what the word *pearl* meant, and
when he explained, they all took it as a great joke. He
strung his great war bow, and they took turns trying to
bend it, and then murmured with awe when he drew the
string to his check. The little girl he had promised the pearls
to crawled into his lap and asked him what his name was.

"Moses," he answered.

They all giggled. "Oh, Egyptian," the little girl said. One
of the boys was bolder and said, "No one has a name like
that."

Another put in, "Moses is half a name. What is the
rest?"

"That's all there is," Moses laughed.

"Then what should we call you?"

"Are you my friends now?"

They all nodded seriously but one, who wanted to know

whether they could be friends with an Egyptian. Moses said he thought they could be because he was a different kind of Egyptian. "Is that why you have half a name?" He nodded, and then they asked him what kind of Egyptian he was, and he told them that he was a prince of the Great House. It was the greatest joke of all, and the children shook with laughter and delight, for they had never met another man who said such things, even to make them laugh. But they still demanded to know what they should call him, and he answered them,

"Call me Moses of the half-name, for that is what people without fear call me—"

So he was hardly aware of Nun's absence, and the time passed and the shadows of the afternoon grew longer. When he heard Nun's voice he stood up, and then when Nun appeared with some of the women, the children scattered as if they had done something wrong. Nun announced with assumed obsequiousness,

"I was too long, O my master. Forgive your slave."

Moses nodded, and together they departed. As they walked back the way they had come, Moses asked Nun,

"What did you tell them about me?"

"I told them that you were a captain of chariots who was now resting and hunting in the marshes for amusement. I told them you were an easygoing master, and because I had fought well in the wars, you had promised that I could see my people."

"Are these all the Levites?"

"There is another village not far from here, but here I was born. We were a great tribe once and we still boast a proud heritage, but now how many of us are left? Eleven or twelve hundred at the most, and we die quickly, even as slaves die." His voice was full of resentment, and Moses asked him, almost apologetically,

"What did you tell them my name was?"

"I gave you the name of that old priest you talk about so much, Amon-Teph."

"I told the children my name was Moses."

"Oh?"

"What do you mean by that?"

"I mean that even a wise man can be a fool," Nun blurted out, and Moses suddenly turned on him and cried,

"You forget you're a slave, Bedouin!"

"I forget," Nun whispered. "Forgive me."

They did not speak to each other again until their boat approached Neph's landing at Tanis. Then Nun offered, half-hesitantly, the information that the woman named Miriam was the sister of Moses. Moses shrugged. It meant nothing, and he could not connect the acid-tongued, bitter and hostile woman he had seen and heard, to himself.

[18]

HE TOLD NEPH of his trip to Goshen, and he said, "I am coming to the end of something. I hope it isn't my life." To which Neph answered,

"How old are you now, Moses?"

"Not far from twenty-three years."

"The oldest time of youth, isn't it?" Neph smiled. "Now you are at the moment when you have lived for eternity, and you must cherish that, because it will never return. From here on, the days and the years move faster and faster, and soon you will ask where is yesterday, while today slips unheeded through your fingers, and you will understand what is always so difficult for us Egyptians to understand, that there is always an end of something and a beginning of something. Don't clutch too hard, boy, and don't pity yourself."

"I don't pity myself," Moses protested.

"I think you do," Neph disagreed, still smiling to take any hurt out of his words. "Do you never tell yourself that you have seen all there is to see and suffered all there is to suffer? You have loved and lost, and you have seen war and slaughter and the death of a great nation. You saw an evil man murder your mother and teachers, and you have been with the noblest as well as with the most degraded of mankind. You have ventured to go where perhaps no Egyptian ever went before, and you saw the holy Mother Nile dry up to a trickle. That is a good deal, Moses, but not all—the great, terrible pain that life judges us with, you have not yet tasted. If this is an end, it's a beginning—as with our old, old Egypt, which thoughtless people deem to have lasted for ever, never giving thought to how many times it perished and rose again from the ashes. Now tell me, as you went among the Levites, did you have it in your heart to return to them?"

"That puzzled me most," Moses said.

"Yes?"

"I stood aside. I watched, and I didn't care. I thought I would be moved greatly, and that something knowing would pass between us, but that was not the case. I told you the story of how Seti-Keph took me to the house of Aton-Moses, the white house that you built on the escarpment. When I saw it—just seeing it and no more—my heart was filled with so much joy and expectancy that I wanted to weep. I felt that finally I had come home, and there was nothing like that feeling when I went to the Land of Go-shen."

"In the first case," Neph answered kindly, "you were not yet nineteen years old, and now you are twenty-three. What happens at nineteen can never happen again, as you know, Moses. And also, let us remember, the house of Aton-Moses typified all that was best in Egypt, the pure worship of Aton, not as a sun-god but as the source of all life and beauty. In the house of Aton-Moses, sweet reason prevailed, and it was full of the heady wine of scepticism and doubt—and there you found a lovely woman who was a joy to look at, to speak to and to be with. But it was not the world, Moses; it was a dream, a retreat, a pretend-game that Egypt's past was not the past and that Egypt's dead were not dead. No—such fancies and dreams are not for you and me. We are plain people, and our feet are dirty with the good mud of Mother Nile, and even if we found such a white house on a cliff, we would not be happy there. Aton-Moses used to berate me with my willingness to bend my skill to any nonsense and conceit that Ramses dreamed of—to build monuments, tombs and temples for fat priests to store away what they stole from the people—while my dream of a dam to harness the Nile was tossed out like so much rubbish. But that was because, for all his wisdom, he never comprehended that unless you are a part of the world of men, your life has neither meaning nor justification in any full sense. I am a builder and I must build—that is essence."

"And what am I?" Moses wondered aloud. "You were already learning your trade when you were a child."

"I think you have another trade, Moses of the half-name," Neph nodded, a trace of a smile, thoughtful, speculative, on his weathered brown face. Almost surprisingly, Moses became aware of the nest of wrinkles that cradled his dark eyes, the deep lines on his cheeks and the whitening of his close-cropped hair. How old was Neph now, he wondered? He had never thought over-much of the difference in age between Neph and himself, and now he was trying to recall when they had first met. That day in the bare, light-drenched studio where Neph stood over his drawings—was that nine or ten years ago? Then Neph would be close to fifty years of age now—old, as age went in Egypt of that time; and for all his wisdom and thoughtfulness, the ultimate knowledge had eluded him. No answers were his to tell; no mysteries his to reveal—

"A different kind of a trade," Neph went on. "We are very different, Moses of the half-name, for it seems to me that I was always much as I am now; but in you there is a process at work, something else. You move in leaps and bounds, and sometimes you seem to be as witless and wild and unpredictable as any young blood out of the Great House. And then, the next moment, there shines out a quality that makes men love you and turn to you. We live in a time that makes me feel, when I am depressed and miserable, that here is the end of all goodness and hope—for under the stone and the gold, Egypt is dying, not going down to defeat before an enemy, to rise up again as in the past, not tearing herself open with civil war, so that the wounds may heal cleaner and better as they have in the past—but being sucked dry of all her blood and strength by these pigs of the House of Seti, who will leave only an empty shell and memory of all we have been. So it is the end of a time, an epoch and a whole world, and maybe that is the way it was all ordered, the way it must be.

Amon-Teph and Enekhas-Amon raised you to be a king, and who knows that they were so wrong?"

"That I know, Neph," Moses laughed. "I tell you I would take my dagger and stick it in my heart before I'd ever sit on the throne of Ramses in the Great House. I know the Great House too well. Ramses hinted that it could be mine; he flattered me by comparing me with his sons—and whichever unlucky one it is, he will have a hundred siblings waiting to put a knife between his ribs. Let Ramses reap his harvest! If Egypt must turn to a nameless Bedouin, a slave-born Levite, then may whatever gods there are weep for Egypt."

"Only a few of us weep for Egypt, Moses—not the gods, who have no hearts, but plain men with eyes to see and ears to hear. But Egypt is not the world, and there are other thrones and different lands. Listen to me now, for these are strange things we speak of and things men say to one another rarely. I am more than twenty-five years older than you, and you are as much of a son to me as my own blood would be. That is why I kept you near me when I could and endured your petty stubbornness, your recklessness, so unworthy of you, your wild humours, your fights and quarrels, your childish pride and boastfulness, which you would cover up with false humility, your sense of being superior, born of the gods, which you denied with words and lived and practised at the same time, going among the plain, poor, hard-working people of Egypt as if they were dirt and now and then condescending to bend your stiff neck an inch or two. No—listen to me, for I haven't said this before and I won't say it again. Remember how you found Nun, a story all Egypt knows now, a prince fighting a chained slave—and put yourself in Nun's place. Would you be so ready to forgive and love? Yet he does—because all this is only one part of you. Yet when will you put it away? You went to see the place of the Levites—and your heart was like a piece of ice. Who put the ice there? Whose heart is it, yours or another's? The Levites are enslaved to me. I bring them to a job to labour with stone and bricks, and I watch the overseers spur them on with the bullhide whips. This is the way it is and I know of no other way it can be, but I don't close my heart to it. I let a part of me cry out for men in such toil and hopelessness, because if I closed that part I would stop being a man. Did you see nothing in the Land of Goshen? Does it mean nothing that your blood is their blood? You are as strong and tall and fair and blessed as any man in Egypt—had you no tears to weep for your brothers and sisters? Do you think that some god blessed you and damned them? Couldn't you look at them and say—There go I, Moses, but for a freak of fortune?"

Brokenly, Moses cried, "That's enough—and now I know! Now I know what you think of me! Worthless, cold, heartless—oh, yes, Neph, you have judged me. It's good to have things clear and open between friends! Why did you let me think—"

"Stop that!" Neph snapped. "You are twenty-three, not thirteen. You are a man—so listen to me like a man! Why do you think I kept you beside me, worked with you, talked to you, became a teacher to you and fought with all my wit and wisdom to make you look at the world with clear and open eyes? Why do you think Amon-Teph adored you so—or did you never know that he worshipped the ground you walked on? Was he only a fat old man to you? Do you think he ever deceived himself into believing that the harebrained schemes of your mother would be successful? I tell you, he did not! He loved you for your own sake, even as all the priests of Aton loved you and cherished you and overlooked all you did that was witless and irresponsible. They gave you the holiest thing on earth, their knowledge and learning, the lore of the skies and the stars, of time and the calendar, and above all the concept of one god, warm and gentle and unknowable, who sent his own son to earth to redeem us all. They gave you Aton, who meant so little to you, so occupied were you with your own hatred of the gods of Egypt and with your wars against them. And when they paid with their lives for this, beheaded and thrown to the swine, you had no tears to shed for them. Yet this I understand—and perhaps more—about you than you imagine. Have you ever thought about what this legend of Aton means? By sending down his son, Aton told us that only man can redeem man. That is why the priests loved you—because they saw something else, a hunger for justice, for right, for truth—the *macaat* that was once the glory of Egypt and is no more; they saw a little flame and dreamed that it could be nursed into a great fire. They saw that, as I saw it, as Nun sees it——"

"And it's a lie, a deceit," Moses whispered brokenly.

"Is it? I don't know, Moses. Time will tell."

[19]

MOSES AND NUN went to the village of the Levites a second time, and Moses told his slave that he would talk with his sister, the woman called Miriam.

The children ran to Moses; they remembered him. This time, Nun lacked the courage to tell him to set aside his

symbols of rank and godhead—and Moses pointed out simply that he would not take off here what he wore in the
streets of Tanis. If he was prince by edict of Ramses, he
told Nun, because he feared to take off the kilt and jewels
where the priests and clerks of Ramses could see him,
should he come to his own people in nakedness and
shame? Nun had reasons and the wisdom of caution as
well, but like his master, Nun also felt that he was riding
a new and strange wind that would take them where it
willed.

Neph should have seen him with the children. They
were not the children of love and of promise; from mothers
and fathers who are slaves, there are only blows and curses
and the sharing of the misery that is and the misery that
is expected—so where, one might have wondered, did they
keep their hunger for love and their hope that it might be
returned? The tall Egyptian was different now. He wore a
pleated kilt of fine white linen and the sandals on his feet
were decorated with gold and silver. A thin band of gold
bound his hair, and upon his breast hung a great neckpiece
of beautifully worked gold links and plates, each separated
from the other by a white pearl or a bead of green jade.
He carried no weapons with him now, only an ivory-hafted
dagger in a golden scabbard at his waist. Yet in spite of
the difference, the children were not awed.

"Here is Moses of the half-name!" they called out to
each other.

He sat with them and showed them his jewels and bangles and laughed with them, while the women and the old
men gathered apart in deep and troubled silence, only
whispering to Nun,

"Why did you lie to us? The children told us—and this

is Moses of the half-name, who will some day, as they say, sit on the throne of Egypt." "Why did you bring him here, to laugh at us in our misery?" "What have we to do with princes of the Great House?" "What does he want from us who are slaves and dirt under the feet of his father?" "We are not round and desirable, to be whores for his father. Why does he look at us as he does?"

To which, for Nun, there were no answers, except to say "He desires to talk to Miriam, the daughter of Amram."

Miriam came to face Nun, and as he looked at her, he realized that the blood and the flesh were knit; for she had the same proud, lean look that her brother wore; the same high-bridged nose, the same long limbs. But beauty, if it touched her, had touched her only briefly. Older than Moses, her belly was loose from childbearing, her breasts flat from hunger and illness, her face pocked with disease, pinched with hunger, drawn with frustration. Her mouth was thin and tight to lock in her sorrows and lost hopes, and her uncombed, lustreless hair was tied back with a string of old cloth.

Now fear took hold of her. "What does he want of me?"

"Only to talk to you. Why are you afraid of him? He is my master, and I know him. Look how the children are gathered around him! Do they run to a bad man?"

"I have done nothing. I tell you I have done nothing. What does he want of me?" A thought occurred to her, and she cried out, "Where is my daughter? Hide her!" Her daughter, a thin child of fifteen or so, had been standing only a few paces away. She stepped forward now, trying to smile to reassure her mother, who slapped her across the face and cried, "Whore! Would you go to the king's bed— to the whoremaster of the whole world! First I would see

Nehushtan swallow you alive!" The child fled wailing to the mud houses, and Nun put in,

"Miriam, daughter of Amram, believe me, for I swear it on Nehushtan and the Holy Ark that contains his presence, this prince of Egypt means only good and no harm. He doesn't want our women or our children. There is nothing to fear from him."

"Then why does he come here?"

"Because his heart goes out to our people and to their suffering," Nun told her. "Because he has seen our tears and heard our cries of misery. Because he has watched us labour and die."

"What is it to him?"

"This is for only him to say. Let me bring you to him, Miriam, daughter of Amram."

She followed Nun, her shoulders bowed with the inevitable, and he took her aside to the well and the palm trees. Moses left the children and came to Miriam and Nun, and when he was close to them, Miriam fell upon her face in the dust, lying there and begging,

"Prince of Egypt, we are slaves, we are nothing, we are the dirt of the ground. Have mercy on us. I have only one daughter, I hold her to my bosom, she is my whole life. My husband, Epher, labours for the glory of the God-King, but there is no strength left in his loins. Two sons I lost in childbirth, and my father and mother are dead. Even my brother was taken as an infant by the god for sacrifice— and how much more must I suffer! Leave my daughter to me and I will lay down my life for you. I will be your slave. I will go out in the streets of Tanis and lay with men to bring you money. Only leave my daughter to me."

Moses was unable to speak, throat and heart choking

him; and as he lifted Miriam to her feet, Nun said, not without annoyance,

"Woman, take hold of yourself 11 told you he doesn't want your daughter and he means no harm to you!"

She stood before Moses, her coarse, sacklike dress covered with dust, splotches of dust on her face, grimy where the tears had mixed with it, her lips trembling; and Moses said,

"Do not fear me, Miriam, please do not fear me."

"I am your slave, O Prince of Egypt."

"I am Moses," he said gently, "who was born to Jochebed, who was taken to wife by Amram, the Levite. I am the child who was put in an ark and cast into the waters of the river. I was lifted out by the mercy of Enekhas-Amon, a princess of Egypt, and by her I was taken to the Great House in Tanis to be her son. You, my sister, are a slave, to chew the bitter cud of slavery, but by some fate which I cannot understand, I eat the food of the God-King and wear the linen of Egypt. I have come here because a man who is torn from his people and his memories, must either find them again or be a homeless wanderer for ever. So dont be afraid of me. We are brother and sister——"

As he spoke, he watched her face and realized that there was no connection between them, no comprehension of a statement so fantastic and unbelievable that to her it could only register as some strange and cruel mockery, as mysterious in its meaning as were a thousand and one other mysteries of the terrible, beautiful, cruel and powerful Land of Egypt. His heart went out to this plain, dirt-stained and work-worn woman as it had never gone out to anyone before, opening with love and a compassion that saw and embraced all the ugliness of the life of these people, the dark and barren ignorance, the vile superstition, the truncated hopes and blocked horizons, the meanness, the selfishness, the ignominious brand of slavery and degradation. That he and Nun were also of the same blood did not leaven his despair; and the thought in his mind that he would bend and kiss this woman, his sister, was blocked by the knowledge that such an action would terrify her and make the puzzle even more unanswerable.

It was with a sense of defeat and despair that he took a gold bracelet from his arm and gave it to her. She held it in a trembling hand and whispered,

"Are you taking my daughter now, O Prince of Egypt?"

"Let us go—quickly," Moses said to Nun.

Nun paddled the papyrus boat and watched his master weep. Not since the climax of the great battle in Kush had he seen Moses shed tears, but now the tears flowed freely, the Prince of Egypt's body racked with sobs, with the deep-rooted grief of man.

[20]

THESE DAYS, NEPH lived at his project, ate and slept there and, as Moses knew from the times he was with him, often awakened in the middle of the night and went to look at the work in the light of the desert moon. It was not easy for Moses to comprehend the fascination and spell exerted upon Neph by the colossus, for Moses could only guess at the power of the wedding between a builder and his work. He knew that Neph hated and despised Ramses, perhaps more than he himself did—for the depth of feeling that had existed between Neph and Amon-Teph was only now being revealed to him—and he also knew that Neph had only

391

contempt for the ego that would perpetuate itself for ever as a giant mass of stone.

But given that, Neph could discard the meaning and purpose of his work and immerse himself in the problem. The purpose mattered, but the problem was all; and Moses had come to understand that this grave, ascetic man burned with a fierce, unrelenting passion to know, to discover, to reveal another little bit of the truth, to demonstrate a new law of mechanics, of mass, a new possible way to cope with the impossible. He had once watched Neph solve a problem that no other engineer in all Egypt could unravel. Ramses had taken a notion to build an obelisk on a pinnacle of stone which the weather and time had separated from the Nile escarpment. The pinnacle, which was seven feet lower than the edge of the escarpment and at least thirty feet apart from it, was too slender to permit the building of any bridge that might carry the great cut stones that would form the obelisk, since Ramses had specified that the pinnacle and the obelisk should form a solid union. For months, the engineers on the job pondered the problem—until at last Ramses impatiently summoned Neph from the granaries he was constructing. Moses had gone with Neph, watching the engineer scribble endless diagrams on bits of papyrus—and when they arrived, he had the solution.

Neph ordered a huge mast of cedar to be brought up the Nile to the escarpment, where it was mounted upon a stone swivel. One end of it was lashed to the base of the obelisk; and on the other end of it, great bags of woven rope were attached. These bags were filled with stones until the weight of them made a balance with the base stone.

Then the cedar timber was gently put into motion, swinging in a circle on the stone pivot. When the base stone was over the pinnacle, the bags were lightened until the mighty piece of limestone settled into place.

It was so simple that no one thought Neph either a great innovator or a great hero; but Neph himself was drunk with the achievement, with the knowledge that he had solved a new problem, done something that no one had ever done before. So it was with the colossus in the desert—a mass of stone higher and more imposing than any figure of a man in all the known world.

He sent a message to Moses, telling him that the raising of the sections had begun and asking him to come and see it; and Moses recognized this as in effect something of a greeting, an embrace, Neph saying, "Come and look at my own vanity, for all men preen themselves and wear their pride for all to see. Soften your anger." But there was no anger to soften, and since returning a second time from the Land of Goshen, Moses had longed for the presence and comfort of Neph, for his sober counsel and for his ability to relate a moment of time to all of time. Nun too was relieved that the message had come, for since the incident with Miriam, Moses had not set foot out of Neph's house but had lived tightly with his misery, leaning morosely and silently on the sill of the window that looked out over the Nile and the marsh islands of the Delta.

They had bought a new chariot that Nun was eager to try, and two fine, strong horses from Philistia, but the horses remained stabled and the chariot idle in the dust and sun. Now Nun smiled happily with his good memories, and sang Levite chants as he greased the axles and polished the bronze handrails of the chariot. The horses pranced and reared as he brought them to harness, and he called out to Moses,

"Tell me, O master, is it not like old times? I only have to close my eyes to hear the camp waking up around us, the men grumbling and swearing at each other, the fights breaking out among the Sea Rovers, who must fight among themselves until they could fight in earnest, the captains shouting, each one louder than the next, and that great bull of a Sokar-Moses with his black bullwhip. I tell you, master, I do not think there is a man in the world I am afraid to match my strength with, but I would think twice and three times before I got into a scuffle with Sokar-Moses. Now what? Tell me—shall I throw some javelins into this pretty wagon and we are on our way to Kush?"

"Throw yourself into the Nile," Moses answered, laughing for the first time in days. "We want fruit and water more than javelins, and I shall need at least three fresh kilts. This will be very ceremonial, for now the God-King has convinced himself that he will live for ever as a mountain of stone, even if someone has the good luck to ransack his tomb."

They set out in the cool of morning, and youth awakened as they took turns with the reins, raced the chariot and put it to the swirling motion of battle exercise. At a well where they stopped to drink, they were the admiration of wide-eyed peasant girls, and Nun was ready to begin the love-making when Moses ordered him away. So they journeyed, the carefree and handsome prince of the Great House with his Bedouin slave and chariot-driver. . . .

They were late on the scene, for already the first two courses of the colossus had been set in place, and now in the desert there was a great mound, its flat, truncated top marking the point to which the monument had risen. A veritable city had come into being, overnight, as it were, shelters for the thousands of slaves, kitchens, water tanks, pavilions for visiting dignitaries who had been invited by Ramses to watch this last phase of a miracle of construction—and even one splendid and bedecked stand of cedar and painted linen, should the God-King himself decide to come here at some moment as the colossus neared completion.

While Nun saw to the horses and chariot, Moses wandered through the project. Never before had he seen so many slaves at work on a single job—and he realized why Neph had explained that this part must be done quickly; for food and water alone became a monumental problem under conditions of such heat and dehydration. Long lines of slaves were carrying baskets of sand, building up and tapering off the man-made mountain that would rise as the colossus rose, extending one side of it as a ramp, and even as they worked on the ramp side, hundreds of other slaves were grappling with the mighty block of granite that would constitute the next course. It was bound with rope, and on every rope scores of men strained and pulled, the whips of the overseers urging them on. Still other slaves, shoulder to shoulder, were putting their weight against the back of the huge stone—and more slaves guided the rollers on which it crept forward, inch by inch, foot by foot. As it moved up the ramp, a course of granite slabs was laid in front of it, that the rollers might have a firm base to turn on, the base stones themselves weighing not less than two thousand pounds; but the hundreds of slaves on the ramp who drew on the ropes had no footing other than the sand, in which they struggled ankle-deep, even while more slaves emptied baskets of sand around their feet, that the ramp might maintain its shape and surface. And always, without pause or respite, the whips of the overseers laced their skin and pricked them on.

So vast, so confusing, so filled with sound and shout and explosion of the breath of toil beyond endurance was the scene—so full of the moan of strength tried too far, of strength broken, of anger, submission, of effort and punishment entwined—that Moses saw no people at first, no men, no individuals, but only a squirming, whimpering entity made up of thousands of parts, all radiating from a monstrous, senseless block of granite that had to be dragged up a hill and placed on top of it. The slaves were joined into a single work-beast. In sweat, heat and under broiling sun, Moses had the impression of an unholy spider with Ramses' stone midriff as its body and gut, walking in slow steps of pain on the broken legs of mankind.

Only then he was able to look at individual slaves. The pot of the Delta had been emptied for this. It was no wonder that Ramses scoured the world for slaves and more slaves, taking nations, burning cities, sending his slave-buyers to every corner of the earth; for these slaves were short-term animals, filled with death and ready to burst with it, dropping in their tracks and dying as Moses watched, kicked aside, tolled aside, rolling over and over down the man-made mountain of sand, and then covered over with sand by other slaves who made the mountain, men whose humanness had been wrenched out of them, whose souls had been seared beyond feeling, whose hearts were hardened before they cracked, and who had come to the point where they cared nothing about death, since life was so much worse.

The world was there enslaved. Moses saw black men from Kush, yellow-haired Libyans, Hittites, Babylonians, Bedouins, Egyptians sold for debt or for any one of a thousand violations of the tranquillity and dignity of the gods—as defined in the priestly codes that were the new curse of the House of Seti—and many others whose origin was as unrecognizable as their age, for dirt and beard gave these wretches a sameness that defied nation and chronology.

And Moses asked himself, "How is it that I have lived among slaves from my beginning, and now I see them for the first time? What has happened to me?"

He found Neph, who had no time for more than a greeting, but questions pounded in Moses' brain, "Is he blind? He is Neph, my father, Neph, my brother. Is he blind?" "Are you ill?" Neph asked, looking into his face; and Moses shook his head, for this was a sickness that no one could talk about, and no physician could cure.

He wandered on, and Nun saw him. Nun was not blind; Nun was a slave, and he whispered, "Master, if I was one of those who toil with that stone, I would cut my throat and die."

"We are those," Moses said. "We are Bedouin people from the desert—we are they. There is no difference."

They walked on. Nun said it would be better if they got away from this place, but Moses shook his head. "How do slaves go away?" he asked himself.

Nun touched his arm. They were at the edge of the sand mound, and directly before them, a score of paces away and up the side of the mound, slaves toiled on one of the long ropes that led back to the granite block. "There are the Levites," Nun said softly.

"How do you know?"

"I know."

"They look no different."

"To me they do," Nun said chokingly. "I know them."

Moses walked forward, his feet sinking into the loose sand of the mound, and as he moved, one of the men on the rope went down on his knees, and his comrades said thickly and hoarsely, in their own tongue,

"Up! Up!"

He struggled to rise, but his strength was gone; on his knees, he hung on to the rope, his dirt-encrusted, bearded head lolling from side to side; and that way the overseer saw him and came striding with his whip. The bullwhip, broke his hold on the rope, and the overseer kicked his recumbent form so that he rolled once or twice down the slope, coming to rest at the feet of Moses. Moses looked down at the motionless man, so small at his feet, so astonishingly small, knees and ankles knoblike on the fleshless limbs; and then Moses took two long strides, tore the whip out of the startled overseer's hands and flung it away. The overseer started to say, "O Prince of Egypt——" and Moses cut short his words with a blow from his clenched fist to the man's face, a blow that would have felled an ox, a blow that snapped back the man's head with a sharp, cracking sound—so that when his legs crumpled and he fell face-down in the sand, Moses and all others within sight knew he was dead.

Numb suddenly, Moses stood like a figure of stone. Nun turned the man over, the head dangling awkwardly. "He is dead," Nun said, not without fear in his voice, thinking that he had seen many blows, but not one so savage and awful as this. To Moses came the thought that he had killed a man for the first time. Had Kush never been, he asked himself? Had he not fought and killed in that battle? Then why did his soul scream at him, "I have killed! With my bare hands, I slew! I murdered!"

Motion and sound stopped. The slaves stood holding the rope, pulling it no longer, their hollow red-rimmed eyes fixed on Moses. The overseers came running, crying out, "Who killed this man?" But when the slaves pointed to the Prince of Egypt, they too stopped and remained silent. Soldiers came, and then this one and that one, until Moses and Nun stood over two dead men and inside a circle of the living—and then Neph came, pushing through the crowd.

He saw—what there was to see, and then asked Moses, pointing to the overseer, "Did you kill this man, O Prince of Egypt?"

Moses nodded.

"How? You have no weapons."

"I struck him with my clenched fist," Moses answered slowly. "He was merciless to this slave, whom he beat to death. Therefore, I was merciless to him."

Close to him Neph came, and Neph whispered, "You did wrong."

"I know."

"Go back to Tanis," Neph said hoarsely, angrily struggling for each word.

"Forgive me, Neph."

"Go back to Tanis."

Moses bowed his head, and with Nun following, he walked through the circle of men and away. He was a prince of Egypt. They drew back before him and they said no word, for he was a prince of Egypt. He understood now, and he understood why Neph would never look upon him with joy or pride or love again. Not as a Levite had he struck this man and exacted the toll of one life for another, not in the anger that comes of suffering and humility; but as a prince of Egypt, he had turned executioner in his wrath and murdered a man.

[21]

HE SAT WITH Nun in Neph's house, waiting. He sat with his thoughts, his dreams and his ghosts. He sat and said to himself, "I am Moses of the half-name, enemy of the gods, despised of the gods, and cursed by the gods. I am Moses of the half-name, who destroys what he touches. I am the wanderer who has no home nor homeland. I am the man of no country and no god."

"Master, what are we waiting for?" Nun asked him.

"Go away, Nun," he said. "Run from me. Death is on whatever I touch."

"Now is that any way to speak? Your heart is the heart of a Levite, master, but your head is filled with this Egyptian nonsense about death. It is not enough for Egypt that death comes when it comes; they must fill their houses with it from the day they are born. It seems to me that instead of these wild thoughts that come when one has nothing to do, we should harness the horses and look at the pyramids at Giza, or something of the sort, and stay away until this business of the overseer blows away. The overseers are a stink in the nostrils of any honest man, and I don't see what difference one more or less makes. You sit there and brood as if you had slain the High priest of Isis."

"I have slain a man."

"Not a man, a swine. We slew better men in Kush."

"It was not like this. In Kush, the blood washed off, but now the stains remain." He stared at his hands, and Nun shook his head bewilderedly. . . .

And then the time of waiting was finished, and Seti-Moses, the steward of the Great-House, came, not alone but with a guard of soldiers—and with his own short-winded exhaustion to underline the importance of an occasion that had taken him through the streets of the city to the home of Neph, the engineer.

"You will come with me, O Prince of Egypt," he said to Moses, "for the God-King summons you."

Moses rose but said to Nun, "Go away now", to which Nun smiled and shook his head. Then Moses asked Seti-Moses whether he might have a word alone with his slave.

"Very well, but shortly. It is not good for the God-King to wait on us." He left them alone then, and Moses faced Nun, his servant and friend, and said to him,

"Of all men, it is you who are closest to me now. I give you now your freedom, which I swear upon all that *macaat* meant when I was an Egyptian. I am an Egyptian no longer. I want you to take half of all the gold and jewels in this house that are mine, and take your weapons, and take my iron knife with the silver handle, and go away where you can make a good life for yourself, where you can build a house and marry a maiden of your own and have children of your own. I want you to go to Babylon or to some city in Canaan, where the cursed king of this land can never seek you out or hurt you, and live there and have whatever happiness a man can find in this life."

"You forget that I am your brother—our blood is mixed and one blood, O Moses of the half-name," Nun answered, more tenderly than he had ever spoken before.

With great and significant formality, Moses said, "You call me by my name, Nun, the son of Ephala," giving him the address used in the speech of the Levites, "and does that mean that you accept your freedom?"

"It was always mine, Moses, my brother, for I swore in the slave pens that I would die before another man owned me. I chose to be your servant. In the old days among the Levites, when a child was born beautiful and full of promise, they anointed him with olive oil and sweet scents. So it seemed to me that you were anointed, and I made an oath with myself that I would never leave you, so long as there was life in your body and in mine."

"Was it a strong oath?" Moses asked, tears filling his eyes. "If it was an oath by Nehushtan, I cast it aside. Neither do I serve nor do homage to any of the dark gods that are born out of the fears and the agonies of mankind."

"It was an oath to no god, but only to myself," Nun said.

"Then I will honour it."

"And I will sit here until you return."

"And if I don't return?"

"Then I will take your chariot and arm it with the weapons of war and ride up against the Great House and either hew my way into it or die."

"Now you talk as wildly as I do, O Nun—and you know that I have turned my face from this business of war and slaying. Wait here for me, if you will, and I shall come back."

"I know that, my brother," Nun said. Then Moses went to Seti-Moses, and told him that he was ready; and with the guard of soldiers around them, they went to the Great House and into the glittering throne room of Ramses, the God-King of Egypt.

In the desert, the stone visage of Ramses sat upon the sand, neck and head without body, waiting to be the last crowning glory of the mighty colossus, when the sand mountain the slaves built was finally high enough; and this face of the God-King was like the stone face that lay in the desert, calm and terrible, aloof from Moses and from itself too, but calm and terrible.

"Clear the room," Ramses said, after Moses had entered, his voice so cold and bitter that no man left with lagging feet; and then the two of them were alone among the painted linen hangings, the garish mosaics and the shining marble—alone in the emptiness of the great room; and as he spoke now, Ramses' voice echoed strangely,

"Come here to me, Moses!"

Moses walked to the platform, but made no obeisance.

"Am I no more your king that you come with such insolence?" Ramses demanded.

Moses remained silent.

"Is it death you look for? Or is there a place where my hand will not reach you?"

"You sent for me. I am here," Moses said.

"I sent soldiers to drag you here!"

"I am not yet to be dragged. I came as I would have come, soldiers or no."

"Was it for pleasure or to test me that you killed the man?"

"You have sons who have killed men. It is no new practice for the blood of the Great House."

"I have no other son who has made such a name as you have. You have blasphemed against the gods and you have profaned holy things and holy places. You have made yourself a thing for Egypt to laugh at and mock at. No man is a thing to himself—not you, not that overseer you slew. He has family, friends in high places, priests and scribes who will never rest until you are in your tomb. You have mocked me and insulted me more than any man—and still you live to come before me without honour and without respect. The crown of Egypt is the holiest and most venerable crown on earth, yet you spurned it and laughed at it—just as you spurned my house and my blood and took yourself to live in the wretched shack of an engineer of low peasant blood, one Neph, whom we both know well. You have plotted against me, cursed the gods of my ancestors, and you have done obscene homage to the cursed Aton of Karnak. And now, to crown all, you murder a man with as little reason as you have lived your life. And this from my son!"

"Not from your son, King of Egypt," Moses said, without fear or passion, feeling nothing—caught wholly in the grip of an inevitable finish, hiding no more, free and lost of his princeliness, free and lost of the burden of shame and pretence and of the whole lie that had been his life, free for the first time in what he was, child of the Levites, whom they would address as Moses ben Amram, child of a slave tribe of desert wanderers, not elated, not saddened, but free in a strange peace of body and soul, free to die without shame and without mysteries, yet not afraid.

"What do you mean?" Ramses demanded.

"Has no one ever told you? Have you really never suspected?" Moses asked in honest incredulity—sensing that was the cruellest punishment he could inflict upon the man, yet taking no joy from the judgment. "The throne must be isolated indeed for a king not to know what is common talk to every palace whore. Or was it your need which made it impossible for you to believe what you did know?"

"Know what?"

"That I am no son of yours and no son of Enekhas-Amon, whom I loved as my mother. But she was not my mother. I am a Bedouin of the Tribe of Levi, and when I was born, they made me a sacrifice to their god and set me afloat in the rushes in the river. There Enekhas-Amon saw me from her barge and sent the priest Amon-Teph to take me. She raised me, and it was her lie and mine too that I was of the blood of the Great House."

For a long, long moment, Ramses was silent; but in his silence his body trembled, his bull neck thickened, and the blood rushed darkly to his face. Then he burst out,

"You lie now! It is not enough to degrade yourself—you have become bold enough to degrade me! Do you know what you have done?"

"I know," Moses nodded.

"You have spoken your life away."

"I know."

"Yet you lie!"

"Look at me, Ramses," Moses said. "Look at me and tell me whether I am lying to you."

His rage broken by the indifference of the man before him, Ramses stared at Moses—and the moments went by and still he stared, trying to comprehend the soul and mind of a stranger. At last, he asked,

"Why did you tell me?"

"You called me your son, and I told you. Not for revenge—I want no revenge. I am tired of being a stranger. All my life I have been a stranger. I sought for gods because there were no people for me to call my own, and yesterday I went as a stranger and murdered a man who whipped the Levites, from whose seed I came. But when they fixed their eyes upon me, their eyes were the eyes of strangers, and their eyes said—Who made you, a prince of the Great House, to sit in judgment on us and our masters? What do you know of us and our toil—and the salt that waters our wounds? Have you lessened our toil? Have you brought us hope or cheer? What do you want with us, Prince of Egypt? Their eyes spoke and ripped me free from myself—and I am no longer a prince of Egypt. I killed, and there is blood on my hands. I ask for no mercy."

His brows knit, unable to comprehend either the purpose or meaning behind this strange confession, Ramses listened, puzzled, disturbed; and then asked,

"Do you want to die?"

"I want to live," Moses answered.

"Yet you must die," Ramses stated, not anger but sorrow and defeat in his voice.

"I know. So that no man will laugh at Ramses for the great hoax of Moses of the half-name."

"Perhaps. Or perhaps because I will know no peace while you live. Who else knows this?"

Moses shrugged. "My mother, Amon-Teph, the priests of Aton—they are all dead."

"You said before that many knew."

"It was a guess. Even your sons taunted me with a birth in water."

"Now you are lying. Does Neph know?"

"He doesn't."

"You lie!"

"On my honour."

"You sold your honour, Bedouin!" Ramses cried. "Get out of my sight. Go back to the roof of Neph, the engineer, for I will not have you profane this Great House. I give you the night to make ready—and perhaps tomorrow you will go to your death with the dignity and courage of an Egyptian. I ask no more—only that."

"You have no right to ask anything of me, Ramses."

"But that I have"—almost pleadingly—"for it was more than this holy throne that was betrayed! Egypt was betrayed, for I thought I gave her a son and king, and instead I gave her a dirty Bedouin assassin." And, suddenly, he rose up from his throne and struck Moses across the face. "May you be accursed of the gods for ever!"

Moses stood rigid, the stinging pain of the blow awakening him as from a dteam, while Ramses roared, "Guards! Guards! Take this man away and out of my sight!" And then, as soldiers, priests and scribes and noblemen poured back into the room, the God-King tore the royal neckpiece from Moses and hurled the bits of gold and precious stones across the polished marble floor.

IT WAS NOT strange to Nun that a man should await his death without considering an alternative, and even if there were no soldiers stationed around the house of Neph, where he and Moses sat, the thought of flight would have been difficult, uneasy in his mind, and full of nameless terrors and impossibilities. His talk of driving the chariot to the Great House was an invention of emotion; the very stones of the Great House would have presented a barrier; and while it was one thing to serve a prince of Egypt whose golden symbols opened all doors, it was something else to serve a Levite condemned to death. Not that he loved Moses less or honoured him less; but the mind of a slave is a long time remaking, and if Moses could not leave, he, Nun, was bound as bitterly.

Thus, with the soldiers barring the doors of the house, the two men sat, each wrapped in his own thoughts, his own dreams lost, his own mystery of the strange, feckless and witless experience called life. Thus they sat while the sun dropped toward the desert and the house cast its dark-green shadow over the slow-moving Nile—and thus they were, alone, the houseslaves fled, when the door opened and the soldiers cast a body into the front room as one casts away a sack of rubbish. It was the body of Neph, the engineer, dead from the raw thrusts of a quick and brutal killing, blood-encrusted and sprawling with loose limbs, mindless and lifeless, no more to think and plan and ponder, no more to understand and pity the folly of men, no more to challenge the gods with reason and compassion, no more to challenge nature with skill and reason, no more to teach, to lead, to unravel, no more to build—no more to defy time and the elements with mighty works of stone that in generations undreamed of would be the wonder and admiration of men.

For, as Moses had come to understand, the murder done by tyrants was as witless and vile as the rule of tyrants; and when he knelt by the body, took Neph's bloodstained, bruised face in his hands and kissed it tenderly, he knew that he touched the last of Egypt.

He stood up and, even in the half-darkness, there was something in his manner that filled Nun with terror. "Cursed be Egypt!" he shouted, "and cursed be Ramses the son of Seti!" His voice boomed from his heaving chest, deep and frightening, like the drums of Kush. "Cursed be this land which fattens on the blood of men! Cursed be the gods of Egypt for ever, and may they be forgotten of men! And may the day come when all that men remember of Ramses is the stone that this dead man raised in the desert!"

And then he stood in silence, his chest heaving; and the soldiers outside were silent—long silent before they were able to laugh and mock at the man condemned to death. But even their laughter and mockery were tempered by fear of the terrible curse.

The cloak of Egypt had fallen from Moses. All of its splendours and wonders, its science and culture, its noble art and ancient literature, its pantheon of dark and grudging gods, its tombs of immortality, its wonderful cities and towering temples, its wealth and might, its armies and its power—all of this had let go of him, with no single thread left to deny that he was a stranger in a strange land, a wanderer out of the desert, a Levite who had never been a

slave or bowed his head under the lash. No more was he
Moses of the half-name. As if he had perished and been
born again—so was he filled with life, his mind lashed, his
soul seared with grief and loss, his memory bright and
clean in anger and even clearer with the substance of his
anger. No more was he a prince of the Great House, and
there was no denying him or doubting him when he turned
to Nun and said,

"We will go away from this place and leave it for ever.
We are young and full of life, and it is not for Ramses, the
son of Seti, to select the moment for our dying."

And Nun answered, "Yes, master."

"Go then and bring the gold and jewels we have in the
house. We will need to buy bread and other things too, for
when we have taken this, there will be no more. Divide it
in two and put it in our hunting pouches, and if there is
bread and olives and dry fruit, take as much as our bags
will hold, and take a skin for water."

"Yes, master."

"And move quietly. They are listening outside."

"Yes, master."

Himself, Moses gathered weapons, an iron sword of
Hatti, their war bows, their hunting knives, two quivers of
arrows, and his long, Kushite stave. With strips of linen,
he bound the weapons together and strapped them to his
back, and then flung off his kilt, standing only in a loincloth, as Nun was. Nun appeared with the bags, which he
had tied together and hung around his neck. Then, without
words, Moses led him to the window at the back of the
house, in the wall built on the water. Moses motioned for
Nun to go over the sill, and then he took Nun's wrists and

let him gently down into the water. He himself hung from the sill until Nun grasped his feet, and handled him down and into the water. Slowly, step by step, their feet sinking into the muddy bottom, they walked downstream, keeping in the darker shadow of the house—until at last they came to their papyrus boat, moored at the little stone quay Neph had built. Here, as they loosened the mooring ropes, they saw the guards only a few feet away, but the Egyptians looked at the house, not at the river; and, soundlessly, Moses and Nun let the boat drift downstream, each clinging to one side of it.

About a hundred paces down the riverbank, in the darkness of the old and ramshackle houses that lined it, in the darkness of the night, they found footing again, tossed their gear into the boat and then climbed in themselves. Quickly and quietly, they plied the long paddles—and soon they were out in midstream, approaching the wilderness of marsh and channel on the eastern shore. They looked back now—at the dark bulk of Tanis, called the City of Ramses, at the flicker of lights that outlined the Great House of Ramses, son of Seti, at the Land of Egypt.

"We are safe now," Moses said, and Nun answered simply,

"The air is sweet."

Moses let Nun steer the boat, and the Levite steered by feel and instinct, even as the helmsman of Neph's work barge had guided it through the marshes so long ago. Hooded by the tall papyrus, they crept through channel after channel, slowly at first and then with more speed when the moon rose and gave them light to see by. Instead of steering due east, toward the Land of Goshen, Nun headed into a maze of channels that bent toward the south, riding sometimes so shallow that the bottom touched their boat, but always able to find water to go on.

They were both of them without any desire for sleep, wide-awake and strong of body and elated with the promise of life and the excitement of their escape. Hours of their long, sweeping strokes did not tire them, and as dawn greyed the sky, they pushed through stunted reeds into a wide, brackish marsh.

"Here," Nun said, "is the northernmost lake of the Red Sea, and here alone are no border guards. Here Egypt ends."

"But not the power of Ramses."

"No, master—he has a long arm."

The sun was up, burning into their faces when they reached the farther shore; and there they broke up their boat and threw the pieces into the lake. They divided the gear between them, Nun taking the iron sword of Hatti and Moses the long black stave of Kush.

"To the east," Moses said, "are the cities of men and civilization, the Land of Hatti and the Land of Canaan, cool water and wine and savoury food. But in every city will be the men of Ramses to seek us out and slay us, for if I know him at all, he will put gold on our heads and never rest until he finds us."

"And to the south?"

They gazed to the south—and in the distance they could see the grey mass of mountains, grim, bare desert mountains, forbidding even in the light of the morning sun.

"The Wilderness of Sinai, where there are no cities and no roads, where there is nothing to call the armies of Ramses, nothing to conquer, nothing to take."

Then they turned their faces south.

"It is good to live, to breathe the air of morning, and to think about tomorrow," Moses said.

Nun looked at his companion, and saw that for the first time since they had known each other, Moses was at peace with himself. For the Prince of Egypt no longer tore at his heart.

Side by side, the two Levites set forth into the Wilderness of Sinai.